LEGION II:
SONS
OF TERRA

VAN ALLEN PLEXICO

WHITE ROCKET BOOKS

This book is dedicated to the memory of Ian Jerome: Student, friend, and proud Son of Terra.

This book is also available as a limited edition hardcover from White Rocket Books.

This is a work of fiction. All the characters and events portrayed in this book are either products of the author's imagination or are used fictitiously.

LEGION II: SONS OF TERRA (THE SHATTERING)
Copyright 2014 by Van Allen Plexico
Cover art by Mark Williams
Cover design by Van Allen Plexico

A White Rocket Book
www.whiterocketbooks.com

ISBN-13: 978-0692021439

ISBN-10: 0692021434

New paperback edition: April 2014
First hardcover printing: April 2014
First paperback printing: February 2014

0 9 8 7 6 5 4 3 2 1

AFTER THE GODS,
BEFORE THE SHATTERING...

It It is the dawn of the 17th Millennium, and the great Anatolian Empire, mightiest successor state to the old Terran Alliance, finds itself beset on all fronts, by enemies both human and alien.

The Emperor is dead, killed along with most of his family by demons from the underverse known as the Below. Former General Hideo Nakamura has been proclaimed Taiko, chief administrator and supreme military commander, ruling in his place. Nakamura has surrounded himself with a "Hatamoto" of close advisors, but in recent days has withdrawn and become distant from them.

Nakamura's old I Legion, The "Lords of Fire," now commanded by General Marcus Ezekial Tamerlane, has been dispatched to the frontier to battle the waves of invaders who seek to overrun the Empire. They have been joined there by the III Legion, the "Golden Phalanx" (also known as the "Kings of Oblivion"), led by rising star Arnem "The Golden" Agrippa. Meanwhile the II Legion, known as the "Sons of Terra" and led by the fanatical General Ioan Iapetus, stubbornly remains in position closer to home, claiming they must be ready to defend sacred Earth and its surrounding core worlds.

But enemies have arisen both outside the Empire and within. Disaffected planetary governor Amon Rameses has turned his back on the Taiko and retreated to his base world of Ahknaton, there to lay his own schemes. And—potentially much worse—at least one of the malevolent old gods yet lives, and has begun to make his presence known among the human worlds once more...

"Our planet is a lonely speck in the great enveloping cosmic dark. In our obscurity, in all this vastness, there is no hint that help will come from elsewhere to save us from ourselves."
—Carl Sagan, 20th Century Earth scientist and educator

"A good commander can beat the odds. A great commander can beat the gods."
—Jack Kirby, 20th Century Earth dramatist

"Who watches the watchmen?"
—Juvenal

DRAMATIS PERSONAE

Hideo Nakamura, Taiko (supreme leader) of the Empire.

Legion I: Lords of Fire
Colors: Red and gold
General Marcus Ezekial Tamerlane, "The Relentless."
Hatamoto.
Colonel Konstans Belisarius, "The Belligerent."
Colonel Niobe Arani, Special Forces officer
Captain Harras Dequoi, commanding officer of the I Legion
flagship *Ascanius*

Legion II: Sons of Terra
Colors: Blue and silver; later black and gold
General Ioan Iapetus, "The Unyielding."
Colonel Berens Barbarossa, "The Daring." Hatamoto.
Colonel Piryu, officer aboard the II Legion flagship *Atlantia*

Legion III: The Golden Phalanx (Kings of Oblivion)
Colors: Green, white and gold
General Arnem Agrippa, "The Golden." Hatamoto.
Colonel Yevgeni Vostok, "The Cold."
Colonel Selim Iksander, "The Lightning."
Major Darius Torgon, Colossus commander
Captain Felix Dakkan, hovertank commander
Lt. Liefer, hovertank commander
Harker and Obomanu, Colossus crewmembers
MacInnish, hovertank crewmember

The Holy Inquisition
Gabriel Stanishur, Grand Inquisitor
Sister Leisle Delain, Inquisitor and aide to the Grand Inquisitor

The Ecclesiarchy—the Holy Church of Those Who Remain
Teluria, Ecclesiarch and vizier to Nakamura
Jasur, Warrior-Priest

The Old Gods (selected)
Aurore, goddess of distraction and deception
Goraddon, god of persuasion and disciple of Vorthan
Lucian, god of evil and mischief who once rebelled against the other gods
Solonis, the seer
Vorthan, god of toil; later labeled a death god

Others of Note
Amon Rameses, Planetary Governor of Ahknaton
Zahir, emissary and later vizier
Iyesu Tokugawa, Planetary Governor of Edo
Suleyman Mehemet, Planetary Governor of Bursa
Titus Elaro, Special Forces officer
Yadsen Erricht, procurer of specialty items
Glossis, tank commander

So close.

So close I came to placing a demon prince on the Emperor's throne.

How perfect it would have been. As the galaxy descended into catastrophic warfare from the tip of one spiral arm to the farthest reaches of the other, a lord of the Below would have reigned over the blazing ruins—a demon lord who owed me everything.

So close!

Alas, it was not to be. A handful of individuals interfered and disrupted my plans. Insignificant insects, all of them, of course, but I will recount their names here lest we forget upon whom our greatest wrath must now fall: Hideo Nakamura. Arnem Agrippa. Ioan Iapetus. Niobe Arani. Gabriel Stanishur. And perhaps most of all, the new supreme general of the Imperial military, Marcus Ezekial Tamerlane.

Each of them has incurred my eternal enmity. Each will discover—far too late—that my machinations against them are well underway, and that their fates are sealed. For some of them, the process is quite advanced; Hideo Nakamura, for example—the so-called *Taiko*—yet walks the halls of his flagship, but in truth he is already dead—a fact he will discover for himself soon enough.

Now the time has come to dispatch two of my most faithful servants to complete the preparations I have begun. Each will take a position close to the ear of the most powerful pieces on the board. Each will play upon that figure's greatest strengths—and weaknesses. Hope. Resentment. Arrogance. Hubris. Despair. And each will be brought low—even as he drags his armies, his worlds, and the galaxy itself into cataclysmic, apocalyptic war.

And then there is the wild card; the aberrant; the unpredictable Iapetus and his II Legion. Potentially the most dangerous of all. The bloody-handed Sons of Terra, fanatical defenders of the human homeworld. For them, a different lever will be required.

And for them, I have something very special set aside.

The board is set. The pieces are ready to move. The endgame is about to begin.

Take heed, for there will be no mistakes, no disruptions, no interference this time.

The Empire of Man is about to fall.

The lords of the Below are preparing to rise.

The galaxy is about to burn.

—Unattributed fragment of document recovered from the data storage units of Ahknaton, 21st Millennium

PROLOGUE:
Six Months Earlier

You have it, I trust?"

Yadsen Erricht allowed a wry smile to creep over his scarred, unshaven face. His eyes flicked from the customer before him—a big, tough-looking, muscular, military type, wearing a heavy suit of black smartcloth and a pair of omnigoggles—to the rest of the bar and back. There was a small crowd in tonight; not as many as Erricht had hoped, given what he was up to, but better than nothing.

"I said, have you *got* it?"

The customer was acting cool and collected, but Erricht could see that, just beneath the surface, he was actually quite antsy. The tone in his voice was unmistakable. He wanted to do the deal and get out quickly. Clearly the man was out of his element down here in the slums of Candis. A soldier he might be, but his uniform—if uniform it was— lacked any sort of insignia to identify exactly which army he served.

Ordinarily, doing the deal and getting away quickly suited Erricht just fine. But not this time. This time, he was curious. This time, he'd been asked to procure an object so rare, so specialized, he'd actually believed for a time that he wouldn't be able to get it. That, of course, would have been unthinkable, because there was nothing in the galaxy that Yadsen Erricht couldn't procure, given enough money, resources, and time. And determination, too—but that came as part of the package deal.

Yadsen Erricht could find anything for anybody. That was the reputation he had built for himself over the years, and that was doubtlessly the reason the big soldier-pretending-not-to-be-a-soldier in the black smartcloth had come to him, six months ago, with the job.

It hadn't been easy. In fact, it had quite possibly been the single hardest item to locate in all of Erricht's many years in the business. In the end, it had been exactly as he'd expected. He'd had to come to Candis. All the most difficult, most expensive, most challenging cases seemed to lead to Candis, eventually. Because nothing could be stolen from Candis.

"You don't have it," the customer growled. He made to rise.

"I have it," Erricht hissed at him. "Sit."

The man glared at him for a second, eyes bloodshot and narrow. Then he lowered his bulk back into the rickety wooden chair.

"Then produce it."

Erricht smiled again, this time broadly, warmly. "I shall indeed," he said in a soft, smooth voice. "I shall indeed. But first—you have brought the payment?"

"It's right outside," the big man replied. He leaned forward. "Now let me see the goods."

Erricht hesitated for a moment, considering the situation, making sure he felt comfortable about it. No, he concluded, he did not feel comfortable. Something was nagging at him about it, though he wasn't entirely sure what it was.

When the man opposite him had approached him half a standard year ago, he had made a rather unusual request.

Now, many of the items Erricht was hired to locate were unusual, but this one set a new standard in that field.

Why would he want it? What good would it do him? Something still nagged at him.

"If you've caused me to fly all the way here from—from my homeworld—for nothing," the man in the black uniform was saying, "I'll—"

"No, no," Erricht quickly told him. "Settle down. Here it is. Right here."

He reached under the table and lifted a small briefcase, setting it on the table. He touched a small rectangle on the edge of the case and the locking mechanisms inside gave way. Then he turned it around to face the other man. "Here you are," he said with another smile.

He sat back and waited as the man opened the case and looked inside. Mentally he was already counting the money he would make from this assignment. It would be considerable. He had figured the client behind it—and there had to be some other client; the big man in black was too dumb, too rank-and-file soldier-ish, to be the brains of the operation—must have engaged any number of other procurement specialists before coming to him. After all, Yadsen Erricht was the most expensive agent of his type in the Empire. Probably in the entire galaxy.

He looked around, taking in the sights, one eye always looking for trouble. He rarely found it on Candis, of course. The planet was almost ridiculously safe.

Indeed, it had worked out quite handily for Erricht that the trail had ultimately led to Candis. That was where he preferred to do most of his transactions with his customers anyway, so it saved him a trip. He liked doing business there because it was safe and secure—or as safe and secure as any location in the Empire could be, given the continuing existence of gods who could simply walk through portals right into any spot in the galaxy, take things, and leave again.

The one place they couldn't do that was Candis. For whatever reason, the walls of reality separating the "normal" universe from the Above and the Below—dimensions higher and lower than ours—were particularly strong and thick in the vicinity of that world. In short, the gods couldn't come there except aboard spacecraft, just like anyone else. Consequently, all the most valuable items in creation resided in private or government-run vaults somewhere on the planet.

No, nothing could be stolen from Candis—but lots of things were bought and sold there, every day.

No laws of nature prevented anyone, god or man, from simply making a transaction there and carrying the goods away. And that was how Erricht made his living; he bought and sold items of particular rarity and value and handed them over on Candis, where no one could walk through a sudden hole in the universe and take them from him without paying.

And the thought of payment brought Erricht back to the present. Blinking his eyes, he looked across at the man in the black uniform. "Is everything to your satisfaction, then?" he asked earnestly. He was absolutely sincere; he had a reputation and a livelihood to maintain.

The other man was smiling too, now. He had lifted a small item out of the case and was holding it up before him, though not so high that anyone else in the bar could see. He examined it carefully, turning it this way and that, appearing to be checking items off on a mental list as he did so.

The item was a pistol, though it was unlike any other pistol Erricht had ever laid eyes on. It looked more like a toy. Its body was made of what looked like plastic, and it had none of the heft and solidity of a good slug-thrower or even a blast pistol. Why anyone would want it, and would be willing to pay so much for it, he had no idea. And so he made the mistake of asking.

"Because it's the most powerful weapon in creation," the man answered.

Erricht laughed, thinking the reply a joke. "Funny—it doesn't *look* like the Sword of Baranak."

The man regarded him with dead eyes.

"Sorry," Erricht mumbled, looking away. "It just—it doesn't look like it could kill a fly."

"It kills gods," the other man said, his expression remaining utterly flat.

Erricht gawked at him. He felt his bowels go soft.

The man returned his attention to the pistol. Opening a small chamber on the top, he looked inside and nodded. He clicked the trigger a couple of times and nodded again. Then he frowned and gazed directly at Erricht. "What about the other thing?"

Erricht frowned for a moment, then brightened. "Ah! Yes. The gemstone. Of course." He reached into the pocket of his tunic and drew out a small black bag, handing it over with an ingratiating smile.

The man took the little bag and opened it, reaching inside. He drew out a jewel barely more than a centimeter in length. It sparkled red in the dim light of the bar. Carefully he slotted it into the pistol's chamber; it fit perfectly. Satisfied, he drew the stone out and returned it to the bag. It vanished into one of his pockets.

"You've done well," the disguised soldier told him. "Come and take your reward."

The man in the black uniform stood and began to walk away from the table. Erricht was on his feet instantly. He looked down at the table and the drinks he'd already finished, empty glasses standing in a small semicircle, then hastily enacted a transaction via the local commercial Aether to pay. That done, he ran after the customer.

The man had already passed through the doorway and out into the cool Candis evening. Erricht pushed the door open and followed him out.

Twin bright lights shone at him, nearly blinding him. Because of that, he nearly ran into a virtual wall of black-clad soldiers, all carrying blast rifles aimed his way. He stopped himself in his tracks in rather cartoonish fashion and gawked.

At the center of the formation stood the man with whom he'd just met. That man was handing the briefcase and the little bag over to another, rougher, tougher looking man who accepted it without comment or expression.

"Umm," Erricht began. He continued to stare in shock and growing fear at the soldiers pointing their guns at him. "I—I haven't been paid yet."

For a long moment no one made a sound. The wall of soldiers stood unmoving and unyielding, their eyes all dark and piercing. Erricht despaired of ever being paid for this transaction; at this point, all he really hoped to depart Candis with was his life—and even that wasn't looking like a strong possibility at the moment.

Then the man at the center—the one now holding the case and the bag—stepped forward. He handed the two items over to a woman behind him who wore the same uniform. Then he looked back at Erricht.

"*You* found these for me?" the big, rough man asked, and his voice was not unkind.

"I did," Erricht replied almost defiantly. He couldn't help but sneak glances at the soldiers lined up, firing-squad-style, behind the man. *This is it*, he thought to himself. *You always knew that, sooner or later, you'd attract the wrong customer. And that would be that.*

He met the other man's gaze, and a glint of recognition echoed through his mind. He'd seen this man somewhere. *Somewhere…*

The man reached out a hand. "Then you have my thanks."

Astonished, eyes wide, Erricht automatically took the hand and shook it. The grip was strong and firm—almost too strong.

When they had unclasped hands, the man gestured casually to one of his compatriots. That one—the woman who had accepted the two items moments earlier—approached Erricht. She reached out and for an absurd moment he thought she wanted to shake hands, too. But no—she was carrying a small plastic card which she handed to him.

"Payment in full," she said.

"I—" Erricht stared down at the plastic square in his hand, then up at the woman. For a second he thought she was smiling. Then the expression was banished. She turned on her heel and moved smoothly away.

"Good luck killing your god," he blurted after her, barely aware he was even speaking. Then, to himself, "Of course, who *isn't* one, these days..."

Another second and then the twin lights snapped off. When his eyes had adjusted and he could see again, the veritable army of statue-like soldiers was gone; the street outside the bar was empty.

Yadsen Erricht stood there for approximately three more seconds, peering into the darkness. Then he took one more look down at the payment card in his hand, jammed it down into his hip pocket, and ran back into the bar, making a direct line for the bathroom.

BOOK FIVE
THE BLEEDING SKY

1

His back arched, his square chin jutting out, General Ioan Iapetus stood like a god at the center—at the very heart—of the galaxy. Stars twinkled all around him, obscuring his extremities like clouds of mist floating all about. The great spiral arms of the Milky Way extended out in slow curves, with him at the epicenter.

The commander of II Legion—the Sons of Terra—was, as always, clad in black. His short, dark hair was brushed back and his expression was grim. A golden stylized eye emblazoned on the chest of his uniform gleamed in the simulated starlight. Watching, always watching.

He turned slowly, eyes sharp, seeking one particular region of that cluster of a trillion stars. He found it easily; it rarely strayed from his thoughts or his plans. There, along the farthest reaches of one galactic arm, lay the homeworld of Mankind and the core of all of humanity's conquests.

Up came his right hand, making a quick, sharp gesture in precise fashion. In response, the holographic image zoomed in until the human-occupied portion of the galaxy—the Empire and its three major rivals—filled most of the space around him. The broad, circular room in which he stood now held only hundreds of stars instead of trillions.

He smiled as he located a particular yellow sun near the center of this array. Brushing it almost lovingly with his left hand, he then cupped its attendant blue-white planet. He peered down at the little world, as though he himself had transformed into some wrathful deity, weighing its worth and passing divine judgment.

"Show me the strategic overlay," he called, his voice echoing through holographic space.

The stars around him darkened into various colors, representing the human and alien empires that controlled each of them. Turning slowly, he took it all in. His frown deepened as he considered just how precarious the situation had become—how precarious it had been *allowed* to become.

Once easily the largest of the four human empires, the Anatolian Empire had been eroded in recent months by attacks from her three rivals: the Riyahadi Caliphate, the Chung Federation, and the Dominion of Allied Core States—a bastardized conglomerate of smaller powers that went by the absurd acronym of DACS. Beyond those incursions, the two alien races that generally gave humanity the most trouble had also become more hostile and were now engaging in border raids further out on the fringes of the Empire. The technocratic Rao were an ever-present threat and always had been, but now even the ancient, enigmatic Dyonari had begun to behave like some young, immature, land-hungry force. It all defied Iapetus's understanding. It was as if something—or someone—had stirred them all up simultaneously, causing everyone who might be in a position to cause the Empire problems to all attack at once.

Whatever the cause, though, the resulting situation was clear enough. Iapetus turned once around again, slowly, weighing priorities as he saw them.

"Nakamura is a fool," he stated in a loud, clear voice—and the treason of the statement sent an electric thrill through the room. "If he wasn't before, he certainly has become one since ascending to the role of *Taiko*—and ascending to godhood." This last he spat with contempt. "Godhood. Well." He turned slowly to face the officers arrayed around the room, his expression sour. He nodded toward the stars that danced in his grasp. "The galaxy at my fingertips," he said to them with a flat smile. "That, gentlemen, is as close to godhood as I will ever come."

"How is he a fool, General?" asked one of the II Legion officers who stood along the edge of the strategium.

Iapetus didn't bother to look that way. He simply chuckled. "Our great *Taiko* is fighting this conflict as if it's all one single war. Sending his forces everywhere at once—but never enough to get the job done in any specific theater of operations. As a result, he is *losing* everywhere." Iapetus stepped around to regard the galactic display from another angle. "We have passed the tipping point. The Empire is lost. It is beyond saving."

No one responded to this statement. Iapetus waited patiently for his words to sink in, the galaxy spinning slowly around him.

"Why do you suppose we are being attacked by everyone at once, General?" came the same voice again from the sidelines, after a long and uncomfortable silence.

Iapetus shrugged. "You will recall that our late Emperor, in his complete lack of wisdom, chose in the recent past to seize territories from our neighbors and engender conflict with most of these other governments. In short, our Empire brought this upon itself." He smiled grimly. "I believe the ancient term is 'blowback.'"

"What should the *Taiko* do, then? Sir?"

Iapetus shrugged. "He must be willing to let the Outer Worlds go—write them off as lost—and focus on defending that which matters most." Iapetus gestured to several clusters of stars closer to the Earth. "At this stage we can only pull back—back to the Inner Worlds, those closest to Holy Earth—and dig in there, protecting what is most vital to us. At least until this fever of conflict and expansionism all around us burns itself out, as it quite likely will."

"What if the situation doesn't change, though, General? What if it continues indefinitely? What if retreating—even strategic retreating—only *emboldens* the enemy? *All* the enemies?"

Now Iapetus looked up, gazing out through the clusters of holographic stars to the ranks of officers and techs who stood along the edge of the room. He found the speaker easily enough; he'd recognized the voice from the start.

"Colonel Barbarossa," he called to the man across the gulf of simulated space. "You live up to your nickname—'the Daring' indeed. But I do not consider your questioning of me impertinent. I welcome it." His gaze moved slowly from the Colonel back to the star field. "So—you believe I am misreading the situation entirely?"

"Not misreading, General," replied the tall, brown-haired officer. "But perhaps misdiagnosing the illness, and thus the treatment."

"How so?" Iapetus asked—not roughly but with a sort of mild curiosity evident in his tone.

Berens Barbarossa stepped forward, the pale light illuminating him somewhat as he stood on the fringes of the display. "I believe the *Taiko* is correct in viewing this as— how did you put it? As one single war. A single conflict spread across a number of fronts."

Iapetus scoffed at this. "Impossible." He shook his head. "A coordinated attack? How could it be? Three different human empires—three that hate each other at least as much as they ever hated us—and two alien races that regard one another with utter contempt? No—there is a difference between antagonizing several of our neighbors at once and

24

facing a coordinated set of opponents. This cannot be the latter. It cannot."

"So this is all some random coincidence, then?"

"What else could it be?" Iapetus shook his head again. "Nothing in the universe could pull all of those forces together in a unified effort."

"Under normal circumstances, I would agree, General," Barbarossa stated. "But, as you yourself have admitted, these are hardly normal circumstances. And if you are wrong, then pulling back to the core of our Empire will only draw our unified enemies in closer and closer to the heart of our civilization—and eventually to Earth itself."

Iapetus appeared to consider this for a moment. Then he faced Barbarossa directly. "Let them come. If our enemies dare approach the sacred Earth, there they will find the Sons of Terra arrayed against them." His voice deepened, almost booming. "And the gods help them all."

The officers around the chamber murmured their approval of Iapetus's words, and even Barbarossa couldn't help but smile at them.

"Before that can happen, though, General," Barbarossa continued after the sound had died down, "do you think the *Taiko* will come to you for assistance along the borders? Will he ask for II Legion to step up as a frontline force?"

Iapetus snorted. "I have no doubts that they will come to me. Nakamura will come—as will Tamerlane, his lapdog. They will have no choice. Their armies are being ground down on a hundred battlefields at once, all along the borders, and they are losing control of our own governors and territories within the empire as well. The fool Rameses on Ahknaton is but the first; more will follow." He offered the officers who were watching him an elaborate shrug. "But what is to be done? What help can II Legion offer? We are the Sons of Terra. Our job—our stated mission, made quite clear by the *Taiko* himself from the beginning—is to defend the Earth and its immediate environs. To preserve humanity's homeworld and the heart of our civilization, even if all the rest of the Empire should fall."

Barbarossa gazed back levelly at Iapetus. "So, you are saying that even if the *Taiko* himself comes to you and asks for—or orders—II Legion to move up and fight in the current theaters of action, your response will be—"

Iapetus didn't blink. His face was cold and his eyes hard. "What," he asked by way of reply, "do you suppose my response will be?"

Barbarossa stared back at the man for a long moment, saying nothing. No one looking on could predict how the confrontation would end—but, perhaps fortunately for both men and for those others in attendance, they were interrupted by a tech who entered the room, almost breathless.

"General," he called. "You need to see this, sir."

Iapetus turned slowly away from Barbarossa and regarded the short, stocky man in the white lab coat. His voice was cold as ice. "Yes?"

The tech seemed to shrink down to an even tinier size. "Um—there are comets approaching a number of Imperial worlds..." His voice trailed off under the withering glare of his commander.

"Comets?" Iapetus was incredulous. "You interrupt the strategium for...*comets*?"

The little man gathered up his resolve and stood straighter. "You—you need to see them, sir."

Iapetus raised one eyebrow.

The tech signaled to his brethren behind the glass and the holographic display that filled the room gained another layer of depth. Now numerous red streaks could be seen closing in on stars all along the edge of the Empire's anti-coreward border. The image zoomed in on one of them at random; now Iapetus could see that it was indeed a comet—a massive conglomeration of ice and rock moving at high speed inward toward the local star, and the Imperial planet that orbited it.

"Their courses are all very precise," the tech stated. "Each is headed for one of our planets."

"Another coincidence, General?" Barbarossa asked, the skepticism evident in his voice. "A coincidence that those things—whatever they truly are—are headed directly into the Empire?"

Iapetus shot him a look but then returned his attention to the comet. "Pull back," he barked.

The holographic image returned to displaying the local region again, as it had done moments earlier. Iapetus counted nearly two dozen of these comets.

"What do you make of this?" he asked Barbarossa and the other officers.

No one replied.

"Why was I not informed sooner?" he asked the tech.

"We only spotted them in the last few minutes, General."

Iapetus stared at the man, almost dumbfounded. "You're saying you only *just* noticed these things? Comets do not normally move all that quickly, nor do they carry stealth technology. How could you possibly have not noticed them until now?"

The tech hesitated. "We, um—" He bit his lip. "We believe they all just dropped hyper a few moments ago. All at the same time."

Now Iapetus appeared completely astonished. "These...*comets*...dropped out of *hyperspace*? Out of the *Above*?"

"Err—yes, General." The man was sweating profusely. "It all seems rather—*unusual*. We thought you should know."

"To say the least. How soon until they begin to reach our worlds?"

"The first will enter the Eingrad system in the next twenty-four hours."

Nodding, the General strode in a slow circle around one of the comets, frowning down at it.

"Pull back further," he said then. "Show me the entire galaxy. And leave the comet overlay in place."

Everyone's equilibrium was momentarily disrupted as the image lurched, and suddenly they were back where they had begun the meeting—viewing the entire spiral of the Milky Way as it nearly filled the round room. But now the image looked strikingly different. Now a veritable wave of dark red streaks invaded it. Many more than the few that were already closing in on Imperial worlds. And all coming from beyond—from outside the galaxy itself.

And there were hundreds of them. Perhaps thousands.

Iapetus swallowed slowly, blinking at this unexpected and unprecedented revelation. Then he gestured toward the techs. "Enough. Get rid of this. Lights."

The strategium's main lights came on, their bright yellow glare replacing the dreaminess of the galactic holography— and the eeriness of the crimson streaks invading it. The officers who stood on the opposite side of the room blinked and shielded their eyes from the rapid transition; Iapetus seemed unaffected.

"So," he said. His flinty eyes met those of Barbarossa. "Colonel. I'm now willing to admit that your position may hold somewhat more merit than I was previously willing to allow."

Barbarossa couldn't help but smile at that. "Should we alert the *Taiko*?"

Iapetus hesitated, pursing his cruel lips. "No," he said at length. "No—assuming he doesn't already know. It is only a matter of time—hours, or even minutes—before our esteemed leader comes to us to beg for assistance. Given the possible threat this new development represents, I believe our position is even stronger than before. We dare not abandon the core worlds now. And I would prefer to have one more ace up my sleeve when the request to do so arrives."

Barbarossa frowned at this but nodded once.

"In the meantime, ladies and gentlemen," Iapetus continued, addressing all the officers now, "ready all our forces. Highest alert." He clasped his hands behind his back and turned to where, moments earlier, ominous red streaks had filled the space along the edges of the galaxy. "We may not be going out to do battle on the frontier, but it looks to me as if the battle is very rapidly coming to us."

2

General Marcus Ezekial Tamerlane stood laughing within a swirling cyclone of flame. His arms were raised like a conductor before a symphony and, in a way, that's exactly what he was—a conductor, creating and controlling and shaping a symphony of blazing fire that roared all around him like some elemental flame spirit, ready to destroy anything in its path but somehow leaving Tamerlane himself untouched and unharmed at its center.

The training room around him had been evacuated for this occasion, no one else safe from the power he intended to unleash. He wanted to test himself; to push his new powers to their limits and discover exactly what they could do— what *he* could do. Now the walls were hazy, rippling in his distorted vision, and he could hear alarms sounding as he pushed the levels of heat beyond even the precautions his engineers had taken in preparation. He knew he needed to back off—back the power level down—to keep from endangering the ship itself, and everyone else aboard. He knew that, and he wanted to do it—or at least part of him did. But another part of him exulted in the full exercise of his abilities. He could feel the fabled Power flowing into and through him, manifesting itself as sheets and waves of fire, surging from just beyond his fingertips; from another level of reality into this one.

Through the thick transparent window set into the far wall he could see the technicians who had been assigned to monitor the test waving frantically at him, and he understood immediately what they meant, what they wanted. He was using too much power, creating too much fire, too much heat. He needed to stop. He simply didn't want to.

Water was spraying from nozzles set into the ceiling now, but it was evaporating to nothingness before it could come anywhere near the fire that swirled in a rapidly spinning vortex around him. He was the eye of a mini-hurricane; a hurricane of fire.

Warning lights were flashing and the people behind the window were jumping up and down in their frantic fear. Slowly he forced his mind to pull itself back to reality, away from the mad reveling in serving as the conduit for so much raw power. He lowered his arms and, as if slowly turning a knob to shut down a mighty flow of water, he watched as the flames dissolved and dissipated to nothingness, as if they had never been there at all.

No, not entirely so, he realized immediately. The metal walls of the room were scorched and some spots appeared half-melted. The ultra-dense transparent window separating him from the techs in the adjoining room looked to have become warped. His own skin was hot to the touch, and he felt flushed.

Just then he felt the sting of water on his face and hands. He looked up and saw that the nozzles were still gushing water down into the room, and now it was actually being allowed to reach the floor without being evaporated first. It was reaching him, as well, and just as much steam was rising now from his own body as from the rest of the room.

Lights on the walls slowly switched back from red to yellow. The door—a massive, thick, reinforced affair—slid open and two figures in silvery suits and helmets entered. They approached him, both attempting to meet his eyes, as if to ascertain whether he had lost his mind. He smiled at them and gave them a thumbs-up, followed by, "Sorry, folks. Sort of lost control for a minute there. I hope no harm was done."

They moved quickly past him. It struck Tamerlane that they looked at him as if he were somehow…inhuman.

Perhaps the Taiko was right to assert our godhood after all—even despite saying previously that he wouldn't, Tamerlane thought as he exited the chamber. *Clearly we have become something more than mortal now. But—just how different are we?* He frowned. *Are we still human at all?*

Back to a normal temperature now but soaking wet, Tamerlane strode quickly down the corridor to his quarters. As he walked, he reflected on how quickly Nakamura had reversed his position on their alleged "godhood" and, publicly, at least, come to embrace it.

Early on, the *Taiko* had maintained that these flame-based powers he and Tamerlane had gained during their journey into the alternate dimensions of the Above and the Below were simply that—powers; abilities. Like suddenly being able to juggle or walk on one's hands. General Iapetus, who famously took great exception to anyone claiming to be a god, was mollified by Nakamura's words to that effect. Thus the transition from the royal Rahkmanov regime to Nakamura's new military government was made smoother. Within weeks, however, rumors had begun to spread across the worlds of Man that Nakamura and Tamerlane had, like the late Emperor and his guardsmen, been possessed by demons, and that their flame powers came as a result of that unholy investiture.

32

Soon riots and rebellions were erupting on dozens of worlds across the Empire. They were focused in part on these rumors about possession, but were fed as well by anger and grief over the fate of the Emperor and fear of the many enemies now laying siege to the Empire's borders and worlds. In response, Nakamura had suddenly reversed his stance. In an official statement released to the media and the churches of the Empire, he had claimed for himself and for Tamerlane divine heritage, and presented their new abilities as a natural manifestation of their inherited godhood. Shocked at first, Tamerlane had never liked this idea but he had, thus far, gone along with it. So had the Inquisition, of late Nakamura's strongest ally in the Imperial bureaucracy. The Empire's official church, the Holy Ecclesiarchy, had accepted Nakamura's and Tamerlane's proclamations of divinity as well; surprising, perhaps, but not as shocking when one considered that most of their leadership had been replaced in the days following the transition of power to the *Taiko*, and that the new crowd in charge there was trying desperately to find favor with the new leaders of the Empire.

It all gave Tamerlane a headache to think about. Barely a year ago, he had been a colonel working on the fringes of the galaxy. Now he commanded I Legion and held nominal authority over the other two—and the Empire's Church called him a god. It made his head spin to consider it all— so he tried very hard not to think about it, whenever he could avoid it.

As it happened, there was plenty else for him to be concerned about at the moment.

Entering his luxurious cabin—a cabin befitting the military figure second in rank only to the *Taiko* himself—he stripped off his sopping and scorched clothes and toweled off, then donned a fresh dress uniform—the deep red and gold of I Legion, the Lords of Fire.

A chime sounded within his Aether connection and he noted that it was almost time for his meeting with Nakamura. *At last. It feels as if he's been ducking me for days.* Frustration welled up inside him. *But this time I'll make him confront the reality of our situation. The dire reality we face.*

He paused to glance in the mirror and run a brush through his still-damp black hair. *I don't look much like a god,* he observed. *But then—what does a god look like? I've never met one before. "Those Who Remain," we call them. There aren't many left, and even fewer that ever turn up in public.*

Out the door and back down the corridor he went, saluting the ship's officers he passed along the way. It seemed to him that some of them gazed back at him with awe, others with simple respect, and a few with overt fear. *Is this what it feels like to be seen as a god?* he wondered. *I'm not sure I like it. Not at all.*

As he neared the bridge of the new Imperial flagship, *Ascanius*, he sent ahead via the Aether link to make certain Nakamura was there and was ready for the meeting. To his immense consternation, the reply came back from the *Taiko*'s executive secretary that he was unavailable and that they would have to reschedule.

Tamerlane paused as this news arrived, standing stock still just outside the doors of the bridge. Then, slowly shaking his head, he inhaled deeply and moved forward. The doors slid open and he entered.

Sure enough, Nakamura was nowhere to be seen.

The bridge stretched some forty meters in every direction ahead of him, rounded across the front with massive windows that revealed the depths of space ahead of them. Techs and officers worked at recessed stations along either side. At the center of the room rose a broad, elevated platform partially surrounded by railing with various control panels situated around it—an area for the command crew to stand as they worked.

As Tamerlane strode the length of the bridge, the ship's captain, Harras DeQuoi, noticed him and saluted. "General—how can we be of service?"

Tamerlane turned right and stopped before the door that led into the captain's office. "He's in there, isn't he?"

"I—I'm not certain who you are referring to, General Tamerlane."

"Please. You know precisely who I mean. Open the door."

The captain—an older man with gray, thinning hair and a dark complexion, appeared uncertain of what to do. "I—I—"

"Let's say you've done your part, Captain. You've tried to arrest me, you've sicced your officers on me—you've even tackled me yourself, but I slipped loose. So—no bad reflection on you. Now—let's skip past all that and just open the door."

The captain dithered another few seconds, torn between two sets of conflicting orders and his own conscience. Fortunately for him, he was absolved of the need to make a decision, as at that moment the doors opened of their own accord.

"Ezekial. Well. It would appear there's no avoiding you today."

Tamerlane looked inside and beheld the *Taiko*—Hideo Nakamura— standing in the captain's office. At first he wasn't entirely sure it was Nakamura; the man had clearly gone days without shaving and perhaps without showering. His short hair was matted and his uniform stained and wrinkled.

"*Taiko*? Are you not well?"

Nakamura waved a dismissive hand. "I am fine," he said, his voice hoarse and almost raw. "What do you want?"

Tamerlane fought the urge to rush to the older man's side and hold him up; he looked as if he might collapse at any moment.

"The strategic situation has grown precarious," Tamerlane replied, "and I wasn't sure you were receiving all the reports."

Nakamura looked back at him through bloodshot eyes. "Precarious," he repeated. "Meaning what?"

"Meaning that our empire is besieged from every direction. The other human states—the Chung, the Riyahadi, even DACS now—rush in to take advantage of our weakness. And with the alien powers on the march as well—"

"I am aware of the many enemies we face," the *Taiko* replied, cutting him off. "Do you not realize I have dispatched all of our available armies to meet them in battle? To defend the Empire?"

"Yes, of course," Tamerlane said. "But even so, the numbers of the enemy and the number of separate conflicts have become so vast, I'm afraid we are about to be overrun along at least two or three of our fronts, and—"

"And what?" the older man demanded, a bit of fire appearing in his eyes now.

"And we must take action," Tamerlane stammered.

"Action. Yes." The *Taiko* nodded. "And do you know of any other secret armies with troops and weapons available to us, that I am not aware of?"

Tamerlane stared back at the older man for a long moment, his eyes narrowing as he sought to detect any hidden meanings. Then he shook his head. "No."

Nakamura nodded. "I thought not. So—what would you have me do, then? Our forces are perilously extended. Our enemies are at the doorstep. Our stewardship of this realm is failing as we watch." He gazed back at Tamerlane, his face pale. "What would you have me do, Ezekial?"

Tamerlane was for several seconds at an absolute loss as to how to respond. Hideo Nakamura was the closest thing he'd ever had to a father. The man had practically raised him—had moved him up through the ranks rapidly. Conflict between them wasn't just distasteful to him; it felt utterly wrong. And yet the entire Empire—and possibly the fate of all Mankind—was at stake.

Tamerlane inhaled deeply, exhaled, and responded: "I would have you act, *Taiko*. I would have you remind everyone, friend and foe alike, of why you first rose to become the supreme commander of all our forces. I would have you deploy and direct our forces in a careful, considered, and above all strategically smart manner—not just throw everything we have at our enemies in every direction at once, willy-nilly, as we do now."

Nakamura took this in and he reddened severely. "You believe I am mismanaging this war?"

"With respect, sir—yes," Tamerlane replied.

The *Taiko* glared at him for a long moment, and flames actually popped into existence along his arms as he did so. Seeing them, he frowned and concentrated, causing them to vanish. The air seemed to go out of him after that. He slumped against the hull, bringing one hand up to his face. He had begun to sweat profusely.

"What can I do, Ezekial?" he asked in a ragged voice. "Our Empire finds itself at the heart of a maelstrom. I fear we cannot win this time."

"The Hideo Nakamura I knew would never succumb to defeatism," Tamerlane snapped back. "He would never give up before the battles have even been decided."

"Then what—?"

"We must regroup," Tamerlane said. He pressed on quickly. "We have to rally our forces, reassess our strategies, and redeploy our legions in the most effective manner possible." He turned and gestured toward the forward windows of the bridge, and the sparkling arm of the galaxy arrayed beyond. "And we must call upon every legion to step up and do its part. *Every* legion."

When Tamerlane turned back to the *Taiko*, he became aware of another presence. A figure in dark red robes now stood at the older man's side, apparently having followed him out of the captain's office. A hood concealed its head and features in shadow.

Nakamura was blinking, still mopping at his brow. He stood up straighter, his eyes seeming to focus intently on Tamerlane for the first time.

"Ezekial?" he whispered. "What—?"

Moving as smoothly as a cat, the new figure stepped close to the *Taiko*. As Tamerlane looked on, puzzled, slender hands with red nails reached up and drew the hood back to reveal a woman's pale white face and long, dark hair.

"Who—?" Tamerlane started to ask. Then he realized who she was. The recently-appointed new Ecclesiarch—head of the Holy Church of Those Who Remain.

"Teluria?" he said, staring at her with a puzzled expression. "Why are you here?"

The woman ignored his presence and leaned over to whisper in Nakamura's ear. The *Taiko* nodded once, nodded again, and the woman moved away. In the time it took Tamerlane to blink his eyes, she was gone.

"I appreciate your words, General," Nakamura said a moment later, "and I will take your suggestions under advisement."

"What?"

"That will be all," Nakamura said. He turned and walked back into the darkened office.

"*Taiko*?" Tamerlane called after him. "Hideo?"

The door slid closed in Tamerlane's face.

Several seconds ticked by before he could move. Slowly at first, he turned away from the blank gray doors and faced the sprawling bridge. No one was looking his way. Very intentionally, no one was looking his way. The captain was standing behind one of the seats at the navigation station, quietly discussing something with a tech. For a split second he glanced up at Tamerlane. Then he looked away again, seeming very busy with ship's business.

Tamerlane considered what had just happened. The *Taiko* had at least talked to him. For a few seconds, he'd even seemed to be listening—to hear what Tamerlane had to say. To take his concerns into consideration. But then something had happened. *Something...*

Had there been someone else? Had someone...?

No, that was ridiculous. Who else could there have been?

Yet a little voice buried deep in Tamerlane's subconscious continued to nag at him, trying to remind him of...something. *Someone.*

Shaking his head, Tamerlane stalked across the bridge and around the lift to the strategium chamber that filled the space behind it. The tech on duty looked up at him and saluted. "Can I help you, General?" the young woman asked.

Tamerlane nodded. "Indeed you can," he told her. "I need an Aether link to Second and Third Legion command bases."

Wide-eyed, the young officer scrambled to obey.

"I'm calling a meeting," Tamerlane added, his hands clasped behind his back. "A meeting of the *Hatamoto*—the top leadership."

"Of course, General," the tech replied. She manipulated the bank of controls before her and a holographic haze began to form throughout the circular room.

"We will act," Tamerlane added, his voice low and aimed only at himself, "even if the *Taiko* himself refuses to do so."

3

The man to Arjan Dev's right screamed, his right arm shorn off just above the elbow, even as the sentry to his left exploded.

The volley of blasts came seemingly from nowhere. A moment earlier, the scene had been one of busy but calm preparation, as legionaries of the Golden Phalanx—better known to most as the Kings of Oblivion—dug trenches and set up mounted weapons and carried supplies and ammunition here and there. The sounds then had been benign: Servos whining softly from the gleaming white Deising-Arry Mark V plate armor some of the officers were privileged to wear, as it increased their muscle power and enabled them to do the work of a half-dozen or more normal men. The low murmuring of a thousand well-trained veteran soldiers discussing the myriad things men of war talked about—some meaningless chatter, some the exchange of vitally important information—in the hours before an expected battle. Orders being passed from trooper to trooper, bickering over slights real or imagined, and good-natured banter. The smells had been of the churned earth, the forest, engine exhaust, machine lubricants, and sweat.

An instant later—only a couple of seconds after the sentries to either side of Arjan Dev were struck by a high-discharge energy lance blast—the sounds became shouts of alarm and screams of shock. Shock and *pain*. The smells of the forest and the earth were utterly overwhelmed by smoke from projectile weapons and fires, ozone from energy blasts, and blood. Death—death *en masse*—had smells all its own that only veteran soldiers knew, and it was those smells that now suffused the camp, heralding the onslaught to come.

Arjan Dev moved instinctively. He was moving before he fully understood what was happening. He threw himself backward from the raised earthwork and rolled, even as sizzling energy blasts struck the ground around him or whizzed past. There was little immediate cover nearby; only a scant few of the tall, slender, tropical trees remained standing in the entire camp. A great deal of the forest that filled and surrounded III Legion's landing zone had been ripped up, burned, or chopped down. At last stumbling past a parked hovertank, he scrambled behind it and accessed the Aether link, intending to sound the alarm. He needn't have bothered; the attack itself had raised plenty of alarm, and the local Aether was filled with urgent reports, orders, and exclamations.

In a flash, everything on Eingrad-6 had changed. General Agrippa, having led the assault force down from orbit and having taken command of them personally, had been preparing for a major assault that he had planned to launch with the following dawn.

He would not get that chance.

Arjan Dev sat crouched behind the hovertank for three seconds—seconds that seemed both as brief as the blink of an eye and as long as an eternity. Gathering his wits and his courage, reminding himself that he was a lieutenant in III Legion, with all that such a distinction carried with it, he stood and drew his blast pistol. Then he leaned around the tank and peered into the smoke and dust, in the direction of the attack.

What he saw surprised him, to say the least.

"We are under attack," came a voice over the Aether link, overriding the other signals. It was General Agrippa himself. "All legionaries stand ready to repel enemy advance."

"This is very unlike the Riyahadi," came the voice he quickly recognized as Major Kursk.

"Yes," Agrippa agreed. "Does anyone have any intelligence as to what they're trying to do—or why? Sentries—have you seen anything that—"

Arjan Dev interrupted his general. He felt under the circumstances it was warranted. "It's not the Riyahadi, General," he reported.

"What?" A pause. "Lieutenant Dev? What are you talking about?"

"I can see the attackers now, sir," Arjan Dev replied, leaning out from behind the tank again and pulling his head back again just before three devastating blasts narrowly missed him. "It's the Rao."

"The *Rao*?" The shock in Agrippa's voice was obvious and pronounced. It was clear that he didn't entirely believe Dev's report. "Why would *aliens* be helping the Riyahadi attack us?"

The blasts grew more intense, and now were coming from more than one direction. The Rao soldiers—humanoid in general, but somewhat shorter than the average human, and pale blue in skin color, on those rare occasions when they were seen outside of their high-tech orange body-armor—were flanking his position. He couldn't stay there much longer. In mere moments they would have him surrounded. But—what could he do? Where could he—?

He looked at the big hunk of metal behind which he had been hiding. He blinked his eyes, registering exactly what it was, then smiled. A second later, he was scrambling up the side of it and back down through the open turret.

The inside of the hovertank was dark, but just enough light from the planet's moons was shining down into the interior that he could make out the controls. He moved his hands over the ignition and main power boards, kicking the big machine to life. Lights in a rainbow of colors lit up on the consoles all around him. Reaching up, he grasped the hatch lid and pulled it closed. Simultaneously, the tank reached nominal power output and rose smoothly into the air, living up to its name by hovering approximately three feet off the ground.

Shots rang off the vehicle's armored hide. This didn't worry Arjan Dev terribly much; though he himself was not a tanker and had never trained extensively in one, he knew the basics. The armor of a III Legion hovertank was thick and very strong, made from a single force-grown crystal of hyper-dense molecular structure, lined with a mixture of light, strong metal alloys and exotic ceramics. The weaponsmiths of the Kings of Oblivion had developed this particular formula themselves and had never shared the full details of the process with even their counterparts in the other legions. The tankers who manned the vehicles, likewise, trained long and hard, in the most rigorous of environments and simulations. As a result, Agrippa's tank corps had achieved a reputation unmatched in the realm of armored cavalry. The soldiers of III Legion took great pride in this. Even those who, like Dev, were not assigned to tank duty.

Arjan Dev manipulated the controls of the tank deftly, spinning the big machine around. His first thought was to use it to retreat back to the main camp from the front line— the spot where, as a sentry infantryman, he had been posted to keep an eye on the Riyahadi. But then he hesitated, looking around him. He was sitting inside a hovertank. Someone in III Legion had parked it there for some inscrutable reason, but there was no sense in turning down a gift like that now.

Dev spun the tank back around, presenting its most heavily-armored section of hull to the advancing Rao aliens in their orange armor. They were charging on foot, already climbing over the raised earth embankment Dev had spent the earlier portion of the evening sitting behind. Their energy lances and power rifles were spitting blindingly bright blobs and streaks of superheated gas and barely-contained pulses of energy, along with solid projectiles and slugs. Their assault was impressive indeed—as long as their opponents consisted of mere sentries with sidearms.

Laughing now, Arjan Dev swung the main turret around and lined both the heavy cannon and the smaller anti-personnel weapon up in the direction of the enemy. He fired.

The main cannon blasted first. A huge, shimmering cylinder of raw energy lashed out, smashing into the center of the Rao advance. It vaporized the half-dozen alien soldiers it struck directly, then hit the earthworks mere inches from where Dev himself had been crouching before. The embankment exploded, further shredding the Rao line.

Before the alien attackers could recover, Dev's smaller automatic gun that was positioned just to the right of the main cannon began to spit sizzling death. It carved into the stunned and reeling Rao on either side of the ragged hole in the embankment, slicing them down one by one. Scarcely ten seconds after Arjan Dev had climbed into the tank, he'd taken out half of the attacking force at his position.

"What's happening there?" demanded Agrippa over the Aether link. "I'm seeing firing from our side of the line."

Dev keyed the link. "This is Lt. Dev, General. I have commandeered a hovertank and am attempting to blunt the Rao advance."

A pause, then, "Good man, Dev. Excellent work. We are on our way now."

The link closed. Dev shrugged to himself and continued to fire, sweeping the turret around forty-five degrees to carve into the right flank of the assault force. The Rao looked surprised now—or as surprised as aliens in armor and helmets that totally covered their bodies and faces could look. Their well-organized ranks were shattered, and individuals scrambled here and there, not unlike what Dev had done some moments earlier. Watching them from inside the tank as he fired, he relished how the shoe was now on the other foot.

Feeling increasingly confident, he stood from the driver's seat, moved one step to his right, and reached for the driving controls, moving the big vehicle forward slowly. It wasn't easy to do that and work the weapons controls at the same time, but he moved incrementally, taking every opportunity to break up any concentration of enemy troops as he went. It looked to him as if the Rao were falling back now. The thought that he might have single-handedly won this battle before anyone else from his side had even arrived began to bounce around in his brain, and he grinned.

The hovertank moved over the earthworks, angling upward as it went, then back down the other side. It bounced momentarily as it reacquainted itself with gravity and proper orientation. Stopping again, Dev returned to the gunner's seat and peered out the main site. He gasped.

Instead of the backs of a few dozen retreating Rao, he found himself face-to-armored face with a veritable ocean of Rao troops. From just ahead of him practically to the horizon, all he could see was pale orange armor. They looked like ants that had been stirred up from their hill.

"We're here, Dev," came the booming voice of Agrippa over the link. "Coming up just behind your position."

Arjan Dev opened and closed his mouth soundlessly for a second, in shock.

"We'll finish off the stragglers," Agrippa was continuing. "I'd like a few prisoners to interrogate."

"General," Dev all but shouted over the link. "Stay back! There are too many!"

Silence for a moment. Then, "What's that, Lieutenant?"

Arjan Dev spun the turret around so that it was facing towards the approaching troops of III Legion, so that he could get a look at them. They were already there, though, rushing past his tank on either side. At the head of the force ran General Agrippa himself. The big man leapt to the top of a still-intact section of earthworks, raising his quad-rifle high in one hand and his gladius in the other. "Advance, men!" he boomed. He looked to Dev like a god among men, tall and majestic and powerful.

A barrage of energy blasts came at him from beyond, and at least two of them glanced off his white armor. He tumbled off the rise and fell heavily to the ground.

As attendants rushed to Agrippa's aid, Arjan Dev keyed the Aether link again. "There are thousands of them," he cried over the mental communications network. "It's an entire army!"

The legionaries hesitated in their advance, looking to the fallen Agrippa, uncertain.

Agrippa pulled his massive, armored form back up onto his feet. "The Lieutenant is right," he sent. "Pull back! We must regroup and prepare a more effective force." A pause as various subordinates acknowledged the order. Then, "You too, Dev. Bring that tank back to the main camp with you. We'll need it."

"Understood, General," Dev replied.

"I've already called in a little help," Agrippa added.

As energy blasts in increasing force and number continued to ring off the hull, Arjan Dev hauled the tank around and accelerated back toward the base. At that moment the Aether link crackled to life again on a private channel. Eyes widening at what he saw in his virtual vision, he keyed it. "Yes, General?"

"That was good work back there, Dev," the big man told him. "You may have saved a good portion of our army—not to mention me."

Dev smiled. "My pleasure, General." He hesitated a moment. "But—"

"What is it, Lieutenant?"

"Are we retreating, sir? I thought we never did that. Never."

"Retreating?" The incredulity in Agrippa's voice was powerful and heartening. "Don't be silly, Lieutenant. Take a look at about two o'clock, and up—toward the sky."

Steering the hovertank deftly—he was better at it than he'd expected he'd be—Dev snuck a quick look through the viewscope in the direction the general had indicated. At first he couldn't understand what he was seeing. It appeared as if about a dozen men were floating in the air, slowly descending. But that couldn't be right; they were too far away. The shape of what he was seeing fought with the sense of distance and scale within his mind for a couple of seconds before suddenly it all snapped into place. In spite of himself, he gasped.

A group of man-shaped Imperial Colossus walkers were settling to the ground. The heavily armed and armored machines had two legs, two arms, a torso and a head, but beyond that all resemblance to a human being ended—not least of which because each of them was some two hundred meters tall. They were engines of pure, unadulterated destruction, and the general had just committed a dozen of them to this battle.

"Retreating?" Agrippa repeated over the link, laughing. "Son, I'm simply reloading."

4

The huge double-doors of the throne room swung open with a crash, instantly dissipating the previously oppressive, almost palpable gloom that had filled the chamber.

Caught by surprise, ceremonially armed and crimson-robed Sand Kings guards reacted with a start, moving away from their usual positions along the walls and hurrying forward, their ornamented but effective golden energy rifles at the ready.

On his throne, the planetary governor, Rameses, jerked awake from the latest of his recent string of nightmares and sat up straight. Scowling at the interruption, he peered through the dimly lit space and attempted to understand exactly what he was seeing.

Through the now-open doorway glided a figure all in black. A peaked hood covered its head and obscured its face in shadow. A few paces behind came a quartet of muscular, bronze-skinned men, all partially clad in black metal armor of some unrecognizable sort, each holding up one corner of a rectangular palanquin.

LEGION II: SONS OF TERRA

The Sand Kings guards hurried to interpose themselves between the intruders and their ruler. Scarcely had they moved into place, however, before the man in black gestured at them with his right hand and they began to fall back, making way.

"What is this?" demanded Rameses, now fully awake and seeing his troops moving aside for this newcomer. He smoothed the wrinkles in his luxurious purple and red robes, the woven gold trim gleaming in the dim candlelight. His voice cracked but was still strong. "Who are you?"

The figure in black ignored him for the moment. Instead it gestured to its right in silent command and the four bearers instantly obeyed, carrying their burden to the area indicated. The figure gestured and spoke a soft word, inaudible to Rameses only a short distance away. The four slaves instantly knelt in one smooth movement, lowering the rectangular platform to the cold marble floor. As it touched down, Rameses could at last fully see what was carried upon it: a small cube of dark red, roughly six inches to the side, and a broad but shallow bowl or basin of gold, slightly more than two meters wide.

Rameses' eyes darted from the objects to the silent figure and back again. "What is the meaning of this?" he called down, but the force of his words had already faded somewhat. His eyes were now locked onto the two objects that had been revealed. Standing, never taking his eyes off them, he hurried down the steps of the dais which held his throne.

"Gifts," the dark figure stated, breaking its silence at last. The voice was low and gravelly. Spindly fingers drew back the hood. "Gifts from my master."

With seemingly great effort, Rameses tore his eyes away from the two objects and glanced quickly at the man whose head was now revealed. He looked at him just long enough to get a general impression—very pale, very slender, angular face, short and spiky hair—and then turned back to

49

the palanquin. "Who are you, then—and who is your master?" he asked. He felt somehow he should know the answer to the second question, but no name came to his mind as he considered it. "You are in my throne room, on my world," he said. "You will answer!"

"I am called Zahir," replied the man in black.

Still distracted, Rameses nodded at this. "Zahir. A good name. A godly name." He glanced very briefly at the man again. "It was carried by one of the Seventy-Five, the lost gods. The gods who died the final death."

"No," the figure in black stated.

Rameses blinked at this unexpected response. He frowned. "No? No *what*? The name Zahir is well-known as having belonged to one of the dead gods."

"No," the figure repeated.

Rameses's anger grew. It was enough now to drag his attention away from the two shiny objects on the palanquin. "No? What do you mean by 'no?'" he demanded. "Do you dispute the fact that the name you bear was also borne by a god?"

"Certainly not," the figure in black replied. He looked up at Rameses and his mouth split into a smile both humorless and disturbing. "I merely dispute the claim that I am *dead*."

Rameses stared back at him for a long moment, then blinked, shook his head, and laughed sharply. "Ah. I see what you are saying now. Very clever—very funny."

The man in black simply stared back at him, his gaze flat and almost lifeless. "You know my master, do you not?"

Rameses' smile faded. For a moment he said nothing. Then he looked away, saw his soldiers standing idly by with glassy eyes and vacant expressions, and nodded. "Yes," he said, as an image swirled into and back out of his consciousness. "Yes, I believe I do."

Zahir chuckled softly. "And, knowing his identity, you would yet believe anything impossible?"

Rameses stood up to his full height, turning his back on the palanquin with great reluctance. He loomed nearly a foot taller than Zahir. "So I am supposed to believe that you are a god?"

"What you believe of me is immaterial," the dark man replied. "What matters is that you understand I am here in the place of my master, and that I have been sent to advise you. You will follow my instructions as you would his, and you will follow them implicitly."

"*Instructions*?" Rameses bellowed. "I am the ruler of this entire world—and soon of much more besides. You would have me *follow*?" He practically spat the word. "I follow *no one*!"

Zahir's eyes met Rameses' and held them. The temperature in the room dropped noticeably. Ice began to form on the stone floor and along the walls. "Yes," the dark man said, his voice hard now. "Yes, precisely. You follow no one. For, as far as this empire is concerned, I do not exist— I am indeed no one." Though not a tall figure, Zahir now seemed somehow to loom over the governor—to tower over him.

Eyes wide, Rameses shrank back, shivering from the cold. A moment later, his face slowly relaxed. At last he nodded. "Yes. Yes, of course. I—I will follow."

Zahir stared at him, his dark eyes cold and penetrating. "What of the girl?" he asked, his voice intense.

"The girl?"

The dark man said nothing, merely waiting, his gaze seemingly locking the governor to the spot.

"You mean the princess, of course," Rameses said, as if remembering something long-forgotten.

"Indeed. The Princess Marens. My master gave her over into your care."

"Yes. It didn't take long for us to discover who she was."

"You have kept her safe?"

"Yes, yes—she is fine. Too young to fully understand what has happened. Growing impatient to see her family." He snorted at that. "But still firmly under control, of course."

Zahir continued to hold Rameses with his eyes for a long second more, as if judging his words. Then he released him and turned away.

Rameses blinked, gasped, then exhaled slowly, his face darkening. "You—how *dare* you—?"

Zahir ignored the anger and gestured toward the palanquin. Now his voice was relaxed and almost casual in its tones.

"My master sends his greetings, his regards—and three gifts. Gifts of immense value."

"Gifts?" Recovering himself, Rameses turned back to the rectangle where it now sat on the floor. "Well. Most generous of him." Squinting, he moved closer, as though trying to get a better look at what sat upon it. "But—I only see two objects here."

"Yes. The third will arrive shortly." Zahir paused. "It will not seem a gift at all at first. But shortly thereafter, you will learn to your wonder and awe that it is the grandest gift of all."

Zahir strode over to the palanquin and reached down, grasping the crimson cube in his clawlike right hand. He held it aloft, the frightening smile back on his face. It began to glow, brighter and brighter by the second, as if from some hidden internal source of light.

"Only twelve of these were ever made, when the Ancient Ones were at the height of their power and their craft. Most have been lost for eons. My master gives you this—one of the very few remaining—as his first gift."

Rameses moved forward and frowned, his eyes locked onto the object, his expression one of deep desire. He tried to sound flippant as he replied, "A lovely music box or puzzle, I'm sure"—but there was no conviction in his voice.

He was entranced by the box, with its dazzling radiance and swirling intricate patterns across the surface.

"Take it," said Zahir, holding it out for him.

Rameses needed no further prompting. Greedily he seized the cube and clutched it to himself. He had no idea what it could be, but something about it utterly entranced him.

For several seconds nothing happened—though that scarcely seemed to bother Rameses, as he appeared content merely to hold the thing. Then the light radiating from within it spread, quickly enveloping his entire body. It flared almost blindingly bright for a moment. Crying out, the Sand Kings guards—now recovering their wits, at last—hurried forward, at the defense of their ruler. But the brightness faded as quickly as it had appeared, and Rameses still stood there, unharmed.

Unharmed—but different. The Sand Kings all exclaimed in surprise and astonishment.

Rameses, planetary governor of Ahknaton, now stood encased in a dark red metallic armor that nearly covered his entire body. Only his face was exposed from within a helmet that blended seamlessly into the rest of the suit. His musculature appeared drastically increased, bulging against the seemingly pliable surface of the suit. The ornamental line work that had covered the cube now covered the armor. The arms and legs featured dull rivets along the sides, epaulets stood out at the shoulders, and two vanes or blunted blades protruded out from either side of the helmet. In sum, the armor appeared at least as impressive as anything worn by the Imperial Legions, and far less bulky and heavy than the crystal armor of the old Emperor's Guard.

Rameses looked down at himself in shock. He raised one arm, flexed the fingers, then did likewise with the other. He moved his head back and forth—there was no resistance, as if the material were smartcloth and not some hyper-dense and strong metal, as it appeared. Then he looked up at Zahir. A smile slowly formed on his face.

"You approve, then?" the other asked.

"I—yes," Rameses answered. "It is remarkable—marvelous. But—why?"

"There is more to that armor than you yet know," the man answered. "Patience. All will be revealed soon."

Rameses nodded. "Very well." He moved as if to pull the gloves of the armor off, only to discover that there were no seams, no divisions in the cool metal material. "How—how do I—?"

"You have but to desire it."

Rameses frowned, then closed his eyes. A second later, the armor was gone from him, and the crimson cube back in his hand. Holding it aloft before his face, he smiled at it, then at Zahir. "Well," he said. "One can only hope all of your master's gifts are so interesting." And saying that, he looked back at the palanquin, and the golden basin that still rested upon it.

Zahir motioned again, and two of his servants lifted the object. They carried it off the palanquin and set it down gently on the marble floor at the center of the chamber, a short distance away from the steps leading up to the throne.

Rameses followed them and stared at it, studying it. Broad and round and golden, it looked like a sort of overgrown bowl or dish, more than two meters in diameter and less than a meter high. Its sides sloped gently in and down toward a depression at the center. Leaning down and reaching out, Rameses ran his fingers along the edge.

"So—what is it?"

Zahir smiled. "It is a doorway."

Rameses reacted to this news with a start. "A *doorway*? It's the strangest looking doorway I've ever seen."

"And the most marvelous doorway you will ever see."

Zahir leaned out over the basin and stretched out his clawed hand, moving his fingers in a series of odd gestures.

Then he reached into his robes and brought forth a gleaming silver knife. As Rameses and the Sand Kings looked on in alarm, he drew the blade across his palm. Blood dripped out and down into the basin—blood that sparkled and shimmered with some sort of contained energy.

As the drops splattered onto the shining surface of the bowl, the air suddenly seemed filled with a soft, persistent, buzzing sound. Rameses and the others looked around, half-expecting to see swarms of insects descending upon them. But that was not the case. The buzzing, as they quickly realized, was coming from all around—from the air itself. From reality itself, as it was being torn asunder.

A flash, a blast of fire erupting from the basin. When it had died down, a shimmering circle remained floating vertically in the air above it.

"A doorway," Zahir repeated.

Rameses gawked. "A doorway," he said, agreeing now. "But—to where?"

"To *everywhere*," the pale man answered.

5

Am I to understand, General Tamerlane," the big, blond man boomed across the Aether connection, "that our *Taiko* is unaware of this meeting?"

Tamerlane smiled humorlessly and nodded once. "That is correct, General Agrippa."

The blond general floated as a holographic ghost directly across the strategium chamber from Tamerlane. He seemed somewhat distracted, if not downright annoyed—a condition Tamerlane chalked up to his being called away from an apparently increasingly bad military situation in order to sit in—virtually—on a sort of committee meeting. Tamerlane could hardly blame the man for such an attitude, given the circumstances. He studied Agrippa, noting with a degree of relief how the man appeared to focus at last on the matter at hand. After a moment's consideration, Agrippa shrugged. "If what I have heard of late is even half-true," he said, "it is probably for the best that he doesn't know."

A reaction of surprise at such blatantly disrespectful talk instantly appeared on the face of the third and final member of the *Hatamoto*—the top circle of trusted advisors to the *Taiko*. Just to Tamerlane's right stood Berens Barbarossa of

II Legion, in the flesh. Only a colonel, he had been selected by Nakamura for this role over the higher-ranking General Iapetus simply because Nakamura did not like or trust Iapetus. He'd needed the mercurial general on his side, however, and he'd known it, so he'd assigned him and his Legion to the defense of the Earth and its near environs. Iapetus had immediately rechristened II Legion the Sons of Terra—and, by all reports, effectively shut Barbarossa out.

"What do you mean by that, General?" Barbarossa demanded. "For the best? How?"

Agrippa rankled at being spoken to in such a manner by a lower-ranking officer, but he refrained from issuing a rebuke. From the very beginning, months earlier, the understanding among the three of them had taken root that rank would be set aside while they met as the *Hatamoto*. Here, in this formal gathering, each held equal voice and equal power. Consequently, Agrippa's flickering form merely replied, "I trust Ezekial will make that clear presently."

Tamerlane grimaced at the degree of rancor that had crept into their dealings, even here amidst the gathering of the *Hatamoto*. He motioned to the other two men to settle down.

"No one here intends disrespect toward the *Taiko*," Tamerlane stated firmly. "We all love him greatly, and none more than me. But we also all have eyes and ears, and have heard and seen what is becoming of our Empire."

"Yes," Agrippa agreed, his insubstantial eyes flickering from Tamerlane to Barbarossa and back. "Something must be done. Actions must be taken. And I fear our beloved *Taiko* is, for whatever reason, unable to take those actions."

Tamerlane had to nod. "And so it falls to us."

Agrippa nodded at this.

Barbarossa shook his head. "This might be considered treason," he suggested, his voice tremulous.

"It is *not* treason," Tamerlane barked back at him. "Treason would be a betrayal of the Empire and its people—a betrayal of Nakamura. This is quite the opposite. We are acting to preserve the Empire and protect Nakamura, despite his own...*weakness*, of late."

"The fate of the Empire—and of untold billions of lives—is at stake," Agrippa added, his voice deep and sonorous and very compelling.

Barbarossa bit back a reply and looked at the other two, considering. After a few seconds he asked, "So—what are you proposing, then? Not that I am granting my consent, of course."

"Not yet, no," Tamerlane acknowledged. "But explaining why you should is one of the reasons I asked you here." He gestured and the holographic display expanded to fill the strategium, surrounding himself and the other two men. Now their entire sector of the galaxy was laid out in three dimensions all around them. In rapid succession Tamerlane pointed out the many key locations where the Empire's enemies were pushing inwards, subsuming the outer worlds and moving into position to threaten the inner ones.

"These are the key points where the incursions must be resisted and halted," he stated after the display had slowly spun about them once. Red arrows marked the locations he was indicating. "The problem, of course, is that we lack the troop strength to boost our numbers at more than two or three of those theaters of war."

"General Iapetus has been privately discussing a different option," Barbarossa stated in a quiet voice.

"And what would that be?" both Tamerlane and Agrippa asked simultaneously.

A small smile crossed Barbarossa's features at that. "He believes that a pullback—a strategic withdrawal of elements of both your legions from the Outer Worlds—would yield many thousands of new troops with which to defend Earth and the Inner Worlds."

Tamerlane parsed this statement out, then frowned at Barbarossa. "You're saying Iapetus would have us abandon the Outer Worlds—simply give them up to the enemy without further struggle?"

"Not as such," Barbarossa said, gazing off to one side. "Not entirely. At least, not permanently. Perhaps."

Tamerlane was shocked. He turned to the image of Agrippa, only to see that the big man did not appear entirely discomfited by the suggestion.

"Perhaps Iapetus has a point," Agrippa said. "Perhaps—"

"You, too, Arnem?" Tamerlane asked, eyes wide. "You would have us simply *hand over* the Empire?"

"Of course not, Ezekial. But perhaps some degree of strategic withdrawal from less important areas is warranted."

"And who decides what areas—which worlds, with our people living on them—are 'less important?'"

Agrippa frowned, looking down at the floor. He nodded slowly, sadly.

"I for one am not ready to give in to the enemy," Tamerlane insisted.

"That's just it, General," Barbarossa said, leaning toward him, his voice intense. "There is no *single* enemy. The 'enemy' you speak of is comprised of virtually every other human empire and alien government that shares a border with us. We cannot fight all of them at once. We simply cannot."

"To even contemplate withdrawal galls me, too, Ezekial," Agrippa stated in deep, stentorian tones. "But the alternative is that we could lose everything. *Everything.*"

Tamerlane took this in, his mouth open but no sound coming out. Finally he looked to Agrippa and said, "We would not be in this predicament if other forces were available to us on the frontier."

"And you know of some?" the big man replied. "I would love to hear of them."

"I know of two different possibilities, actually," Tamerlane said. His gaze shifted from Agrippa to Barbarossa. "If their commanders can be persuaded to bring them directly into the conflict." He waited.

Barbarossa looked mystified for a moment. Then recognition dawned in his eyes. "Ah. You speak of my own legion. The Sons of Terra."

"That is one, yes," Tamerlane said.

Barbarossa smiled at this and even chuckled a bit.

"Something is amusing, Colonel?" Agrippa asked, annoyed, reverting to calling the man by his rank even though they met there as *Hatamoto*.

Barbarossa met Agrippa's hard blue eyes with his own brown ones. "In point of fact, and with all due respect, *sir*—yes." He turned to Tamerlane. "The thought that you include II Legion in your calculations is, to me, amusing."

"Amusing?" boomed Agrippa, his annoyance growing.

Tamerlane waved this aside impatiently. "You think that Iapetus will refuse to deploy them as I request?"

"I *know* he will refuse, General."

"And if I order?"

Barbarossa merely laughed again and shook his head slowly.

"He will refuse a direct order?" Agrippa asked, almost glaring at him. "You are so certain of this?"

"Absolutely certain," Barbarossa replied, turning back to the big blond man. "He will not budge."

Tamerlane and Agrippa exchanged troubled glances. No one spoke for a moment, and tension filled the air.

Barbarossa raised a hand. "If I may—you said there were *two* possibilities. What is the other?"

Pushing down his anger, Tamerlane forced himself to set all thoughts of the Sons of Terra and Barbarossa's statements about them aside. He turned and pointed to a location in the holographic display above him and to his right. At his silent signal over the Aether link, one star there began to flash bright red.

"Ahknaton," Barbarossa said. "Of course."

"The Sand Kings have, by all reports, grown quite formidable of late," said Agrippa. "They are no longer a mere planetary defense force but an actual army now, with troop strength and weapons to rival any of the legions. That being the case, we must insist that Governor Rameses do his share in the defense of the Empire and bring them into play."

"He had no business expanding their ranks or their armaments in that fashion, of course," Tamerlane pointed out, "and certainly not without the permission of the *Taiko*."

"It's treason," Agrippa summarized.

"We can prosecute him for his actions in creating essentially his own legion after the war is won," Tamerlane said. "For now, we should make use of them for the good of all."

Barbarossa had listened to all of this and considered it, and now he nodded slowly. "Alright," he said, "I understand the gravity of the situation and the particular strategic plight we face. If the *Taiko* is not acting to address it—"

"He is not," Tamerlane interjected.

"—then yes, we must move. Immediately."

Tamerlane smiled grimly at him. "Good. I'm glad we are all in agreement."

"So you will speak to Iapetus, then," Agrippa's holograph said. "Persuade him to add the ranks of the Sons of Terra to our new offensive."

"No," Barbarossa replied.

The other two men were dumbstruck.

"What—what do you mean, '*no*?'" Agrippa demanded a moment later, as Tamerlane looked on, puzzled.

"I mean what I said. I will not bring such a request before General Iapetus."

"Why?"

"Because I know precisely what his answer will be. So there is little or no point in asking."

"But—"

"Additionally," the colonel pressed on, "I have worked very hard these past few months to earn some degree of trust with Iapetus—to secure my place as a somewhat valued member of II Legion. Your request for me to come here in person was not well-received by him, and I have work ahead of me simply to recover from it—from what is effectively a secret top-level meeting that excludes him." Barbarossa paused, then, "Were I to go to him with your proposal, knowing full well that he will reject it, he would think me a fool. He would turn the request down flat, and afterward he would effectively banish me from the Legion—restrict me from any position of power within it." Barbarossa looked from Agrippa to Tamerlane. "And then what use would I be—to him, or to you?"

Taken aback, Tamerlane found he had no real answer for this. He glanced at Agrippa but the big man only shrugged.

"Very well," the I Legion commander said after a few seconds of silence. He turned away from the other two *Hatamoto* and called, "Colonel!"

For a moment nothing happened, and Barbarossa looked about in puzzlement. Then the clouds of holographic imagery parted and Colonel Konstans Belisarius, a tall, handsome, dark-haired man and second-in-command of the Lords of Fire, emerged into the open space already occupied by the three *Hatamoto*.

"Sir?" Belisarius asked, saluting.

"I have a new assignment for you," Tamerlane said. "You are to go to Earth and meet with General Iapetus. Find a way to convince him to acquiesce to my request for at least some portion of the II Legion to move up to the front lines."

From his spot off to one side, Barbarossa suppressed a laugh. The others glanced at him but no one commented.

Belisarius took this order in but didn't reply at first. His Latin features grew darker, his expression confused.

"Something the matter, Colonel?"

Belisarius pursed his lips, started to reply, then hesitated again.

"What is the matter, man?" Agrippa demanded.

Belisarius inhaled deeply, then addressed his superior, Tamerlane. "I have been monitoring the conversation, as you requested, General," he said, "and I believe I would be of better use traveling to Ahknaton and seeking to persuade Governor Rameses in the way you described."

Tamerlane frowned at this. "Why do you say that, Colonel?"

Belisarius again appeared to be wrestling with himself and could barely answer. At last he managed, "I'm...not entirely sure, General. But... I feel strongly... that I could make a difference...if I were allowed to go to Ahknaton."

Tamerlane was clearly surprised by this reaction from his trusted second, but could only agree. "Very well, Colonel. Our need is great, and the time grows short. So, if you feel so strongly in the matter, then fine. You will go and explain the state of affairs to Rameses." He stroked his chin for a moment, then stepped closer to the man and continued, "Be forceful. Don't take no for an answer. Make the case very clearly to him that he must answer to the Imperial government. Explain to him in no uncertain terms that this 'legion' of Sand Kings he has created—for whatever reason—is as much a part of the Empire as any other unit, and not his personal and private army to do with solely as he pleases."

"Understood, General," Belisarius answered quickly, snapping a salute. "I will depart immediately."

Tamerlane nodded and the colonel moved back through the clouds and out of the strategium.

"Well, that was odd," Agrippa observed. "Why would he feel so strongly that he should go and talk to Rameses instead of Iapetus?"

"Perhaps he understands what I have been attempting to explain, General," Berens Barbarossa suggested innocently. "Perhaps he didn't wish to engage in a pointless mission."

Tamerlane gave Barbarossa a look, then sighed. "I suppose it's understandable."

Silence descended for a moment.

"Are you still thinking of sending someone to Earth to make the case for action to Iapetus, Ezekial?" Agrippa asked quietly. "And if so, who?"

Tamerlane shook his head again. "Sending someone? If what the good colonel here tells us is true, there's no point."

"Indeed," Barbarossa agreed. "That is sensible."

"So I will contact him myself," Tamerlane added. "Now."

As Barbarossa looked on, surprised, Agrippa laughed heartily. Finally the blond man turned to Tamerlane and smiled. "Best of luck with that. I trust you will tell me how it goes. I cannot wait to hear." He chuckled again, then looked away for a few seconds, speaking to someone off-camera— at his own physical location, but not within the visual holographic field. After another moment he turned back. "The enemy is advancing. Which one it is this time, I have no idea. But, in any case, I am needed with my troops. I believe it is time to employ my heaviest ordnance. I will take my leave now, if that is agreeable, Ezekial."

"Good hunting, Arnem." Tamerlane sent a signal through the Aether, ending the recording of their meeting and officially declaring the *Hatamoto* recessed for the time being.

With a nod and a slight bow, the big general vanished in a sparkle of holographic haze.

Tamerlane issued an order over the Aether link: "Connect me with Earth, please. II Legion command. General Iapetus."

Barbarossa stepped forward. "Should I excuse myself, General?"

Tamerlane considered this. "No," he replied after a second's thought. He motioned toward the shadowy area of the strategium where Belisarius had lurked earlier. "Wait over there, if you would, Colonel." He smiled flatly. "I suspect I may desire a witness for this conversation. One not affiliated with the Lords of Fire."

Barbarossa bowed his head and chuckled. "I suspect you may be right about that, sir," he responded, before stepping into the darkness.

Titus Elaro stepped off the Imperial transport craft and quickly took in the sights.

He was a big man; well over six feet tall, with solid muscles and a square jaw. Blondish-brown hair, cut very short, covered his head. His uniform was not of any legion but the neutral tan of a planetary defense militia—in his case, Gaurean, a world far out on the spinward fringe.

As he turned his imposing head this way and that, his eyes moved across a sea of other soldiers milling about on the broad landing field. A short distance away, the nearest set of half a dozen transport shuttles was lifting off in smooth, choreographed movements after having disgorged another cadre of recruits. Beyond them stood a smooth gray stone wall, the outermost defenses of a towering, ancient fortress that lay beyond and within. In all, not the most imposing of locales at which to gather a collection of mercenaries, disaffected soldiers, pensioned guardsmen and trainees from all across the Empire. And yet that more or less described the crowd that had been aboard the transport with him. All of them here because they'd heard a scrap of a hint or a whisper of a new force being gathered; each of them seeking to make a new start in a new army—a *Nizam* Legion, itself a secret and with a secret commander—rumored to be outside of the normal chain of command. All of them, of course, except for Elaro.

Elaro very unobtrusively studied the faces and clothing of a quick random sampling of the men and women around him. A few of them matched with one another in ethnicity and dress, and those tended to stand together in little clumps; likely they had departed the same homeworld together and had arrived here together, and were clinging to the familiar—to each other. The rest of the crowd though... Elaro studied them a bit more closely and allowed himself a tiny smile. They were from all over the Empire.

Elaro's smile was for one simple reason: his first gamble had paid off. He'd been forced to hope that, whatever this gathering was intended to be, it was made up of personnel from all across the Empire that had never worked or fought together before. If that was indeed the case, no one could stand out as a stranger, because it would essentially be a gathering of strangers. No one would suspect where he actually came from, or for whom he worked.

The danger wasn't over yet, of course. Not by any means. Elaro quickly looked for the people in charge. He figured, if he was going to be caught and exposed, better to get it over with quickly.

It didn't take long to find the individuals running the show. A table had been set up some distance away on the tarmac and two officers in the red smartcloth uniforms of I Legion were checking in the arrivals. A sign on their table read: TRANSMIT ID CODE TO SGT VALUS.

Elaro moved away from the transport and followed along with the flow of troops. A heavyset man wearing sergeant's stripes who had been observing the crowd just as carefully but much more openly turned his full attention in Elaro's general direction. The man's eyes flicked from one soldier to the next, and Elaro realized they were following the instructions and sending him their identification code. Ah, Elaro thought. That must be Sgt. Valus.

So. The first test of the skills of the covert action division. Elaro had been assured he was fully prepared for any contingency, but one could never be certain of such things until they were put to the test in the real world.

Elaro met the stare of the sergeant and accessed the Aether. Instantly a red square appeared in the corner of his vision—Sgt. Valus's icon. He focused on it and transmitted the file he had been given that contained his forged identity codes. Valus looked at him, blinked, and shifted his gaze to the next man behind him.

Elaro didn't sigh with relief, didn't smile, didn't do a little dance. He simply continued to shuffle along with the crowd. The line at the officers' table was long but it was moving rapidly. Most of the business was handled via the Aether link, and Elaro figured the two men behind the table were merely a sort of formality. He stepped up, seventh in line now, and rehearsed his lines just in case they asked him anything specific. He felt ready to—

"You there!" came the cry from behind him. "Stand out!"

Elaro tensed, but he kept himself entirely contained. He waited a moment before turning and looking back. By that time, nearly everyone else was doing it.

A soldier in the red and gold of the Lords of Fire was approaching at a good clip, his hand moving down to his sidearm. Instinctively, Elaro's hand moved down for his. He spared a half-second to take in his immediate environment, realizing that whatever happened next, it would cause quite a few people to be killed and do a great deal of damage to the facility.

The man stalked right past Elaro. He roughly grasped a shorter, older man nearer to the front of the line and yanked him out into the open. Angry words were exchanged; Elaro heard something about a robbery aboard one of the shuttles. Accusations and denials flew back and forth. Finally a pair of men who were very clearly military police arrived and took the older fellow away.

Elaro waited, still tense, to see if anything further developed. Time seemed to move very slowly, and he couldn't hear a thing. In situations like this, he tended to almost turn off the senses he wasn't particularly using, as though that allowed his other senses to become somehow heightened. Was the danger over? Was that man the only one they were looking for?

"Do you hear me? You're next, soldier," the officer on the right side of the desk was saying.

Elaro looked up, coming back to reality. The officer had called him twice now.

"Yes—sorry, sir," he said, flashing a white smile as he stepped up and turned to face the men behind the table.

The officer who had called him was frowning. He nodded to Elaro's right hand; it hovered over his belt in the spot where his gun would've been holstered, had it been permitted here.

Recovering quickly, Elaro moved the hand away and smiled again. "Don't like thieves, sir," he offered by way of explanation.

The officer regarded him for another second, then nodded distractedly. He marked Elaro's ID code via the Aether link and gestured for him to continue on past the table. "Next!"

"I'm in," Elaro whispered to himself as he strode casually from the landing field and into the camp proper. "Everything they promised me would work—actually worked."

He passed through an arched entryway and into a broad, flat courtyard covered in ancient-looking, rust-red cobblestones. A dozen or so armed soldiers wearing I Legion uniforms stood at roughly equidistant spaces around the perimeter. The number of recruits crowding into the center was hard to estimate, but Elaro guessed it was something like a thousand, at least.

"What's this all about?" one of the rougher-looking men to Elaro's left asked, almost rhetorically. The man clearly didn't expect to receive an answer and Elaro didn't attempt to supply one.

A few minutes later, a big guy in red tramped up a metal stairway to a sort of stage at the far end of the area and surveyed the crowd. At the bottom of the stairs, almost lost in the sea of muscular bodies, stood a young, dark-haired woman in a skin-tight smartcloth uniform of dark red and black. Seeing the two of them, the recruits buzzed louder in speculation for a few seconds, then quickly quieted down.

"Welcome to Mysentia," the big man on the stage boomed. He gazed out at them, waiting as they muttered to one another at that particular revelation. Elaro realized then that he hadn't even thought about what planet they were on, and no one before now had bothered to tell them. His every thought had been about the mission, and about overcoming the many security hurdles. The actual location he was traveling to hadn't mattered to him at all.

"This is a nice world," the soldier continued when the crowd quieted down. "Maybe not one of the Seven, but it's civilized, and all that. So—try to act that way yourselves. Best behavior. Or else."

"Else what?" asked a recruit close to the front of the crowd.

"Else the fines start kicking in." The soldier snorted. "You'll find it doesn't take more than a few violations before your entire paycheck is gone."

The recruits mostly nodded or mumbled grudging assent. Elaro almost laughed. They wanted to cut up. They were as rough a crowd as he'd ever seen. But they wanted to be paid even more than they wanted to cut up.

"You'll be shown to your billets in a few minutes," the soldier said. "But first, our commander has a few inspiring words for you. So listen up."

LEGION II: SONS OF TERRA

The recruits all looked around, attempting to spot the commander. No one was prepared when the young woman in the tight uniform sprang up the steps and stood before them, her dark eyes peering out with grim appraisal.

"I'm Colonel Niobe Arani," she told them. Her voice was strong and clear but not terribly loud; nonetheless they found they had no trouble understanding her.

"*She's* the commander?" muttered the man next to Elaro who had spoken earlier. Again Elaro didn't figure the guy expected an answer and didn't volunteer one. To himself, however, he thought, *No. She can't be. She's just a colonel. And I've never heard of her. There has to be someone else—someone above her.*

"My officers have devised a very demanding series of tests for each of you," the dark-haired woman was saying. "Those of you who fail the tests will be expelled. Your memories will be wiped. You will not remember any of this. You will wake up on one of the Outer Worlds with a severe hangover and a wad of consolation pay in your pocket, wondering what you were doing for the previous week."

A smattering of grumbling from the crowd.

"If that scenario disturbs you overmuch," the woman stated, "you can drop out now. You'll still be mind-wiped, but you'll only have a day or two to wonder about. And a much tinier wad of pay."

The grumbling settled down.

"Those of you who make the cut will be allowed to become a part of the greatest military force in the galaxy. And I don't mean the Kings of Oblivion," she added. "Or the Sons of Terra. Or even the Lords of Fire."

The crowd buzzed at this. The man to Elaro's right snorted. "So we're joining the Sand Kings, then?" This time Elaro deigned to look at him, and the expression he wore shut the man right up.

More buzz. The woman, Arani, raised one hand and the crowd quieted.

"As you have doubtlessly come to understand by now, this entire operation is top secret. Your ability to keep it secret will directly impact your acceptance into its ranks— or your rejection, hangover, and small wad of money."

Now the crowd actually laughed. For his part, Elaro smiled. The woman was winning them over. He found himself somewhat impressed.

"You will be separated into three divisions," she continued. "Three majors will be chosen and designated from your ranks after careful evaluation of your skills and abilities, to lead them."

"What's the mission?" one brave soul in the thick of the crowd shouted.

Colonel Arani gazed out in the general direction of the voice, then shrugged. "A fair question. Unfortunately, not one I am able to answer quite yet." The grumbling reappeared, and Arani held her hand up again. "Rest assured—if you make the cut, you will know. And you will not be disappointed."

With that, she hopped down from the stage and stood to one side as the big soldier moved up into her spot. "Check your Aether displays," he shouted. "You'll see a number now. If you have a *one*—over there." He pointed. "Twos in the middle. Threes over there."

Slowly the crowd began to divide itself into three clumps as the recruits found their number floating in their artificial vision. As they parted, Elaro suddenly had a direct and unimpaired view of Colonel Niobe Arani, roughly a dozen meters ahead of him. She was striding forward with purpose, clearly deep in thought, mostly oblivious to the soldiers in their mismatched uniforms all around her. Acting on pure instinct, Elaro took a step in her direction, and then another. He wasn't sure why he did it.

She looked up and became aware of him, standing like a roadblock in her path. She started to frown.

Movement from her left and just ahead of her. A scuffle. A shout.

Time slowed down. Elaro's vision acquired a strobe effect.

Someone—a woman in dark green, with very short, blonde, almost white hair—was emerging from the crowd. She had something in her right hand.

A knife.

She swung it at Arani.

Arani, distracted by her own thoughts and by Elaro's presence before her, didn't fully appreciate the danger in time. By the time she realized what was happening, the blade was on its way down, toward her chest, her neck.

It didn't arrive at its target.

Elaro surged forward, moving very quickly despite his size and weight. His right arm came up, blocking the blow before the knife tip could reach the colonel. It struck his arm instead. The smartcloth material of his jacket hardened, bending the point.

The assassin spun about and produced another blade from within her clothes, tossing the ruined one away.

Arani drew her pistol and attempted to aim at the attacker, but Elaro was blocking the way.

"Move!" she cried.

Elaro blocked the second knife's swing—this time it had been directed at him—and backhanded the assassin. She stumbled away, blood flying from her smashed nose and mouth. He stayed on her, driving her back, grasping her wrist to force her to drop the second blade. Disarmed now, she shrieked wordlessly at him. He grasped her clothing by the waist and the collar, lifted her high up in the air, and tossed her almost effortlessly across the clearing. She smashed into the wall of the enclosure and lay stunned.

"I'd secure her before she finds a third knife somewhere in there," he told Arani, brushing himself off.

The colonel almost gawked at him for a second, then spun on her heel and barked orders to the I Legion soldiers that had rushed up to her defense—and had done so a few seconds too late to have saved her. "Lock her down!" she shouted. "Check for suicide devices and booby traps. I want her alive!"

"Very wise," Elaro said, nodding, when she turned back to him.

The dark-haired commander appraised him for a moment. "Well done..." She hesitated again, and he could tell she was accessing the Aether for his personal information—in reality the false information he'd planted upon arrival.

"Elaro," he told her with a nod.

"Titus Elaro," she confirmed, closing out the Aether link. "Former captain in the planetary defense army of Gaurean. Well. I'm very glad you chose to join us, Elaro. And glad you were paying more attention to my safety than I was, just now."

He smiled and laughed a quick snort of a laugh. "You had a lot on your mind. It's your officers' job to keep you safe."

"Clearly they weren't up to that job," she replied, eyeing the men in red and gold who now half-surrounded her in a semicircle. Most of them were staring openly at Elaro and regarding him with some combination of curiosity and distaste.

He shrugged. "What can you do?" he asked rhetorically. "You go to war with the officers you have."

"Not necessarily," Arani replied. Now she smiled at him, and he found himself taken aback by this woman he'd been sent to spy upon. "Sometimes you find your officers—and find them in the most unexpected places."

He gave her a quizzical look.

One of the red-clad I Legion officers leaned in, clearing his throat. "Excuse me, Colonel," he said, "but there is a call coming in from—"

Arani shushed the man with a quick wave. Her eyes remained locked firmly on the man who had saved her, appraising. "Report to the officers' quarters, *Major* Elaro," she said at length. And, as he and the others stared after her in surprise, she marched back into the fortress. The heavy iron door clanged closed behind her.

7

You can't have them," said the holographic ghost of Ioan Iapetus. "And—with all due respect, General—you're wasting my time. And yours."

Tamerlane was taken aback. He stared at the flickering image of the commander of II Legion standing there before him within the strategium and sought for the most appropriate response. A number of rather *inappropriate* responses suggested themselves—and did so very forcefully—but, aggravation aside, he knew the situation was so delicate and so critical that he dared not launch immediately into an angry rebuke.

In fact, he reflected a second later, perhaps that was precisely what Iapetus was seeking to provoke.

And so Tamerlane calmed himself, breathed in and out, and forced a seemingly warm smile onto his face.

"I cannot have *what*, General?" he asked pleasantly.

"My legion," Iapetus said. "You wish me to hand it over to you, or at least to place some or all of my troops at your disposal. I will do neither."

Tamerlane could not help but be startled by Iapetus's instant recognition of what lay behind this call.

"You would refuse to obey such an order if I issued it?"

"If *you* issued it? Of course."

The anger was surging back already. "Why?"

"You are not the *Taiko*," Iapetus said with a slight shrug. "Nor—despite all the propaganda emanating from high command—are you a god. As we both know." He clasped his hands behind his back and leaned in, his holographic form now only a matter of inches away from Tamerlane. "You may command I Legion, but you have no authority over me or my army. You are not my superior officer—and you most certainly are not my god. Or anyone else's."

"The god thing was not my doing," Tamerlane conceded, "and I will not argue with you about it. But," he went on, "the rest is debatable." He faced Iapetus squarely and didn't flinch. "When Nakamura headed I Legion, he held authority over all Imperial forces, and now that I have assumed that role—"

"You are not Nakamura," Iapetus interjected, "and the circumstances—as you are well aware—have changed since then."

"Not entirely," Tamerlane said, his voice now a low growl.

"Oh, I believe they have—and in more ways than you might imagine."

Tamerlane didn't respond to that.

"But, at least in terms of issuing orders to me or to the Sons," Iapetus concluded, his cold, dark eyes peering out of the holographic mist, "they most certainly have."

Tamerlane looked from those cruel eyes to the golden one emblazoned on the man's black uniform—the new uniform the officers of II Legion had adopted following Iapetus's rise to command of it, and his re-christening of it as the Sons of Terra. *Watching, always watching.*

He met Iapetus's gaze again. Neither spoke for a long moment. Finally Tamerlane crossed his arms and offered the other man another humorless smile. "Given the present dire circumstances faced by our empire," he said, "we can perhaps agree to disagree about that point—for now. The larger issue looms, however: I require at least a portion of your legion. The Empire requires it. Our very *survival* is at stake!"

"The Empire will survive or it will not. Neither is my direct concern."

Now Tamerlane's eyes widened. "What?"

"My task—my sworn duty—is the defense of sacred Earth and its environs. Your precious *Taiko*, Nakamura, assigned me that duty himself." Iapetus paused, then, "Let us be frank here, General—he wanted me out of the way, safely ensconced on the homeworld while your legion and Agrippa's were free to go wherever you like, here and there across the galaxy. I agreed to that arrangement—to every bit of it—and I intend to live up to the obligations it entails." He crossed his arms over the golden eye—the effect was of the eye closing, shutting Tamerlane out. "My Sons of Terra defend the Earth. Period," he said. He stared back at Tamerlane with his own eyes with undisguised contempt. "If the rest of the Empire falls in the process, then the rest of the Empire be damned."

Tamerlane almost gawked at him. "You...come close to treason, General," he said at length, his mouth dry.

"I disagree," Iapetus replied. "I do my duty. Nothing more and nothing less."

Tamerlane licked his lips, his mind racing. This man was even more stubborn, more intransigent, than he'd expected. He glanced over at the shadows, where Iapetus's second, Colonel Berens Barbarossa, watched and listened. He could imagine what the man must be thinking. *He was right all along,* Tamerlane realized. *He said there was no way Iapetus would comply. I didn't fully believe him, but he was right. And he can justify everything in such a way that I can't order his arrest for disobeying orders, because he's right—he is obeying the prime order the* Taiko *issued to him.*

The Taiko, Tamerlane thought then. *If only Nakamura were himself; if only he would snap out of whatever this condition is that has bewitched him. He could* order *Iapetus to comply.* Tamerlane resolved to make the case again to Nakamura—and even more forcefully, this time. The Empire could no longer afford for its *Taiko* to avoid the issue. The galaxy was burning down around them.

As if reading his mind, Iapetus spoke up then. "I assume that since it is you making this request, and not the *Taiko*," he said—and Tamerlane noted the use of the word request and not order—"you yourself are acting outside of Nakamura's orders. That being the case, I believe our business here is concluded." Iapetus made to sever the connection.

"Wait!" Tamerlane called. He couldn't let it end like this. It could mean the end of everything.

Iapetus halted midway through turning. His holographic image looked back at Tamerlane. "Yes, General?"

"All of these issues between us can be resolved in time. But, for now, will you at least contribute *something* to the defense of the Empire? Anything at all?"

"There are no issues between us, General," Iapetus replied with a smile that was at once both warm and chilling. "There is only duty. I seek to do mine; you seek to divert me from that."

Tamerlane forced himself to breathe evenly. "Again—we can discuss that subject at a later date. But, as to my... *request?*" He hated himself for using the term Iapetus had substituted, but the safety of the Empire's billions of inhabitants had to come first.

"I have already sent you one, General," Iapetus replied.

"One?" Tamerlane frowned. "You've sent me one what? One *division?* One *regiment?*"

"One Son of Terra."

Tamerlane blinked at this, uncertain at first what the other man meant, unable to speak for a second.

"And he is there now, lurking in the shadows, no doubt." Iapetus chuckled. "I hope you have found this conversation enlightening and useful, Colonel Barbarossa. And I hope General Tamerlane can put you to good use."

Before Tamerlane could respond to this—and he had no idea what he might say, in any event—Iapetus cut the link. The strategium fell into darkness.

For a long while no one spoke. Tamerlane stood there, half his mind poring over possible actions, the other half still in shock at Iapetus's attitude and refusal to help. *And he knew Barbarossa was there*, he thought. *Has he infiltrated my own legion? Or is he just that canny—that smart?*

Barbarossa moved forward a tentative step and coughed softly.

Tamerlane chewed his lip for a moment, still lost in thought, then turned to the colonel. He regarded him, seeming to size the man up.

"Shall I return to my legion, then, General?" the colonel asked, after waiting for a few seconds.

"No," Tamerlane replied, pursing his lips. He was still deciding exactly what to do next. "Not just yet," he said at length. "Since General Iapetus has been good enough to lend you to I Legion for a time—and since you are, in fact, the sum total of all the assistance he appears willing to provide—I'd like to make use of you." He smiled. "I have another assignment in mind."

"Might I ask what that is, General?"

Tamerlane laughed.

"I'd like your assistance and advice on a small matter," he said. "It directly pertains to General Iapetus. You have been in his presence on a regular basis, correct?"

"Daily, General."

Tamerlane moved in closer, sobering. "I have enough on my plate, dealing with officers I believed perfectly rational and reasonable only weeks ago. I don't need trouble from the ones I have never trusted. So—with regard to the good General Iapetus: Would you describe him as sane? As stable?"

It was a startling question, asked about a commander of one of the three legions of the Empire, and asked of a man who served as second in command of that legion. And yet, despite those facts, Barbarossa did not answer immediately. He took the question in, appearing somewhat taken aback, and frowned for a few seconds. At length he replied, "I'm afraid, General, that any answer I could give would be highly subjective."

It was Tamerlane's turn to be surprised. "How so?"

Barbarossa began to speak, and now his voice was much softer, lower. "One's view of General Iapetus's sanity very much depends upon the context involved. Is he the most normal, the most conventional of men? Certainly not. But—" He paused, thinking carefully, choosing his words with equal care. "But is that what you want, occupying his role? Is there anyone better equipped—in every sense of the word—to defend our mother world? To fight to his last breath, his last drop of blood, for it?" The colonel shook his head. "Iapetus is perhaps eccentric, but he's also brutally efficient and effective."

Tamerlane considered this. Reluctantly he nodded. "Yes. I believe that's what the *Taiko* saw in him. *Sees* in him. All right. That will do for now." He paused, then added, "Perhaps we will revisit the topic when the present crisis is over. If anyone's still alive then." He hesitated, then, "In the meantime, Colonel," he said, leaning in and speaking in a softer voice, "I would be interested in hearing any additional impressions you gain of him."

Barbarossa stared at the general, considering his words. "Sir, are you saying what I think you're saying?" He gave

Tamerlane a half-smile. "You wish for me to spy on Iapetus for you? To spy on my own commander?"

Tamerlane at first appeared taken aback by Barbarossa. He eyed the other man strangely, as if attempting to ascertain his true reaction. "Spy?" he said at length. "I wouldn't use that term."

"No," Barbarossa said.

"But if, as Iapetus likes to say, he and his legion are 'always watching,' does it not make sense that someone else, in turn, watch him? I believe the old saying is, 'Who watches the watchmen?'"

Eyes narrowing, Barbarossa nodded slowly.

"You are in possibly the best position of anyone to...*evaluate* Iapetus on an ongoing basis," Tamerlane went on. "I would appreciate your thoughts along those lines, from time to time."

"I see," the colonel replied.

Tamerlane continued to study Barbarossa for another few seconds, then gestured toward the holographic display of the galaxy that still filled the center of the chamber. It showed the main deployments of the three official legions, the markers highlighted in their traditional colors of red, blue and green. Enemy units of many different other colors overwhelmingly outnumbered them. "As you can see," the general said, "and as you surely knew already, we suffer from a lack of troops. I need every unit at the Empire's disposal to fight this war. I have to be able to count on every legion equally—including the Sons of Terra. I have to have confidence that they will respond when I call for them— that they will obey orders that are issued to them."

Barbarossa smiled. "Of course, sir. I understand."

"I thought you would. You are a loyal soldier of this Empire, and a dedicated member of the II Legion."

"Indeed I am, General."

"And all of us, regardless of our legion affiliation, serve the Empire and the *Taiko* above all else."

"Certainly we do, General," Barbarossa said. His smile deepened. "Certainly we do."

8

The comet filled the nighttime sky of Eingrad 6 like some blood-red herald of the apocalypse.

It had appeared suddenly, as if dropping through a heretofore-unseen hole into our universe from out of some other, nightmare realm. That description was, as it turned out, not entirely inaccurate.

Beneath it, moving in what at first appeared to be a slow, deliberate, plodding gait, towered an Imperial Colossus—two hundred meters of gargantuan war machine, cunningly crafted in the general shape of a man but fitted out with massive weapons and defenses. Mostly painted white, the green and gold of III Legion adorned its scarred and pitted metal surface here and there as trim and detailing.

Within what passed for its head rode three human beings, two seated at the controls and the third standing behind them, issuing orders and occasionally consulting the holographic tactical display that filled the balance of the small cabin. The two working the brightly lit and tactile-sensitive control board wore helmets that completely obscured their heads and faces, generating an immersive three-dimensional operating environment for them as they steered the mighty machine. The man who stood behind them, however, wore no helmet, and his blond hair and rough-hewn, handsome features were easily recognizable to anyone in the Legion: Arnem Agrippa, recently promoted general of the Third—the Golden Phalanx, better known in casual parlance as the Kings of Oblivion.

Oblivion was indeed what they and their Colossus were delivering to the enemy at the moment, leading the charge as the Phalanx blasted its way through the defensive lines of the Riyahadi. Massive plasma cannons arrayed around the right forearm of the Colossus took aim and fired repeatedly, as quickly as permissible given the awful accumulation of heat with just one volley. Each blast tore into the ranks of the foe with the force of divine lightning, melting hovertanks and evaporating whole rows of infantry with instant and horrific suddenness.

Enemy fire deflected harmlessly from the crackling defensive fields that protected the most sensitive sections of the huge walker, while ricocheting off the ultra-hardened upper limbs and torso. Weapons existed that could hurt a Colossus, but the Riyahadi Caliphate apparently had not, it appeared to Agrippa, deigned to deploy them here in the Eingrad theater of operations. And for this, the big man was exceedingly grateful.

After rechecking the general condition of all systems for the hundredth time since the attack had begun, the General spun the holographic display to reveal the situation directly behind them. He frowned.

"The others are falling behind," Agrippa barked as he took in the tactical situation.

"Should I slow our advance, sir?" asked the helmsman, Obomanu.

Agrippa considered this for a moment, weighing the dangers of becoming isolated with the success they were having by pressing their advantage. "No," he replied. "I will deal with this quickly enough."

Accessing the Aether network, he opened a link to the next Colossus in line. "Torgon—what's the hold up? You're over half a click behind us now."

"Aye, sir—sorry—but the Riyahadi are using gravitic shields to block our path, and then hammering us with heavy artillery. They must not have been ready when you came through, but they have us hemmed in pretty good."

Agrippa took this in, then cursed to himself. Checking the broadest-angled display he could access, he saw that their column of walkers was now strung out dangerously thin, their initially tight formation long since disrupted. "Alright—do what you can. We will swing around and hit them from behind, and spring you loose."

"Thank you, General," Torgon answered. "My apologies."

Agrippa closed the link and issued terse and angry new orders to his helmsman. "You heard," he barked. "Let's help them out."

Obomanu acknowledged the order and manipulated the controls. In response, the engine deep within the walker's torso roared, sending surging waves of power down to the legs. The mighty beast strode to its left in a broad curve, one step at a time, Harker the gunner continuing to blast away at enemy targets all the while. As it advanced on Torgon's machine in the distance, Agrippa activated the horn, blasting a nearly-deafening wail across the battlefield. "No sense trying to be sneaky," he stated as Obomanu gave him a puzzled glance. "Nothing this big ever snuck up on anyone."

The walker drew nearer and nearer to the position where Torgon's machine was trapped. Agrippa studied the holo display intently, taking in the situation. Indeed the second walker's commander had been correct: the Riyahadi in their inventiveness had positioned gravitic shield generators in careful alignment such that the legs of the Colossus were blocked from moving in any direction. And now the enemy—humans, but of a rival empire to that of the III Legion—were pouring everything they had, weapon-wise, into the attack, seeking to break through Torgon's defenses and destroy the walker while it was held firm.

"The shields themselves are preventing Major Torgon from destroying their generators," Harker the gunner reported, "but I can get a fine bead on them from here, sir."

"Open fire," Agrippa ordered, nodding.

The plasma tubes surrounding the Colossus's forearm lit up like neon bulbs. Bolts of shimmering raw energy stabbed out, one after the other, striking the Riyahadi emplacements between Torgon's position and their own. Explosions lit up the smoke-filled battlefield, great gouts of flame towering into the sky. The soldiers manning those sites looked to the men of the walkers like tiny ants scampering frantically around before dying ignominiously; their screams, coming from so far below, never reached the ears of the Phalanx officers, who towered far above them like grim and uncaring gods.

After fifteen seconds of bombardment by Agrippa's walker, the last of the enemy gravity shields flickered and died. Torgon's machine wrenched itself loose and blasted out of the trap that had held it, looking none the worse for the wear.

"Many thanks, General," the Major sent over the Aether link.

Agrippa was already switching over to link to the infantry that trailed behind them. "Colonel Iksander," he barked. "If you would be so kind, please have your men sort this mess out. Torgon and I will be pressing on."

"Certainly, General," replied the voice of Agrippa's oldest friend and the head of the ground forces. "We won't be a—uh oh."

Agrippa frowned at this. He knew Iksander far too well to think the man would react so blatantly to anything that wasn't a horrific threat. "What is it, Selim?"

"Check your reverse view," Iksander replied.

Agrippa realized his machine was still aimed back the way they had all originally come. He spun the holo display around even faster than Obomanu could actually rotate the walker a hundred eighty degrees. What he saw gave him pause, to say the least.

"Shields to maximum!" he cried. "Divert all energy to the—"

The impact of the first shots rocked the Colossus back on its heels. The second volley, an instant later, knocked it off its balance.

The mighty machine teetered for a very long moment, its metal joints creaking as it fought for control. It failed. It fell.

Looming over it stood three Riyahadi walkers, identical in design to one another but somewhat different from the Imperial Colossus. They were a bit shorter and wider, and their main weapons appeared to be situated atop their shoulder units—almost balanced there, extending in front and behind them. Their gun ports all smoked from the barrage they had unleashed against Agrippa's machine. The weapons flared to life again.

"Evasive!" Agrippa commanded, even as he struggled to regain his feet. When the walker had gone down, the control cabin had likewise been tilted back sharply at a ninety degree angle. The crash webbing that held all three of the crew in place had prevented any injuries, but the disorientation was severe—and particularly dangerous coming just as the enemy was pressing its advantage of surprise.

Obomanu worked the controls with frantic fury. In response the Colossus rolled rapidly to its right, just as concussion blasts from the three attackers speared down into the bare earth where it had lain an instant before, seeking to finish off the taller machine.

LEGION II: SONS OF TERRA

Taking advantage of the wave of dust and debris hurled into the air by the blasts, Agrippa ordered the walker to stay low as it scrabbled away from the trio of enemies. The next round of energy blasts missed by a wider margin; the Riyahadi had already lost their target lock.

"Now," ordered Agrippa. "Bring everything we have on line and hit them—*hard!*"

Rearing up with a quickness that seemed impossible in anything so large, the Colossus brought its main plasma cannon to bear and fired directly into the chest of the nearest enemy walker. Any human standing on that battlefield whose eyesight was unprotected would have been blinded, likely for life, as the column of superheated plasma streaked out and impacted the Riyahadi machine's shields—and shredded them. The last of the blast continued on and melted a hole roughly five meters in diameter directly through the walker's chest. Sparks sprayed out, followed by a gout of flames, and then a billowing of noxious black smoke. The enemy walker rocked back and forth on its feet for another few seconds before creaking and slowly crashing to the ravaged surface of Eingrad 6.

Agrippa didn't wait to see the walker fall. He continued to bark orders, one after the other, to his driver and his gunner. The Colossus leapt to the attack, charging toward the Riyahadi machine on the left. Agrippa was happy to see that Torgon's Colossus had managed to extricate itself completely from the trap that had held it, and now it was fully engaged with the enemy on the right. Together the two Imperial walkers made short work of their foes, short-range blasters ripping them to shreds once the range became too tight for their plasma cannons.

"The path is clear again," Agrippa called back to Colonel Iksander when the third of the three walkers had collapsed, flames roaring from its joints and explosions bursting from its damaged fuel cells. "Bring the Legion up."

Then the Aether channel shrieked in Agrippa's head with heavy distortion and he nearly lost his balance. Reaching out with one muscular arm, he steadied himself as he gritted his teeth and forced the volume down.

"What was that?" cried Obomanu, one hand off the controls and clutching at the side of his head.

The wailing noise faded somewhat as each of their internal links to the Aether struggled to contain the wild and unexpected interfering signal. Agrippa gestured with his right hand and switched the holo display from tactical to electromagnetic, searching for the source of the rogue signal.

"There," he almost shouted, pointing to a spot on the three-dimensional map that hung in the air before him. "It's coming from over there." A low hill, just under a kilometer away, appeared to be the source of the signal.

"The Riyahadi did that?" Torgon called over the link, now that it was working properly again and free of the awful noise. "How is that possible? No one's ever hacked the Aether before."

"I don't know," Agrippa replied. His lips were pulled back in a snarl. "Let's go ask them."

The Colossus stepped forward again, massive legs moving as quickly as possible. Torgon's machine followed closely behind.

The procession hadn't gotten halfway across the battlefield toward their new objective when the signal shrieked out again. Agrippa cursed and ordered his men to ignore it as best they could and continue on, reasoning that the best way to deal with it was to find its source and destroy it as quickly as possible.

As Agrippa looked up again from his men in the cockpit, he beheld a sight that nearly took his legs out from under him. At that same moment, Torgon's voice over the link cried, "Look out, General! More enemy machines!"

Indeed, six more walkers had emerged from hiding places in the rubble, their guns already glowing with energy as they prepared to fire.

"All power to the shields!" shouted Agrippa. "Evasive!"

Too late. The train-car-sized blasters mounted on the shoulders of each of the enemy walkers opened fire virtually simultaneously. Twelve beams of violet light speared the two Imperial machines and met their shields. The defensive energy screens of Torgon's Colossus lasted all of three seconds before failing and giving way in a blinding storm of lightning and concussive force. Agrippa's shields survived for only two seconds longer. Now protected only by their thick metal hides, the two Imperial war machines held out for another ten seconds—ten seconds of failed attempts to dodge and evade—before the barrage of weaponry brought both Agrippa's and Torgon's walkers down.

The two man-shaped war machines crashed to the surface within a few dozen meters of one another. The Riyahadi continued to pound away at them, ripping into the armor with their many smaller weapons.

Inside the control room of the lead machine, Agrippa fought to extricate himself from the crash netting. The Colossus lay on its stomach, face down, and consequently the cabin was tilted at a severe forward angle, making it difficult for any of the three occupants to move.

With a roar, Agrippa ripped the main connector of his netting loose from its mooring and pulled himself free. He reached down and disconnected the corresponding portions of Obomanu's and Harker's netting, allowing them to pull themselves out of it.

Agrippa made one quick and futile check of the Colossus's systems. The holographic display wouldn't function and the main engine was dead.

"Evacuate," the general ordered. "Out!"

Harker tapped a quick code into a panel set into the hull. Nothing happened.

"Uh oh," the gunner breathed. He entered the code again. Still nothing.

"What's wrong?" Agrippa demanded. The hull of the metal monster they inhabited rang with the sound of shells and blasts impacting the surface outside.

"It's jammed—or blocked," Harker replied, his expression growing frantic. "She won't budge!"

"If the hull itself is warped there, we'll never get it open," Obomanu stated, anxiety filling his voice.

Agrippa's own countenance soured. "Move aside," he barked, and the two crewmen scrambled out of the way.

The hulking blond general reached down and grasped the manual locking wheel of the hatch with both his hands, his muscles bunching as he exerted his full strength. For long seconds the machinery resisted, as the sounds of enemy fire grew louder.

"They're concentrating fire on us—trying to blow the fuel cells—to finish us off," Obomanu observed, sweat blanketing his dark face now.

"This machine is already finished," Agrippa grunted, his own face reddening as he continued to wrestle with the hatch. "But we're not."

At that moment the hatch gave way and popped open, swinging out into darkness.

Agrippa gasped in relief and let go, stepping back. He pointed to the newly-opened exit. "Go," he barked.

Harker instantly obeyed, climbing through the hole, Obomanu hurrying closely behind. Agrippa took one last look around the cabin of the big war machine, frowned at the loss, and followed.

The battlefield onto which they emerged appeared apocalyptic in its devastation. A perpetual twilight hung over the landscape as clouds of smoke mingled with stirred up dust and fog; the sun was a tiny red dot barely visible through the haze.

"This way, General," called Obomanu, motioning from behind a half-shattered wall nearby.

Agrippa glanced up, seeing the Riyahadi walkers turning and stalking away, lumbering as if they were normal-sized beings recorded in slow motion. Apparently they had decided the Imperial Colossus was dead and any human survivors weren't worth their trouble. They were moving on to find other, larger targets of opportunity. Agrippa knew that didn't mean he and his men were safe yet, though. The infantry and lighter armor would surely be following along in the wake of the giants, taking prisoners as they found them—or finishing them off.

The big general hustled over to where his crewmembers were crouching behind the wall. A quick look around, and then, "We can't stay here," he stated. "We have to move."

"I've been trying to retrieve the emergency hovercar by remote," Obomanu reported, frowning, "but it's not responding. It may have been damaged when we went down."

Agrippa cursed. "Well, that's how it is, then. Maybe Torgon—"

At that moment, the Aether link crackled.

"Torgon. Is that you?" Agrippa fought to hear through the static. "I'm still getting interference."

The voice of the other machine's commander came to him faintly but just clearly enough. "We're okay, sir, but the Colossus is done for."

"Is your hovercar alright?"

A pause. "Afraid not, sir. Lt. Brantley is just checking it over now, but it looks to be ruined."

"Ours, too, I think," Agrippa replied. "Break out the armor. We're on foot—at least for now."

"Will do. Be there in a moment, sir."

Agrippa nodded and cut the link, then turned to his two crewmen. "This isn't over, gentlemen," he growled, gazing out at the smoking wasteland that had once been a major Imperial population center here on Eingrad 6. "It was my bad judgment to underestimate the Riyahadi here. It cost us two of our best machines. But we're not finished yet." He shook his head and flexed his fists. "No—it's not over by a long shot."

Amon Rameses, planetary governor of Ahknaton, stood on the upper balcony of the Heliopolis palace, overlooking the city's broad main avenue far below. He clutched his staff with its crooked end tightly in his right hand and watched as the vast army of soldiers at his command, officially known as the Sand Kings but now also called by him the IV Legion, marched past in review.

The Sand Kings appeared resplendent in their dress uniforms of dark red and dark blue, with gleaming gold trim everywhere. The soldiers carried ornately decorated and very advanced-looking energy pistols and quad-rifles. Their shoulder plates bore emblems of coiled snakes and regal birds and other traditional Egyptian symbolism, emblazoned in gold and sparkling gemstones. Similar emblems adorned the robes of the newly-constituted cadre of sorcerers who strode alongside the fighters. The columns of hovertanks, sandcrawlers and troop carriers, likewise, shone in the harsh sunlight, their sides and decks adorned with the markings of the Sand Kings. There was no trace of the classic Egyptian eye, though; as soon as Iapetus and the II Legion had adopted the eye as their major symbol, Rameses had ordered it removed from his own troops' uniforms and banished entirely from Ahknaton. For Rameses hated Iapetus, and hated him with a cold, burning fury.

Rameses had reason to hate Iapetus, of course, and he had a long memory. And if everything over the coming days and weeks played out the way he intended, Iapetus and his so-called Sons of Terra would spend their final moments of life wishing they had never gotten on his bad side. On the bad side of a living god.

For that was precisely what Iapetus was intent on becoming: a god among men. The living embodiment of long-dead Amenophis, once the patron of the people of Ahknaton. And the equal of any of the ancient gods who once strode across the Above with power and glory and utter impunity.

At least, that was what he had been promised by the man—the very odd man— who now stood at his right hand. The man he had only just appointed as his vizier, or top minister and advisor. The cloaked and hooded man in dark red robes who called himself by a god's name: *Zahir*.

Precisely how and why he had granted that lofty position and title to the man, Rameses was not entirely certain, and thinking about it too hard tended to give him a terrible headache. Much easier, he had discovered, to simply accept it—go with it—and not ask why. Still, something about it troubled him... And there came the headache again. He let it go, reluctantly but of necessity.

At that moment, as if overhearing his thoughts, Zahir turned and peered at Rameses with dark, hollow, black-rimmed eyes.

Rameses started. Much as he had come to accept the man's value, or at least his constant presence, he could not quite get used to his sheer *oddness*.

"You are not enjoying seeing the full might of Ahknaton on display, Governor?" the hawk-nosed vizier asked.

LEGION II: SONS OF TERRA

Rameses returned his gaze to the legion marching below. "I suppose I'm merely impatient," he replied after a few seconds. "More troops and more guns are all well and good—but how much will they truly matter to me when I have assumed the mantle of great Amenophis—when I have become a god?"

"Patience, O Rameses," the vizier cautioned. "We will begin shortly, and then your time remaining in this frail mortal body will be brief indeed."

Still not looking at the strange man, Rameses nodded. He said nothing aloud about it—he never did—but he found himself once again silently questioning who Zahir truly was and how he could possibly make good on his extravagant promises. He'd arrived days earlier with his two "gifts," plus a promised third—what were they, again? He couldn't quite recall. And with his grand talk of godhood and the Above and...

And then, as he always did, Rameses started to forget his concerns. They simply receded, faded, slipped out of his mind, leaving him slightly muddled but overwhelmingly pleased. Pleased, and anxious to get on with whatever Zahir would have to do in order to make the transformation happen. And he knew it would happen—that Zahir could make it happen, could transform him into a god, because...why?

He could feel the man's dark, haunting eyes upon him again. He glanced to his right and saw that he was correct. He offered a half-smile and a nod, suddenly somehow anxious to earn the vizier's approval—which was absurd of course, except... What had he been thinking about, again?

For Zahir's part, he watched this internal conversation play itself out on the governor's face. It was all so obvious; the man could hide nothing from him. His mouth tightened in a somewhat camouflaged smile. Everything was transpiring as his master—his *true* master—had planned.

After another minute or so, one of Zahir's servants crept quietly onto the balcony and whispered into the vizier's ear. Zahir nodded, then turned to Rameses and gestured toward the double-doors that led back into the palace. "Preparations are complete, my lord governor," he said with a broad smile. "At last we can begin."

Rameses found himself standing beside the golden basin that now occupied the center of the massive throne room. Flames—flames of many different colors—danced in the bowl, though there was nothing burning at the bottom. The effect was almost hypnotic, and Rameses lost all track of time as he watched the flickering tongues of fire.

"We begin the treatments that will make you what you long to be," the robed and hooded vizier intoned. He gestured with one clawlike hand and the flames burned hotter, faster. Moments later they had transformed into a column of pure light and energy, erupting up out of the bowl and flowing, geyser-like, high up into the air before curving back down and falling back into the basin.

"The Fountain," Rameses muttered, eyes wide. "I have seen pictures—paintings—representations from those who traveled there in ancient times. It is the Fountain of the Golden City!"

Zahir smiled. "A close approximation," he said. "Nowhere near as powerful, but effective enough in its own way. Sufficient for our purposes here."

Tiny suns and stars and constellations erupted into the air far above the gleaming marble floor of the throne room.

Zahir stepped closer to the towering torrent of primal energy. He raised both his arms out wide and leaned back his head. As if sensing him, tendrils of forking electricity reached out and raked over his body, sparking in places as they touched him.

"Yes," he muttered. Then, louder, "*Yes!*"

Rameses looked on in fascination and in awe and in a slowly growing fear. "Am I—am I to walk into that?"

"Walk into it? No," the man in red robes answered a few seconds later, as if so distracted by the energies raking over him that he at first hadn't realized anyone else was there. "To do so would annihilate you instantly. No—we must take this slowly. Slowly and carefully." He motioned to his bald, muscular servants, then told the governor, "Remove your robes, if you would, sire."

Frowning, Rameses reluctantly stripped off his red and blue robes and laid them on his throne, leaving him wearing only tight crimson shorts and a thin tunic. He walked forward, leaning over to see into the basin, fascinated by the play of cosmic energies there.

At some unspoken command two of Zahir's servants moved forward again. Before Rameses could react, he found they had bound his wrists with two leather-covered cuffs. Cables and wires trailed from them down to a small box that stood next to the basin.

"Though you may become one, you are no god now, Rameses," Zahir said as the servants attached similar wired cuffs to the governor's ankles. "Your mortal body is weak, frail. It must be infused with the Power before you will be able to walk among the stars."

The vizier gestured and one of the servants touched a series of controls on the box next to the basin. In response, tongues of fire and lightning lashed out from the geyser of energy, flowing along the cables and flaring brightly as they reached the cuffs. The governor cried out in shock and pain, but quieted down quickly as, startled, he began to feel the Power flowing over him and into him.

"Now you understand, yes?" Zahir asked.

"Yes," Rameses replied. "I can feel it."

"And what does it feel like?"

99

Rameses grinned as the energies washed over him, infusing his very cells. "Destiny," he said. "It feels like destiny."

Zahir nodded. "Yes." Then he turned to his servants. "Bring out the girl," he said.

Rameses started at this. "The girl? What do you mean, the—"

The governor's voice trailed off as another of Zahir's servants carried a tiny body out and laid it on a low, flat platform. At first Rameses feared she was dead, but then he detected her shallow breathing. She was sleeping—or had been drugged.

"The princess?" he exclaimed. "What do you want with her?"

The strange vizier favored him with a leering grin. "Surely you did not think you were the *only* one," he said, "with a *destiny*."

10

ou know, I trust, about the comets," Grand Inquisitor Stanishur said as he lowered himself into a broad, cushioned chair in Tamerlane's private quarters. Behind him, his two ever-present acolytes waited motionless in their crisp, black smartcloth uniforms and hoods, standing at attention as if they were soldiers. For all intents and purposes, of course, they *were*.

The trio had arrived via private Inquisition shuttle only a short time earlier. Their flight had been unlisted and unexpected. But of course once their ship had rendezvoused with the *Ascanius* and announced exactly who was on board, Tamerlane had quickly granted them permission to dock. The Grand Inquisitor had wasted no time in making his way to the general's quarters, saying nothing at all en route. The whole business somewhat unnerved Tamerlane. Anything that bothered the crusty old holy man enough to make him sneak around like a thief in the night was likely something that would be bothering everyone else in the galaxy soon enough.

"I'm sorry?" Tamerlane asked, certain he'd misheard the other man. "The…what?"

"The *comets*," Stanishur repeated, as though it were obvious.

The general frowned. He seated himself in a chair opposite the Inquisitor and leaned forward. "Comets. You're saying you came here because you wish to discuss... *comets*."

"Indeed I do," the ancient figure responded, his voice reedy and thin but strong.

Tamerlane regarded him, elderly and gaunt in the black robes and vests and belts that marked his high office. Reflexively he thought back over the last year of their unlikely association with one another. They had emerged as unexpected allies due to their mutual support for Nakamura as *Taiko*—military ruler of the Empire—after the death of the last Emperor, and because of their shared experiences in the Above and the Below, as part of an expedition gone horribly wrong.

"I assumed you asked for this meeting to talk about the state of the wars against us," Tamerlane said, "or perhaps to inquire as to the *Taiko*'s health."

"I am well aware of the state of the wars, General. I could scarcely be Grand Inquisitor of the Empire and not know such things. For instance, I know that we are losing on all fronts, and that our time as the dominant human political entity in the galaxy is nearing an end—unless something dramatic alters our fortunes very soon."

Tamerlane couldn't contradict this. He simply returned Stanishur's baleful stare, waiting.

"And as for Nakamura's health—physical and mental, both of which appear to me to be in deterioration—I am most assuredly concerned. But neither of those things carries the urgency of—"

"Of comets," Tamerlane finished for him, frowning deeper. "Really." He leaned back in his seat. "I must admit, you have piqued my interest, Inquisitor. By all means, continue."

Stanishur allowed a hint of a smile to touch his bloodless lips. "You don't believe me yet," he said. "But you will." Without taking his eyes off the general, he motioned with one bony hand to his acolytes. In response, the woman stepped forward and offered him a small crystal. Stanishur took it and the woman—Sister Delain, Tamerlane remembered now—moved back into her former spot.

"I haven't trusted this to the Aether net," the older man said, handing the crystal in turn to the general. "A hard copy only." He gestured toward the holo console. "Plug it in. See for yourself."

"I can't wait." Tamerlane inserted the crystal in a small slot on the brushed aluminum console before him and activated the holo field. Instantly the room filled with a foggy representation of the galaxy. Red streaks—like claw marks from some insanely vast creature—appeared along one edge of the nearest spiral arm.

Tamerlane's brow wrinkled. He sat forward, then stood, walking slowly through and around the holographic projection, attempting to comprehend what he was seeing.

"Well?" Stanishur asked, impatient.

"They're homing in on Imperial star systems—on our planets."

"Yet they are merely comets," Stanishur said again, smiling his rictus smile that contained no mirth whatsoever.

Tamerlane looked from the red streaks to the Inquisitor. The older man pulled himself slowly to his feet and moved alongside the general. Together they peered at the strange display for several quiet seconds.

"Alright," Tamerlane said at last. "Tell me: What are they? Because we both know they must not be—they *can't* be—mere comets."

"No, indeed," Stanishur replied, shaking his head. "They are something very different."

"What?"

"They are," the old Inquisitor replied, his eyes gleaming in the darkened room, "the very apocalypse itself, made manifest."

Tamerlane took this in, then closed his eyes, weariness creeping over him as he thought of all the obstacles he and his government already faced, before being confronted with...*this*. "Of course they are," he sighed.

Tamerlane led the way through private corridors of the ship, heading directly for Nakamura's quarters. The three Inquisitors followed closely behind him.

Stanishur had insisted on seeing the *Taiko*, despite Tamerlane's warning that Nakamura was in seclusion and likely wouldn't receive him or anyone else.

"I have my suspicions about that," the old man had replied, but wouldn't say more.

They reached the door and Tamerlane accessed the Aether, signaling his presence—the high-tech equivalent of ringing the doorbell. Several seconds passed, and then the door slid partway open. The open space was filled by the slender form of a woman in dark red robes and hood. The robes were drawn tightly about her.

Tamerlane stared at her, blinking, surprised.

"The *Taiko* is unavailable," the woman said, her voice thick and strange to the general's ears.

"You," he said, his voice almost a whisper. "Teluria."

"Our new Ecclesiarch," Stanishur added, his tone clearly disapproving. "Is this the first time you two have met?"

"Yes, it—" Tamerlane hesitated, then, "No. No—you were here before. With the *Taiko*." He looked off to one side, frowning. "But—why did I forget?"

"I cannot help you with such problems, General," the woman said. Her dark eyes flicked from Tamerlane to the three black-robed Inquisitors who stood behind him. Then she reached up and drew back her hood to reveal long,

104

straight, dark hair and pale features. "Well. Grand Inquisitor. A pleasure to see you." She bowed her head ever so slightly. "May I ask—what brings you here?"

"I might ask you a similar question," the older man said. He stared at her blatantly, his eyes moving over her form and all around her, as if searching for something.

"I am here at the request of the *Taiko*," she said, "to offer him guidance and advice." She looked from Stanishur to Tamerlane and back. "I do not believe, however, that he requested the presence of either of *you*."

"We serve the Empire," Stanishur shot back at her. "All of us here do. We do what must be done to protect and preserve it—particularly in difficult times such as these."

Teluria's expression soured. No one spoke for several seconds. Then, "The *Taiko* is indisposed at the moment. Perhaps if you came back later...?"

Tamerlane gave Stanishur a knowing look.

The Grand Inquisitor said nothing for a second. Then he inclined his head slightly and said, "Of course. Thank you, Ecclesiarch." He paused before looking back at her. "And when we return, the *Taiko* will be available to see us."

"Perhaps."

"It was not a question," the pale man told her. "He *will* be. One way or another."

Teluria drew back, her robes fluttering around her. "Was that a veiled threat, Inquisitor?"

"My words are no more veiled than yours," the older man said, smiling thinly. "I hide nothing."

The dark-haired woman nodded at this, then raised her arms and stepped forward a step. Her blood-red robes fell to the deck, leaving her utterly naked before them.

"Neither do I, Inquisitor."

Tamerlane blinked twice, then quickly looked away, clearing his throat.

Stanishur stared at her for a long moment, then cackled a laugh. "Ah, my dear—the days when such a display had

105

any effect on me are long behind us, I fear. More's the pity." He laughed again, then turned on his heel and began to stride back down the corridor. "The *Taiko*. When we return," he called back over his shoulder. The two acolytes hurried to catch up.

Tamerlane glanced back one last time at the Ecclesiarch, seeing her kneeling to retrieve her robes. Then he set off after the others.

The door hissed closed behind him.

"She thought to deceive us," Stanishur said, sinking again into the big chair in Tamerlane's office. "She thought showing us herself completely uncovered would convince us she had nothing up her sleeves—or at least distract us from our purposes."

"I have to admit, she's a very impressive figure of a woman," Tamerlane muttered.

"No, she isn't," Stanishur said, shaking his gray-haired head. "That's just part of the spell."

"Spell?"

"She was doing several things there, all at once. Part of it was a spell to distract us; to confuse us. Making us think she is some sort of raving beauty is just one more weapon in her arsenal. One of many, I believe." He shrugged. "If you'd seen her through my eyes, you wouldn't have been so impressed." He chuckled.

Tamerlane shook his head in wonder. "I suppose I'll have to take your word for that," he said.

Stanishur waved it away with one bony hand. "She clearly has her hooks in the *Taiko*," the old man said. "That much is obvious. But we cannot address that now. Time is of the essence."

"The comets," Tamerlane guessed.

"Yes.   The comets.   They must be investigated immediately. We have to be absolutely certain of what they represent."

Tamerlane nodded. "I will put my best man on it."

Stanishur smiled at that. "Ah. Your best man. I believe I know who that would be." He chuckled. "Big. Blond. Dangerous."

"The very one."

"Excellent."   Stanishur stood, and Tamerlane got to his feet a second later. "Meanwhile I fear I must return to Holy Terra, General," he said. "Urgent business awaits me." He motioned to one of his two acolytes—the woman, Delain. She stepped forward. "But I will leave you my best *woman*, to assist you, in my absence."

Tamerlane was puzzled. "You aren't going to wait a bit and go to see the *Taiko* again?"

Stanishur snorted at this. "I was not serious. I simply wanted to gauge Teluria's reaction to my threat. In any case, I suspect there is little to gain from a meeting with Nakamura now. I believe he has become entirely her creature. Her puppet. He would say whatever she wished for him to say."

Tamerlane appeared stricken at that remark. He started to object.

Stanishur raised a hand. "Save your words, General," he said, not unkindly. "Believe me, we will deal with that situation soon enough. But provoking a confrontation now will likely only result in drawing the real enemy out, and too soon."

"The *real* enemy? What are you talking about?"

Stanishur leaned in closer, his voice now barely a whisper. "Forces are gathering against us, Ezekial," he hissed. "Forces greater than just the armies and navies of our neighboring human and alien empires." His eyes nearly burned into Tamerlane's own with his fervor. "You know

the sort of forces to which I refer. You have seen them—
fought them—yourself."

Tamerlane moved back a step. "You're saying what we
face is more than just a war," he whispered.

"Oh, it *is* a war, General," the Inquisitor replied, his eyes
sparkling. "Just not the sort of war you imagined it to be. It
is a war of the *gods*."

Moments later, the Grand Inquisitor had shuffled out of
Tamerlane's quarters, his male acolyte in tow. The door
closed behind them and the general turned and sank into his
chair, his mind racing in a thousand different directions. It
actually took him several seconds to realize that he was no
longer alone.

"Ah," he exclaimed, looking up at the woman in black,
where she stood quietly in the same spot she'd occupied
during the conversation with Stanishur. "Sister Delain. I'm
sorry—I almost forgot you were there."

No response.

Quickly he accessed the Aether and ordered an aide to
prepare guest quarters for a new arrival. Then he looked
back at the female Inquisitor. "Your room will be ready
shortly," he told her, wondering why he was suddenly
nervous.

"The comets," Delain said by way of reply.

Tamerlane blinked. "I'm sorry?"

"The comets," she repeated, her voice flat and even.

"Yes—of course." Tamerlane stood, frowning. "I will be
contacting the appropriate parties immediately."

Delain nodded. "After you do that, we will discuss the
next steps that must be taken."

"We will?"

The woman's face remained impassive. "The Grand
Inquisitor has briefed me fully on everything that he wishes
for you to do. You may consider my...*advice*...as coming
directly from him."

"I...see," Tamerlane replied, raising one eyebrow. Before he could say anything more, the woman turned and moved to the door. It slid open and she vanished through it.

Tamerlane sank back in his chair and shook his head. *Apocalyptic comets*, he thought. *Mysterious figures conspiring against humanity. And to top it all off, a new assistant, compliments of the Inquisition—and one who makes Stanishur seem like a sparkling conversationalist...!*

11

The shock waves from explosions erupting all around hurled the bodies of the regular infantrymen across the battered landscape, in some cases in more than one direction at the same time. Resolute and unmoved amidst the maelstrom of violence, however, the dozen members of the Golden Phalanx's Bravo Squad pressed on. The forces that washed over them budged them not at all, as though each step they took somehow glued their feet to the ground. Their Deising-Arry Model 5 heavy plate armor, layered as it was over complex exoskeletal components, increased their weight by a factor of five and their strength and power by an even greater number.

"Keep moving," barked General Agrippa over their closed Aether link. "Distortion shields to maximum, everyone. Don't allow them to get a fix on us. *Any* of us."

No one replied; it was expected that they would all simply do as their leader commanded. With their humming distortion shields cranked to maximum output, the only thing the enemy would be seeing when gazing down into this valley—with scopes, scanners, or just the naked eye— was a hazy field of gray fuzz, stretching for hundreds of yards in any direction. There could be no pretense of stealth, of course, with the noise the devices generated; but then, no one wearing heavy plate armor had a right to ever expect stealth to enter into the equation.

The distortion shields crackled and popped whenever the troopers got too close to one another and caused their bubbles to momentarily overlap. Each time, before Agrippa could hurl an admonishment, the offenders would realize their error and pull back into proper spacing. They were good troops, disciplined and well-trained. Agrippa had seen to that for his entire army, and had then chosen only the best for his Bravo Squad.

With the big Colossus walkers out of commission, Agrippa and his crewmen had been forced to walk for a time, crossing the heart of the battlefield clad only in their normal uniforms. Finally, though, they'd managed to break through the Aether jamming and set up a rendezvous with the other members of the squad. Armed and armored now, they represented a force almost as intimidating in many ways as the gargantuan machines they'd piloted only hours earlier.

At the front of the marching formation, only a half-step behind Agrippa, Major Darius Torgon kept his quad-rifle at the ready and his eyes peeled for enemy troops. The landscape, barren and rocky as it was, afforded little in the way of cover, but they'd stumbled across hidden traps more than once already since landing here on Eingrad 6.

Massive bolts of energy streaked overhead, smashing into the line of cliffs in the distance. Torgon glanced quickly backward at the source of those blasts and once again marveled at what he saw: the heavy artillery of Third Legion's main assault force, just unloaded from city-sized carryalls that were now streaking back up into orbit to ferry down the next load. "Artillery" scarcely conveyed a true sense of exactly what Agrippa had ordered to be employed here on Eingrad 6, however. From the Colossus walkers to heavy aircraft to planetary-crust-shattering bombs, the general was leaving no weapon in his arsenal unemployed. "Eingrad will be ours," he had intoned at the start of the campaign to free it from the Riyahadi invader, "or it won't *be* at all."

And yet for all of the bluster he had put on display for the benefit of his men's morale, Agrippa understood that this world represented only one small portion of a much larger problem now faced by the Empire: they were confronting enemies everywhere, and they were losing everywhere.

And the sheer variety of enemies was overwhelming in its own right. In his earlier days, Agrippa had fought against the Riyahadi here and there; simple border skirmishes that had happened from time immemorial. Likewise, from time to time the alien Dyonari had blundered into human space— or vice versa—and armed conflict had resulted. But never anything like this. It seemed to Agrippa that every planet the Empire controlled, short of the core worlds themselves, was being attacked, besieged, or invaded by someone. The Riyahadi, the Chung, the DACS crowd, and various outlaw groups from among the human part of the galaxy, not to mention the alien Dyonari and Rao—if it had a ship that could fly and a gun that could shoot, and it existed somewhere beyond the borders, it looked to be coming after the Empire.

"Enemy forces ahead," one of the scouts reported over the Aether. Agrippa immediately motioned for a halt. He then began issuing orders to the troops to move into position.

Even as the Bravo Squad prepared for battle, a signal suddenly penetrated the static that had dominated the Aether link for hours. The general gritted his teeth at the volume but accessed the signal. "Agrippa here," he answered tersely.

A pause, then, barely audible over the interference, "General, this is Ezekial Tamerlane. I apologize for the level of this communication—it's being boosted to about a thousand times the normal signal strength—but the tech guys here tell me it was the only way to get through to you."

"I believe it," Agrippa replied, his head already throbbing in reaction to the squealing static in his brain. "We've been dealing with a great deal of interference—jamming, or else something natural we haven't encountered before."

"Understood," Tamerlane said. "So I'll keep this brief. I have a new assignment for you."

Agrippa scowled. "What? But—General, the Legion is committed to liberating Eingrad 6! In fact, my Bravo Squad and I are at this very moment about to engage the Riyahadi and—"

"You can leave your Legion in place there, Arnem," Tamerlane interjected. "Colonel Iksander is perfectly capable of leading it to victory. For the job I've just learned needs doing, though, I will require the best. And we both know that's *you*." He paused, as if knowing that objections were sure to come. Then, in a lower, more intimate tone, "Arnem, listen to me. The survival of not just the Empire is at stake, but of all the men, women and children that make it what it is. *Everyone*."

Agrippa bit back his automatic reply—the argument that he didn't want to leave Eingrad with the job not fully done. He wanted to say it, but he couldn't. After all, if Tamerlane had another job—a job that was somehow more important, more critical to the survival of untold billions of people—he could scarcely turn it down.

"What's the job, then, General?" he asked, truly curious.

"I need you and a chosen team to investigate the incursions into Imperial territory that we are now suffering."

Agrippa was puzzled. "General...I thought that's what we were doing now—battling the enemy forces that have invaded across our borders."

"Not those incursions, Arnem," Tamerlane replied. "Not just the usual jealous neighbors. I mean something else.

Something perhaps more insidious." A pause. "I mean the comets."

For a long moment Agrippa was at a loss for words. He didn't know what to say—whether to take his commanding officer seriously or not. Finally he managed to reply, "Comets? You want me to investigate comets?" He shook his head in astonishment. Had the leader of the I Legion lost his mind?

"Trust me on this, Arnem," Tamerlane responded quickly. "There's more to them than we realized."

Agrippa looked up at the darkening sky above Eingrad 6. The blood-red comet was still there, larger than ever. It seemed to grow even as he stared at it. The longer he did so, the more a prickly sense of...*unease, anxiety*...filled his mind and his heart. There was no arguing it; there was indeed something very disturbing about the thing. With great effort he tore his eyes away.

"...Understood, General," he managed after another few seconds; seconds it had required for him to regain his equilibrium. Within his mind, he cursed. *Another threat? Now—when our forces are already divided and spread all across the Empire? Could our luck be any worse?*

"I will send you coordinates of the nearest Imperial world that we know has one in its system," Tamerlane was saying.

"Not necessary," Agrippa said, still looking up. "We have one here."

"There? Above Eingrad? They've penetrated that far into the Empire?"

"Yes, sir," Agrippa replied, still eyeing the comet. It was very close now.

Tamerlane's voice was sharp, clipped. "Investigate, General. But—be careful. From the fragmentary reports I've been hearing from other worlds—just...be very careful."

What Agrippa had at first thought was a joke or perhaps insanity on the part of his commanding general now seemed increasingly serious to him. "Understood," he repeated. "We will proceed with caution and I'll let you know what we find. Agrippa out."

The squealing, static-filled link clicked off and the pain in Agrippa's head lessened—but it didn't entirely vanish. Now it seemed to have been replaced by something else; by a deeper, lower hum that partially registered in his ears and partly within his skull. He looked around at his armor-clad men, all still crouched in their defensive positions, awaiting contact with the enemy, and tried to determine if they were hearing it, too. He couldn't tell; their helmets covered their faces.

"Alright, Bravos," he called over the local link. "Change of plans. We have a new job, direct from the top." He expanded the signal to reach the rest of III Legion. "Phalanx, you're now under the immediate command of Colonel Iksander. Mop these Riyahadi up and reclaim this planet for the Empire."

"Not a problem. We shall have them sorted out in no time, General," the notoriously brash Iksander replied from his position some distance away. "But I suspect the tough part of this fight isn't over yet."

"Why do you say that?" Agrippa asked, even as he signaled for his Bravo Squad to assemble around him.

"The omens have been wrong here from the start," Iksander stated. "It's been there—right up in the sky—all along."

"The comet," Agrippa said, and a chill ran through him. *He senses it, too. The wrongness of it.*

"It's an evil sign. Bad things are coming."

Agrippa wanted to scoff at this naked display of superstition, but he couldn't. He felt it, too. Everything his subordinate was saying was true.

"Look," called one of the squad members, pointing upward with an armored hand.

Agrippa had to force himself to regard the comet once more. It loomed high above, blood red and fragmented, shimmering clouds trailing in its wake, and a very palpable sense of unease—of *fear*—preceded it. As ridiculous as that sounded, Agrippa found he could not deny it. Not one bit.

It was starting to break apart as it encountered the outer edges of Eingrad's atmosphere. And something else. He thought he was imagining it at first, but as he continued to watch, he became convinced it was true: the comet fragments were *slowing*.

Much as he hated to admit it to himself, he knew that Iksander was right. That Tamerlane was right. Something bad was coming. Something worse than a Riyahadi army unit with creative ideas about the deployment of gravity generators. Something worse even than the unexpected arrival of enemy heavy armor. No, something far worse— something *unnatural*—was coming to this planet, and perhaps to every part of their Empire.

And it would arrive very, very soon.

"So—what are we going to be doing, boss?" Major Torgon asked from nearby, his voice echoing hollowly over the local link.

Agrippa swallowed and raised his arm, pointing to where the first fragments of the comet were streaking down some miles away. In a voice he found he had to struggle to keep even, he answered, "We're going comet hunting, gentlemen."

Nobody laughed.

BOOK SIX
FIRE AND ICE

1

The Sand Kings troopers in their golden plate armor stood with weapons at the ready. They were arrayed on either side of the crowd of men and women who were lined up just outside the main doors of the throne room. The people had been randomly rounded up from the streets of the Heliopolis at the orders of Zahir, the recently-installed vizier to Imperial Governor Rameses, and brought here at gunpoint. No one knew why—not the people, and not the soldiers who herded them along.

Now the great double-doors were opening, and the voice of the vizier himself called out: "Bring them inside! Quickly!"

The Sand Kings motioned impatiently for the people to move through, into the vast throne room itself. There was little panic among them now; many among them began to suspect that they had somehow won a semi-private audience with great Rameses himself.

Indeed they had.

"There," Zahir barked, pointing at the golden basin with its column of energy towering up into the cavernous open space of the chamber, far above their heads. A ramp had been constructed that led to the edge of the bowl, looking for all the world like a diving platform for a very small pool. "Line them up there."

"This is absolutely necessary?" came the voice of Rameses as he descended from the throne and stood beside the red-clad vizier. His eyes moved nervously from the soldiers to the citizens to the basin itself.

"It is vital," Zahir replied. "The matrix is not complete. The basin is gathering and channeling the Power from the Fountain in the Golden City, but it lacks the...shall we say, *human* element that will enable it to more fully interact with you, sire." He smiled his wicked smile. "It will most assuredly speed up the process of your apotheosis—and that is something you most assuredly desire, yes? Something worth virtually any price?"

Very reluctantly, Rameses nodded.

Zahir once again attached the cuffs to the governor's wrists and ankles, the wires and cables trailing away to the machine that sat next to the basin. Then he motioned to the guards. "Now!"

At that order, the special operations soldiers of the Sand Kings Legion in their gleaming gold armor began directing the citizens forward, toward the ramp. At first they moved along, uncertain. Then, as they drew closer to the churning energies of the Fountain, they began to resist. A couple of quad-rifle butt blows to the head took the fight out of the first few, but stirred the others up a great deal more than they already were. Finally the Sand Kings were forced to physically shove the people up the ramp, guns in their faces. At last the first of them—a dark-haired man in his forties— stood like a diver at the edge of the ramp, looking down into the coruscating bowl of light and flame and energy.

"Go!" came the electronically amplified voice of the nearest soldier.

"What? But—*no!* What is—?"

The Sand King reached out and shoved the man off the ramp and into the bowl. He vanished instantly in a crackle of light and sparks.

The others cried out. Some began to fight back again. The soldiers beat them down mercilessly.

"Put them in," Zahir cried, his voice growing impatient. "Now!"

The Sand Kings bodily shoved the remaining citizens— all crying out and trying to fight back— up the ramp and off of it, down into the swirling fire of the bowl. None of them had any chance against even one soldier in plate combat armor; against half a dozen, it was over very quickly and with brutal efficiency.

The flames danced higher within the bowl. The column of energy that erupted continuously out of it, geyser-like, appeared to grow thicker, brighter.

Zahir nodded as he watched this occur. Then he touched a set of controls on the machine before him. Waves of energy radiated out from the fountain, even as the cables and wires that connected to Rameses danced with scarcely-contained current. The cuffs around the governor's extremities flared brightly with light, and Rameses stumbled back, the electricity racing through him.

"Bring in the girl," Zahir cried.

Two more Sand Kings, these wearing only beige smartcloth uniforms, escorted the tiny figure out of an anteroom. This time she was awake—though barely. She looked around, dazed, unsteady on her feet, uncertain of her whereabouts. Zahir moved alongside her and began to connect a set of cuffs to her, as well.

Before he could go further, one of the Sand Kings officers strode up and stood at attention. "My Lord Governor," he said, addressing Rameses, "a party has arrived from the *Taiko*."

Despite the waves of raw energy rushing through his body, Rameses managed to focus his eyes on the officer. "A party?"

"Emissaries," the man stated. "Colonel Belisarius of I Legion, along with certain other members of the Imperial bureaucracy."

"Bah," Rameses scoffed. "Tell them I am busy."

The officer hesitated. "The Colonel bears orders directly from General Tamerlane. He warns that failure to receive him immediately is tantamount to treason against the Empire."

Now Rameses grew angry. "Treason? I'll show him treason! How dare he—?"

Zahir leaned in. "My Lord Governor," he intoned, while surreptitiously motioning to his servant to take the girl back out of the room. "We are not yet ready to move. I counsel that you receive this emissary from the *Taiko*, hear what he has come so far to say, make whatever promises are called for, and then send him on his way."

Rameses growled wordless anger deep in his throat. "Very well," he muttered. Then, louder, "Send them in!"

The doors opened to reveal a procession of four men and women. Three of them were older and clad in the brown and tan livery of the Imperial bureaucracy; the fourth was younger, taller, more muscular, wearing the red and gold of I Legion.

"So, Colonel Belisarius," Rameses called from where he stood near the basin. "What errand of the pretender Nakamura has brought you to Ahknaton?"

Belisarius and the others walked slowly into the throne room, their eyes locked on Rameses and the bizarre setting within which he stood. "Governor Rameses," the colonel said, his voice filled with puzzlement, "may I ask what is going on here?"

"You may not," Rameses all but shouted. "You are a guest—for the moment—in my home. What I am doing is none of your concern."

Zahir stepped quickly and deftly between the two. "What message from the *Taiko*, Colonel—and why did he feel the need to send your august personage to deliver it?"

"My message is not from the *Taiko* but from General Tamerlane," Belisarius stated, his eyes flashing from Rameses to Zahir, "and it is for the Governor—not for you, whoever you are."

"I am Zahir, the governor's vizier—chief minister and advisor."

"Oh? Well, a word of advice, Zahir. All the charm in the world can't cover up treason."

Zahir scowled. "And my advice for you," he snapped back at the colonel, his heretofore ingratiating persona dissolving instantly, "is to watch your step while you tread on worlds not your own."

Belisarius regarded the man in the red robes with open contempt, then stepped past him, moving closer to Rameses.

"General Tamerlane has repeatedly requested that you make a portion of your Sand Kings army available to him and to the *Taiko*, for use in defending the Empire. You have as yet failed to respond to him."

"My unwillingness to take such a request seriously is all the answer he should expect to receive," Rameses barked back.

"They are Imperial forces," Belisarius argued, "and as such, they are ultimately under the command of the *Taiko*."

"I beg to differ. They are loyal to this world, and to its ruler."

"Its ruler is the *Taiko*."

Rameses laughed loudly. "Not true, either de jure or de facto," he stated.

"You reject the authority of the Imperial government?" blurted one of the officials to Belisarius's left.

"There *is* no Imperial government at the moment," Rameses scoffed. "Only a general whose reach exceeds his grasp."

Belisarius reddened. "Understand something, Governor, and be completely clear on it," he said, his tone low and menacing now. "To call it a 'request' is politeness on the part of the general and myself. Make no mistake: you are required to hand your forces over for Imperial defense. And if requiring fails, the general will compel."

Rameses began to issue an angry retort, but Zahir moved between them again, cutting him off. "Perhaps we should take a short break before resuming this conversation," the vizier suggested. "It would be tragic for the wrong impressions to be made in the heat of emotion."

The governor glared at Belisarius as he spoke. "I believe the only impressions being made here at the moment, Zahir, are very accurate and revealing ones. On both sides."

The vizier leaned in close to Rameses, speaking in a barely audible whisper. "As I stated before, sire, we are not entirely ready. We lack the resources to go against Nakamura at the moment. I must caution you to not seek to provoke—"

Rameses practically spit his rejection back at Zahir. "Bah! The colonel here knows full well my views on all of this. I won't waste either of our time by being disingenuous." He smiled broadly at the still-angry Belisarius. "And now you may convey that message back to the usurper on the Imperial throne."

"No!" Zahir almost shouted, now moving around behind the colonel and the bureaucrats. "No—we do not wish to give the impression of treason or rebellion to the *Taiko*."

"The impression?" Belisarius shouted. "Not until you're 'ready,' whatever that means? And I believe I know all too well what it means."

Zahir moved in closer to the colonel, readying another line of argument—and then he froze, not moving. His dark, kohl-lined eyes narrowed as they focused intently on the I Legion officer.

Belisarius, distracted by this, turned away from the governor and studied Zahir. "What are you doing?" he asked, his anger blending with puzzlement.

The man in the dark red robes ignored the question. After a few seconds, he moved in still closer to Belisarius and began to sniff.

"What do you think you're doing?" the colonel demanded. "Why—"

Zahir's eyes widened as he continued to sniff the other man. For the colonel's part, sweat began to trail down his cheeks. Within a matter of only moments, he appeared feverish and pale. His eyes grew glassy and he coughed, coughed again.

"Could it be?" the vizier asked rhetorically. "Could it be so easy?"

"What?" Rameses demanded, disengaging himself from the cuffs and cables and stepping away from the basin. He wore only a loincloth of woven gold and clutched a gleaming golden dagger in his left hand. Curious as to what was happening, he strode toward Zahir. "What is it?"

Zahir raised his own left hand, halting Rameses in his tracks before he could approach closer. Then he turned back to the colonel. "It is you, isn't it?" he hissed softly. "Come straight into my lair."

"What's that you're saying?" Rameses demanded, wanting to approach more closely but unwilling for the moment to defy his vizier.

"Nothing at all, sire," Zahir stated quickly.

The three other individuals who had entered the throne room along with Belisarius now spoke up. "Just what is the meaning of this?" asked the woman, the only female of the three.

Zahir ignored her. "Why are you here?" he asked Belisarius, studying the man closely.

"You know why I am here," the colonel barked. "I've made that perfectly clear."

"No," Zahir breathed, his voice low. "Why *you*? You specifically? I must know. Why did Tamerlane choose you to come here, and not some other officer?"

Belisarius blinked at that. He opened and closed his mouth soundlessly. Then, "I—I volunteered," he said. "I wanted to come here."

"Ah!" Zahir gasped. "Yes! You were compelled. You had no choice!"

The colonel blinked rapidly now. He moved back a step, suddenly uncertain. Then he whirled around, bent over, and threw up.

"What is all of this?" Rameses demanded, repulsed, drawing back from the sick man. "Zahir? What are you talking about?"

Meanwhile the three bureaucrats gathered closer around Belisarius. One of them—the tallest, a blond man in his fifties—leaned in close. "Colonel? Are you ill? Can we—"

Belisarius straightened. His eyes met those of the blond bureaucrat and flames danced within them. The blond man gasped and stumbled backward. Belisarius drew his blast pistol and shot the man in the chest twice.

The Sand Kings guards reacted as their training had conditioned them to: they rushed forward, weapons at the ready. Rameses meanwhile gasped and scrambled away. "*Assassin!*" he cried. The other two bureaucrats screamed.

Moving very smoothly and swiftly, Belisarius whirled about and shot them both down where they stood.

A short distance away, seemingly unconcerned for his own safety, Zahir stood unmoving, a grin wide and bright on his face.

The Sand Kings reached for the colonel, grasped him, tore the pistol away from him, and held him securely.

Rameses was livid. He stalked forward, looking at the three bodies on the floor of his palace, then glaring up at Belisarius. When he saw the flames in the colonel's eyes, his angry questions died unspoken in his throat. He turned and looked to Zahir.

The vizier laughed.

"Will you tell me what just happened?" Rameses demanded.

"Perfect," Zahir breathed. "Just perfect!" He gazed into Belisarius's eyes, watching as the flames slowly faded—though they never entirely died away. He nodded.

"I *demand* to know," Rameses shouted now, moving directly in front of Zahir. "I demand to know the meaning of all this!"

Zahir's smile actually grew wider. "I present you, my lord, at long last," he said, "with what I promised you when I arrived." As Rameses looked on, uncomprehending, Zahir nodded toward Belisarius. "I present you, sire, with the third gift."

2

Right there, sir— do you see?"

Captain Felix Dakkan leaned over the shoulder of the scanner operator and squinted at the little screen. As usual, he felt a pang of jealousy for the drivers of the big Colossus walkers; their cockpits were equipped with full holo displays, while aboard his hovertank he had to settle for the ancient technology of a 2-D screen. Forcing that out of his mind, he looked more closely and nodded slowly.

"Looks like a cluster of distortion fields," Dakkan speculated. "Though I suppose the question is, whose distortion fields?" He frowned. "And what are they trying to hide?"

"Shall I maneuver closer, sir?" the driver asked, looking back at Dakkan.

He didn't hesitate. "Yes. And arm the main gun. The side guns, as well."

Loaders clacked to life, echoing through the confined spaces of the hovertank.

Dakkan accessed the Aether and surveyed the available local channels. Finding the one he wanted, he opened a link.

"Lieutenant Liefer," he called. "Are you registering the distortion area to the northeast?"

"Was just about to call you about that, sir," Liefer responded from the other tank. "I read it as most likely covering up a small column of soldiers—though they could have most anything concealed in there along with them."

Dakkan nodded. "We're going to investigate. Arm your weapons and follow us in."

"Will do, sir."

Dakkan left the link in standby mode and peered at the forward viewscreen. His tank was curving around in its path now, approaching the distortion area very quickly. He motioned to the gunner. "Be ready."

"Aye, sir."

The crackling gray field rushed at them, and then they were through it and inside the hemisphere of electrical camouflage. Dakkan blinked and kept his eyes glued to the screen, ready to give the order to fire at a moment's notice.

"You're in, Captain," came the voice of Liefer from the other tank, watching from a short distance away, guns at the ready.

Dakkan continued to stare at the screen. His frown deepened. He glanced over at the driver, MacInnish. "What do you make of that?" he asked.

"I'm not really sure, sir," MacInnish replied. "It looks like... combat suits? Heavy plate?"

Dakkan had to agree. Before them marched a group of figures covered entirely in gleaming white plate armor, edged here and there with green trim. The markings weren't clear yet.

"Attention soldiers," Dakkan sent over the Aether across multiple channels. "Identify yourselves."

Nothing. Only silence across the link.

"Sir," the driver said, his voice carrying almost reverential tones, "That looks like Deising-Arry Model 5 heavy plate they're wearing."

Dakkan agreed, but he couldn't imagine how it could be possible. They also looked to be carrying quad rifles, making the small group at least as formidable as one of his tanks. Perhaps both of them. Dakkan remained on his guard, ready to give the order to fire at any moment.

The tank drew closer, rushing forward with an imposing fury and swerving to a halt directly in the soldiers' path. The gunner directed the swivel-mounted anti-personnel cannons at the head of the formation and waited.

Dakkan watched carefully as the procession of armored, helmeted men halted and stood there, staring back at them. And, despite their heavy plate armor and the helmets that completely covered their heads and necks, they were clearly men; they were too bulky for Dyonari and their suits didn't look anything like what the Rao would wear. But—could they be Riyahadi? Chung? DACS? Their insignia were visible now and read III Legion, but there was certainly no reason Dakkan could think of that a detachment of his own legion's troopers would be out roaming around on foot this far into the battlefield. In the thick of a massive military action, he couldn't afford to take any unnecessary chances.

For several seconds no one on either side of the confrontation moved or spoke. Finally Dakkan grew impatient and decided it was time to take what could be called a necessary chance. He reached up, unlocked the top hatch, and swung it open. He pulled himself up and through, his upper body projecting out the top of the hovertank. He stared down at the group of armored troops—it looked like a dozen, easily, and each as armed and armored as a smaller version of the hovertank he commanded.

"Identify yourselves," he demanded. "Now!"

In the corner of Dakkan's vision, a green diamond flashed. It was a code being transmitted over the Aether link. Dakkan glanced at it, looked away—then looked at it again and blanched. Could it be possible?

No, he concluded. It couldn't.

He returned his attention to the troopers in white and shouted down, "Alright—cut the crap. You don't expect me to believe the General himself is wandering around out here with a few men, do you? I want to know who you *really* are. Deserters, who stole the armor from supply, or—"

His voice trailed off and died in his throat as the lead figure reached up and unfastened his helmet, then pulled it slowly off his head. Dakkan gawked at the chiseled features and short blond hair that were revealed.

"General? General Agrippa? Sir!"

The big blond man grinned back at him. "I appreciate your caution, Captain—" He consulted the Aether personnel database quickly. "—Dakkan."

Speechless, Dakkan could only nod.

Agrippa's grin widened as he saw the other tank zooming up alongside the first. Lieutenant Liefer had been listening and surely now wanted to see for himself that the III Legion commander was there, on the battlefield, in the flesh.

"And I also appreciate you turning up at a very opportune time," the general continued, as behind him other members of the Bravo Squad unfastened and removed their helmets, enjoying a bit of air—not fresh, certainly, but better than what they'd been breathing inside their helmets for the past couple of hours. "Now—open these cans up, soldier," the big man boomed. "I need your men to hop out."

Dakkan was nearly in a daze. After all, members of III Legion—the Golden Phalanx, though they generally preferred to be called the Kings of Oblivion—practically worshipped their powerful, charismatic general. The tank commander tried to pull himself together. "You—what are you doing *here*? Sir? If I may ask?"

Agrippa sighed. "Son, I'm going to assume you didn't hear my order the first time. So I will repeat it, just this once. Out of the tanks. All of you. Now."

The tanker blinked, swallowed, nodded and saluted—and ten seconds later, all of his men were out of their tanks and lined up to one side, standing at attention.

"Now, we'll be taking your vehicles," Agrippa began.

"Taking them, sir?" Dakkan managed.

"*My* vehicles, actually," Agrippa amended. "So I can pretty much do with them as I wish." He regarded the line of tanker troopers. "It's a top priority mission, and we need to move quickly. I hate to leave you gentlemen to fend for yourselves out here, on foot, but the situation isn't as bad as it looks." He pointed back the way he and the Bravo Squad had just come. "Colonel Iksander and the whole blessed Legion are right down that way, and they're advancing quickly. So you just need to find them and hook up with them again."

The tankers didn't look thrilled with this development—with being reduced to infantrymen, in the midst of an active battlefield— but they couldn't very well argue with their legion's general.

Agrippa motioned and the Bravo Squad began to pile into the tanks.

"May I ask, sir," Dakkan said as he watched his two vehicles being appropriated and occupied, "what you will be doing with my—with *your*—tanks?"

Climbing up to the top of the turret of the lead tank, Agrippa glanced back down at the man. "It's very simple, Captain," he said. "Officially and technically, I'm following the orders of General Tamerlane. More specifically—and in reality—I'm probably stepping into a hornet's nest." He shrugged. "Or maybe not. But that's what I'm going to find out."

"I—I understand, sir," Dakkan replied. "I think." He hesitated. "Actually, not at all." He saluted. "But best of luck, sir."

"To you too, Captain. Men." Agrippa saluted, then dropped down into the tank. The hatch clanged closed.

LEGION II: SONS OF TERRA

As the tankers—now *former* tankers—looked on, the two hovertanks pivoted about and zoomed away, heading in the direction of the red glow on the horizon, where the meteors had come crashing down a bit earlier. Then, resigned to their fate, they turned and began to slowly march in the opposite direction, their previously pristine clean boots already coated in a thick layer of mud.

3

He occasionally displays some small bit of reluctance, of resistance," Zahir said aloud, "but I believe I have Rameses firmly under control."

"Good," came a voice in response. It was soft, gentle, barely audible. One might have mistaken it for the hiss and rustle of the wind through trees and grass—had there been any of either in evidence there. There were, of course, neither.

Zahir knelt on the floor of a small antechamber he had ordered prepared just off one wing of the Heliopolis palace. Slowly, cautiously he gazed up at the row of metal religious icons adorning the wall. The newest one, just above and before him and added only since his arrival on Ahknaton, occupied a position of importance second only to the image of the god Amenophis, he who was beloved of the people of this world. The others were of gods long dead.

At least, *most* of them were long dead.

The icon directly in front of him now glowed a bright, almost blinding red, though no heat radiated from it at all. To the contrary, impossibly, a cold wind seemed to blow through the closed room, and spider webs of ice and frost were forming across the marble tiles of the floor and walls.

"He will continue to obey, whether his will is directly enslaved to us or no, so long as he believes I am transforming him into a god," Zahir went on. "Above all things he desires to become the living incarnation of Amenophis, ancient god of this world and its people."

"Amenophis," the voice whispered back at him, its tone mocking, dismissive. "Oh yes. I remember him well. A minor god at best." Laughter echoed softly. "I never considered him worthy of any *real* regard. How he tricked the people of Ahknaton into honoring him above all others has always puzzled me. On those rare occasions when I spared any thoughts for him at all."

"I never knew him, my master," Zahir said aloud, head bowed.

"Consider yourself fortunate. He was a bore. I saw it as a mercy when Vorthan ripped his living spirit out and confined it to that gem. And then into the Fountain, of course—with so many others." Another laugh, cold and cynical. "So many who *needed* to go."

"Needed to, master?" Zahir asked, somewhat startled.

"Indeed," the voice replied. "Great Vorthan was wise to steal their souls, but he would have simply enslaved them. As events transpired, the cosmos saw fit to grant us a much preferable outcome: eternal death for all of them."

Zahir frowned but kept his head bowed. "I—see, master. Yes. As you say." A pause, and the silence of the chamber began to seem like a sort of hollow ringing that gnawed at the edges of Zahir's sanity. Whether it was real or some trick of the mind, he didn't know, but he spoke aloud then, if only to disrupt it. "I know that you do not like for anyone to question your plans, master," he said quickly, in a rush, trying to get to his point before being cut off, "but I must know—are any of the legions poised to strike down upon us here?" He waited only a moment before adding, "I trust the Sand Kings have been built up to the point now that they could adequately defend Ahknaton from any encroaching

135

scraps of Tamerlane's or Agrippa's forces. But I must admit—I worry that *Iapetus* and his wholly intact Second could cause us serious problems. They are encamped on the Inner Worlds now, but if he should choose to enter the fray before we are ready—"

"Calm yourself, Zahir," the voice hissed. "I have taken steps—and further steps are being taken even as we speak— to ensure that Iapetus and his Sons remain firmly in place on and around Earth." The voice changed ever so slightly, reflecting perhaps some degree of admiration, or at least appreciation. "No force in the galaxy can dislodge that man once he makes up his mind. In that way he is like our kind."

Zahir nodded to himself. "Yes—thank you master. I am reassured."

"You doubted me?"

"I—*no*, master. Never."

Silence. Silence and echoes, and the ringing that grew louder in his ears.

"Master? Are you still there?"

Nothing. Nothing—and then, "Yes, Zahir. One thing more."

"I await your command."

"You are to—"

The door of the small antechamber banged open. Zahir looked up, startled.

Into the room charged four Sand Kings of the governor's elite guard, resplendent in their red and blue Egyptian-motif dress uniforms trimmed in gold. They half-surrounded the vizier and pointed their elegant but deadly energy lances at him. For a long second, no one moved or spoke.

"What is this outrage?" Zahir finally demanded, rising to his feet.

"Quiet!" barked the lead officer. He glared at Zahir, anger and determination clear on his face—but he did nothing. His expression slowly changed to one of puzzlement, and he looked down.

Ice from the floor had spread up onto all the soldiers' boots, and continued to climb up their legs. It didn't touch Zahir.

"*He's* doing it somehow," the leader said, panic becoming evident in his voice. "Shoot him," he ordered to the others. "*Now!*"

"I—I *can't*," the Sand King next to him gasped. "I—*can't move!*"

"...Neither can I," the commander replied, eyes widening now in fear.

"Indeed you can't," Zahir barked, standing across from them, hands on hips, red robe flaring around him. "What is the meaning of this? Speak!"

At first none of the four replied, but then the leader's mouth opened—clearly against his will—and he blurted out, "We came here...to *kill* you."

"Oh yes? Why?"

"You...have brought... treason... and heresy...to our world...and to our...governor."

"Oh, please," Zahir scoffed. "Rameses was a traitor from the start. I am simply providing him with a bit of direction—and *power*."

"You...are...a...*devil*," one of the other Sand Kings gasped through lips now frosted over from the cold.

Zahir snorted a laugh. "You scarcely know the meaning of the term," he said.

The ice was up to their chests now, and still spreading. Within a few seconds only their faces were free of it—and then it closed in there, too.

"Shall I free them, master?" Zahir called to the icon on the wall, its metal face still gleaming.

"No," came the soft, hissing voice. "They would require more time and effort to bend to your will than I am able to spare at this time."

Zahir nodded. "I understand."

Slowly he walked across the ice-covered marble floor to stand next to the four men. They now appeared to be nothing more than white statues of soldiers, utterly devoid of any signs of life. With a sly, twisted smile, he drew back his fist and struck the nearest one a light blow.

It shattered into a million shards, the pieces tumbling to the floor.

Laughing, he did the same to the others. Then he stood over the small mounds of ice fragments, gazing down at them.

"You are pleased, master?"

"I am bored," the voice whispered back. "You should not have let the situation come to that. I will not tolerate rebellion or interference in my plans, Zahir."

"Of course, master," the vizier replied quickly, bowing his head again.

"Tend to Rameses. Be absolutely certain that he remains firmly in your grasp. Let no one else interfere."

"Yes, master."

The icon's red glow faded to darkness. Zahir bowed one last time and then hastily departed the antechamber. Behind him, the remains of the four elite Sand Kings warriors slowly melted and disappeared through cracks in the floor.

4

team hissing out all around him, General Ioan Iapetus descended the ramp that led down out of his command shuttle and onto the deck of the II Legion's flagship, *Atlantia*. At the bottom he stopped and waited, standing alone, immaculate in his black uniform with gleaming golden eye emblazoned on the chest.

No sooner had his boots touched the metal floor than the honor guard marched out to welcome him. They moved smoothly, together, as one unit: a dozen soldiers in the black of the general staff and a dozen more in older uniforms of the dark blue that had been II Legion's official color until recently. At the front of the formation, a woman bearing the insignia of colonel stepped forward and saluted smartly.

"Colonel Piryu," Iapetus said. "A pleasure to see you again. I trust all is well with the *Atlantia*."

"General," she said, "the pleasure is ours. We received word of your coming only a short while ago, and there was no indication as to the purpose of your visit. May I ask where will you need us to take you?"

Iapetus strode forward across the broad landing deck. The much shorter woman hurried to keep up. He traveled past the ranks of the honor guard and out into the center of the huge, vaulted space; dull gray alloy ribs arched high overhead, holding up the ceiling and holding out the freezing void. After a dozen more steps he stopped and stood staring at the soldiers and vehicles and weapons that filled a good portion of the hangar deck. All those troops, all those weapons, all at his disposal. The power it all gave him was considerable. Most considerable. He allowed himself a tight smile. Then he looked down at the colonel. "Nowhere," he said.

Whether his answer or his smile was the more disconcerting to Piryu, none could have said. Either way, she was taken aback. She blinked, frowned, and said, "I'm sorry, General—did you say 'nowhere?'"

His smile held on for another half-second and then evaporated. "Yes, Colonel."

The woman considered this, clearly not understanding, and then nodded once. "Very well, sir. Is there any other service we of the *Atlantia* can perform for you, then, while you are here?"

Iapetus exhaled slowly. "You can show me to the strategium, Colonel," he grumbled, "and then you can leave me in peace."

Looking as if she'd been stung by a bee, Piryu involuntarily moved back a step, then recovered, straightened and saluted. "Yes, sir." She nodded toward the lift. "If you will come this way, sir—?"

A brief ride in the lift later, sandwiched between two short walks along dull gray ship's corridors, Iapetus stood alone in the center of the massive flagship's strategium— the cavernous chamber where, when necessary, he and the other top ranking officers of the Sons of Terra formulated and laid out their plans for interstellar war. Sweeping into the room, he had brusquely ordered everyone else out, from tacticians to technicians to the ship's captain himself. Only Colonel Piryu had he ordered to remain behind, if only for a moment, that she might shut down all the electronics, turn out almost all of the lights, and then seal the room tightly on her way out.

That done, Iapetus arched his back and laced his fingers behind his waist, closing his eyes as in prayer or meditation. He reached out with his mind, as if attempting to use the Aether link—but he was not using the Aether. He was stretching his mental faculties beyond that artificial, man-made technology, to something far deeper, far more fundamental to the fabric of the universe itself.

"Are you there?" he asked silently, some time later. "Can you hear me?"

For several long seconds there was no reply. Then the voice came to him—the same one that had woken him up from a deep sleep a few hours earlier: "I am. You are aboard your flagship?"

"Yes." Both his expression and his voice were grim. "As you demanded."

"And the ship remains where it has been for the past three standard days?"

Iapetus quickly consulted the ship's navigational data via the Aether. It took less than two seconds. "Yes," he replied. "I placed it on sentry duty. It has not moved. Why does that matter?"

Silence.

Iapetus quickly grew impatient. "What do you want?" he asked, as calmly as he could manage. Then, as there was still no answer, he couldn't help but add, "You dragged me all the way out here. Speaking with me at my base headquarters on Luna wasn't sufficient. Fine. I have come. I'm here. Tell me what you want." He paused. "And who you are."

Nothing. The strategium remained still and dark and quiet. Only the faint hum of the ship's massive power plant and the dim illumination from a half-dozen recessed lights gleaming off the brushed metal surfaces kept him company.

He stood there, anger and impatience growing within his breast, until he had nearly convinced himself that he'd imagined the entire thing. He turned on his heel and started for the door.

And then the strategium flared to bright, brilliant light and life. A great eye formed in the center of the room, much like a holographic tactical display normally would, and in the same location. The eye expanded until it touched the floor and the ceiling; it was more than twice that wide. At its center, clouds and light swirled about.

Like some feral, predatory animal, Iapetus bared his teeth. He stepped back involuntarily, at the same time reaching for his sidearm.

A human form appeared within the smoke and the lights, moving forward, stepping out onto the deck of the *Atlantia*. A female form, mostly covered by a dark red cloak and hood.

Iapetus didn't flinch. One corner of his mouth did turn slightly down, possibly in surprise, though it could have been distaste or some other emotion entirely.

"General," the woman said, bowing slightly. As she raised her head again, some portion of her face was visible, though clouded by shadow. Behind her the great eye closed and vanished.

"Do I know you?" Iapetus retorted, frowning.

"We have not met," the woman said, her voice smooth and strong. "But I know you well, Iapetus. I have watched you from afar, and have judged your worth."

"Who are you to judge me?" Iapetus snapped. "And why would you be interested?"

"I am Teluria, Ecclesiarch of this Empire and vizier to the *Taiko* Nakamura."

"The new Ecclesiarch?" Iapetus narrowed his eyes, appraising her anew. "And—Vizier? *Advisor?*"

"Just so."

"I see." He paused. "And how did you perform that little teleportation trick just now?"

Teluria smiled. "You have no love for those who claim the mantle of godhood," she said by way of response. "This is well known. But I trust my clumsy display went some distance toward persuading you that any claims I may make about myself are well founded." Her own dark eyes met the general's and held them. "I would be a fool to claim such a thing in your presence— would I not?— if I could not back it up."

Iapetus regarded her anew, openly staring, sizing her up. The curve of her form beneath the cloak only mildly interested him. His mouth had twisted into a sour expression.

"Why should I believe some cheap special effects equate to godhood?" he asked, still impatient. "And, in any case, why tell this to me at all?"

"Because you are necessary and important," Teluria answered.

"Necessary?" Iapetus stared at her. "Necessary to whom?"

"You are the wild card," she went on enigmatically, sidestepping his question. "You are the unpredictable piece—the piece on the board that must be accounted for."

"You're not making any sense," Iapetus protested—but his voice was growing weaker, his words slightly slurred. "Answer me!"

Now Teluria laughed, softly and gently. She reached out one pale, delicate hand and took Iapetus's own. It was scarred, rough, brutal. Somehow he had been unable to prevent her from grasping it.

"I merely wish to converse," she said. "We have much to discuss, you and I."

"We do?" Iapetus was growing unsteady on his feet.

"Come," she said. "Come and let me show you."

"Come where?" the general replied, even as his feet moved him forward, along with the hooded woman, across the open space of the strategium. "Show me what?"

She smiled at him again, and the eye reappeared, filling the center of the room. Teluria led Iapetus towards it.

"Wonders," she said. "Come and let me show you wonders." She paused a moment as he gazed at her expectantly. "And terrors," she added, as the eye opened and swallowed them both.

Iapetus stood upon a large, jagged fragment of ice, careening nightmarishly through space. The universe in all its grandiose majesty, velvet black and speckled with stars, surrounded him. Teluria stood motionless just behind him, her cloak held tightly about her. How he was breathing, how he had come to be there at all, he could not say. Eyebrows knitted, swallowing his fear, he gazed about.

A moment earlier, after passing through the eye portal, the general of II Legion had found himself at the center of a magnificent city square—one he'd never seen or heard of before, its streets literally paved with gold. He'd seen it, experienced it, for only a few seconds. Then Teluria had again summoned the portal and they had stepped through to here—wherever *here* was.

He tried to speak but no words would come. He looked back at her, but she merely stared straight ahead, statue-like. Then she raised her left arm slightly from her side and pointed down at the ice. Iapetus frowned at this but he turned and looked.

The ice sheet on which they stood was mostly cracked and streaked with black but it was translucent in places and fully transparent in others. Iapetus could make out something underneath—shapes, forms—just below the surface, trapped within like flies in amber. He knelt, attempting to see through it.

A wave of horror—abstract, not connected to anything he was seeing—rushed over him, nearly causing him to fall backwards. Teluria's hand caught and steadied him, even as frost began to form on his uniform. He brushed at it absently as he stared down through the ice again.

A face—hideous, skull-like, alien—leered up at him. He gasped. It was made of gleaming metal. And it was *moving.*

He stumbled back, harder this time, falling onto the ice.

The surface ahead of him cracked. A clawed hand reached up from the depths, grasping.

Iapetus looked back at Teluria, almost frantic. Her face remained impassive.

Another claw ripped free of the ice.

Iapetus reached for his pistol, drew it, fired. The bolt of energy struck one of the claws but had no visible effect.

The ice was cracking directly beneath him now. He could feel it giving way.

A tap on his shoulder. He looked up. Teluria held out her slender hand. He grasped it. The eye reappeared, swirling all around them. It consumed them.

They fell.

A timeless time later, there within the strategium of the *Atlantia*, the great dimensional eye blinked open again. From its depths emerged Teluria, leading the way, her blood-red cloak flaring around her, revealing her nakedness beneath. Behind her came Iapetus, his jet-black uniform white with frost.

"You have seen now," the dark woman said, gathering her cloak about her, her piercing eyes locking onto the general's. "You understand."

"Understand? No." Iapetus looked uncharacteristically shaken. Melting frost mixed with sweat ran down his face and neck. "Where did we go?"

She smiled. "First we ventured into the Above. Into the realm of those you call gods."

Iapetus stared at her. His mouth opened and closed once before he found his voice. "I am to believe...*that*... was...the *Golden City?*" He looked away, still not fully himself. His usual skepticism melted away along with the remnants of frost on his uniform. "Alright, perhaps," he whispered. Then, louder, "Why did we leave so quickly?"

"Time moves slowly in the higher realms. In the City it passes much slower," the woman answered. "This universe would have left you behind, had we lingered there but a bit longer." She smiled and reached out, caressing his cheek like some wild animal she had domesticated and grown fond of. "Know, though, that the scant seconds you were there represented a far longer time than almost any other mortal has ever spent within the Golden Realm." She hesitated. "Though I somehow suspect such a distinction is lost upon you." Her expression darkened. "In any case, you are needed here and now, and so here I have returned you—and a mere three hours of local time after we left."

"I'm needed?" He was starting to revert to his old self again. He straightened and gave her a skeptical look. "By whom? When? For what?"

"You saw for what," she said. "You saw the face of the enemy."

He blanched, recalling the face he had seen—the skull. Its exact appearance was already fading like some half-remembered nightmare.

"Those *things*—in the ice," he stammered. "You're saying they represent a danger to Earth?"

"They represent a danger to anything and everything in their path."

Iapetus nodded. After what he'd seen, it didn't take much to convince him of that. "And Earth is in their path?" he pressed.

"Directly in their path. It is their ultimate destination—their primary target."

He exhaled slowly. He hardly found that news surprising. "What *are* they? Where do they come from?"

"All in good time, General," the woman replied. "But as to your question of *when* you will be needed, I'm afraid the answer is now. You have been gone too long and your crew members are jealous of your absence. They are concerned. They will break through a bulkhead or the hatch here any minute, thinking to save you somehow, from something." She smiled wanly at him, and for perhaps the first time he could see all of her face beneath the hood. She was beautiful. And terrible. "We have little time left to talk," she continued. "Your last questions must be well-considered."

A sudden realization struck him. He snapped his fingers and looked hard at her. "The comets," he said. "That was one of them. I understand now. We were standing on one of those comets. And they're..." He frowned, his eyes staring past her at the blank metal wall. "...They're filled with those...*things*."

"Yes," the woman replied. "They are called many things in many corners of the universe. Most commonly they are known as Phaedrons. You needed to see them. To experience them. To understand the magnitude of the danger they and the comets that carry them represent."

Iapetus met her gaze and his scowl softened. He nodded once.

"You understand?" she said again, and this time it was clearly meant as a question.

Iapetus's eyes flicked from the woman in red to the swirling portal that filled the center of the chamber, then back to her. "Yes," he rumbled. "Yes, I believe you are who you say you are, and I believe what you showed me."

Teluria smiled a flat, emotionless smile. "Then, if you understand those things, understand this: Soon only you

147

will stand between the Phaedrons and sacred Earth. Your legion is called the Sons of Terra, and you swore a holy oath to defend the homeworld from any and all threats. Will you stand firm against this enemy?" She moved closer to him and her eyes narrowed. "Will you resist all entreaties to move your forces away from Earth and the other inner worlds—to leave them vulnerable—no matter who requests or orders it?"

Iapetus, now fully himself again, snorted. "That you can count on."

Teluria nodded. "Excellent. Excellent." She gazed away for a moment, then blinked, looked at him and smiled. "The people of the empire will rest easier in their beds at night knowing that you and your legion protect them from the many horrors this universe has yielded up."

Iapetus ignored this. He studied the woman in the dark red robes closely, his eyes moving up and down her form.

She appeared to take umbrage at this. "You have other questions, General?" she asked imperiously.

"Yes," he said. "Many. But later." He nodded towards the hatch; the lock mechanism was being cycled from outside. "For now, I'd say it's time for you to go."

Teluria followed his gesture, saw the hatch being unlocked, and turned back to him. She executed a very slight bow. "Until we meet again, then, General."

He nodded his head slightly to her and watched as she stepped into the swirling eye. A second later, she and the portal were both gone; gone as if they'd never existed.

The hatch completed its cycle and slid open. A half dozen armed soldiers rushed in, with Colonel Piryu just behind them, her pistol drawn. She seemed particularly exercised.

Iapetus met her and her forces just inside the room. Fully recovered from his experiences, he summoned up his most authoritative voice and seemed to almost loom over the others. "Stand down," he commanded in a deep, resonant voice. "All is well."

The soldiers stood ready, glancing from Iapetus to Piryu, uncertain of what to do. The colonel moved to the front of the formation and looked him up and down. "Sir—I'm sorry to barge in like this, but... you were in here nearly three hours with no communications whatsoever."

"Three hours?" Iapetus frowned at this, then nodded. The woman had spoken the truth. "I appreciate your concern, Colonel," he said to Piryu, favoring her with a half-smile, "but I assure you I am quite alright."

"I see that, yes, sir," she said. She hesitated a moment, then, "If I may ask—what happened, General?"

"You may not," Iapetus barked, dismissing the question along with the rest of the soldiers. Once the squad had filed back out of the strategium, he turned to the flustered Piryu.

"Contact the bridge, Colonel," he ordered, his voice exuding authority, and she instantly moved to comply. "We must set a new course, and with all possible haste."

"Aye, sir," she said as she accessed the ship's local Aether link. Then she looked up at him. "For where?"

Iapetus was already moving toward the exit. He had no further need of the strategium. His plans were set. "We travel to where we are most needed. And we will recall the entire legion along with us."

"Yes, General?"

"Our enemies are closing in on us, Colonel, from all sides. We have been most fortunate—the entire human race has been fortunate—to have received an advance warning." He glanced back at her, his eyes burning with conviction now. "Set course, Colonel, for Holy Terra." He smiled, and it was the first genuine smile Piryu had ever seen on his face. "The Sons are coming home. Earth will be defended."

o you have no idea what has become of Colonel Belisarius, then?"

The holographic, red and blue robed ghost of Governor Rameses spread his arms wide and shook his head. "I understand that you dispatched him some time ago, but he has yet to arrive here on Ahknaton."

General Tamerlane appeared taken aback by this. "He hasn't even arrived?" He glanced back over his shoulder at Sister Delain, who stood impassively as ever just behind him within the strategium of the I Legion flagship, *Ascanius*. Then he looked back at Rameses. "You've heard nothing from him?"

"Nothing," Rameses replied, and now he glanced momentarily off to one side, out of frame of the hologram. A second later he looked back at Tamerlane. "Perhaps he had other duties to attend to along the way—?"

"No," Tamerlane said. He turned back to Delain again, this time nodding once to her; a not-so-subtle signal, delivered using a simple visual cue rather than a thought transmitted across the Aether. Sometimes the simplest ways were still the best, he reflected. A nod can't be intercepted, recorded, decoded.

Delain closed her dark eyes for a moment and then reopened them, and Tamerlane assumed that meant it was done.

As he watched this, he was struck by the fact that, with Nakamura more or less incapacitated, Stanishur dealing with matters back in the imperial capital, and Agrippa away fighting at the head of his legion, the enigmatic lady Inquisitor was the only person near to him that he felt he could trust. *An Inquisitor is the only one I can trust.* He shook his head. *To think it has come to that.*

Delain's expression remained as impassive as ever. Her thick, blood-red lips were closed and her dark eyes peered straight ahead, giving the appearance that she was seeing right through Tamerlane. Somehow, he suspected she could do just that—among many other things. Beneath the surface, meanwhile, she was very busy.

"Ah," the holographic representation of Governor Rameses was saying. "Well, we have received no word at all since he departed your ship. We have been growing concerned ourselves."

Tamerlane turned back to him. "I—yes, I see. Well. Thank you for the information, Governor. I will of course have this investigated immediately."

Rameses nodded solemnly.

Delain leaned forward and whispered something in Tamerlane's ear.

"One moment, if you would, Governor," the general said before Rameses could break the connection.

"Yes?"

Still listening to Delain, the general frowned, then looked back at the flickering image of Rameses standing a few meters away—life-sized, sparkling, floating in the clouds that filled the strategium. He pursed his lips, seeming to appraise Rameses anew.

"Something the matter, General?" the governor asked, the slightest hints of impatience beginning to show.

"I'm not certain," Tamerlane replied. "You see, I have received conflicting information about Colonel Belisarius."

"Conflicting? From whom?"

Tamerlane inclined his head. "From Sister Delain here."

The image of Rameses leaned forward, probably meaning he was looking more closely at the holographic image on his end of the connection, and becoming aware of the figure in black who lurked just behind the general. "Ah. And she is...?"

"A top operative within the Holy Inquisition," the General replied, "and special assistant to the Grand Inquisitor himself."

Rameses flicked his eyes from Tamerlane to Delain. For the first time, his confident demeanor faltered. "Oh yes? And what is the nature of this alleged conflicting information, if I may ask?"

"The conflict, Governor," Tamerlane said, his voice growing suddenly hard, "is that Sister Delain tells me Colonel Belisarius most assuredly did arrive safely on Ahknaton. In fact, he even entered your palace. And spoke with you."

Rameses' face grew as red as the trim of the Egyptian-style headgear he wore over his shaved scalp. He stammered an attempt at a reply, then gathered himself. "And why would she think such a thing?" he demanded.

"She *knows* it because, while we have been conversing, she has been sending Trojan horse files back along the Aether link and into your palace's automated systems and computer banks. She has already examined many of your records—she is very fast, I assure you!—and has seen that the Colonel *did* touch down on Ahknaton, *did* enter the Heliopolis, and *did* meet with you shortly thereafter." He paused, allowing the revelation to sink in to Rameses' mind. "Therefore," he went on a few seconds later, "as we have now established that the Colonel did arrive, and further that you are lying about that fact, I must ask again—what has become of Colonel Belisarius?"

Rameses had reddened as Tamerlane lay out the case against him. Now his face was nearly purple. His mouth worked soundlessly for a couple of seconds, and then another figure—slender, gaunt, robed in red—leaned in, whispering words in his ear. Rameses nodded.

Tamerlane made a mental note: *Find out who that is. Find out who is giving advice to Rameses.*

The expression on the governor's face slowly softened, and within a few seconds it had moved from anger to portraying a look of sympathy. "General," he said, "I must confess—I was attempting to spare your feelings."

"What?"

"I know that Colonel Belisarius is close to you, and I knew you would take it hard to learn of what has happened to him. I had hoped that my people here on Ahknaton could help him a bit—have him on the road to recovery, so to speak—before I reported to you exactly what had happened."

Tamerlane frowned. "And what would that be, Governor?"

Rameses shook his head sadly. "It seems the Colonel went mad upon his arrival here. I regret to inform you... he...*murdered*...his own party, those who accompanied him. He threatened me and my officials and court. We were barely able to restrain him. You can check the records you have already stolen from me fully; it should all be there."

Scowling deeply now, Tamerlane glanced back at Delain. Clearly she was doing just what Rameses had suggested, and at very rapid speed, within her mind. She offered Tamerlane only the faintest of expressions, but its message was clear: *"There may be some truth to what he is saying."*

"Perhaps it was caused by the stresses of his office," Rameses went on. "Certainly we are all under enormous

153

pressure, what with the utter failure of your military initiatives on our frontiers."

Angry now, Tamerlane turned back to the holographic Rameses. "And so you're holding him?" he demanded. "Giving him some kind of treatment?"

Rameses spread his hands. "We were not entirely sure what to do with him at first, General. Obviously he had to be taken into custody. From there, well..." He trailed off, eyes wide, shrugging.

Tamerlane was about to ask Delain to dig deeper in the Ahknaton records when she leaned forward and whispered, "I've lost the connection."

"You've what?"

"Something on their end just severed my connection. I would have said that was impossible—until it happened."

Tamerlane kept his eyes on the holograph as she was speaking; the slender figure in red had been whispering something to Rameses at the exact same instant Delain had reported the loss of connection. Now Rameses wore a half-smile on his face, and he nodded once. The other figure moved out of frame again.

He thinks he's getting the better of me, Tamerlane knew. *He's about to have to think again.*

"So we will continue to give the Colonel the finest treatments available," Rameses was saying. "If and when there is any change, I will of course alert you personally."

"No. I will have a ship on Ahknaton within the day," Tamerlane replied. "You will hand the Colonel over immediately, and make all of your records fully available to agents of I Legion."

Rameses reddened again. "I think not."

Tamerlane almost gasped. "You—you *think not?*"

"Not yet, at least," Rameses said. His eyes narrowed as he spoke. "We would like to be certain that this was an isolated incident of a madman, and not, shall we say... imperial policy at work."

Tamerlane could scarcely contain himself. "I assure you, Governor," he growled, "I have no reason to wish you or anyone in your court any harm. Thus far. But I also assure you that if 'imperial policy' did include your assassination, you and I would not be able to have this conversation right now. You would already be dead."

Now it was Rameses' turn to grow angry. "Are you threatening me, General?"

"I am expecting and requiring cooperation from you, Governor," Tamerlane shot back. "The cooperation I have a right to expect from the head of one of the Empire's major worlds. Do you not see what is happening around us now? The entire Empire is besieged from every direction, and—"

"Due to the incompetence of our political and military leaders," Rameses barked.

Tamerlane bit back a sharp retort and forced himself to remain as reasonable as possible. "The Empire must be protected. We must all do our part, or it will disintegrate beneath our very feet. Surely you see this."

"And what would you have me do?"

"I know you have been building up your forces in secret," Tamerlane said, stepping closer to the holograph. "I am well aware that your Sand Kings now in effect represent a fourth legion."

"As is my right."

Tamerlane nodded. "And we have tremendous need of such forces at present. You must hand over control of them to central imperial command and—"

"Never."

Tamerlane's eyes widened. "What did you say?"

"I will *never* hand over control of the Sand Kings. Not to you—not to *anyone!*"

Tamerlane ground his teeth. "Governor, are you blatantly disobeying my orders?"

"Your orders? No," Rameses replied, "because I have never recognized or acknowledged your authority in the first place." He snorted. "You and Nakamura seized power illegally; it was nothing more or less than a coup. Everyone knows it."

Tamerlane had to fight the desire to grab the holograph and strangle it; possibly only the knowledge that his hands would pass harmlessly through the ghost form prevented him from trying it. "We can debate the legitimacy of the *Taiko*'s regime once the danger to all of the Empire has passed," he growled. "For now, I cannot be placed in a position of having to fight both the enemies at the gates and my own governors at the same time. It could lead to the death of us all! Surely you can see that."

Rameses scoffed. "I see only a fool trying to hold onto his own personal power, even as it crumbles away beneath his feet."

Tamerlane started to shout his answer but a hand gently laid on his shoulder restrained him. It was Sister Delain, he realized and, while the action surprised him, he was suddenly very grateful. There was no telling what he might have said to the rogue governor if she hadn't interrupted him. One more attempt at persuasion, he told himself firmly. Nice, polite, reasonable persuasion.

Instead of the furious rant he had likely been about to unleash, Tamerlane breathed in and out once and then said in a level voice, "Governor Rameses. I know not what you had planned for your newly-expanded army; perhaps you'd thought to engage in open, armed rebellion, and perhaps not. But that is beside the point now. The Empire faces its most dire challenge, and all of us—*all* of us, and all of our worlds—risk being overwhelmed very soon. I therefore order—" He caught himself, thought better of what he was saying, breathed again, and started over. "I therefore *ask* that you contribute your forces to the defense of the Empire. Immediately."

The holographic image of Rameses glared back at Tamerlane with kohl-rimmed eyes. "No," he said.

Tamerlane's own eyes widened. "No? You're simply rejecting outright the order—the request—and the entire concept of defending the empire of which your world is a part?"

"I am rejecting *you*, Tamerlane. You and your corrupt, illegitimate regime."

All pretense of politeness evaporated from Tamerlane's demeanor at that. He darkened. "This is your last warning, Governor," he hissed, "and your last chance."

As Rameses started to issue his inevitable retort, Delain leaned in and whispered something quickly into Tamerlane's ear. Upon hearing it, Tamerlane instantly cut the governor off.

"Wait, wait." He raised a hand. "What exactly are you up to, Rameses? What game are you playing that involves cosmic energies?"

"Excuse me?" the suddenly wrong-footed and very suspicious governor replied, frowning. Now the slender man in red robes moved into frame again, whispering to him.

"Sister Delain tells me that a rift in the fabric of the universe has opened on your world, in your capital city—within your palace itself! And someone or something is somehow channeling massive amounts of cosmic energies through that rift and into our universe. It appears to be disrupting spacetime itself." He paused, scowling. Then, "I can only assume you would be *aware* of something of that magnitude, happening right inside your palace," he added sarcastically.

"What I am doing within my own palace, on my own world, is none of your concern," the governor snapped. He listened to one last bit of advice from the man in red, then straightened. "I have made my position clear, Tamerlane," he stated flatly.

"Indeed you have," the general replied. "And you will receive my own...shall we say, *official* response shortly."

He leaned in closer. "I very much doubt you will like it when it arrives."

Rameses scowled and cut the connection at last.

Tamerlane laughed, but it was a bitter laugh. He turned to Delain. "We cannot have rebellion within our borders if we are to defeat the many enemies outside them," he said.

"What will you do?" the Inquisitor asked, her voice soft but strong.

"I will unleash a legion upon Ahknaton," he replied.

"A legion?" she inquired, visibly surprised. "My understanding was that all your legions are tied down on the borders."

"One remains unengaged," the general stated. He offered her a half-smile. "I will, as they say, kill two birds with one stone."

The Inquisitor raised one eyebrow in curiosity, waiting.

"I will dispatch the Sons of Terra," he said, before turning and striding through the doorway of the strategium. "One way or another."

Delain watched him go for a few seconds before gliding along after him. What she thought of his declaration, however, she kept to herself.

I t is done, master," Teluria whispered as she knelt in her quarters aboard the *Ascanius,* her head bowed as if in prayer. Patterns of ice formed and slowly spread on the floor all around her. "Iapetus has been shown the comets, and the danger to the worlds he is sworn to protect," she said. "I cannot imagine he will budge now—no matter who asks, or even *orders*, him to do so."

"Excellent," came a voice from nowhere, dry as old leaves blowing in the breeze. "You have done well."

"Thank you, lord."

"But I think it is not enough."

"What?"

"Iapetus is a wild card. He is a powerful piece on the board—a capital piece, at least—but I cannot yet tell which side he plays for."

"I suspect he plays only for himself," Teluria said.

A pause. "Yes. I believe that is true. As such, he serves only to disrupt the game."

"I have neutralized him, sire."

"It is not enough," the voice repeated. "I would see him *dead*."

"Dead?" Teluria frowned. "That—would be exceptionally difficult, my lord. I could perhaps—"

"You will dispatch someone else to tend to it. I have other plans for you."

"I—see, sire."

"Send your best agent. Have Iapetus taken somewhere that it can be done as an...*accident*. We do not want his death to serve to rally his legion. Quite the opposite. I desire a lonely death for him and a loss of spirit for his Sons of Terra. I want them tied firmly to Earth, when the time comes."

Teluria considered this. "Very well, sire, if that is your wish. I will see to it."

"Indeed."

She hesitated a moment, waiting. Then, "You said you had some other task for me?"

"Yes," the voice hissed. "I have recently become aware of another threat—another legion. A *secret* legion, being assembled without the knowledge of most of the Imperial government."

"Another legion?" Teluria was startled at this revelation. "Assembled by whom, sire?"

"By one who has thwarted my designs before," the voice replied. "One who must be dealt with once and for all."

"Yes. What am I to do, then?"

"You will offer your assistance, of course, as any Ecclesiarch would. And then..."

Teluria listened to the words of her master. Slowly, a smile crept across her face.

"It will be as you say, master."

"Of course."

The connection broke.

7

Waves of heat. Clouds of smoke. A glaring red light radiating from somewhere ahead in the distance. And, overlaying all the rest of it like some thick, palpable fog, a sense of disturbance, of danger—of fear. None of the men and women of the Bravo Squad spoke of it, but they all felt it, and they all wondered what it meant. They worried what it meant.

As the lead hovertank came to a halt approximately a kilometer away from the site, Agrippa raised the hatch and peeked carefully out, wanting to appraise the situation with his own eyes. What he saw disturbed him greatly.

A wasteland, even here in a region of a planet already battered and beaten down by a prolonged war. Whatever buildings had stood here once were now shattered and broken and almost entirely gone. Trees, grass, and the like were also churned under. Only a sea of dirt and mud lay ahead, sloping gently down into what, from this distance, clearly was a shallow valley filled with impact craters. And all of this under a sky grown dark and angry from days of bombardment hurling tons of particulate matter into the atmosphere.

"That's definitely where it all came down," Agrippa growled back down through the hatch opening. "In several fragments, it looks like."

Indeed, the comet had separated as it passed through the planet's atmosphere and at least seven distinct pieces had crashed down, all confined to this area.

"Contact," called the trooper manning the scanner. "East by northeast."

Agrippa instinctively turned to face that direction; the Aether link confirmed that he was facing the right way. He squinted but could see nothing. He considered donning his helmet just for the enhanced optics it offered, but before he could reach down for it where it lay inside the tank, the scanner man snapped, "Check that. Reading has vanished."

"Vanished?" Agrippa asked, puzzled.

"Yes, General. Possible ghosting from atmospheric effects, or—"

"Or some kind of distortion field," he finished for the man. "Or cloaking of some other kind."

A pause, then, "Entirely possible, sir. Scanning again."

Agrippa nodded, waiting.

"Still nothing, General. Scope is clear."

Agrippa pursed his lips, then nodded his head forward once. "Alright. Let's move in."

At the controls, and as deft at driving a tank as he had been at directing the path of a Colossus walker, Obomanu re-engaged the drive. The big armored vehicle surged to life, its small but massively powerful fusion engine directing barely-contained energies into the propulsion system. As it zoomed into the valley, the second tank cruised along in its wake.

"Are you reading anything unusual back there, Major?" Agrippa called over the link.

"Unusual?" Major Torgon's voice conveyed almost a sense of disbelief at Agrippa's question. "You mean, sir, aside from the obvious?"

Agrippa snorted. "Yes, Major. That's precisely what I mean."

"Well, then—no, nothing at all unusual here, sir," he replied.

Listening in, the others in the tank's cabin laughed—but it was a tight, tense laughter, and Agrippa understood it. They were venturing into the unknown, and the tension was high among them. And beyond even that, there was *something*...

The two hovertanks, each floating almost two meters above the shell-scarred ground, rocketed down into the valley, their gun turrets traversing this way and that, in search of foes or ambush. Just ahead, the crimson glow radiated brightly from the craters where the comet fragments had crashed down to the surface of Eingrad-6.

"Contact," shouted the scanner officer again, this time more definitively. "Sir, there is definitely something off to our right."

Agrippa was still looking that way. "Still not seeing anything," he muttered. "How far back?"

"Approximately half a click."

"I'm getting something, too," came the voice of Torgon from the other vehicle. "I think it's—"

Impact. The blast struck like lightning and skewed the tank around sideways as it continued along its path. Inside, Agrippa had to grasp the sides of the open hatch with both hands to keep from being hurled out. The other troopers cried out and the metal tank rang like a bell.

"What in the Above and Below was that?" the general demanded.

Obomanu recovered quickly and seized the tank's controls, wrestling them into submission. Within a couple of seconds, the heavy vehicle was back under control, and he slowed its velocity, curving around to aim in the direction of the attack.

"Riyahadi tank, almost on top of you," Torgon called over the link. "They're bearing down, but I think I can—"

The second blast was only a glancing blow. Obomanu was using every evasive trick in the book to keep the big metal vehicle from making itself too easy a target.

"Whatever you think you can do—*do* it!" shouted Agrippa over the link.

As Agrippa's tank topped the rise again, coming back out of the valley, the Riyahadi vehicle suddenly appeared in their path, about half a kilometer ahead. Its gun—a larger piece than the one atop their tank, Agrippa could see immediately—was aiming right at them.

"Brace!" the general cried.

A vivid, nearly blinding blast struck the Riyahadi tank and blew a chunk out of its rear left corner.

"There you are, Torgon!" Agrippa shouted, grinning. "I don't think he saw you back there. Give him another!"

Before Torgon's tank could fire again, however, Harker took aim and blasted away with their cannon. The enemy vehicle, already becoming aware it had interposed itself between two opponents rather than simply ambushing one, was caught with its gun halfway between the two, trapped in indecision about which to fire at next. The column of violet energy that speared out of Agrippa's tank's gun skewered the enemy dead center, carving its way through layers of metal and ceramic armor. An explosion blossomed as the fusion drive was hit. Torgon followed this a second later with his own second blast, which sheared the main cannon off at the turret.

"She's done for, sir," Harker reported as he peered through his gun sight scope. "They're abandoning ship!"

The hatch was open and three survivors were scrambling out, their white and gold Riyahadi Caliphate robes fluttering around them. They were barely clear before the tank went up in a horrific blast that hurled them forward and down into the mud.

"I've got them, General," Torgon called over the link. His tank zipped around and positioned itself alongside the three Riyahadi survivors.

"What's our status?" Agrippa asked Obomanu. "How badly are we hurt?"

The driver checked a series of displays and looked up at the general. "It's not great, sir, but we can still move. And fire."

Agrippa nodded. "Very well. We—"

There was a sudden sound of gunfire over the link, and shouting.

"What happened, Major?" Agrippa demanded once the sounds had died down.

Silence for a moment, then, "Two of the Riyahadi tried to get cute, sir," he said. "They wanted to take a few of us with them. Suicide fighters. They definitely got the 'suicide' part right, but the rest didn't work out too well for them. We're okay."

Agrippa acknowledged this. Then, "You said *two* of them...?"

"We have a prisoner, sir. He doesn't seem as anxious as his two brethren to move on to the afterlife."

"You have him secured?"

"Yes, General."

Agrippa frowned at this but nodded. He wouldn't admit it, but he would have preferred that all three of them attempt a foolish action of that type, so they could all be justifiably eliminated. He wasn't really in a position to tend to a prisoner at the moment. Nonetheless, a prisoner he had, and he'd deal with that as best he could.

"Very well, Major. Let's get back to business, then. I'm assured that my tank is still operable, so we're headed back into the valley."

"Right behind y—"

A squawk of static.

"Major? Torgon, are you there?"

More static. Then, "—hear you, sir. Something is—"
White noise.

Agrippa gritted his teeth in frustration and glanced over at
Harker. "Are you hearing Torgon?"

"Just barely, sir," the gunner replied. "How is that
possible?"

"Something is interfering with our Aether link," the
sensor officer reported. "Some kind of outside signal or
wave. And it's growing stronger."

"How is that *possible?*" Harker repeated.

"I don't know and, at the moment, I don't care," Agrippa
snapped. He glared at the sensor man. "Whatever it is, I
want it eliminated."

"Working on it, sir," the officer replied quickly, with just
a hint of fear, before turning his full attention to the
interface boards in front of him.

Agrippa thought for a moment, then turned to Obomanu
at the main controls. "Let's go," he barked.

The hovertank raced forward in the direction of the valley
and the craters.

They had barely traveled two hundred meters when the
scanner man called out, "Contact! Dead ahead!"

"Again?" breathed Agrippa. "Is this a Riyahadi base or
something?"

"Not Riyahadi, General," the scan man stated. "Alien."

"Alien?" Agrippa raised one eyebrow and looked over at
Harker. The gunner in turn brought the main weapon
controls on line again and stood ready.

"You—are General—Agrippa. Yes?"

The voice had sounded within his head, very much the
way an Aether connection worked. But it hadn't come via
the still-jammed Aether. Agrippa stood up straighter, his
upper half still projecting out of the tank's upper hatch, and
looked around.

"Who is there?" he said aloud.

Obomanu and Harker looked up at him. "What was that, sir?"

"You didn't hear it?"

The two men exchanged glances, puzzled.

The voice came again. *"You wish...that all...can hear. And see. Very well."*

At that same moment, Harker spoke up: "There's the contact, General. And—oh..."

Directly ahead of them hovered a gleaming vehicle of very otherworldly design. Agrippa stared at it and almost gasped.

It was circular and smooth and looked as if it had been formed entirely of glass. It hovered only centimeters above the ground; its transparent hull radiated every color of the rainbow in waves of light so pure and clear they almost hurt the eyes to look upon them. Agrippa recognized it. It could hardly be mistaken for anything else.

"Dyonari," he whispered.

"Indeed," came the voice in his head. *"We are that which you call the Dyonari."*

Agrippa nodded. His fingers flexed involuntarily and he glanced down at Harker to make sure the gunner was prepared and ready to fire. "And you're looking for a fight, right?"

"Not at all," the ethereal voice replied. *"I am—Glossis. You would know me as the commander of this unit."*

"Why are you inside my head, Glossis?" Agrippa asked, suppressing his anger at the seeming violation of it.

"I am communicating with you in this manner— mentally—because of the effect that is preventing both our parties from accessing the lowest level of the Above—what you call the Aether. In short—we are, both of us, being jammed." A pause. *"A fight—as you put it—may well be coming—and that for both of us, as well,"* the Dyonari went on. *"But—not... with... each... other."*

"Not each other? We have a common enemy?" Agrippa found himself, if not entirely willing to accept this, at least willing to listen. Given that the Empire was currently at war with virtually everyone around it, the likelihood seemed not so remote. "And who might that fight be with, then?" he asked.

The image of the blood-red comet appeared in his mind then, doubtlessly placed there by the Dyonari. A wave of very palpable fear washed out over the general and his men, and all of them shuddered. Beneath Agrippa's fingertips, a thin layer of ice began to form around the ring of the hatchway.

"With them," the alien voice said. *"Though,"* it added after a couple of seconds, *"it may already be too late. Too late—for both of us."*

8

The time draws near, my disciple," whispered a barely-audible voice that nevertheless somehow filled the entirety of the room. "The pieces are now in motion. Soon all that we have prepared will come to fruition."

Zahir was back in the antechamber, again kneeling before the red-glowing icon, his hands clasped together in supplication. He now wore an ornate Egyptian headdress, as was the style on Ahknaton, and a golden loincloth; his chest was bare and smooth, his wiry muscles standing out.

"What would you have me do, my master?" the slender figure asked.

For several seconds there was naught but a dull buzzing as with a bad connection over an ancient telephone. Then the icon flared brighter and the voice whispered, "Give the servants of our enemies a welcome befitting those who challenge my authority."

Zahir nodded slowly. "Of course, of course." Then he hesitated, frowning. "Servants of our enemies are coming? And—I will know them when I see them?"

This time the response was virtually instantaneous. "Oh yes," the voice said. "They will appear in your very midst, and with most hostile intent. And very soon."

The vizier nodded more earnestly. "It will be as you command, my lord." He paused, then, "As for Rameses—"

"You continue the treatments, yes?"

Zahir nodded. "Yes, my master." A smile played about his thin lips. "Rameses believes he will soon be a living god."

Laughter rolled out and echoed around the room.

"If that is enough to cause him to voluntarily submit to the treatment, then by all means encourage that belief," the voice said when its laughter had subsided. Then, "As for the girl—have you begun the procedure yet?"

Zahir hesitated. "Actually, master, I wished to speak with you about that—especially in light of the events that occurred of late on Ascanius."

Anger crept into the tone. "You have not begun the transference yet?"

"All is made ready, master," Zahir hastened to say, "but I have not fully begun the procedure just yet."

"Why?"

"I have certain...*concerns*...that—"

"Your concerns are groundless, my disciple."

Zahir cast his eyes downward, frowning at being treated so dismissively by his master.

"Still," the voice said a moment later, "If you have reservations about our great work, I would hear them."

"I—um—thank you, lord." Zahir gathered his thoughts. "These humans—Rameses and the girl—I am not entirely certain their mortal frames can long bear up to the Power that you have commanded me to infuse within them. Human bodies cannot long tolerate the presence of the divine. Recall, as I mentioned a moment ago, the events during the Council on Ascanius—"

"The situation was different there," the voice boomed. "A unique set of circumstances conspired to cause the demon form to emerge from Janus prematurely."

"And yet, already, after only a few doses of the Power, Rameses' physical form grows distorted and begins to deteriorate," Zahir said plaintively. "If I continue—"

"If? You *will* continue," the voice barked, louder now and filled with anger, "because I command it."

Zahir recoiled, nearly falling over backwards.

A few seconds passed and when the voice sounded again, it was back under tight control. "Your concerns are not entirely without merit, my servant," it said. "No human can long contain a demon form within itself, any more than it can contain large doses of the cosmic energies some call the Power."

Zahir nodded, almost overwhelmed by his master's acknowledgement.

"But," the voice went on, "once infused with a precise amount of the Power, their mortal bodies will hold together a while longer," it said, "and that will be enough." A laugh, deep and sinister. "*More* than enough."

"As you say, master."

The voice echoing around the chamber softened, but its malevolence only increased. "None of this should have been necessary," it said, now seeming to speak to itself as much as to Zahir. "I could not have anticipated the very premature emergence of the Emperor's demon from inside him—which resulted in his death and in the disruption of my plans, as well as in the wholly unexpected and troublesome rise to power of Nakamura as '*Taiko*.'" A pause, during which Zahir waited, unmoving, listening. "But, once the young princess has been successfully made host to a demon lord, and has then assumed her rightful place as Empress over these human worlds," the voice concluded, "all will be as it should have been all along." A pause, then, "You will insinuate the demonform into the princess slowly, Zahir—oh so slowly. Allow it to acclimate to its mortal body. Patience is key!"

"Yes, sire."

"She will rule as I instruct her, and without question. And then, when the time is ripe, she will consume humanity from within even as my forces consume it from without, and glorious chaos will reign over all."

"Yes, my master—it will be as you have foreseen," Zahir said after the echoes had faded. No reply came back to him, and so he gazed up at the icon. The metal was cold and dark.

Zahir fled.

Rameses was screaming when Zahir glided into the throne room. As the vizier drew near, he saw that the planetary governor's eyes were warping, with first one of them and then the other growing to cartoonishly large size. The man held up his hands, wires and cables trailing down from them, and gazed in horror as the fingers rippled and distorted, extra digits appearing and then disappearing by the second.

"What is happening to me?" demanded the governor, his voice raw and rough. "What are you *doing* to me?"

"I assure you, sire," Zahir said in his most placating tones, "all proceeds as it should. This is but a mere side effect. Soon you will be what you have always desired to be: a living god—the living embodiment of the great Amenophis!"

Rameses appeared to be mollified by this. "Yes," he hissed. "Good. I must have the power to deal with my enemies—to visit destruction down upon Tamerlane and Iapetus and all their lackeys—to sweep their forces from the universe!"

"And you will, dread lord."

Rameses nodded and ceased his complaining, but his expression remained one of shock and horror at what was happening to his body.

"Now relax, lord," Zahir murmured, leaning in close. The energies of the cosmic basin churned all around the governor's body, tendrils of it actually passing through and out the other side.

Zahir waited until Rameses had closed his eyes and sunk back against the side of the basin, as though enjoying a nice hot bath rather than the raw cosmic fires of the Above. Then he turned and gestured to his four servants who lurked in the shadows along the far wall. Instantly two of them, muscular and bald, stepped out into the light—the light that gleamed off their dark skin and golden belts and vambraces.

"Bring out the girl," Zahir hissed to one of the minions.

The brutish man bowed and disappeared into the shadows again. A moment later he reemerged with a small form in his arms. It was a young, blonde girl of about twelve standard years. She wore a dark green dress of very fine silk and linen and appeared to be asleep.

Zahir looked her over once. Then, without saying a word, he gestured to the small cot-like arrangement depending from chains that disappeared up into the dark ceiling of the throne room. The minion bowed again and, carrying her over, laid the girl on the cot. Zahir moved next to the basin, ignoring Rameses, who now looked to be dozing. He executed a series of gestures, his fingers held in a very precise manner, and muttered several arcane phrases. In response, jets of cosmic energy leapt from the basin and streaked toward the girl, impacting her and disappearing within her body.

"What are you doing?"

Zahir started, nearly jumping a foot in the air. He turned and saw Rameses sitting up, wide awake. The distortions of his flesh continued, but now it was as if he had become used to them, at least to some degree. His eyes were cloudy and bloodshot but clear in intent and purpose.

"This girl," he said, gesturing towards her. "The Princess."

"Yes," Zahir snapped. "You did well to keep her here these last few months, as my master requested. But now the time is ripe, and the designs begin to unfold."

Rameses shook his head at this bit of seeming nonsense. "What are you talking about? What are you doing with her?"

"Preparing her," the vizier said by way of answer.

"Preparing her? For what?"

Zahir smiled, and flames danced in his eyes. He motioned again, and two of his other servants brought in a catafalque, this one larger and longer than the cot that held the princess, and this one bearing the now unmoving and seemingly unconscious form of Colonel Belisarius.

Rameses saw the colonel on the cot and got to his feet, cables dangling around him. His expression now reflected utter bewilderment.

Zahir was already answering his previous question. "We are preparing the Princess Marens for the most important task of all," Zahir said. His gaze moved from Belisarius to the young girl, and then to Rameses himself. He grinned. "We are preparing her to usher in... *the future*."

he *Ascanius* and the *Atlantia* glided smoothly alongside one another, tractor beams bringing them into perfect alignment. A moment earlier, the *Ascanius* had emerged from its hyper lane at the prearranged coordinates only to find Iapetus's II Legion flagship already at the rendezvous point, waiting.

"Iapetus doesn't like anyone getting the drop on him," Tamerlane said to Harras Dequoi, captain of the *Ascanius*. "Not even a fellow general of the Empire."

"If you don't mind my saying so, General," Dequoi responded in a low voice, "I don't believe Iapetus considers himself to be a 'fellow' of anyone or anything."

"That may be so, Captain," Tamerlane replied with a tight grin. "But I'm going to do my best to remind him that we're all on the same side. And we have to cooperate, if any of us are to survive."

Dequoi chuckled. "Good luck with that, sir."

Tamerlane said nothing. He waited until the signal came that General Iapetus had boarded, then turned and strode from the bridge, Sister Delain trailing along behind him.

Together they made their way the short distance to the strategium. Iapetus was to meet them there.

This time Tamerlane arrived first.

"Come in, General," he called as the man in black appeared in the doorway. "It's good to see you again in the flesh. I tire of conversing with everyone only via holographics."

Iapetus entered. He was alone, and clad as ever in his jet-black uniform with the golden eye on the chest. "Your eccentricity is costing me a good deal of time, having to come here in person," he responded. "I trust we are here for a reason consequential enough to justify that."

Tamerlane swallowed his initial reaction to Iapetus's insolence. He reminded himself that it wasn't entirely personal. The commander of the Sons of Terra had always been that way; Nakamura had known that and had still chosen him to lead II Legion. The *Taiko* had had his reasons for that selection, and Tamerlane trusted them— whether he fully understood them and agreed with them or not. For his own part, he would have as soon seen Iapetus put out the nearest airlock.

"I noticed the invitation to this—*whatever* it is—came directly from your office, as a polite request, rather than from Nakamura's, as an order. Should I draw any conclusions from that, with regard to the health and well-being of our esteemed *Taiko*?"

"He's not well," Tamerlane replied. "That should be obvious, and it's all I can say right now."

Iapetus considered this for a moment. He nodded once. "Very well. So—what have I come this far to see and to hear, General? Particularly bearing in mind that I am not *Hatamoto*, and so there are others whose opinions you would doubtless prefer to entertain."

Tamerlane ignored the remarks. He signaled via the local Aether link and in response the round, empty chamber of the strategium darkened, filling with a holographic display

176

of the galaxy, the stars of their Empire highlighted in blue. Next came bright orange blobs and markers all along the fringes of that territory, each annotated with a box of text that floated there in midair. Finally came the comets, some of them having impacted their targets and thus now missing from the display, but others still lit up blood red.

"If your purpose with this," Iapetus rumbled, "is to show me our strategic situation, General, and to instruct me as to its utterly hopeless state, then you're wasting my time and yours. I am all too aware."

"That is merely my starting point, General," Tamerlane replied. He signaled again. "I show you that, to show you *this*."

Near the heart of the Empire, one star began to blink rapidly. Its color changed from blue to yellow. Faint lines traced out from it in multiple directions, linking it to Earth and to other key worlds.

Iapetus frowned at this and walked into the display, approaching the flashing yellow one. He stood next to it and read the text that floated beside it.

"Ahknaton," he read. "Ah. Yes."

"You know about Rameses?" Tamerlane asked.

Iapetus shrugged noncommittally. "I know a good bit. Probably as much as I want or need to know about him."

"He's openly rebelling."

"Is he now?" Iapetus snorted. "Not surprising."

Tamerlane faced Iapetus. "You don't seem terribly...*exercised*...about it."

Iapetus turned to face the other general, and now only a scant meter separated them. "Should I be?"

"I would think so. We face a tough enough challenge holding the borders against our enemies. If we begin to lose authority over our own planets, our own governors, too—?"

Iapetus didn't look convinced.

"Where will it all end?" Tamerlane asked. "Where will we find ourselves if people like Rameses can get away with this?"

"Probably in about the same predicament we already find ourselves in," Iapetus replied. "If the rest of the Empire is about to be overrun by the Chung and the Riyahadi and the Rao and all the others, what matter if Rameses is overwhelmed while swearing allegiance to our great *Taiko* or while striking out on his own? It all amounts to the same thing."

"I do not intend to allow our Empire to be overrun by *anyone, anywhere,*" Tamerlane snapped.

Iapetus offered him a dubious expression. "That's all well and good to say, but I have to proceed from the assumption that the outer worlds could succumb and fall at any time, leaving Sacred Terra and the other inner worlds to fend for themselves, with only the Sons to protect them."

"If we stop our enemies at the borders, you and your Sons won't have to fight them at Earth."

"But you *won't* stop them there," Iapetus rumbled. "We both know it. There's no chance."

"That's not true."

"It is absolutely true."

Tamerlane waved a hand. "Put that aside for a moment," he said. "In any event, we can agree that sedition and rebellion by our own worlds and our own governors cannot be tolerated, particularly at a time as sensitive as this."

"This is still about Rameses?" Iapetus scoffed. "You're that concerned about his childish antics?"

"I'm concerned that he's doing something involving the Power itself. Here is something you perhaps don't know: He's ripped a hole in the fabric of reality. What do you suppose he's up to?"

This brought Iapetus up short. He stared at Tamerlane for a moment. "He's done what?"

"I don't know yet. Not precisely. But there can be no doubt—he is tampering with the boundaries between our universe and the Above. And perhaps the Below. The Inquisition has confirmed this." Tamerlane turned and looked to the silent, motionless, hooded figure of Delain where she stood, off to the side. As Iapetus looked at her, she simply nodded once.

The commander of II Legion appeared to consider this new information for a moment as the other two looked on, waiting. At last he nodded and turned back to Tamerlane. "It is disturbing, I will grant you that. But," he said, eyes narrow as they met those of the I Legion general, "ultimately it changes nothing."

"Nothing?" Tamerlane nearly shouted the word, so shocked was he by Iapetus's response. As he did so, flames spouted from his hands and flared all around him before he was able to get them back under control.

Iapetus didn't visibly react at all. "Oh, spare me your literal pyrotechnics, Tamerlane," he said, his expression sour, once the fires had vanished again. "If you intend to kill me, get on with it. Otherwise, make your case. I have other duties to attend to."

"Duties? You speak of *duties*?"

"Certainly I do."

Tamerlane clenched and unclenched his fists, anger rising again. "And yet you side with Rameses?"

Iapetus barked a laugh. "Side with him? Of course not. Rameses is an idiot and deserves to be deposed. He's scarcely qualified to lead a kindergarten class, much less a planet—or a Legion. Especially if he's engaging in forbidden activities. But," he went on, "if you are looking to me and mine to do something about it, you're going to be disappointed. I've made it perfectly clear to you that I will not dispatch the Sons anywhere other than their current defensive positions around Earth and the inner worlds."

Tamerlane cursed. "Then what am I to do? Rameses has to be arrested and his Sand Kings placed under direct Imperial control. And we have no more time to waste."

Iapetus shrugged, then offered him a wry half-smile as he laid his final cards on the table. "Why not use your *own* legion?"

"I've told you—the First is tied down fighting our enemies on three fronts!"

"Oh, I don't mean your precious Lords of Fire," Iapetus said contemptuously.

Tamerlane frowned but said nothing, waiting.

"Come now, General. We both know of whom I speak. Your so-called *Nizam* Legion is available, and by all reports fully trained and armed."

"My—?" Tamerlane blurted the one word, then closed his mouth and simply glared back at Iapetus. For his part, the II Legion commander stood still, arms crossed over the golden eye on his chest, his expression blank. *Always watching*, the eye seemed to be saying. Apparently watching even more than Tamerlane had realized. He cursed inwardly, knowing he shouldn't be surprised.

Tamerlane glanced back at Delain. "Why," he asked softly, rhetorically, "do I feel as if everyone in this Empire knows more about what's going on than I do?"

"I'm not certain that fact makes you the most qualified to run it," Iapetus observed.

"I never *asked* to run it!" Tamerlane almost shouted, whirling on Iapetus. "I'm not the Emperor. I'm not the *Taiko*. I'm just a soldier—just a *man*."

"So now you're just a man again? Not a god?"

Tamerlane held Iapetus's gaze. "Yes. A man. But I am the man to whom, for better or for worse, the task has fallen of defending all our worlds and all our people. And I'm going to do the best I can at that, even if I have to die trying."

Iapetus took this in and nodded. "Commendable." He looked Tamerlane up and down, as if seeing him anew.

"Perhaps I have misjudged you," he allowed. "A tiny bit, at least." He shrugged one last time. "Perhaps you and your forces will hold the line longer than I expected. If so, that will give my legion a marginally better chance to prepare for the enemy before they reach the Earth." The "inevitably" that preceded "reach the Earth" was unspoken but obvious to everyone present.

Tamerlane stood there, saying nothing. Iapetus pursed his lips, then said, "So—if there's nothing else, General?"

Tamerlane shook his head. He was angry and felt somehow defeated. He offered Iapetus a dismissive wave. The II Legion commander turned on his heel and strode easily out of the strategium. Minutes later, the *Atlantia* had separated from the *Ascanius* and was turning to jump to hyper once again.

Tamerlane exited the strategium, Delain in tow. As they walked, Delain shocked Tamerlane by actually speaking. "How did Iapetus know about your secret *Nizam* Legion?"

The general practically gawked at her, then recovered, happy at least that she seemed to be growing comfortable enough around him to engage in conversation.

"I don't know. I suppose I shouldn't be surprised, but I have to admit it concerns me. It can't possibly be good." He stopped walking and turned back to her. "But...*you* knew, too?"

The woman in black smiled. "Come now, General. You are well aware of the organization I serve—and the resources it possesses." She shrugged slightly, and to Tamerlane's surprise he found it somehow endearing. "Besides—how could I be of any real service to you, if I didn't know everything already?"

Tamerlane found he had no answer for that. He merely nodded, then stood there in the corridor, rubbing at his eyes, his head suddenly pounding. "I'm going to my quarters for a bit," he told her. "I have some important decisions to make, and very soon. I need to think things over."

The walk to his quarters was fairly short. When he reached the door, he turned back and realized with a start that the lady Inquisitor had silently followed him. As the door hissed open, he said, "Delain, I'm sorry—I must not have made myself clear. I won't be needing you for a bit."

"I disagree," replied the woman in black. She strode past him, through the open doorway.

Puzzled, he followed her in. "Um—is there something you need, Inquisitor?"

"Just the opposite," she said, her voice smooth and soft now. "As you said, you have important decisions to make very soon. And you are entirely too distracted, too wound up at present to adequately consider them. And so—" She pulled back her hood, unfastened the clasp at her neck, and let her cloak fall to the ground. Then, bending over, she unzipped her skintight black bodysuit in one quick motion and let it fall to the ground.

He stared at her, astounded. Quickly he recovered and, his throat suddenly dry, asked, "So—this is merely duty, then?"

"There is that component to it," she replied. "But I will not lie and say there is nothing more. If so, I would've merely challenged you to a game of chess."

"I...see."

She stepped closer, gazing at him, meeting his eyes almost defiantly, as though daring him to object.

He did not.

So content was Tamerlane, so at peace for the first time in a very long time, that he didn't even notice the door chime sounding. On perhaps its third repetition he opened his eyes, grumbled something unintelligible, and crawled out of bed, grabbing a crimson robe from where it lay draped over a nearby chair and pulling it on. He stepped around Sister Delain's uniform, boots and cloak; they still lay where she had left them. He opened the door and peered out. "Yes?"

LEGION II: SONS OF TERRA

Teluria, Imperial Ecclesiarch and vizier to the *Taiko*, stood just outside, hands on hips, resplendent in her silky red robes. Her hood was drawn back and he realized with a start that her straight, dark hair almost eerily resembled Delain's. Her expression was one of impatience at first but then, as her gaze moved from the disheveled general to the clothing and boots on the floor and the curved shape still in his bed, she smiled wickedly.

"Well, General—I see that I may have misjudged you. Perhaps you are more fully... *human*... than I had come to believe."

Tamerlane didn't bother to reply to this. He moved to position himself between Teluria and the woman in his bed. "Can I help you?" he asked gruffly.

"To the contrary," the woman in red stated, still smiling, "I believe *I* may be able to help *you*—and the Empire, in the process, of course."

Delain was awake and sitting up now, a sheet clutched to her chest. As Tamerlane glanced back at her, she became aware of the other person's presence at the door. Realizing the identity of that person, she reddened. Slipping out of the bed, she quickly retrieved her clothing from the floor and began to dress. Tamerlane raised a hand, motioning for her to stay back.

Teluria paid all of this no attention. She spoke directly to Tamerlane. "You are considering sending military forces to assault Rameses on Ahknaton," she said, "but you hold back because you are concerned with overcoming his quite formidable orbital defenses, and what such an operation would mean in terms of potentially massive losses to your legion. Your *personal* legion."

This time Tamerlane didn't bother to act surprised. He'd come to grips with the idea that, in this Empire, there simply were no secrets. He merely nodded.

"I believe I can offer a solution to that dilemma," the woman in red went on.

"You have access to Rameses' security codes, then?" Tamerlane asked, intrigued. "You can disable his orbital defenses—open the front door for us?"

"Oh, I can do better than open the front door, General," Teluria replied, and now the smile was back, broader than ever. She gave Delain one more quick, amused glance, then turned back to Tamerlane. "How would you like for your legion, in all its glory, to walk right into the heart of the Heliopolis itself?"

10

Elaro was nearly knocked out of the bed as Niobe Arani sat straight up and gasped.

"Nightmare?" he asked, but she shushed him with a quick sound and a wave. He realized then what was happening: a message across the Aether network.

Awake now, he sat up as well and then stood, reaching for his uniform. Still groggy, he was puzzled at first by the clothing that lay on the floor on his side of the bed. It was neither of his uniforms; not the Gaurean planetary defense force outfit he'd arrived in, and not his actual legion's uniform. Then the events of the last day clicked into place and he remembered that, as far as anyone here knew, he was now a loyal member of...of whatever army this was. Not only that, he was now a major. And getting very close in particular to its commander, Colonel Niobe Arani.

The assassination attempt had been exactly what he'd needed. It was hard to believe it had just happened, given that it had worked so well to boost his standing here. As far as he was aware, it hadn't been part of the operation. For all he knew, the deadly woman he'd taken down the day before really had been a hired assassin aiming to kill Arani.

Then again, knowing who he actually worked for, Elaro had to admit there was a strong possibility the entire thing had been staged. If the latter was true, the would-be assassin would never admit it.

Elaro finished donning his uniform; it was a charcoal-gray number with a thick, heavy texture, but it was remarkably soft and light. He strapped on his belt with holster and fitted his blast pistol into it. Then he looked over at Arani. She was still engaged with someone via the Aether.

He sized the woman up, appreciating her fully. She was remarkably young for a colonel in the I Legion; perhaps late twenties. Rumor had it she had been directly involved in the events that led to the death of the Emperor and the rise of the *Taiko*, Nakamura. If that was true, it explained a lot. Moments of massive turmoil and change usually provided the best opportunities for junior officers to very rapidly become senior officers.

He studied her while she "spoke" telepathically over the link. Her lips were bright red and full, and were moving ever so slightly as she communicated. Her hair was at least shoulder-length and straight and black, and her face reflected predominantly Asian features. She was slender and very athletic, as he'd confirmed over the past few hours. He found he liked her a lot. He hoped he wouldn't be ordered to kill her. Prior to meeting her in person, he'd assumed he could do it if he had to, but now he found himself beginning to question whether he could, and whether he would.

The conversation ended and she shook her head, coming back to reality, then looked up at him and smiled. "Sorry," she said. "I had to take that."

"New orders from the highers-up?"

She nodded. "I have to assemble a strike team."

"Okay. Where are we going?"

"We?" She laughed. "Pretty confident you'll be chosen."

He shrugged. "Sure am. So—?"

"I can't tell you where," she said.

"Hmm. Then what's the objective?"

"Can't tell you that, either."

She moved across the bed on her knees, the sheet wrapped around her. He leaned down and kissed her. "At least, not quite yet," she added, smiling again.

"Right." He straightened and walked to the door of her quarters, opening it slightly. He peeked out at the broad courtyard; it was still early and the troops hadn't been called out yet for exercises and training. "A mission to nowhere, to do nothing. Got it. Sounds like every mission I've ever been sent on."

She laughed again. "Then I suppose you *are* qualified. Fine—you're on the team."

"Thanks."

"You knew when you came here—when you signed up for this army—that everything we do, everything we are is top secret. Right?"

"Oh yeah, I knew that. It was made very clear by the guys who recruited me back home."

"And you still wanted to join. You didn't ask too many questions—or they would've ruled you out, sent you packing."

He shrugged. "They said they were part of a new military force, secret even from most of the Imperial government, but with the objective of keeping all the worlds of the Empire safe. Sounded good to me." He snorted. "Plus, they said they had access to the best weapons and equipment—better than anything I'd ever get my hands on as a member of a planetary defense force." He grinned at her. "I told them they might be surprised what I've gotten my hands on, over the years."

She laughed with him at that.

"They wouldn't tell me who was behind it, or what it was called, or just about anything else," he went on. "They just said to report to the spaceport at such and such a time, and board that shuttle. I thought about rejecting the whole thing outright, what with all the secrecy."

She nodded. "I'm sure a lot do."

"Still," he said, "it sounded like a good opportunity. And an important thing to be doing. So—here I am."

"Yes. Here you are." Her eyes sparkled.

He came back across the little room to her and they kissed for a few seconds. Then she broke away and began to dress. When she was done, she started for the door. He got there first and opened it for her, waiting as she passed through. She paused halfway, looked back at him, and grinned. "Okay," she said. "You've tortured it out of me. I'll tell you two things. One: we are called the *Nizam* Legion."

"*Nizam?*"

"There's a historical connection of some kind," Arani said, waving it away impatiently. "And two: we're going to—"

"Ahknaton," Elaro said over the private, encrypted Aether link. He stood under a tree, off to one side of the practice and exercise field, facing away. The sound of gunfire echoed all around, from troops training with various sorts of weapons being provided to them by their new organization. Colonel Arani was back at the center of things, as always, barking orders and organizing the strike team.

Silence on the other end of the link for a moment, then, "Ah. Of course," came the reply. "Hardly surprising, given Tamerlane's recent obsessions." A laugh followed. "I didn't believe he would actually take me up on that suggestion. He must be even more desperate than I assumed."

Elaro waited patiently, not particularly clear on what the other was talking about and not particularly anxious to know.

"Alright," came the voice. "You have done well, Major. Or—should I address you by your rank in your *current* force?"

"She actually promoted me to major yesterday, sir," he replied. "It helps keep things straight, I must say."

Laughter. Then, "Keep up the good work, Major Elaro. Keep me informed. Perhaps, when this is all over, you'll gain a promotion from me, too—a promotion that actually matters."

Elaro nodded to himself. "Thank you, sir."

"Do your best on Ahknaton. I have no love for Rameses. The man is a fool, and a charlatan, and deserves to die. If I can't do the work myself, I'd be pleased to hear that you did it."

"Understood, sir."

Just like that, the link closed. Elaro turned. Colonel Arani was standing there. She was staring up at his face, her own expression slightly puzzled.

"Everything alright, Major?" she asked.

"Yes. Fine," he said, flashing her a half-smile. "Just taking a little break. How is the organizing of the strike team going?"

"Very well, I believe," she said. She looked at him for another lingering moment, then turned and started back toward the center of the field, clearly expecting that he should follow. He did.

"We leave in an hour. The shuttles will be arriving at any moment."

"Understood."

She pointed toward a group of soldiers, mostly male but with a few females mixed in, who were standing apart from the others near the center of the field. "That's the team. Get to know them as best you can, before we go."

"Will do." He separated from her and headed toward the group.

"Major?" she called to him a couple of seconds later, halting and staring back at him.

He stopped and looked across the short distance at her. "Yes, Colonel?"

"I can count on you, can't I? I would hate to find out I have misjudged you somehow. On any count."

Elaro blinked, then smiled. "Absolutely, Colonel. I am yours to command. Entirely."

She continued to regard him for another moment, then nodded and continued on her way.

She suspects something, he told himself. *She's a lot sharper than I was led to believe. She's a lot more a lot of things than I was led to believe.* He walked the rest of the way over to the assembled team, but his mind was still on Niobe Arani. *I hope, for her sake, she isn't that sharp. Because I don't want to have to kill her. I would, of course,* he quickly reassured himself, *but I would hate having to do it.*

As he reached out and began to shake hands and clap backs with the chosen men and women of the strike team, however, his thoughts remained on Arani. *Is anything I just told myself true?* he wondered. *Could I kill her?* Would *I?*

To his utter bewilderment, he found he had no answers.

11

Agrippa made his decision.

Minutes earlier, after his brief mental conversation with the representative of the Dyonari, he had attempted to contact General Tamerlane aboard the flagship *Ascanius* and fill him in on the strange new developments. No link could be made, however. Then he tried to reach his second, Colonel Iksander, currently in command of the bulk of III Legion's forces here on Eingrad-6. No luck there, either. Something in the area was blocking all Aether connections. Thus the decision fell to him alone: Should he meet with the Dyonari? Should he trust the Dyonari? Should he expose himself to the ancient aliens and whatever scheme they might be carrying out?

Or was the alternative—refusing to even talk with them face to face—even worse?

He deliberated internally for all of two minutes before reaching a conclusion.

"Stay here," he ordered the others in the cabin of the hovertank. Then, fitting his helmet over his head, he snapped the locks in place and reached out to grasp the rim of the hatchway, ignoring the thin layer of ice that had formed around it. With surprising quickness and strength he hauled his massive, armored bulk up through the opening and out onto the turret.

Dense, smoky air swirled around him as he climbed down onto the deck and then hopped down onto the muddy ground. He looked down, saw that he was still holding his quad-rifle in one gloved hand, considered that fact for a moment, and set it down on the tank's rear deck. Then he strode forward, moving like a tank himself as he set off across the field; moving like a god; like one of Those Who Remain come to do battle.

He sincerely hoped quite the opposite—that he would *not* have to do battle. Not this one time. Not if, as the Dyonari leader had seemed to imply, a mutual foe threatened them both.

In the distance, a panel opened on the side of the crystal alien vehicle that faced him, and one of the Dyonari stepped smoothly out.

The Dyonari were truly as alien as anything the human race had encountered since first venturing out into the galaxy, back in the days before the fabled Terran Alliance. Tall they were—taller than most humans—but almost impossibly thin, with elongated skulls and probing, sharp-pointed fingers. Whenever they were encountered by humans, they wore armor, and that appeared to be made entirely of glass, like their vehicles and their weapons. This representative of their people that approached Agrippa was no exception, though his armor was decorated in particularly ornate fashion. Agrippa mentally paused there, thinking, "Is this creature a he? A she? Perhaps simply an it?" After mulling that over for a moment, he decided to go with "he" until presented with evidence to the contrary. Besides, the term "it" seemed to carry too much negative connotation, and Agrippa was sincere in his efforts to reach out in as friendly a manner as possible under the circumstances.

Still, he intended to be very, very cautious.

When the two were roughly twenty yards apart, Agrippa stopped and held up one hand. "That's far enough, for now."

The alien looked at him sidelong, his head moving in eerie fashion, and halted as well.

"You are the one called Glossis, leader of this force—yes?"

The alien bowed his bizarre head. His voice sounded entirely within the general's head. *"I am."*

Agrippa saw the long, curved, glasslike sword hanging at the alien's waist. He nodded toward it. "I left my weapon back there," he said, pointing toward the nearer of his two tanks where it hovered above the mud. "Did I err?"

The Dyonari didn't move, didn't make a sound, didn't react—but, a second later, another of the species hurried up from their vehicle and waited respectfully as the leader drew his sword and handed it, pommel-first, to him. The underling hurried back out of sight with it, leaving his leader apparently unarmed.

"You come for the comet," the Dyonari said then. He spoke aloud this time, but the voice still sounded louder in Agrippa's mind that it did to his ears.

The blond general nodded, his bulky helmet moving along with him. "I've been ordered to investigate," he replied. He considered saying more, but decided to wait and see what the alien might reveal first.

"You sense its evil—its wrongness," the Dyonari went on.

Agrippa frowned at this and hesitated. He hadn't exactly attempted to quantify it yet, but there was no question that something—something in the very air itself, in the atmosphere, in the ground they stood on—felt wrong now. Had felt wrong ever since the comet had fallen. It was as if the planet itself had been wounded by the impact, and was not yet recovering. "Yes," he finally said. "I think that's fair to say."

The Dyonari looked at him for another few seconds, as if somehow appraising him. As if reading his insides as well as his outside, even through the plate armor. Then he nodded once. "You...understand. I sense it. For all your...bluster, human, you are with...the light."

Agrippa considered this. He thought he might understand. "I suppose so, yes. With the light."

"We, too...battle... the darkness," the Dyonari said. "We should be allies in that fight."

"Fine by me," Agrippa said. "But of course this planet we're standing on right now is Eingrad-6, a human world—part of the Empire ruled by my superior, the *Taiko*, Hideo Nakamura. And you are trespassing." He smiled flatly. "So, much as I'd love to be friends with you, it's sort of hard to see you and your people as entirely innocent and deserving of some kind of alliance when you yourselves have gone and invaded part of our territory."

The alien appeared to be thinking this over for a second, and trying to come to grips with it, as if Agrippa's statements were so foreign as to be almost impossible to understand. "Ah," he said at last. "But you see—we do not—consider this world—to be *your* territory. Or *anyone's*."

"It's not *yours*," Agrippa said. "There's never been a single claim to preexisting sovereignty over it."

"It is—not ours—nor is it—yours—nor is it—*anyone's*," the Dyonari replied. "That, I believe—is the root—of our—misunderstanding—here." He spread his hands, his impossibly long fingers fanning out wide. "No world can be owned. Not in the sense that you mean it. Worlds belong only to themselves."

Agrippa got it now. He smiled. "A fine sentiment," he boomed, his voice amplified to the outside world by speakers in his helmet. "Very nice. But, unfortunately, perhaps, that is not the galaxy—the universe—we live in. Territories are claimed by the various governments and races, and treaties are assembled, and we must all live with their provisions." He chuckled. "It keeps things simple and clear for everyone—especially for military people like me. If we can't draw a line, I won't know when someone has crossed over it, and needs to be put back in their place."

"Yes," the Dyonari said—and Agrippa felt he could detect a softening of the stance, the body language, of the alien now—"I believe we have found the root of the disagreement between our peoples." The Dyonari made a motion that might have been a shrug. "But we cannot solve such cultural problems here today, nor should we try."

Agrippa laughed. "We're soldiers—and thank Those Who Remain for it. We don't have to work out solutions to sociological and religious differences. We just do as we're told—which, often as not, means blowing things up."

"Quite so," the alien called Glossis agreed. "And, as soldiers, we must be forever preoccupied with defending our people. That being the case, you must be aware that other, more immediate dangers now threaten us both."

"The comets," Agrippa suggested. "You mean, somehow—whatever they are—they're a danger to both our peoples."

"Indeed." The alien looked at him more closely. "And you are suggesting you do not know what they represent? What they are?"

"Suggesting?" Agrippa shook his head. "I'm outright stating it." He no longer felt the need for guile. Unless this alien was doing something very subtle and probably telepathic to him, to influence his thinking, he felt the guy was being pretty forthcoming and honest. He wanted to reciprocate as best he could. He reached up and unlatched his helmet, pulling it off. He breathed in and out. The air had grown cooler than it had been the last time he'd been outside the tank, only a short while ago. "All I know," he said to the alien, now in his own voice, "is that the comets are moving in on a number of our planets even now."

The Dyonari appeared to be taking this information in and considering it.

"So, anything you can tell me would be much appreciated," Agrippa continued, being as restrained and diplomatic as he was capable of being, "and might go a long way toward improving relations between our respective governments."

"Tell you? Can you not *feel* it, human?" the Dyonari asked. "Can you not sense the danger—the terrible, terrible danger—now present here?"

Agrippa could feel something, alright. A wave of... anxiety? Something like that, anyway, creeping over this portion of the battlefield. A sense of dread. Of danger, as the alien was suggesting. He could feel something, that was certain—but he simply wasn't convinced yet about its source.

Before answering, he noted that the air had grown considerably colder in the past minute or two. He looked down and blinked in surprise. Ice, all around.

Ice? But it was warm. Or, rather, he corrected himself as a cool breeze struck his uncovered face, it had been warm earlier. True, the temperature had been dropping in the last little while, and pretty rapidly. But, still...

"You see it now, yes?" the alien asked.

Ice now covered a good portion of the formerly warm mud all around, and it was spreading fast.

Spreading out—out from the crater area.

Something nagged at Agrippa's mind as he stared at the thickening patches of ice. Something from the recent past... But.... he couldn't quite recall...

"Perhaps we should pull back a bit, if we are to continue this conversation," the big general told the alien, snapping out of his momentary daze. "I'm concerned that being this close to—to whatever it is, down there—could be hazardous to our well-being."

"Did you not come to investigate, as we did?" the Dyonari asked. "We suspected, oh yes—but we wished to be certain." Spindly fingers motioned toward the nearest crater. "Do you not wish to see the foe we both face?"

Agrippa hesitated, then stepped forward. His boots didn't squish in the mud as they had when he'd first gotten out of the tank. Now they crunched over the thin but hardening layer of ice. He walked past the Dyonari and right up to the edge of the crater, looking over and down. The red glow was much brighter down there.

"I can't really see anything specific," he told the alien. "Just that strange light."

The Dyonari joined him at the edge and gazed down. "As we feared," he said. "They form their own spacecraft around them as they travel through space. Ice. It accompanies them wherever they go. A side effect; residue of their psychic energies. They somehow channel that power for propulsion and for life-support—if they are, indeed, truly alive at all, in any sense that you or I would understand."

Agrippa shifted his eyes from the red glow in the crater's depths to the tall and slender alien in glass armor that stood beside him. "Okay, enough," he said, growing testy. "No more mysteries." He jabbed a thick finger toward the bottom of the crater. "Who is down there? *What* is down there?" He shivered, though whether it was from the weather or some other strange phenomenon, he didn't dare ask himself. There was no question it had become very cold now. "What am I supposed to fear so much?"

The alien leaned over farther and looked down into the light that almost floated like a pool of liquid in the bottom of the crater. "The worst thing there is," he replied.

Another wave of fear washed up and out of the crater. The ice hardened. The very air itself now crackled around them with the cold. And something changed. Something very subtle at first, but very real. A *presence.* Aware of them. *Watching* them.

The Dyonari moved back a step. "No," he murmured. "No—this cannot be correct. Even they are not so powerful."

Agrippa half-turned toward the alien. The Dyonari was backing away now, clearly growing more and more agitated as it went.

"No," he cried, even louder—and a psychic echo of that word bounced around in the general's skull, nearly knocking him over with its sheer force and vehemence. "*No!*"

Agrippa turned his back entirely on the crater and the red light and started toward the Dyonari, growing very concerned for the alien's condition. "What's wrong?" he asked. "Do you need help? Can we call for your people to come and—"

The Dyonari screamed an unintelligible scream, whirled about, and ran back toward its vehicle.

Agrippa started after it, then hesitated.

Doors all around the alien craft were opening and more Dyonari—these all very clearly armed—were getting out.

The general had no idea what was happening, but he had more than enough experience to recognize a hostile party when he saw one. He also understood enough to know he needed to get back to his own troops and their vehicles as quickly as possible.

Before he did, though, he turned back and looked down into the crater one last time. The red light was almost blinding now, but he managed to focus his eyes and tried to discern anything tangible, anything material within it. After a couple of seconds of effort, he found he could just make out something. Something...unearthly. *Unholy.*

A face.

Yet, somehow, not a face.

More like a skull.

An *alien* skull.

Silver and mottled and leering, a skull glared up at him. A cloud of black billowed up, surrounding it, and the malevolent red light seemed to wash around and over it.

Icy fingers of utter dread gripped Agrippa's heart.

By the hardest, by sheer force of will, he pulled his eyes away from the thing in the crater. He turned and raced back toward his squad, moving his big, muscular body and its covering of metal plate armor as quickly as he'd ever moved in his life. As he trudged across the ice, nearly slipping down on numerous occasions, he could hear the sound of the Dyonari troops behind him moving into attack positions.

He opened a link to his men and attempted to warn them, but the interference was still too great, even over so short a distance.

He had almost reached the cover of the nearest tank and was calling aloud to his squad when he heard the sound of the Dyonari behind him bringing their weapons to bear and charging them.

They opened fire.

12

Colonel Arani and Major Elaro were about to lead the strike team onto the two waiting shuttles when the very fabric of reality tore itself asunder.

"We're under attack!" shouted someone from behind them. Elaro instinctively drew his blast pistol and clicked off the safety, his eyes flicking this way and that, searching for enemies. Simultaneously he reached out with his other arm to pull Colonel Arani out of harm's way—but she wasn't there. She'd already leapt forward, her athleticism on full display, and rolled behind cover, coming up with her own pistol at the ready.

Lightning flared. The sky rent. And just ahead of them all, in the center of the courtyard and training grounds, a vertical seam appeared in midair. It split up and down, until it touched the dusty stone tiles and extended some twenty meters up into the sky. Then, slowly, it spread, opening into a gaping maw. After only a few seconds, it came to resemble the open end of a tunnel, with bright light spilling out from within.

A figure appeared in the opening then, coming through from the other side—wherever that was.

Elaro and Arani both trained their weapons on it—and then, as the figure emerged into the bright noonday sun, they lowered them. Eyes wide, they glanced at one another, then back at the person who had just made such a grandiose entrance. He was an olive-skinned, black-haired man in his late thirties, wearing a dark red uniform with gold trim. His face was one known all across the Empire.

Arani gasped. "General Tamerlane?"

Seeing her, he smiled. Then he saw the reaction his method of arrival had caused. He raised both hands. "My apologies," he called in a loud voice. He smiled. "I assure you all—I come in peace!"

Smiling too, now, Arani stood and moved out from behind cover, hurrying over to him. The other members of the strike team lowered their weapons and looked at one another, puzzled.

Elaro holstered his pistol and moved up behind Arani, studying the famous general as unobtrusively as someone of his size and appearance could manage.

"General—how..." Arani pointed to the tear in reality that still stood there, gaping, light shimmering around and within it.

Tamerlane laughed. "Not exactly the conventional means of transport you were expecting me to take, is it?" He motioned in the direction of the portal, appearing to be summoning someone else through it. "Come ahead, please," he called.

Two additional figures appeared within the swirl of light and fog, moving forward. They stepped through onto the surface of Mysentia. Each of them wore hooded robes—one in blood red, the other in black—and each exuded calm, quiet authority. And—there was no mistaking it—each was female.

The woman in red drew back her hood and stood regally, haughty, her back arched and her hands on her hips, as if she were the late Empress herself. She regarded the soldiers before her with what seemed to be icy contempt. Tamerlane nodded toward her. "This is Teluria," he stated by way of introduction. "She is our new Ecclesiarch and also vizier to the *Taiko*. She has agreed to assist us in this mission."

Teluria radiated an almost palpable sense of power, of danger. The soldiers regarded her with a mixture of curiosity and wariness.

Arani nodded to her. She waited for additional information, but Tamerlane left it at that.

What kind of assistance is he talking about? she wondered. Then she gazed at the gaping mouth of the cosmic portal that still stood open behind them and she pursed her lips, thinking.

Meanwhile Tamerlane motioned toward the woman on his other side and she, too, reached up and grasped her hood, pulling it back. While she took a more casual stance, her dark hair and piercing eyes caught everyone's attention immediately.

"This is Sister Delain of the Holy Inquisition," the general announced. "She has been...*loaned*...to I Legion for the duration of the present crisis." He nodded respectfully to her. "I have no doubt she will prove of great value to our efforts."

The general turned slowly, taking in the courtyard and the gathered strike team in their advanced khaki uniforms, their blast pistols and other high-powered weaponry in hand. "I'm pleased to see the *Nizam* Legion is prepared and ready for action," he called to them. "I'm sorry I haven't been able to check in on your progress personally before this. But I was confident that, in the hands of Colonel Arani, you would be forged into as fine a military force as exists in the galaxy."

A slight cheer went up at this. Most of the soldiers were still coming to grips with the idea that their secret benefactor and patron all this time had been General Ezekial

LEGION II: SONS OF TERRA

Tamerlane—the leader of I Legion, the famous Lords of Fire.

"Our Ecclesiarch here," the general continued, speaking so that all around could hear, "is going to provide transportation for you all, directly to the objective. There will be no interminable sitting around aboard a transport ship." He smiled. "And no danger from the orbital defenses, of course. She will open a doorway and you will walk through and be there."

The soldiers murmured to one another at this news. Elaro and Arani exchanged surprised glances.

"Is our objective still the same, General?" Arani asked.

Tamerlane smiled. "Oh, indeed." He spoke louder, for the benefit of all. "Colonel, you and your troops will be doing the Empire a tremendous service today. As most of you know, all of the legions are tied down, either defending the Inner Worlds or battling invaders along our borders. Meanwhile another danger—a different danger—has been growing from within, like a cancer, taking advantage of our forces' preoccupation with those other enemies to work its insidious harm upon the very heart of the Imperium."

Elaro smiled at this. Tamerlane had been generous in his description of why the other legions were tied down; he suspected that, in private, the man wouldn't have been nearly as generous toward Iapetus and the Second.

"Governor Rameses of Ahknaton has been plotting—and is now carrying out—dire treachery," Tamerlane went on. "In our Empire's moment of greatest crisis, when we should all be pulling together behind our rightful ruler, the *Taiko*, Rameses gives us only treason and rebellion. He has refused my entreaties to send his Sand Kings legion to the aid of the Empire. And we believe he is only days—*or hours*—away from attempting to depose the *Taiko* himself."

The strike team's grumbling grew louder and angrier. Elaro nodded in appreciation at the skill with which

Tamerlane manipulated their emotions and played on their loyalties.

"And so your mission is clear and straightforward," he concluded. "You will step through this portal and out into the palace of Rameses, on Ahknaton. You will depose him as ruler of that planet, capture him—and, if need be, kill him. Deadly force is most assuredly authorized. One way or another, his treason ends today."

Tamerlane stood straight and still for a moment, gazing out at the troops of the *Nizam* Legion—the secret army he had been assembling ever since the *Taiko* had begun to grow erratic and Iapetus and Rameses had begun to assert their rebellious natures to their full extent. Sister Delain stood motionless at his side, like some three-dimensional shadow. "Men and women of the *Nizam* Legion," he cried, "Are you ready?"

A shout went up. It was loud, but not terribly enthusiastic.

"I asked you if you were *ready*," Tamerlane called.

The shout was much louder this time, and much more enthusiastic.

Tamerlane nodded, looked at Arani and smiled. "You may begin your mission, Colonel," he said. "May the gods be with you all."

Arani saluted and Tamerlane returned it. The general then looked up, his eyes momentarily locking with those of Elaro. Tamerlane hesitated, a slight frown creasing his brow, as though he somehow recognized the big man, or perhaps simply sensed something about him. Elaro quickly smiled a hard, flat smile and saluted. Tamerlane hesitated a second longer, then returned the salute and gestured toward Teluria

The red-robed woman stepped forward. She reached up and threw back her hood. Her hair was black as night and her eyes flared brightly, as if refracting some internal light source. She raised one hand and the portal opening behind her shifted colors dramatically, lightning flaring around it again.

Elaro involuntarily moved back a step, bringing up one hand before his eyes in reaction to the bright flashes. He watched the woman, wondering who she really was and what she was doing. He assumed she possessed some measure of the power of the gods—*the Power*, as it were—and was currently changing the location that the other end of the portal reached, from wherever she and Tamerlane had come from, to where he and his team were about to go. Presumably to Ahknaton itself.

The strange woman moved up behind Tamerlane and Delain and whispered something. The general nodded and motioned in turn to Arani. Elaro couldn't help but note a slight smile that played about Teluria's mouth. He didn't know why, but he found it made him extremely nervous.

Then everything happened very quickly.

"Form up!" shouted Arani. "Two columns!"

The *Nizam* strike team, to their credit, didn't hesitate, didn't question their leaders. Alas, if only they had.

"Weapons at the ready. *Go!*"

As Tamerlane and the two robed women stood to one side, watching, the troops formed twin columns and marched quick-time into the gaping mouth of the portal. Arani walked through in between the columns, at the rear, and Elaro strode just behind her.

The rift in spacetime swallowed them up, hurled them across the galaxy, and spat them out—directly into the murderous line of fire of a thousand guns, all blasting away at them.

13

Deep within the Heliopolis complex, the vizier Zahir made his way back into the royal throne room, returning from another session of "prayer" during which he'd received more orders from his true master.

Much of the session—he flattered himself by thinking of it as an actual "conversation," implying some form of give and take—had consisted of the master impressing upon Zahir the danger and the opportunity that had arrived with this stage of their operation. Tamerlane was falling into their hands even now, and handing over his last army as he fell. If everything went as planned, soon the last of the armies of the Empire would collapse and its government—a government unnaturally prolonged by the unexpected rise of the *Taiko*—would fall into ruin, only to rise anew shortly thereafter in the hands of the young princess— by then the Empress— who would in turn be the slave of the master and his loyal servant, Zahir.

It was all happening just as the master had said it would, so long ago when he had whispered to Zahir through countless layers of the Below and the Above, calling him back into his service and laying out his vision for the future—a future in this, the mortal universe.

Before that it had been centuries, if not millennia, since he had last heard the master's voice. Over the ages of time Zahir found his memory growing dim in spots, with certain events and individuals blurring together with other, similar ones from other times and places. He could clearly recall, however, the Revolt in Heaven, when Lucian had sought to overthrow the great golden god Baranak and his clique, who had at that time more or less ruled the Golden City. That was back when the City was a bustling, well-populated center of highest civilization, and not the ghost town it had been ever since the time of the murders and the fall of Baranak. Zahir had favored Lucian's cause back then, and had thrown in with him briefly. But then the master had approached him and quietly warned, with great assurance, that the Revolt would end badly for Lucian and anyone on his side. Luckily for Zahir, he had found the master's arguments... *persuasive*.

Zahir caught himself and paused. Something about that thought puzzled Zahir for a moment, and he blinked, but couldn't quite put his finger on it or why it should bother him, and so finally he shook his head, forgetting about it.

And so when the day of Lucian's Revolt dawned in the City, Zahir had been many layers of reality away, carrying out the first set of orders of his then-new master. He had served him ever since, loyally and well. All of which made Zahir feel somehow strange when he thought back to the just-ended session. *Session? No*, he reminded himself—*conversation*.

Because something about what his master had just said nagged at him. There had been his standard admonishment to Zahir: "Remember. We do not *control*. We —that is, *I*," the voice had amended, "and through me, you—*persuade*. We persuade each of them along lines they are already contemplating, no matter how privately."

Of course Zahir understood that. Only the master truly possessed the power—*the Power!*—to control the minds of mortal men and women. Zahir's talents lay in other areas. But by channeling a fraction of his might through the Aether, the master could bestow a weaker but similar ability upon his servants. Thus Zahir now possessed the limited power of persuasion, and he used it in the service of he who had granted it to him.

That was all well and good, and so far Rameses and the others on Ahknaton seemed to be perfectly willing to obey most, if not all, of his "suggestions." But then the master had said something else; something that planted a seed of doubt, of suspicion, of concern within Zahir's mind.

His analogy in discussing the situation had been a game of chess—an analogy he often used. This time, however, he had suggested that not only pawns would be sacrificed in the name of ultimate victory. Some of the more powerful pieces would also be swept off the board before checkmate was achieved.

This troubled Zahir deeply. He knew full well that he was not a king nor—gender aside—a queen, nor even a bishop, but he liked to believe he was at least a knight in his master's service.

And in chess, when powerful pieces were lost, knights were often the first of them to go.

Would the master truly sacrifice him in the name of winning the larger game?

Zahir feared he knew the answer to that question, and knew it all too well.

Barely paying attention to his surroundings, he emerged from the hidden side-corridor and swept out into the throne room. With all these thoughts racing through his mind and his master's final words still ringing in his ears, he at first didn't hear Rameses calling to him from the basin where he stood, coruscating rivulets of energy washing over him.

"What's the matter with you?" the governor of Ahknaton demanded after his vizier failed to respond. Rameses stepped forward, almost out of the bowl, cables stretching out behind him from where they were attached to his arms and legs. His eyelids and lips spasmed from the waves of current running through him, making it difficult for him to speak. "Zahir!"

The vizier remained oblivious to his surroundings, all of his attention directed inward. "They are coming," he murmured. "The master in his wisdom has arranged it on the other end, to draw all the armies together and eliminate them all at once. But...surely he does not intend to eliminate his most faithful servants at the same time..?" He shook his head. "No. But, still, we must prepare, just to be certain." And if the plan did call for the removal of Zahir from the board, the master might just find the script had been slightly rewritten when it came time to act out that phase. No, if the coming storm bearing down on Ahknaton was as great as he feared, he resolved to meet it with an equal storm of his own.

"What's that you're saying?" Rameses called, frowning, growing irritated. "I can't hear you. Speak up!"

The vizier blinked and looked up from his musings. Seeing Rameses, the flesh of his face appearing to flow in almost liquid fashion for an instant, brought him back to himself. He hurried over. "Sire," he said, bowing obsequiously, "I have reason to believe you are in grave danger."

"What?" Rameses glared at his hollow-eyed advisor. "Danger? Here? How is that possible?"

"I believe it is very possible," Zahir replied. "An enemy approaches. An enemy that can harm you. Even here."

Rameses scoffed. He gestured at the ranks of Sand Kings in their gleaming golden plate armor, lining both sides of the long entryway. "I am protected by the finest soldiers in creation—and to reach even them, an enemy would first have to approach Ahknaton from space, where he would be met with the devastating power of hundreds of high-orbit weapons platforms and surface-to-air beam and missile installations." He laughed. "I am quite safe here, my friend."

"Not if they approach Ahknaton from some other avenue than space, sire."

Rameses simply stared back at him, uncomprehending. "Other than...space? But..." A second passed, and another. "You... you mean from the Above? Or the Below?" Slowly he frowned. "Are you suggesting I could face an attack... from...one of... *them*?" He staggered back a step. "How— how would you *know* something like that?"

"I have access to certain...*sources*, sire."

"Sources? What exactly does that mean?"

"Perhaps, sire," Zahir said by way of reply, and exerting the smallest fraction of the Power, "you should don your armor."

Rameses looked at him blankly, and then his complexion ashed over. Nodding, he pulled at the cables connecting him to the basin and the equipment that sat beside it, yanking them loose. Then, as the waves of energy flowing around and over him subsided somewhat, he climbed out of the basin, even as two Sand Kings hurried forward, one of them bearing the crimson cube. Kneeling, the soldier offered it to the governor, who accepted it and held it up.

"You recall how to—?"

"Of course," Rameses snapped. He clutched the cube closely to his breast and closed his eyes. Bright crimson light flared. An instant later, the seamless armor covered him entirely.

"And now let us get you to a safer location," Zahir was saying, tugging at the Governor's metal-covered arm.

"Wait," Rameses said, pulling away. "The girl." He turned and pointed across to the other side of the basin, where the little blonde child lay unmoving on her golden bier, tendrils of energy reaching out almost tentatively to brush against her and through her. "What about the girl?"

Zahir waved a hand vaguely in the air. "She and Colonel Belisarius will be tended to directly, sire—never fear." He reached out to clutch at the Governor's arm again. "But our first priority must be removing you to safety."

Rameses frowned at the slender vizier, seemed about to object, then almost reluctantly nodded. "Very well."

"You should also have the Sand Kings go to high alert," Zahir suggested. "If you'd prefer, I can issue the orders myself..."

"No! That is *my* task, and I am doing so now!" Rameses had his eyes closed, clearly tapping into the local Aether network. He opened his eyes a moment later and faced Zahir directly. "Do your precious sources tell you where the enemy will strike first—where on this planet they will arrive?"

"Unfortunately not, sire," the vizier replied. "But I fear that even this royal chamber is not safe. That is why I wish to move you—immediately—to a more defensible location."

"Yes, yes—fine," Rameses growled. Encased in the unimaginably advanced armor, only his face was revealed, and he scowled at his advisor. Zahir was relieved to see that the physical distortions had subsided now that he was no longer receiving the "treatments" in the basin.

Zahir gestured and two of his hulking servants hurried forward, taking up bodyguard positions on either side of the governor. Half a dozen elite Sand Kings soldiers joined them, energy spears charged and held ready at their sides. Together the entourage hustled Rameses out of the throne room, leaving only Zahir, the other two muscular servants, and another dozen Sand Kings behind, along with the now seemingly comatose bodies of Colonel Belisarius and the Princess Marens lying prone on their catafalques.

Zahir strode across the now nearly empty throne room. He made his way around the broad basin that was serving as a miniature representation of the great Fountain of the Golden City, gazing as he went upon its blazing, glorious radiance. On the other side of it, he stood between the two catatonic figures—one large and powerfully built, the other small and delicate—and stared down at them, stroking his smooth chin all the while. For nearly five minutes he did that, as his minions looked on, waiting and pondering all the while, unable to decide how best to proceed. Dare he begin the final process now, before the vessels were truly ready for the transference? Dare he wait longer, and perhaps lose everything? Then the sounds of battle came to him through the walls and windows of the inner palace, rousing him to action. Instantly a new set of alarms began to sound and lights flashed throughout the throne room.

"That's it," he muttered to himself. "No more delays. The time has come."

At his barked command the two bald servants hurried forward and dragged sets of heavy, insulated cables across the floor, positioning them between the two prone bodies. One hurried to fasten the near ends to the two catafalques while the other hurled the far ends over the side of the basin.

The tasks completed, the two servants stood at attention and waited. Zahir ignored them and took a position between the two bodies. Raising both his arms in dramatic, conductor fashion, he brought the lightning down out of the empty air. Forks of energy played across the colonel and the princess.

"Awaken," he called from bloodless lips. "Arise from your slumber within the human soldier!"

The lightning continued to play across both bodies a few seconds longer. Then a dim, red luminosity seemed to erupt right out of the body of Belisarius. Seeing this, Zahir grinned and moved back to the foot of the colonel's catafalque. Now he could just discern another shape, another entity, becoming visible, its form somehow superimposed over him. It was a horrible, horrific form. As the vizier watched, the shape enlarged even as it remained ephemeral.

"Welcome into this universe, oh demon lord!" Zahir crowed. As the lightning crackled down in waves, in sheets, he stood there, seemingly oblivious, and at last gestured toward little Marens where she lay. "A new host body has been made ready," he shouted in ecstatic glee. "The future Empress of Mankind awaits you!"

14

The sounds of firing came to Tamerlane very clearly and distinctly as the last of his *Nizam* strike force troops disappeared into the portal. He frowned. So soon? They had opened fire the instant they were through? That didn't seem right.

"*Betrayal*," cried Teluria. "The Sand Kings were lying in wait for your forces, General. You have been betrayed!"

"What?" The sheer shock of the woman's words—the incomprehensibility of what she was saying—caused Tamerlane to hesitate for an instant.

Teluria had raised her left hand and was beginning to make the gesture that he recognized as the one that would close and dissolve the portal. He reached out and grasped her wrist, yanking her hand down.

She whirled on him, glaring, teeth bared. He ignored her display and barked, "Stop! What are you doing?"

"I am sealing the breach," the woman in red replied angrily, "before the armies of Rameses force themselves back the other way, and attack us here!"

Again taken aback, Tamerlane frowned at this, considering the ramifications. "But—what of my forces already on Ahknaton?"

"They are lost," Teluria replied, her expression hard. "You must realize that—you must accept it."

"No!" He moved in closer to her. "Leave it open, for now. I mean it!"

Her expression sour, Teluria obeyed.

Quickly Tamerlane called up an Aether link, searching for Colonel Arani's signature on the other side of the portal. For some reason, he couldn't get a reading on any of the strike team. Something—some sort of interference—was playing havoc with the Aether as it touched on Ahknaton. Then, almost miraculously, he managed to connect. Before he could "say" a word to her, asking what was happening there, she called back at him, her mental voice frantic. He couldn't understand most of what she was sending to him. One word, however, repeated several times, came through clearly enough: "Ambush!"

Tamerlane whirled on Teluria. "You led them into a trap," he almost shouted at her.

"*I?*" Her dark eyes widened in seeming astonishment. "I have done nothing but open a path, just as you requested."

Tamerlane bit back his anger as best he could. "Bring them back! Get them back here *now!*"

"I cannot bring them back," Teluria replied, her voice filled with anger. "You know that very well, General. I can only open the way; they must choose to return—and be *able* to."

Furious, Tamerlane hesitated on the threshold of the portal to Ahknaton. The younger, more impetuous side of him wanted to race through it—to gather up his forces, who were being subjected to the gods knew what sort of violence on the other side, and bring them home. But the older, wiser part of him counseled restraint. He did not at all trust Teluria, and suspected she might well choose to close the portal with him on the other side, trapping him in the ambush along with his men, and cutting him off from the rest of his troops, with no way to escape. Torn, he stood there, uncertain.

The portal rippled, and a figure stumbled through it, falling to the ground at his feet. More came through behind it, many of them bloody and burned.

The one at Tamerlane's feet started up, and the general helped him. Seeing the big man's face, he recognized him as the major that had accompanied Arani— Elaro, it was.

"What happened, Major?"

"They were ready for us—*waiting*, General," the big man said, in between coughs. "They knew we were coming. They knew exactly where we would appear." He coughed again, hard. "They were butchering us. One company volunteered to fight a rearguard action while the rest of us withdrew, and—"

"Where is Arani?"

Elaro's eyes widened. "What? She was with me a moment ago—" He straightened and looked all around. Not seeing her, he instantly turned and started back toward the portal.

"Stop right there, Major," the general ordered.

Elaro hesitated, turning back and looking at Tamerlane. "I have to find her—*help* her," he said.

"She can help herself," Tamerlane replied. "She's a very good soldier. I don't need to lose any more men today."

Elaro glared at the general. "With respect, sir—you don't command me. I don't belong to your Lords of Fire."

"You belong to the *Nizam* Legion," Tamerlane retorted. "And I command *it*, too. So I command *you*." He stepped forward, grasping Elaro by the upper arm. "Major, I understand that you want to help her. Believe me—so do I. But this isn't the way. Either she's dead—"

"She's not dead!"

"—or else she's held prisoner, or she's on the run from Rameses. If she's dead, that's that. And if it's one of the other two, we have to think carefully about how to get her— and the others—back." He motioned toward the portal. "And blindly charging through there isn't the way to do it. It's not remotely safe."

Elaro gave Tamerlane a vicious look. "Don't I know that," he growled. "But—we have to do *something*!"

Before Tamerlane could answer, someone else did decide to do something. Sensing movement behind them, the two angry men looked up—just in time to see the black-robed form of Sister Delain racing through the portal.

"Stop!" shouted the general, but it was too late. She was through to the other side. Tamerlane cursed and turned to Teluria, but what he would have said to her, no one would ever know. For at that instant a barrage of energy blasts erupted from the mouth of the portal, coming from the other side. Staring into that swirling abyss, Tamerlane could make out the shapes of Sand Kings troops rushing his way, quad-rifles and energy lances up and firing. He opened his mouth to issue an order—but before he could say a word, Teluria gestured sharply and the portal slammed closed, vanishing as if it had never been, entirely severing the link with Ahknaton.

Tamerlane dropped to his haunches and cursed again, dust and debris and the smell of sweat and blood swirling around him. He looked up at the stricken Elaro and shook his head wearily. Along with Arani and Delain, more than two thirds of his army was gone.

15

Aboard and around Agrippa's hovertank, they all braced for impact.

It never came.

The sounds of weapons fire—of blasts from alien energy pistols and rifles—was almost deafening. But those blasts, beams and bullets didn't streak out toward the humans.

Realizing the shots weren't connecting with him or his Bravo Squad, Agrippa halted in his headlong race for his tank and turned, looking back toward the Dyonari position, trying to determine what was happening.

In the smoke and gloom, it was hard to tell. His eyes flicked frantically here and there. His heart was beating quickly, his respiration ragged. Fear clawed at his insides. Desperately he tried to calm himself. *I am General Arnem Agrippa*, he told himself with a firm determination. *I do not panic on the battlefield—or anywhere!* He pulled his helmet off and gasped in air. *What is the matter with me? I have never reacted in such a way before. Never!*

The light. It had been the red light. And—something within it. A face. A skull-face, rising. But even that— possibly a simple holographic illusion by the Dyonari, or someone else—shouldn't have been enough to frighten him. Not like this! Not at all!

Something else. Something...telepathic. Psychic. A force of pure fear—of pure *evil*—rising up out of that crater.

He looked down. Ice. Ice all around them. Sheets of it, covering the ground and growing thicker by the moment.

The Dyonari are psychic, he reminded himself, *but not like this. There's never been any report of them creating fear—terror!—in their enemies. Certainly not an artificial fear that begins to dissolve as soon as one recognizes its presence.*

Agrippa frowned, shaking his head to clear the last of the psychic residue.

"What are they doing, General?"

Agrippa looked back. Obomanu, his driver, was leaning out the hatchway, staring out across the murky valley.

"They're shooting one another, it looks like," came a voice from the other side of the vehicle.

With a whoosh of air, the second hovertank, commanded by Major Torgon, glided around Agrippa's vehicle and came to a halt just next to it. Torgon was standing in the open top hatch, studying the Dyonari position through high-tech field glasses.

"Shooting each other?"

Agrippa leapt up onto the second tank and took the field glasses from Torgon. He pointed them toward the odd, crystalline vehicle that had carried the alien force.

"I realize this isn't proper spacing for battle conditions, sir," Torgon was saying, "but I was growing frustrated with not being able to contact you via the Aether."

Still looking through the glasses, Agrippa nodded. "You did well." Then he grunted. "You're right, Torgon. They appear to have gone insane. They're firing their weapons at one another. Using those swords on one another. Fighting hand-to-hand with one another!"

"What should we do, General?" Torgon asked.

"I...honestly don't know," Agrippa breathed, watching the alien soldiers slaughtering one another. "Perhaps we should—"

"The enemy," came a now-familiar voice within Agrippa's head, *"is driving us mad. Making us kill each other—kill everyone."* Glossis, the leader, sounded much more strained and strident than he had before. *"We Dyonari are especially susceptible to psychic influence. It is our greatest weakness as a people. The enemy is exploiting it now—driving us into a rage. It is taking all of our remaining reserves of psychic restraint to avoid firing at you."* A pause, as Glossis seemed to gather his wits and his strength. Then, *"You must leave this place at once!"*

"We do not run from a fight, Glossis," Agrippa mentally replied. "And if we can help you, we will do so."

"You do not know this enemy, General."

"No, we do not. And I am still waiting for you to enlighten us. What do we face here?"

"The worst foe imaginable."

"You said that before. Who is it?"

"They do not want me to tell you. They are exerting great psychic influence to stifle me. They enjoy having yet another advantage over their enemies. That is why I have been unable to name them thus far. But—I am fighting it. I will—" Glossis cried out, and the sheer mental force of his anguish nearly took Agrippa's feet out from under him. Reeling, he steadied himself against the armored plating of the tank.

"General! Are you alright?" called Torgon. He started to climb out and hurry to his commander's side, but Agrippa waved him back.

"No, no—stay at your post, Major. We may yet need all of our firepower—and at a moment's notice."

"Yes, sir," Torgon answered. He followed that with, "Sir! The battle seems to be over."

Agrippa looked out toward the alien vehicle. He could still see movement here and there; perhaps they hadn't all killed one another.

A second later, Glossis's voice returned. It was steadier now. *"They are no longer provoking us, General,"* the alien said. *"Only a few of us survive."*

"Why have they stopped?" Agrippa asked.

"I believe they... no longer care... if I divulge their identity to you. Apparently they have grown supremely confident of their power, and of their chances of victory."

"Then who—?"

"They...are called... Phaedrons," Glossis stated. *"Masters of psychic combat. The ice comets invading your worlds are simply outer shells that form about their ships as they travel, as a side effect of their mental powers."*

"I...see. Where do they come from? We have never encountered their like before."

"They come from outside of our galaxy. We fought them, ages ago—we and the other, older races. We believed them to have been banished forever. But something has stirred them up—driven them back into our galaxy."

"What do you mean?"

"There is another force at work, beyond just the Phaedrons," Glossis said. *"We have felt it. We know it is there, but we do not know what it is. But it is powerful, and it is driving the Phaedrons forward, urging them to attack all in their path—perhaps, we fear, as a vanguard for some larger invasion."*

Agrippa absorbed this information, his expression grim. He thought of what he had seen in the crater. Of the absolute and utter terror that had surrounded that bizarre, skull-like face.

At that moment, Glossis cried out across their mental link. *"They are coming! You must flee!"*

A visual image flooded into his mind: A metal, skull-like face, swathed in black and shot through with baleful red light, in the depths of a crater. And it was rising... *rising...*

Glossis's soundless voice had become unhinged. *"The Phaedrons come!"* he cried within Agrippa's mind. *"They rise! They rise! Flee!"*

The link was severed.

"Sir! The Dyonari—they're—" Torgon was watching them through the glasses. He shook his head. "What are they doing?"

Just beyond the crystalline vehicle, a shimmering circle of light had formed. The surviving Dyonari soldiers were very quickly climbing back aboard their craft.

"Sir—look there!"

Agrippa shifted his eyes to where Obomanu was pointing. Despite himself, he gasped.

From out of the craters—all of the craters, all dozen of them—black clouds were rising, billowing up. And the red light that blazed up from each of them was growing brighter and brighter. The temperature dropped again; it was growing intolerably cold now, even within the heavy plate armor.

"The Dyonari have opened some kind of portal—a dimensional gateway, like the gods can do," Torgon said, pointing toward the aliens' position. "They're going through!"

Indeed, the crystalline alien vehicle spun about on its axis and zoomed toward the shimmering circle of light.

"A portal." Agrippa didn't hesitate. He leapt back onto his own tank and dropped halfway inside. "Follow them," he barked. "Quickly!"

For their part, Obomanu and the driver of Torgon's tank only hesitated for the tiniest of moments before slamming the big hovertanks in gear and racing along after the alien craft.

"What are we doing, General?" called Torgon aloud from the second tank, his voice barely carrying over the roar of the engines. "Pursuing the Dyonari—or fleeing this new foe?"

Agrippa bit back an angry retort.

"We cannot contact our other forces because of the psychic interference blanking out the Aether link," he barked. "And right now we are the only humans, as far as I know, who have any information whatsoever about this new enemy. We have to get that information to General Tamerlane and the *Taiko*—*immediately*."

"But—where are we *going*?" Torgon asked, as Agrippa's tank closed in on the circle of light.

"I don't know," Agrippa replied, though he was unsure now if the Major could still hear him. "I don't have any idea. But—if the Dyonari think it a safer place than the one we just left—the Dyonari, who are never afraid of anything—then that's good enough for me."

The two tanks roared into the portal. Just after they passed through, the circle closed, vanishing from the surface of Eingrad-6.

Agrippa and his men plunged through darkness—the darkness between the stars.

16

I don't know how you're doing this—how you've done any of the things you've done," Tamerlane was saying to Teluria, even as he clasped her hand in a firm grip, closed his eyes, and concentrated. "But there is obviously more to you—much more—than you've let on."

The mysterious woman in red only smiled enigmatically.

"Whose side are you on?" the general asked her, opening his eyes and meeting hers. "In truth."

"You must concentrate, General," the woman replied. "Focus all of your thoughts on Colonel Arani."

Scowling, Tamerlane closed his eyes again and did as he was told. "As soon as this business is resolved," he murmured, his voice already growing distant, "we will have a reckoning between us."

"As you say, General," Teluria said. She didn't appear particularly concerned.

They sat at the table inside Arani's office tent. Elaro, meanwhile, had been ordered to reorganize the remaining troops for immediate action. Tamerlane, though, had been determined to make one more attempt to contact his missing soldiers and Inquisitor Delain before they took any new action.   If any of those forces remained alive, the intelligence they might offer could make the difference between a repeat of the ambush they'd walked into the first time and actual success.

"Arani," Tamerlane whispered, even as he pushed that thought through the Aether in what he hoped was the direction of far-away Ahknaton. "Can you hear me?"

Channeled through the higher dimensional realm of the Above, the Aether provided a virtually instantaneous link across great distances of the normal universe.   No one, though, had ever tried to send a message through it across anything like the distances involved now.   Or, if they had tried, they had entertained no hope of success, and had found none.   Tamerlane, however, believed that in this one case he might be successful.   Teluria had demonstrated remarkable powers when it came to manipulating the fabric of reality; one might almost describe her as a god—as one of Those Who Remain. If so—if she truly was a creature of that variety—she must possess untold personal reserves of power—of *the Power*.   The Power of the gods.   With that energy now at Tamerlane's disposal, as he clutched the woman's hand, he hoped it might act as a sort of booster to his own signal, forcing the message through to—

"General!"

Tamerlane recoiled, nearly severing the connection. Arani's voice had come loudly—very loudly—back through the connection.   He clung to Teluria's hand and called back over the untold light years, "Yes! Arani! Yes, it's me! Are you alright? What's your situation?"

A pause, then, "I'm sorry, General—your signal is barely reaching me. But know: I'm still alive, as are some twenty-four other soldiers of the *Nizam* Legion. Sister Delain is with us, as well.   She has done an amazing job of camouflaging us, helping us to avoid the Sand Kings patrols."

Tamerlane's guts churned at this news. Arani and Delain—alive! And with a decent-sized force behind them. It was the first good news the general had received in quite some time. But—so many others were dead. So many.

"We are just outside the city," Arani continued. "We can see the Heliopolis clearly from here." She read off a string of coordinates. "The Sand Kings have moved on to other areas in their search for survivors, so we should be safe for now. We await further orders or an extraction attempt."

Tamerlane's grin only grew. *Safe*, he thought. *They're safe, and it sounds as if they can remain that way for at least a little while.* He started to reply, then considered the situation. It appeared their connection was somehow able to convey her messages to him much more clearly than it carried his words to her. He opened one eye and glanced across the table at Teluria; she was pale and sweating under the strain, and he guessed she couldn't hold a connection of this distance open much longer. He had to consider what he was going to tell Arani carefully and convey it in a very concise manner.

"Stay where you are, Colonel," he sent back to her. "Stay alive." His smile grew grim but determined. "I am on my way.

Tamerlane gathered the remaining few dozen members of the *Nizam* Legion on the broad plain beyond the training facility. The shuttles that were already parked there had been joined by another group of them; more than enough to hold every soldier of the legion that yet lived.

Those remaining troops now stood at attention, weapons at the ready, khaki smartcloth uniforms crisp and clean on some, torn and bloody on others.

"We will be boarding shortly," Tamerlane called. "We are taking the shuttles directly to Ahknaton. Our mission is simple: we will strike hard and fast. Priority one is the extraction of survivors from the previous mission. Once that is accomplished, we will attempt infiltration of the Heliopolis and the palace itself. As before, our primary target is Governor Rameses. I want him alive if possible, but dead is perfectly acceptable."

"You will never get past the planetary defenses," Teluria observed, her red lips pouty. "You must allow me to open a portal for you and your—"

Tamerlane shook his head. "Don't take this the wrong way, lady," he said, "but, at this point, I feel more confident in our ability to survive a sky filled with anti-ship weaponry and orbital mines than in our ability to survive a doorway opened by *you*."

Teluria scowled. She moved back a step, anger flaring on her face.

"To the ships," Tamerlane called, ignoring her. "The faster we get out of here, the faster we bring our people home—and the bad guys to justice."

The *Nizam* Legion boarded their shuttles and seconds later the boxy vehicles lifted off. Only Teluria remained behind, having declined all offers of transport. She stood there on the dusty surface, watching as the last of the ships roared up into the Mysentian sky and disappeared.

"He must be told," she whispered to herself. "I have no choice." Even so, for several long minutes she waited there, staring up at the sky, uncertain.

"Yet I do chafe at simply obeying orders—from whatever direction," she whispered. Fear seized at her then; she never knew if *he* was listening in. He was with her always, it seemed.

Finally, cursing again, she waved a slender hand, opened a portal directly in front of her, and walked through, gone.

17

An exuberant Amon Rameses reentered the throne room on Ahknaton. "That was the best Tamerlane and Nakamura could do?" he crowed as his Sand Kings and Zahir's two servants escorted him in. "What comedy! Am I to respect, to fear, the mighty *Taiko* and his lapdog, when all they can bring to bear against me is a force such as that?"

Zahir bowed deeply to the governor. "Indeed," he said, straightening. "Your victory would now appear assured."

"Of course it is," Rameses laughed. He had removed the crimson armor—it was back to being a small red cube again, which he carried almost casually in one hand. He strode across the broad marble floor, its whiteness veined with crisscrossing lines of gray and black, and set the cube atop an ornamental granite pedestal. All of the tension—the fear—that had filled him earlier had utterly evaporated as he had witnessed his Sand Kings obliterating the ranks of the invaders. He felt exhilarated. He felt *freed*, somehow, though he wasn't entirely certain what that might mean.

And then he registered what he was seeing in front of him.

He opened his mouth to speak, but no sound at first would come out. Eyes widening, he approached Zahir more slowly now, stopping some ten meters away. He stood there, staring.

Lightning was flaring down from within the high arched dome of the ceiling. It didn't strike the floor, however; instead it was playing across the prone bodies of Colonel Belisarius and the young girl.

And, as Rameses looked more closely, he became aware of something else—something truly terrifying. A strange, ethereal, blood-red humanoid form was in the process of separating from Belisarius's body and rising up to float in the air over him.

"Governor," Zahir started to say as he swept forward. "Perhaps you shouldn't—"

At that moment a warning alert sounded, vibrating and echoing throughout the big chamber. It was followed by a strident voice: "Alert! Alert! Starships dropping hyper in high orbit!"

Zahir whirled about and raced over to a monitor. It displayed a visual of a number of large spacecraft exiting the hyperspace pathways of the lower Above and moving into Ahknaton airspace. The vizier blanched. "Governor," he called, "we may be under another attack!"

Rameses dismissed the words with a casual wave. "If Tamerlane has been stupid enough to send part of his starfleet to the same grim fate as his legion, so be it. The orbital defenses will deal with them in short order."

His eyes still on the monitor, Zahir shook his head slowly. "I don't think these are Tamerlane's ships..."

Rameses wasn't listening. He ignored both the vizier and the alert and returned his attention to the humanoid shape now hovering horizontally above Belisarius. The more Rameses stared at it the more disturbed he became. It looked somehow frightening, terrible, horrific. It appeared, in short, demoniacal.

As Rameses looked on in fascinated horror, the crimson form began to solidify and slowly it moved into a seated position on the edge of Belisarius's palanquin. It waited there for a few moments—long moments during which Rameses wondered exactly what was happening and what would happen next—and then it stood upright, its feet still not touching the floor, its height now much greater than the average human even as it continued to grow. It floated across the space separating Belisarius and Princess Marens, pausing about halfway, gazing down at her.

Seeing that, Rameses at last found his voice.

"What in the name of Those Who Remain is going on here?" he demanded.

Fearing the situation was about to unravel, Zahir had no choice but to abandon the orbital display and hurry over to the governor. "Nothing untoward, I assure you," soothed the slim vizier. His voice hardened slightly. "Nothing that has not long been planned."

Rameses stumbled back a step. The horrific figure floating in midair had become almost completely solid now, standing upright between the two platforms, yet still floating like some awful apparition. It looked entirely unearthly and terrifying with its dark red color, twisting horns, fangs, and narrow eyes.

"Planned?" Rameses exclaimed. "This is nothing *I* ever planned or approved," he all-but-shouted. "I don't know what you think you're doing, but that—" and he pointed with his right index finger— "is a demonform, and it has no business on my world."

The vizier was now growing visibly concerned. He hurried over to Rameses. "My lord," he said, "this is nothing that you should allow yourself to get upset about." He attempted to move closer, into the governor's field of view—to capture his full attention. "All goes as it was meant to go."

"Meant to go?" Rameses was almost shrill now. He stomped past Zahir, never giving the vizier an opportunity to ensorcell him. "How is bringing a demonic creature onto my world helping anything conceivably go, as you say, 'as it was *meant* to go?'" He whirled on Zahir, anger and outrage spilling out of him. "And exactly *whose* plan are we talking about? Certainly not mine!" He moved in closer to the vizier and brought a finger up in the slender man's face. "This is base heresy," he growled. "Heresy perpetrated on *my* world, in *my* name! I will not *tolerate* it!"

"Heresy?" Zahir reddened. "What care you for accusations of heresy? You are beyond the reach of the Inquisition now! You are master of this world. Heresy on Ahknaton is what *you* say it is!"

"Blasphemer!" Rameses backhanded Zahir, sending the man tumbling to the hard marble floor. The stunned vizier lay where he had fallen, mouth hanging open, as if he couldn't quite believe what had just happened.

Tension in the throne room had become almost overwhelming. The Sand Kings troops instantly moved up behind Rameses, weapons ready, even as Zahir's four minions closed ranks behind him, one of them leaning over and helping him up. In the background, the orbital alarms continued to sound. For a moment, no one could have predicted what would happen next.

On his feet, Zahir—now flushed and sporting a deep red mark across his left cheek—started forward, clearly ready to fight. An instant later, however, he restrained himself, apparently rethinking the situation. He breathed deeply in and out and motioned his servants back. His expression softened, his complexion growing ashen. "My lord," he began, "I apologize for any impudence on my part. I understand that you were not expecting to see what you have seen here today, and I should have better prepared you for it."

"Silence!" Rameses bellowed. "Do not seek to talk your way out of this now, vizier!"

Zahir started toward the governor again. "My lord," he said imploringly, "if only you would listen for a moment—"

"Guards!" shouted Rameses. "Arrest Zahir and hold him. Sand Kings! Prepare to destroy the demonform!"

"No!" cried Zahir. "It is not yet fully in this universe—it is still vulnerable!" He hurried toward the governor, almost frantic now, arms raised.

Reacting instinctively and protectively, the nearest of the Sand Kings directed his energy lance at Zahir and fired. An expanding sphere of superheated gas and energy erupted from the tip of his weapon and shot point blank directly at the vizier.

It never struck him. A heretofore invisible barrier flared to life a short distance beyond and fully surrounding the vizier. It absorbed most of the blast and deflected the rest away.

"How did you—?" Rameses stumbled back, away from Zahir. As he did so, he finally caught a glimpse of the orbital display monitor. He gasped.

The image of the space above Ahknaton revealed a veritable armada of vessels. Only a few were of human origin and none of them were I Legion ships under Tamerlane's command. Most were very alien indeed.

"What—what is *happening*?" demanded Rameses, turning frantically from the display to the demonic form hovering over the princess to Zahir standing there unharmed after being shot point blank by an energy lance. He raised his hands to his eyes, grinding the palms into the sockets, crying out in confusion and dismay. A few seconds later, something about his face, his expression, changed. He lowered his hands, moved a step closer to Zahir, and frowned, appearing extremely puzzled.

Zahir, still surrounded by Sand Kings, started to speak, but Rameses cut him off.

"Who *are* you?" he asked, scowling. "How did you come to be my advisor—my *vizier*? I have no memory of ever hiring you or assigning you." He moved another step closer, and this time his voice was loud and strong: *"Who are you?"*

Before Zahir could formulate a response, the entire throne room was filled with blinding light.

Turning to discern its source, Rameses had to raise a hand before his eyes to block the worst of the glare. Quickly enough he could tell that it was coming from—radiating from; *pouring out* from—the golden basin, and the small geyser of raw energy that constantly flowed up from it. That modest flow had in the past few seconds become a mighty geyser of energy erupting far up into the air of the throne room.

And somehow, astonishingly, out of that light and energy stepped a figure.

Rameses continued to shade his eyes from the awful light, but he struggled to make out exactly who this person was. He found the man looked somehow familiar.

For man he was, at least superficially. Human. Male. Dark hair, dark eyes, black clothing.

Seeing him fully, Zahir fell quickly to his knees. "My master," he cried.

The man in black had now fully emerged from the fountain, and subsequently its magnitude and radiance reverted to what they had been before. The man, meanwhile, strode confidently across the marble floor and spared the now-prostrate Zahir only a slight glance before standing directly before Rameses and pursing his lips.

The governor stared at the man in black, astonished, but could find no words. He felt as if he'd seen—met, even talked with—this person before. The memory eluded him for a long moment before he suddenly gasped. "You! I remember! After the Council of Ascanius—you spoke with me. You brought the princess to me. You—"

"Indeed," the man in black replied, "you remember well. In fact, you remember far too much." He glanced back momentarily at the kneeling vizier. "That is entirely Zahir's fault. His ham-fisted approach to managing you has brought us to this juncture."

"*Managing* me?" Rameses grumbled, confused.

"Yes—or attempting to. But instead he has allowed you to break free of your conditioning. And now I have been forced to come here to set things right again," the man continued. "And that I shall do."

"My master," Zahir said, "forgive me. There was a great deal of confusion here—we were attacked by Tamerlane's forces, who somehow were able to travel directly here, in the manner of our people."

"I am well aware of Tamerlane's actions," the man in black barked. "Who do you think *instigated* them?"

"What? Zahir gasped.

"And it played out precisely as I foresaw that it would. Did you not deal with them swiftly and surely?"

"I—well, yes, but—"

"And the balance is restored."

Zahir, now frowning, shook his head as if in a daze. "But, master—"

The man ignored him and continued. "The situation has reached a critical juncture. I cannot allow your ignorance and incompetence to jeopardize my goals."

At that point, Rameses had had more than enough. "Who are you people?" he demanded. "What are you doing here? What do you want with me—and my world?"

Zahir leapt across the distance separating them and returned Rameses' backhand slap, knocking the governor down. "You will address our lord Goraddon with respect!" he shouted.

Recovering, looking up from where he'd sprawled, Rameses' expression conveyed the depths of his shock. "Goraddon?" he gasped. He looked around the chamber, as if somehow he could spot some piece of evidence that this was all a ruse, a joke, a performance. Alas, no such bit of evidence presented itself. "That—that's not *possible*! Goraddon was one of the old gods—he died along with most of the others. Everyone knows this!"

"To the contrary, it is *entirely* possible," declared Zahir, hands on hips, standing over the governor. "Some few of the gods merely used that event as an opportunity—an opportunity to retreat for a time, gather their strength, and—"

"Enough, Zahir," said the man in black. He turned from the slender vizier in the Egyptian headgear to the fallen Rameses. He extended a hand and Rameses reluctantly took it, and he pulled the man back up to his feet. "What your vizier says is true, Governor."

"He is *not* my vizier," Rameses hissed, eyeing Zahir sharply.

"He *is*," the man in black stated, "because I willed it to be thus." He offered Rameses an almost apologetic smile. "What I want with the princess is what I wanted with her father, the Emperor, before. Unfortunately, his mortal shell was not able to withstand the force of carrying a demon lord of the Below within him for very long, particularly when provoked by the unexpected interference of certain other parties, and..." He shrugged. "We all recall the unfortunate outcome, at the Council on Ascanius."

"Yes! I do remember seeing you there," Rameses blurted. Then he blanched. "You—you were responsible for that atrocity—that unspeakable—"

The man in black nodded slowly. "Oh yes. And without the untimely intervention of Nakamura and Tamerlane, all would have happened as I envisioned it." He laughed once, sharply, and looked around at the ornate, opulently decorated, Egyptian-themed interior of the vast throne room, regarding it as if it were the lowliest cave of some hermit on a backwater world. "But, in any case, here we are now, doing it all again. Fortunately, we have one last demon lord at our disposal." He nodded toward the grotesque, blood-red form hovering nearby.

"Yes," chimed in Zahir, grinning madly. "The demon that traveled out of the Below inside the old Ecclesiarch, Zoric, and then hopped into Belisarius's body during the Council." He looked away, distracted for a moment, and muttered, "If only we'd known all along that it had jumped inside Belisarius. We had no idea where it had gone." He *tsked.* "It would have saved so much time and trouble." Then he shrugged and turned back to the governor. "And we also have one last royal alive to receive it. The heiress to the imperial throne." He laughed. "And this time, we have taken a number of precautions to be certain there will be no interference—to be sure that both the so-called *Taiko* and his lapdog Tamerlane have been rendered impotent and removed from the picture."

"Indeed," stated Goraddon.

By the hardest, Rameses was able to tear his eyes away from the man in black and stare at the apparently comatose young girl lying on the catafalque. The horrific shape of the demon hovered over her now, and the meaning was clear: it was preparing to possess her. Rameses fought down the urge to throw up.

Goraddon watched the governor's reaction and chuckled. "As to what I want with you and your world, well..." His smile broadened. "You and your Sand Kings are important pawns on the board. You have already served to confuse matters with Tamerlane—to keep him off-balance and concerned with his internal security as well as all the external attacks I have engineered." He smiled warmly at Rameses and shrugged. "But now I am afraid the time has come for the sacrificial move."

"Sacrificial?" Rameses was both utterly confused and completely terrified now. He stumbled back a step. "What do you mean?"

LEGION II: SONS OF TERRA

The man in black gestured toward the monitor screen and Rameses followed with his eyes. He gasped. He had forgotten the wave of starships that had been dropping out of hyperspace into high orbit just before this alleged Goraddon had appeared. As he stared at the screen, his mind reeled: Now there were scores of ships—*hundreds* of them; *thousands*— of every conceivable known race and empire, alongside many that were entirely unfamiliar.

"I mean that the imminent immolation of Ahknaton will serve as a blazing beacon across the galaxy," the man in black declared, his body now seeming somehow taller, bigger, more luminous than before. "It will act as herald of the news that I have returned from my long exile, and that I bring with me a gift—a gift for all creation." He raised his hands and they seemed to stretch right up through the domed roof and into orbit, where a thousand starships now waited, their arsenals directed at the planet below. "I bring," Goraddon cried, "the sweet embrace of chaos and death!"

18

I t's a snowflake," breathed Lt. Harker.

"A bloody big one," Obomanu amended.

"No denying that," Harker agreed.

It hovered there before them, filling half the sky. It was bright and it was huge and it nearly made the members of General Arnem Agrippa's Bravo Squad forget about everything else. Considering everything they'd just been through, that was saying something.

They had followed the Dyonari hovercraft through a shimmering circle of light, and in the process had left the scarred surface of Eingrad-6—and the horrific alien Phaedrons—behind. For a timeless time they had seemingly fallen through darkness. And then they had emerged here—wherever *here* was.

Agrippa himself recovered first. He had to will his eyes to close and force himself to turn away, facing in the opposite direction from the vast crystal snowflake that blazed so brightly in the dark. The rest of his troops continued to gawk. There had to be something psychic at work, he understood then; something that impelled his soldiers to focus monomaniacally on the thing in the sky.

Having succeeded in breaking the attraction, he found himself gazing across the deck of what seemed to be a gigantic space station. Towers and columns of slender crystalline beauty extended upward into the darkness. At their bases, hundreds—perhaps thousands—of tall, spindly Dyonari stood watching them, seemingly as fascinated by the humans as the humans were by the object that floated out in space.

Agrippa swallowed and instinctively reached for his quad-rifle, only then realizing he'd set it on the tank before they had so rapidly exited from Eingrad-6.

And there was no doubting that they were no longer on Eingrad-6. In fact, they were probably nowhere in the Eingrad star system. The stars far up above seemed wrong, or at least different. *Very* different.

Settling for the blast pistol he'd left in its holster all this time, he climbed fully out of the tank and hopped down onto the surface of—of whatever they were on.

The others were still staring at the gigantic glowing snowflake-like object in the sky. He cleared his throat. "Ladies, gentlemen—I believe the more immediate concern is *this* way."

Slowly, reluctantly, the other Bravos turned to face the way Agrippa was looking. They recognized the situation instantly.

"Uh oh," Harker breathed. "We've followed the boogers right into their lair."

Indeed, in addition to the large number of Dyonari now staring back at them, the crystal hovertank-like vehicle they had followed from Eingrad was now parked just in front of them, its crew standing outside it. Several of them started toward the humans. They carried objects that could only be weapons—exotic pistols and rifles in addition to the long, curved, glasslike swords they favored.

Agrippa raised one hand in as peaceful a gesture as someone wearing heavy combat plate armor could reasonably manage. "I apologize for the intrusion," he said. "I was under the impression that we were being invited to follow you through the portal. If I was in error, I apologize."

Behind Agrippa, the turret of Major Torgon's tank whined as it turned, directing the heavy energy-beam cannon toward the aliens. Agrippa called back to Torgon sharply. "Stand down, Major. We're all friends here. I imagine that just needs to be clarified a bit." He smiled at the approaching aliens. "Do you concur?"

The four that had approached the closest to the human position stopped in their tracks. They seemed distracted, as if someone was speaking to them inaudibly—or over a sort of Aether link. Then they bowed quickly and turned, moving back to their vehicle. A second later, a lone Dyonari strode out, moving in very deliberate fashion towards the humans.

Agrippa studied him. "Glossis?" he asked.

The alien drew near, then nodded once. *"I am happy that you and your soldiers survived the Phaedron incursion,"* he stated in silence, his voice entirely within Agrippa's head. *"Unfortunately, your presence here is...* problematic.*"*

Agrippa nodded. "I was afraid that might be the case."

"Yes. No human has ever set foot on one of our glo'chas *before. There are some among us who consider this an act of great blasphemy—the final straw that will inevitably result in a destructive war among our two peoples."*

Agrippa almost recoiled. He gathered himself and met the alien's eyes; while a very tall human at over two meters, he still had to look up to see Glossis's face. "That was not my intention. Far from it."

"I understand," the Dyonari replied. *"And I cannot deny that I was glad to provide an avenue of escape for you."* He looked back at the crowd of his fellow aliens standing in the distance, appearing for all the world now like a lynch

mob. *"Nonetheless,"* he went on, *"if that view prevails, you will likely all be executed."*

Agrippa's expression soured but he said nothing for the moment.

"I have countered," the alien went on, *"that humans would not send so tiny a force here if their objective was to attack us."*

"That's the truth."

"I have put forth a competing narrative. I have suggested that your team coming here is the opening move of a new era of potential cooperation between our two species."

"That suits me fine," Agrippa said. "My people already have about as much conflict as we could ever ask for. We aren't looking for new enemies."

"Yes," the Dyonari commander agreed. *"We have been observing your empire and its conflicts for nearly a...* year, *as you measure time. We have evaluated them carefully. You are losing."*

"Losing?" Agrippa snapped.

"Your ultimate defeat is inevitable. You cannot hope to prevail against so many foes at once."

"Time will tell," Agrippa growled. "We aren't done yet." He paused. "Tell me this. Have you put any thought into why so many different forces have chosen to attack us all at once?"

Glossis was silent for a few seconds. *"We have assumed they are all behaving in an opportunistic manner,"* he said at length. *"To use your vernacular, which I hope you will not mind that I have borrowed from your mind—they smell blood in the water, and they each wish to strike you while the opportunity is there—while you are distracted with other enemies and with your internal leadership crisis."*

"Leadership crisis?" Agrippa frowned at that. He raised an eyebrow and almost smiled at Glossis. "You may have better access to inside information than I do," he snorted.

The Dyonari said nothing in reply.

Agrippa looked from Glossis to the multitude of aliens arrayed behind him. "So," he rumbled. "When will a decision be made? When will we learn if your people wish to execute us, or welcome us as ambassadors, or whatever?"

Glossis made a sound—an actual, physical sound, rather than a psychic projection—that Agrippa quickly decided must be a kind of laughter. *"Oh,"* the alien said once he had recovered his composure, *"your fate was decided nearly twenty seconds ago."*

Agrippa let his hand slide slowly down to the grip of his pistol. "And?"

"And you are welcome here," the alien concluded.

Agrippa released the grip and smiled. "Thank you."

"Of course."

The crowd of Dyonari moved in, waving and greeting the humans. Their guns and swords were now nowhere to be seen. Agrippa motioned for his troops to put their own weapons away and climb out of the tanks.

Glossis turned back to Agrippa and started to say something, then hesitated.

"Yes?" asked the big human commander.

"The fact that you had to ask about the verdict is telling as to your lack of knowledge about my people," the alien told him. He nodded toward his pistol in its holster. *"Your little gun would not have saved you. Had the deliberations resulted in a different decision, you and your soldiers would already be dead."*

Whatever had caused the distortion that had prevented communication via the Aether link on Eingrad, coming to the Dyonari space station seemed to have remedied it—and somehow even boosted the signal. Agrippa closed his eyes and reached out, accessing his Aether implant and triggering it, tapping it into the bottom-most layer of hyperspace—of the Above, to use the religious terminology of the Ecclesiarchy—in order to achieve near-instantaneous communications. He selected the link for General Marcus Ezekial Tamerlane and made the connection.

"Arnem," came Tamerlane's exclamation as he accepted the link. "Thank the gods. I was beginning to worry you had run into something out on the battlefield that you couldn't handle." His voice carried a tone of humor tinged with relief.

Agrippa started to answer in a flip manner, then hesitated and rethought his reply. "That may well have been the case, actually, General," he stated reluctantly.

Tamerlane sobered at this. "You?" he asked, incredulous. "Something *you* couldn't handle?"

"It was definitely something unexpected, and quite formidable," the big blond man said over the link. "And troubling." He thought back to the leering metal skull-face in the crater and had to suppress a shudder. "It's a new race—one we haven't encountered before. The Dyonari call them 'Phaedrons.'"

"Another hostile race. I see," Tamerlane said, and Agrippa noted to himself that he had never heard the man sound more weary or frustrated. "I'm very anxious to hear your report on what you found out there, and how it connects to the comets. But before you go into detail about that—where are you now? And why couldn't we contact you for the past three hours?"

"Jamming, sir," Agrippa reported.

"Jamming? Of the Aether?"

"Yes, sir." Agrippa gazed out across the deck of the station, seeing his troops shedding their heavy plate armor and enjoying a bit of time outside of their hard shells. The Dyonari were moving among them, providing ornately curved pitchers of water and trays of food. Agrippa didn't trust the aliens at all—not yet, at any rate—but so far they were behaving perfectly hospitably, and he was grateful for a bit of down time before his squad inevitably was ordered back into the action.

"By whom?" Tamerlane was asking.

"At first I believed the Riyahadi forces or the Dyonari were jamming us, General," Agrippa said, "but I now suspect that it may have been psychic interference caused by the Phaedrons themselves."

"Psychic interference?" Tamerlane sounded puzzled. "Is that even possible?" He was quiet for a moment, as if thinking it through. "Can mental power alone block our access to the Aether link?"

"I have no way of being certain," Agrippa replied. "But, given its critical importance to us, and the absolute denial of access we experienced back on Eingrad-6, I believe it is a possibility we should be aware of, and should get the eggheads in the Science Ministry looking into."

"So noted, General," Tamerlane said. "Thank you for the information. I am of course pleased you and your squad survived."

Agrippa nodded. "It was entirely thanks to the Dyonari, sir," he said.

"The Dyonari? They *helped* you?"

Agrippa laughed. "They *saved* us. Provided us a way offworld just when the Phaedrons were about to—" He trailed off, frowning.

"About to what, General?" Tamerlane asked.

Agrippa struggled to sort through his thoughts and feelings. "I—I don't know, actually, sir," he managed. "At the time, I was certain these new aliens were going to wipe us out—that we stood no chance at all. That death was inevitable. Now, though—looking back on it all—I'm not entirely certain why I believed that." Agrippa reddened. "I'm concerned now that I may have...*panicked*, sir. It's not like me, but—"

"It's not *you* at all, Arnem," Tamerlane shot back at him. "Think, man. You said these Phaedron aliens were psychic—possibly powerful enough to block access to the Aether itself."

"Yes, but—"

"So just imagine what they must have been able to do to your *head*—to the heads of all your troops. What if they projected intense feelings of fear, of hopelessness...?"

Agrippa considered this. He nodded slowly. His fingers bunched into fists and he reddened further. "I think you're right, General," he grumbled. "I think they got into my head and made me think they were invincible and horrific and deadly, but—"

"Oh, they sound pretty deadly to me, Arnem," Tamerlane said. "I do not for a second think you acted improperly by getting out of there. We needed this information, and we needed you and your squad alive. Everything else is secondary."

"Yes, sir," Agrippa replied quietly, still very angry at himself for being taken in by a bunch of telepathic aliens. That thought caused him to start, and he looked around. The Dyonari—telepathic aliens themselves, though nothing like the things they'd encountered on Eingrad—were still mingling with his troops. Agrippa tried to think it through rationally—to be sure he wasn't being mentally manipulated again. The commander, Glossis, had been straightforward with him. The Dyonari had honor, there was no question about that. And now they were showing great generosity in welcoming this element of III Legion to their private space station. Even so, every fiber of Agrippa's being told him it was time to get out of there, before something else unexpected occurred.

"I have a bit of information to share about the Dyonari," Agrippa said over the link. "But I'd prefer to wait until I'm no longer on one of their spacecraft before I go into it."

"Understood," Tamerlane replied. "As it happens, I have a new assignment for you anyway—if you're able to travel across interstellar distances at this time."

"I'm...not entirely certain about that, General," Agrippa said. "Our route to our present location was...*unorthodox*, to say the least. How we will depart this place is something of a mystery to me at the moment."

"I trust you will find a way," Tamerlane said. "I need you on Ahknaton, and as soon as possible."

"Ahknaton?"

"I'm on my way there now myself, and I would appreciate your help. Your orders—and a brief about the situation—should be coming through on the sub-channel now." Tamerlane paused. "I look forward to speaking with you in greater detail very soon, Arnem, and in person. Best of luck."

"Thank you, sir."

The link closed. Agrippa checked that the file Tamerlane had mentioned had indeed downloaded into his memory, and then turned back to face his troops.

"Alright, Bravos," he shouted. "Time to get your suits back on. We have new orders."

A particularly tall, slender Dyonari strode toward Agrippa, stopped and bowed slightly. He recognized Glossis.

"You will be wanting to take your leave of us now, I suspect," the alien said, speaking as usual via mental projection.

Agrippa nodded. "Your hospitality has been much appreciated, Commander," he said, returning the bow. "I hope this will be the beginning of a new and warmer relationship between our two peoples." He glanced at his men; they were grumbling and not happy, but they were obeying his orders. Most of them were already halfway back into their white and green Deising-Arry Model 5 heavy plate armor. "But, for now, I would settle for a way back into Imperial space."

Glossis made the noise again that Agrippa had decided must be laughter. *"Oh, General,"* he said, *"that is a very simple request to grant."* He gestured off to his right with one impossibly long, slender arm. Instantly a circle of light appeared, standing on its edge like the mouth of a cave. As the seconds ticked by, it grew brighter and brighter. Within twenty seconds, the outer ring of the circle had taken on an appearance of solidity, while the inside of it swam with lights and shimmering out-of-focus images.

"Where would you like to go?"

Agrippa simply stared at the alien. "Where?" he managed to say after a few seconds of silence. "You mean—"

"I mean I can direct this pathway to any location you desire—with certain limitations," Glossis replied. *"After all, the walls between the worlds are of varying thickness, and even we Dyonari cannot pierce all of them. Your Candis, for example..."*

Agrippa nodded, still practically gawking at Glossis and then at the ring of light. Behind him, the two hovertanks fired to life again, their fusion engines purring as they lifted up off the deck.

"All aboard, General!" shouted Obomanu, his driver, from the turret opening.

"Am I to understand," Agrippa asked the alien commander, "that your people can simply...*walk...anywhere*? Just like the gods?"

"The gods?" Puzzlement crept into Glossis's telepathic "voice." *"Ah—you are referring to those of your people who, ever since the incident, can tap into the* elemental— *into the* Sourcefire. *The* Power.*"*

Agrippa was now staring directly at the Dyonari. He wasn't sure what to say.

"Ah," Glossis said again. *"You think of those individuals as supernatural. I see."* He made a gesture that might have been a shrug. *"Perhaps they are. Certainly they are above and beyond the 'nature' of your people's normal state."*

"They're—they're not gods?" Agrippa whispered, leaning in toward the alien.

"Oh dear," the Dyonari muttered. *"Perhaps I have said too much. You really should forget the last few moments of our conversation, General."*

"I should—*what*?" Agrippa blinked. "I—what were we saying?"

"You were telling me where you and your soldiers need to go," Glossis said.

"Yes—I—yes, of course." Agrippa hesitated, feeling there was more being said but unable now to recall exactly what it had been. "Ahknaton," he murmured. Then, louder, "Ahknaton. We have been ordered to Ahknaton."

Glossis motioned ever so subtly with his slender, needle-like fingers, then bowed again. *"Safe journey, General Agrippa,"* he said. *"Perhaps we will meet again someday."*

Agrippa looked at the circle that floated in the air. He could see a desert landscape stretching into the distance within it. Then he turned to the Dyonari one last time. "Thank you again for your assistance today," he said. "It won't be forgotten."

Glossis bowed more deeply.

Agrippa turned and hopped up onto his tank. Obomanu in turn dropped down through the opening and into the driver's seat. Agrippa assumed his usual spot, his upper half projecting out of the hatchway. He saluted Glossis and nodded toward the other Dyonari now gathered around behind the commander, then barked orders down into the tank.

The big vehicle lurched forward and shot smoothly through the portal, Major Torgon's tank just behind it.

As they passed through the gateway, Agrippa glanced back one last time. His vision was filled with impossibly big, bright, shining snowflakes.

BOOK SEVEN
THE GODSLAYERS

1

The desert beyond Anakh City was cloaked in the still, cold darkness of deepest night. Even so, shapes moved across its rolling hills.

Colonel Niobe Arani made a quick, sharp gesture with her left hand and the two dozen troops behind her froze. A second later, they had slipped into near-invisibility behind whatever cover was available, there on the scrub-covered, sandy hillside beyond the gleaming pyramids of the Heliopolis. She adjusted the settings on her visual implants and studied the landscape between what remained of her *Nizam* attack force and the nearest visible Sand Kings soldiers.

They had come through the portal some two hours earlier and walked directly into an ambush and a withering crossfire. It was a miracle any of them had survived. Arani had ordered as many back through to safety as possible before that avenue of retreat had been cut off. That number had included Titus Elaro; though she wished he was with her now, she was glad that her ruse had worked and he'd run back through before noticing she wasn't coming right behind him. She had wanted him to get away; he was in truth just a new recruit, while she had duties to the troops she had spent so much time and effort training. She was never going to leave until all the others able to do so had made it back through.

"What do you see?" asked a feminine voice to her right. Despite her training, she nearly jumped straight up. She hadn't thought anyone was there, and certainly hadn't heard anyone approaching. She looked to her right quickly and, even with the vision augmentation, could only barely make out the shape of the Inquisition woman, Delain, crouched down in her black robes and hood.

"Not a lot," Arani whispered back. She gave the woman one more quick look. She hadn't at first been sure if she should trust her, when she had come running through the portal from Mysentia even as Arani had been trying to funnel her people back the other way. But then she had recalled that Delain served as assistant to Stanishur, and the dour Grand Inquisitor was one man she trusted implicitly, following their harrowing shared experiences on Ascanius. That had been enough to set Arani's mind at ease—for the most part.

Delain made a gesture before her own face—casting a spell? Adjusting her visual implants? Both? Neither?—and then nodded. "There are a few Sand Kings gathering further to the east," she whispered, pointing.

"Right," replied the colonel, impressed. She possessed what she believed were high-quality optics—the kind only available to officers of the legions—and even she was having difficulty making out what Delain was referring to. "But they don't look to be heading this way." This was as much a guess as anything, and she waited to hear how the Inquisitor would reply. As it happened, the woman in black said nothing.

The wind whipped over them, howling as it came through the tall glass and steel buildings of Anakh City and blew along the canyons just beyond, making it tough to hear anything for a few moments. They weren't using the

Aether to communicate on the off-chance the local forces could somehow intercept or overhear them. Arani wasn't sure that was even possible, but she didn't want to take any chances. They were making do, but it made things ever so slightly awkward.

As the wind died down again and silence descended, Arani thought back to their escape and had to stifle a laugh. Delain glanced at her, one dark eyebrow raised and just visible under her hood.

"Just thinking how surprised Rameses' troops must have been when we literally vanished from the *cul de sac* they thought they had us trapped in," the colonel explained quietly.

Delain didn't smile; she merely nodded once.

"How did you know about that hidden passage?" Arani pressed, curious now. "Even *they* didn't appear to know about it—and it's their world!"

Delain shrugged. "The Grand Inquisitor trained us all well. He has shared all of the hidden ways with us. If there's a secret passageway anywhere in the Empire that he doesn't know about... then I assure you, no one else knows about it either."

Arani nodded at this. "That doesn't surprise me in the least," she chuckled. Still smiling, still thinking over their next actions, mainly including how to stay alive and out of the way of the Sand Kings patrols until Tamerlane and Elaro came to rescue them, Arani leaned back her head and gazed up at the star-speckled night sky.

She frowned.

The stars were moving. And there were a lot of them. Far more than she had expected to see.

"Ummm... Inquisitor," she murmured, "what do you make of that?" She pointed straight up.

Delain pulled back her hood and looked up. She made a slight sound of surprise in the back of her throat.

"Yeah," Arani breathed, "me too."

The space above Anakh City—over Ahknaton itself—was filled with starships. Hundreds, perhaps thousands of starships.

"Those aren't patrols looking for us," the colonel concluded quickly. "Those are big ships—capital ships— way up in high orbit." She shook her head. "But—why? Do they belong to Rameses?"

"That is not possible," Delain replied. "Ahknaton possesses virtually no navy."

"As far as we know."

Delain shrugged. "The most optimistic projection would not put them close to affording that many ships, nor constructing them in such a short time— let alone doing so in secret."

"Then what are they? Where did they come from?" Arani stared at them, pushing her optics to the limit. She still couldn't make out any details.

"They are an odd mixture," the Inquisitor said, continuing to stare upwards and obviously seeing much better than the colonel. "I recognize human ships—the Chung, naturally, and the Riyahadi—as well as a few Rao. Three or four larger Dyonari vessels. And—" She hesitated, as if unwilling to believe what she had to say. "And also there are quite a few ships of completely alien design—ships I am utterly unfamiliar with."

This took Arani aback. "Aliens other than the usual suspects?" A chill ran up her spine. "Where could they have come from?"

"I don't know," Delain said. She blinked, then added, "There is also a comet."

Arani looked at her, puzzled. "A comet?"

"You don't know," Delain said. "Trust me. It could be the worst news of all."

"Right," the colonel said, clearly not convinced. She started to say more, but then felt a signal coming in across the Aether. She recognized it as Tamerlane and knew she had no choice but to answer it—even if it meant revealing their position to anyone who might be able to trace such things.

"General?" she sent back across the link. "We're still here."

"Very happy to hear that," Tamerlane replied. "We will be joining you shortly."

"You will?" Arani suppressed a grin. "Excellent news, sir. Will you be opening another portal?"

"No," Tamerlane said, and the distaste was evident in his voice. "We are taking ships. ETA at Ahknaton is twenty minutes."

"Ships? You're *flying* here?" Arani nearly choked. "Sir— I don't think that's advisable."

"I'm well aware of their planetary defenses, Colonel," the general replied. "We will deal with them in short order." He paused. "At least well enough to slip our little fleet through and down to the surface."

"No, General," Arani warned, "not the orbital weapons. I'm talking about the armadas currently occupying almost every bit of airspace over the planet."

The link seemed to go dead for a moment. Arani waited patiently. At last Tamerlane's voice returned. "Did you say 'armada,' Colonel?"

"Yes, General."

Another pause, then, "And...what might you mean by that?"

By way of response, Arani simply selected a stored frame of video from her memory and transmitted it via the Aether link. A couple of seconds later she heard Tamerlane gasp.

"Colonel—what you sent me—those ships are in orbit *now*, as we speak?"

"Yes indeed," she said. "Right over our heads."

"I...see," Tamerlane said. "I knew Rameses was ambitious, but..." He paused. "Alright, very well. Let me—" He went away for a couple of seconds, then came back, his voice a bit more strident. "I'm sorry, Colonel, but it appears it is too late. We are dropping hyper just beyond Ahknaton now."

"Oh dear," Arani said. She looked up at the night sky again.

"We will see you soon," Tamerlane said. Then he added, "I hope."

The link closed. Arani blinked and looked back at Delain. The Inquisitor looked troubled. Arani found she didn't have anything to say that might change that.

"The Sand Kings must not have detected that communication," Delain said after a few seconds, as she continued to watch the local soldiers patrolling along the edge of the city.

"That's one good break for us, then," Arani breathed. She looked up at the tiny lights in the sky; lights that signified what had to be an impenetrable wall between Tamerlane's approaching ships and the planet. "Now, if nothing else can happen to bring any attention our way, we can—"

A blinding light flared just beyond their position on the hill.

"Oh, come on!" Arani growled, even as she spun around and drew her pistol. She recognized what was happening and she could only assume it was a bad thing.

A portal was opening—an inter-dimensional pathway very similar to the one that had brought her and the others to Ahknaton.

"Could it be the general's rescue?" Delain called, standing up from her place of concealment.

"Pretty sure not," Arani said. "Up and at 'em!" she called over the Aether link to her half-dozen remaining soldiers. As she did so, she leveled her pistol and made ready to fire.

The light flared brighter still, and then an army of heavily armed and armored troops rushed out of the portal, tanks arrayed behind them.

2

With a lurch, the transport craft slid back into normal space. Standing on the flight deck between the two pilots, Tamerlane watched as the brown disc of Ahknaton took shape directly ahead.

"All ships accounted for, General," the co-pilot reported.

"For now," Tamerlane muttered. "Alright," he replied, "good work. What is the tactical situation?"

The co-pilot studied her display for a long moment and then gasped.

"Lots of ships, right?" Tamerlane asked.

The co-pilot turned in his seat to look back at the general. "You know?"

"I was just told."

The co-pilot turned back to the screen. She was wide-eyed as she studied the numbers coming through the computer. "By the stars! Thousands of them! Human ships, alien ships—"

"And unknown ships," Tamerlane finished for her. "Yeah—I know."

The co-pilot glanced quizzically at Tamerlane but didn't reply.

The general moved up behind the lead pilot. "Can we get through?" he asked.

The pilot made a wordless sound that didn't seem particularly positive or encouraging. "I don't see how, to be frank with you, sir," he said. "There are just so many..."

"We don't know they're hostile," Tamerlane pointed out. "At least, to *us*. Not yet," he added.

"They don't seem to be attacking Ahknaton or its orbital defenses," the co-pilot reported. "In fact, no one is firing at anyone at the moment."

"That strikes me as a bad sign, if you don't mind me saying, sir," the pilot observed. "If they're not shooting at each other..."

"Yeah," Tamerlane finished for him. "They all may be waiting to shoot at us."

Suddenly the proximity alarms shrieked.

"What's that?" Tamerlane demanded. The only answer he received at first was a violent shaking of the craft, nearly hurling him across the small bridge. He pulled himself to his feet and moved back next to the pilot who, along with the co-pilot, had been spared the rough treatment by various belts and crash webbing. "What just happened?"

The pilot was incredulous. "A—a *comet*, sir!" he said. "A comet just blasted right through our formation. Somehow our instruments didn't detect it before. And now—"

Tamerlane shifted his gaze from the tactical display to the main window. They had gotten close enough to Ahknaton that the waves of starships were visible ahead of them—joined now by a spinning, tumbling mass of blood-red ice, streamers of steam trailing away from it as it barreled on toward the planet. The starships lying in its path were already igniting their maneuvering engines to move out of the way as the shuttle-sized yet deadly chunk of ice approached.

While the two pilots looked on in astonishment, Tamerlane recovered his senses and barked, "Behind it!

Now!" He activated the Aether link to the other pilots of his little armada. "All ships," he called, "follow us—follow the comet! As close as you can get!"

Moments later, the Imperial transports had formed up in an arrowhead shape, rocketing along only a short distance behind the comet. One of the ships positioned itself just far enough to one side of the formation to effectively see past the icy escort and beam tactical data from ahead of them to the rest of the ships. What they saw shocked them all over again.

One of Ahknaton's major orbital defense bases floated motionless just ahead. Fighter craft clung to its gantries like wasps around a nest, yet none of them had launched. Massive particle-beam cannons and missile launchers lined its external decks, yet none of them were firing yet.

And the platform was directly in the comet's path.

"What are they waiting for?" Tamerlane breathed, watching in grim fascination as the comet swept on and on, closing the distance with the platform in mere seconds. "Are they all asleep? Why don't they fire?"

The Imperial transports followed along in the wake of the comet and slipped easily past the waves of starships. Not a one of them fired. It was as if no one even noticed them there, in the shadow of that blood-red harbinger of doom.

One second ticked past. Another.

Now, so belatedly as to be entirely pointless, the platform opened fire. Its particle beams shot out, ripping into the massive comet. Small fragments were torn away, sent tumbling into new and nearly as deadly trajectories. The main body of the comet tumbled on, inevitable as death.

And then came the impact.

The comet struck the orbital station like a high-caliber lead slug from an old-fashioned musket tearing through a melon. The platform disintegrated, fire blossoming everywhere, secondary explosions touching off as the munitions stored within it were ignited. Another two seconds and all that remained was a cloud of debris—and a hole right through the alien fleet and the planetary defenses.

Tamerlane whooped. "Go!" he cried. "Go!"

The two pilots glanced back at him, grinning, and punched the accelerator.

The comet continued on toward Ahknaton. Just behind it came Tamerlane's little fleet—untouched and undeterred.

"This is going to work!" he shouted to the pilots and to the universe itself. "It's going to work!"

And then the big alien starships behind them seemed suddenly to come awake, all at once. The nearest ones curved down and opened fire, and Tamerlane's fleet began to explode.

3

General Iapetus strode out of the heavily-armored shuttle that had carried him and a battalion of his Sons of Terra down from the *Atlantia*.

Just behind him came a young man clad in the white uniform of the Ecclesiarchy—a soldier-priest of the Empire's religious order, under the direct command of the Ecclesiarch, Teluria. He went by the name of Jasur.

"This had better be worth my time," Iapetus growled as he led the black-clad II Legion soldiers out onto the rocky surface of Tolkar.

"The Lady Teluria assured me that this was something you needed to see, General," Jasur responded, "in person."

They marched a short distance away from the shuttle, passing a small village that was situated just off to their right. Moments later, Jasur led them up to the crest of a low hill. The Ecclesiarchy officer crouched down and leaned out over the edge, peering down. Iapetus moved alongside him, also looking.

At the bottom of the hill, the ground had been ruptured by some sort of impact. A crater, Iapetus recognized immediately. And a red glow shone up from its bottom.

It took Iapetus only a couple of seconds to realize what he was seeing.

"The comets," he whispered. The thought of what he'd encountered before, with Teluria, gripped him, and he had to fight down a very uncharacteristic sense of panic. "One crashed here."

"Yes," Jasur said, his voice low, soft, dreamy.

Iapetus looked at the man in white. His face was blank, slack.

"Dammit!" he cursed. "Back to the shuttle," he barked at his men. "Now!"

The two dozen Sons turned and started back toward their ship, only to discover that a large crowd had interposed itself in the way. It was a group of the local townspeople—at least a couple hundred of them—but something was very definitely wrong with them. They shambled forward as a single mass, eyes wide and faces as slack as that of Jasur. As they drew nearer, Iapetus could see frost had formed all over their bodies, with icicles dangling from their chins and noses. A red glow emanated from their eyes.

"The creatures from the comets," Iapetus whispered to himself. "They're controlling these people somehow. They're psychic."

The wave of townspeople rushed forward, arms outstretched.

Iapetus didn't hesitate. He drew his sidearm and opened fire. The other Sons did likewise. Streaks of coherent light, deadly blobs of superheated plasma, and old-fashioned projectiles tore into the possessed townspeople, shredding their forward ranks. Scarcely noticing this, the people pressed on, surrounding the black-clad little army and assaulting them with superhuman strength. Screams came from a few of the legionaries, though most that died met their fate in stoic silence, as was the way of the Sons of Terra.

LEGION II: SONS OF TERRA

"Cut a path back to the shuttle," Iapetus demanded. "Remember who you are! You are the Sons of Terra!"

The soldiers in black set aside any reservations and opened fire with everything they had. Energy lances, quad rifles, and blast pistols all chewed into the oncoming wave of people and obliterated them. For a few moments the outcome of the battle hung in the balance. Then the Sons gained the advantage and broke free, erupting out of the broad circle of humanity.

"Go!" shouted Iapetus, pointing toward the shuttle. "Clear a path!"

The Sons of Terra fought with the utter, ruthless ferociousness that was their calling card across the galaxy. They slaughtered townspeople by the dozens—by the hundreds. In the process, they died, too. Soon only a half-dozen of them remained alive. Iapetus raced through the tunnel they were effectively creating, at last reaching the shuttle.

The ship was surrounded by another group of zombies. Iapetus had retrieved a blast pistol from a fallen soldier and now he fired away with a gun in each hand, his teeth bared and his dark eyes flashing as he cleared away the final obstacle to reaching the shuttle. Two more of his men went down to his right as he advanced.

The delay was costly. The massive group of townspeople from whom they'd just broken free was now closing in. Iapetus barked commands even as he shot down the last three zombies that barred the way to the shuttle hatch. In response, the four surviving Sons whirled about and took a knee, firing into the approaching wave of humanity.

The hatch opened and Iapetus leapt inside. Another shape moved past him as he tumbled through the entrance. Behind him, the last of the Sons of Terra kept firing, keeping the ship as free as possible of the onslaught of zombies until it could lift off. He mentally saluted them and their sacrifice on his behalf.

The hatch slammed closed. The shuttle blasted into the sky. The last of the Sons on the surface fell to the rampaging attackers, who then stood stock-still, staring up at the ship as it soared up and away. They reached for it, clawed hands pawing after it. Then they all stopped moving and dropped to the ground, like marionettes with their strings all cut at once.

In the sky above them, the shuttle raced for orbit and for the vast *Atlantia* flagship that awaited them.

Iapetus collapsed, exhausted, into a padded seat. Blood ran down the side of his face from a wound suffered when one of the crazed people had clawed at him. He dabbed at it, then remembered seeing someone else boarding the shuttle behind him. He looked up.

Jasur the Ecclesiarchy officer sat in the seat opposite him. His eyes had reverted back to normal and his complexion was flushed. He held a pistol aimed directly at Iapetus.

The general ignored this last bit. He was too angry— though he refused to let it show. "Why exactly did I *need* to see that, Jasur?" he asked, his voice restrained and almost casual in its tone.

"You...you weren't supposed to *survive* it," the man in white replied, frowning. "Now—now, I'm not certain what—"

"Oh, I'm sure your orders are perfectly clear," Iapetus said, interrupting the stammering man. "You're to see that I get myself killed. Failing that, you're to do the deed yourself."

"I—"

"Who exactly are you working for?" Iapetus asked, again in a calm, casual tone. "Do you serve those creatures down there? Are you a traitor to the entire human race?"

Jasur's expression changed instantly to one of shock and horror. "What? No—no, of course not. Not *them*—no! But..."

The man's voice trailed off. Iapetus simply stared at him, trying to figure him.

The hatch from the cockpit area slid open and a trooper in black—a lieutenant by his insignia—entered the cabin. Upon seeing Jasur holding a gun on the general, he reached for his own weapon—but Iapetus waved him back. "No, no, Lieutenant," he said. "This man is no longer a threat to us."

Jasur looked extremely confused now. He blinked his eyes rapidly, looked down at his pistol, then back up at Iapetus. Frowning suddenly, he aimed his gun at the other soldier and pulled the trigger.

Nothing happened.

Iapetus laughed. "You didn't think I'd trust you to have an armed and ready blast pistol on my shuttle with me, did you?" he asked conversationally. "The first thing I did when you came aboard was have your gun remotely disarmed. It will only work now when *I* decide it can work."

Jasur's expression soured further. He set the gun down on the seat beside him and continued to stare at Iapetus.

"You know, this was truly a poor play by your masters," the general said after a few seconds of uncomfortable silence. "Because I think I know who's behind all of this now, and they should have left well enough alone."

Both Jasur and the third man looked at the general, both of them puzzled.

Iapetus laughed. "Your mistress, Teluria, had nearly convinced me that the danger to Earth and the Inner Worlds posed by the comets was sufficient to keep my legion stationed there, and not come to the aid of Tamerlane or anyone else."

"Nearly?" the Ecclesiarchy officer asked, regarding Iapetus through slitted eyes now.

"Nearly." The general smiled. "But because she feels the need to up the ante—to actually arrange my death—now my interest is piqued. Now I know something more is happening." He shrugged. "If she's so determined that I not set foot on Ahknaton, well..." He spread his hands wide before him and smiled again.

Jasur breathed out slowly. Then he reached for something at his belt.

Iapetus only watched as the man drew a small, exotic-looking, rectangular device from its compartment and manipulated a control on its surface. "This is Jasur," he said into it. "I must speak with the Ecclesiarch immediately! I—"

Iapetus drew his own pistol and shot the man, then shot him again. Red blood spread slowly across the snow-white uniform as the Ecclesiarchy agent stared back at him in shock, then crumpled to the floor.

The other soldier in the cabin didn't flinch as his general fired. When it was over, he turned to Iapetus as if nothing out of the ordinary had happened and reported, "We will dock with the *Atlantia* in two minutes, General."

Iapetus nodded. "Thank you, Lieutenant." He gestured vaguely toward Jasur's body where it lay in the floor. "Put this in storage, please. We may need it for evidence later. Or something."

The lieutenant saluted and leaned down, grasping the body by the feet. Quickly he dragged the remains of Jasur through another hatch and into the rear cabin.

Iapetus stared down at the blood stains on the floor of his shuttle and pursed his lips in thought. If Teluria had wanted him dead earlier, she could have easily killed him on the comet—or allowed the creatures there to do the job. Something had changed. The stakes were being raised. Someone behind the scenes was playing a game—a very large and very deadly game—and apparently they had decided they no longer wanted Iapetus and the Sons of Terra in play.

Iapetus chuckled softly.

"You lose on that score," he whispered. "Now you've only made me curious. And angry."

LEGION II: SONS OF TERRA

There came a clanging sound as the shuttle docked with the mothership. Iapetus rose and strode from the cabin, through the hatchway and out into the *Atlantia*. Ranks of black-clad Sons of Terra stood at attention as he emerged.

"Prepare yourselves," he called to them as he strode past. "We have a new objective."

Moments later, the *Atlantia* disappeared into hyperspace.

4

The white-knuckle trip down from orbit to the surface of Ahknaton was a brief event that for Tamerlane seemed to go on and on like some endless, demented nightmare.

As the nearest starships circling the planet—each representing a different alien race or human empire—apparently became aware of his little squadron of transports hiding in the wake of the comet, they came about and opened fire. Almost immediately, in response and without being ordered—for no such order would've been given—transports at the rear of the formation closed in tightly behind the lead vessel. There they absorbed the brunt of the attack. Their shields could scarcely hold up against the massive firepower being directed against them and all too quickly they began to explode.

Aboard the lead transport, Tamerlane stared at the tactical display in consternation. "What's happening?" he demanded of the two pilots. His eyes swept from the monitor to the forward viewport—the massive brown orb of Ahknaton looming, filling the window, with the comet dead center, just ahead—and back to the side-mounted tactical screen that displayed his ships being destroyed behind him. He struggled to comprehend what he was seeing. "We're taking losses?" he asked, dismayed, not wanting to accept it.

"We are, sir," the co-pilot replied, his voice tense. "Terrible losses."

"They've seen us," the pilot added.

"The Sand Kings?"

"The ships in orbit."

The tactical screen now revealed only four *Nizam* Legion transports left, including the one the general occupied. A blinding flash; now three.

Tamerlane cursed. "What's our status?" he demanded. "Can we stand up to—"

The pilot interrupted him. "We're entering the atmosphere," he all-but-shouted. The ship was beginning to vibrate. "It's going to get rougher. Hang on!"

This time Tamerlane was able to grasp the back of one of the pilots' seats just before the man's warning came true, and thus avoid being hurled about the cabin. The little ship rocked violently as it carved its way through the atmosphere of the planet. The pilot was fighting the controls for all he was worth.

"No need to follow the comet all the way down," the pilot shouted over the roar of the hull. "We wouldn't want to be anywhere near the spot where that thing hits."

Tamerlane nodded. "The city," he said. "Take us near the city."

The transport veered off, diverging from the comet's trajectory. One of the two ships behind it peeled off and followed; the other exploded as it was nailed by a broad-spectrum energy blast from high above.

A few moments later the capital city came into view, its glass towers and pyramids gleaming on the horizon. Tamerlane's transport rumbled along like some out-of-control ox, its twin trailing along behind it. Atmospheric friction flames lined the exteriors of both ships as they shed velocity. Blinding energy beams speared down from above, only narrowly missing as the pilots of each ship attempted desperate evasive maneuvers.

Tamerlane accessed the Aether net and attempted to contact Colonel Arani and the *Nizam* Legion survivors. His efforts were met only with static, filling his brain, loud enough to make him claw at his skull before he managed to shut off the link. He cursed. "What in the name of the gods was that?"

The co-pilot looked quickly up at him, eyebrows raised in question.

"The Aether is nothing but static," he said, still recovering. "Just deafening white noise. Nothing else."

The pilots had no explanations.

Tamerlane turned back to the tactical display. The ship shook violently from another near-miss. He cursed again.

"We have to get down or we're dead," he muttered.

"Where to, sir?" the pilot asked, the strain in his voice from fighting the controls belying the innocuous question.

Tamerlane had to make a decision, so he did. "Over the city," he said, pointing.

The two pilots gaped. "Wha—?"

"Take us over the city. Now!"

Acknowledging the order without further reaction, the pilot banked hard and curved them around again, angling down. The other remaining ship, flying along just behind them, was struck by another shot from above and spouted flame. It listed to starboard, lost control entirely, and hit the ground in a tumbling, disintegrating, fiery crash.

Tamerlane watched the exploding ship's dot on the tactical display wink out. He grunted.

"It's just us," the pilot stated, not looking up from the controls. "We're the only target they have left."

"Then let's hope I'm right."

The pilot glanced at him quizzically but said nothing.

The transport was nearly to the city. Tamerlane watched the glass towers and steel pyramids grow larger and larger ahead of them even as two massive shots barely missed them from above. And then they were over the city, and the shooting stopped.

"Ah. They won't shoot while they risk hitting the city, it looks like," said the pilot.

Sure enough, the wide-angle display revealed the lone major warship that had been pursuing them and that had destroyed most of the rest of their squadron was now leveling off, holding its general position, possibly waiting for a clear shot again.

"Where to, sir?" the co-pilot asked.

"I—don't know," Tamerlane admitted. He realized then that he had no choice; there was no other way to locate Colonel Arani. Scowling, he inhaled deeply, exhaled slowly, and nodded to the pilot. "Give me one minute," he said, "and I'll try to find out."

Gritting his teeth, Tamerlane closed his eyes and mentally reopened the Aether link. The wall of shrieking static that erupted nearly blew the top off his head; certainly it felt as if it had, at any rate.

He staggered back a step, almost fell, stuck out a hand blindly and caught himself on a bulkhead. The noise was undiminished. He sank down into a squatting position, eyes still closed, and attempted to gather himself. The co-pilot, seeing his distress, leapt to his feet and started over, but Tamerlane recovered his senses enough to wave the man back. With the greatest of effort, he managed to pull himself up to his feet again and somehow force the waves of raw noise down, out of his consciousness. Slowly, so slowly, millisecond by millisecond, the excruciating pain receded.

"The ground defenses have seen us," the pilot announced almost matter-of-factly. "Surface guns are locking on to us."

Tamerlane continued to calm his mind, visualizing the static as a bundle of threads, excluding each wave of sound thread by thread. At last there was only a single, faint tone coming through. Not noise—a signal. He seized upon it, examined it, recognized it.

Arani.

"General," the pilot said, "we are taking ground fire."

"Get us out of here," Tamerlane barked, now himself again. Quickly he located the general position of the source of the signal. He pointed at a spot on the tactical display. "There. Take us that way."

The pilot looked, nodded. "Aye, sir."

The transport swung around.

Arani, we are coming. Don't shoot. And, if that's you, give me some kind of signal.

The ship curved down toward the sandy hills just beyond the city. As they dropped, they could just make out a lone figure waving a quick-pulse light.

"There she is," Tamerlane almost shouted, pointing. "Take us—"

At that moment the ground fire found their range. Energy bolts pounded the vessel, rupturing the hull and slicing off half the rear engine. The transport dropped.

"Brace for impact!" called the pilot over the intercom to the passenger cabin. This time the warning came too late for Tamerlane. He stumbled backwards again as the floor dropped away and then caught him again. As the ship stabilized one final time, for just an instant, he took the opportunity to lie flat on the cabin floor and loop his left arm around a metal strut that supported one of the pilots' seats. That probably saved his life.

The transport was already low before the blazing shots chewed into it. Only a scant two seconds later it hit the ground, sliding, skidding, somehow managing not to tumble end over end as the pilots wrestled the controls for all they were worth. After what felt like eternity to everyone aboard, it came to a halt at the base of the low line of hills they had seen from over the city.

LEGION II: SONS OF TERRA

The pilots had had an easier time of it than Tamerlane. They unfastened themselves from their seats' crash webbing and stood, saw the general lying dazed against the bulkhead, and hurried over to him.

"I'm alright," Tamerlane said, wiping a streak of blood across his forehead from a shallow cut. "Just some bruises." He gave the two men a smile. "You two need to work on your landings."

The two pilots blinked and then laughed simultaneously. It didn't last long; all three men were up and moving a second later, hurrying into the passenger cabin.

"General!" Titus Elaro called, turning from where he was helping another of the soldiers disengage his seatbelt and harness. "What happened?"

"We got shot down," Tamerlane growled. "And now we need to get out of here before the Sand Kings come looking for their prize."

The last survivors of the mission clambered out the emergency exit hatch. They constituted a motley collection of dark-red-uniformed Lords of Fire troopers that had originally flown in aboard the transports, alongside khaki-clad *Nizam* Legion soldiers who had made it back from the earlier failed assault. Tamerlane and the two pilots followed them out.

As soon as their boots touched the rough, sandy surface of Ahknaton, they realized they were not alone. A squad of dusty, dirty, well-armed soldiers who didn't look terribly happy were standing there, weapons at the ready. Their faces were covered with makeshift masks, either to hide their identities or, more likely, to filter out some of the cloying dust that filled the air after their ship had come crashing down.

It took a second before Tamerlane recognized the underlying khaki of their damaged uniforms. When he did, he relaxed a bit and smiled. "Very happy to see you all again," he said.

The *Nizam* Legion's refugees recognized him and lowered their weapons. "General!" a couple of them shouted. One added, "Welcome to Ahknaton!"

"Not sure how welcome I actually feel," Tamerlane muttered under his breath. He started to turn and address the men behind him, when suddenly someone practically shoved past him. He looked up and saw that it was Elaro.

"Where is Arani?" the big man demanded. He grasped the nearest soldier and pulled him closer. "Where is the Colonel? Is she alright?"

"I'm right here, Major," came a feminine voice from just ahead. "And I'm fine."

The dusty ranks of khaki parted and Colonel Niobe Arani pushed through, followed closely by Inquisitor Delain.

Elaro reached out and grasped her in a bear hug, actually lifting her a few inches off the ground in the process. The others looked on and some offered a lewd comment or a wolf whistle. Arani started to protest but then gave in halfway through and just went with it.

Tamerlane moved forward and gave Arani a hug, too—albeit a much more restrained one. Somehow, despite the appalling losses they'd both suffered, seeing her alive—and Delain, too, of course—made things ever so slightly better. As he separated from Arani he gave the young Inquisition woman a wink, perversely enjoying the raised eyebrow and overall look of bemusement this produced on her face.

"We don't have much time," Tamerlane said once the greetings were done. "They'll be coming out here to check on their prize. We have to move."

Arani nodded. "How many more ships are left?" she asked. "Where are they?"

Tamerlane's expression was grim. He shook his head.

"All gone?" The colonel stared back at him, blinked, looked off into the distance. "I can't believe it," she said.

Tamerlane nodded. "We've made a lot of sacrifices to get here," he said bitterly. "To get this far." He ran his hand back through his dark hair; bits of gray had begun to appear there in recent weeks. "We have my flame power, and our combined forces, but..." He shook his head. "I just don't see how we have enough manpower or firepower left to do any damage at all to Rameses."

"If it's manpower—and firepower—you need, General," game a familiar, deep voice from behind him, "then look no further."

Tamerlane whirled. Elaro drew his pistol, ready.

From around the other side of the transport strode General Arnem Agrippa, his white and green plate armor scuffed and smudged and a battered quad rifle strapped over one shoulder. He saluted and flashed a wicked grin. Behind him came the rest of the Bravo Squad, similarly armed and attired. The tops of two hovertanks could just be seen in a depression beyond the nearest hills.

"Oh, yes," Arani laughed as she addressed Tamerlane. "I neglected to report—General Agrippa arrived just before you did."

Tamerlane restrained himself from wrapping the big man in a bear hug—or at least attempting to. He grinned back and extended a hand, clasping Agrippa's warmly. "So— you made it," he said to the blond man. "From...*wherever* you've been."

Agrippa snorted a laugh. "Honestly, General, I have no idea where we've been, or how we got here, beyond just walking through a whole lot of lights and clouds." He chuckled. "But it worked, so I'm not knocking it."

Still smiling, Tamerlane nodded. "I take it you experienced the same problem with the Aether we did."

"If by 'problem' you mean deafening, skull-splitting white noise, then yes," Agrippa replied. Arani nodded as well.

"This is problematic," Tamerlane said. He paused and bit his lip for a moment, thinking. "Then again," he said, "if we play it correctly, it could also be very useful."

Agrippa brightened. "You're assuming our enemies can't communicate, either," he laughed.

"Precisely." Tamerlane cast his gaze across the soldiers gathered there, doing a quick estimate of their force size. Barely over sixty, all told. Not overwhelming numbers. But, he reminded himself, with certain distinct advantages, including Agrippa's men with their armor and their tanks, his own powers and whatever Delain could now do, the highly trained I Legion specialists he'd brought, and the skills of Arani's *Nizam* troops... It wasn't as entirely hopeless as he'd first feared.

"The first thing we need to do," he told the soldiers as they gathered around, "is move. Right now we're sitting ducks. Rameses will surely dispatch ground troops to look the wreckage of our ship over."

"You would think so, General," Arani said, "but actually, I suspect something has their whole army distracted."

Tamerlane frowned at her. "Distracted? What do you mean?"

She shrugged. "I'm not really sure, sir," she said, "but they withdrew back into the city right after pulling that first ambush on us. They never followed up to be sure they'd gotten us all."

"I'm glad to hear they're so incompetent," Elaro interjected with a grin.

"They aren't," Tamerlane stated firmly. "Not normally."

"And then," Arani continued, "from the time we took up this position, we haven't seen much in the way of patrols at all. I don't know what's happening inside the Heliopolis, but *something* is, and it surely seems to have everyone's attention in there."

Tamerlane nodded. "Nevertheless," he said, "we don't want to take any reckless chances. We have this one transport still intact. We can probably fit everyone aboard and launch an attack by—"

"An attack?" Arani asked, surprised. "You still want to attack the Heliopolis? Sir?"

Tamerlane started to answer angrily, then caught himself. "Colonel," he said after a moment's pause and calming himself, "the situation across the Empire is grim. There may be no one left to offer us reinforcements, and we may not be able to penetrate this far into Rameses' defenses again." He turned to gaze across the short distance to the walls of the Heliopolis. "We have to seize the opportunity while we can."

"Agreed," boomed Agrippa. "Also, note that we have few other options at the moment." He gestured toward the crashed transport craft.

Tamerlane nodded grimly. "That's true. Each of the avenues our three groups took to get here is now closed. And with the Aether jammed, we can't even call for help."

"We need none!" Agrippa patted his quad-rifle as the servos within his Deising-Arry Mark V armor whined. "We will hit them hard and fast and decapitate the leadership before they know what's happening. After that, the Sand Kings will surely collapse, leaderless." He shrugged. "I daresay a small, efficient strike team can succeed where a larger force would fail."

Arani reluctantly nodded.

Tamerlane smiled at his big blond friend. "You give us all hope, Arnem. Thank you." He turned to Arani. "Colonel, if you would have your troops—"

Lights flared across their location. At the same instant the sentries outside cried out and then were silenced. The whine of a turbolaser washed over the little camp.

"They are here!" came the shouted voice of one of Arani's sentries. "The Sand Kings are upon us!"

5

The meeting broke up instantly, with everyone dashing for cover. Tamerlane positioned himself behind a low patch of brush and stuck his head up very briefly, just long enough to get the lay of the land.

Soldiers—a dozen, at least, in ornamental, Egyptian-style armor of red and blue enamel over gold metallic sheen— were advancing on their position, coming up the hill. Apparently they'd taken a more circuitous route and avoided the gaze of Arani's sentries until they were directly upon them. They were carrying energy lances and void swords along with their standard, snub-nosed blast rifles. As they climbed the sandy hill they opened fire again, murderous blasts streaking past the *Nizam*, I and III Legion positions all around.

"They're coming!" cried someone from the ranks of Arani's soldiers, stating the all-too-obvious.

Arani cursed quietly. Her hopes had not come true: Rameses' forces were moving in to investigate the downed ship, and she and the others had been caught, sitting ducks. She turned to face her troops and issue orders, only to hear a wordless cry of fury just behind her. She spun back around just in time to see a Sand King in desert-camouflage smartcloth cresting the hill and swinging a deadly, curved void sword at her. The shimmering blade tore through the air with an unearthly wail, only to stop in its arc suddenly as a blast caught the warrior in the shoulder and spun him backwards, dropping him to the sand.

Arani, her pistol in hand, rose up to engage with the wounded enemy, but another Sand King moved in almost instantly, his own gun in hand, aiming.

A shape moved past her then and she realized it was the person who had shot the first attacker. Titus Elaro brought his energy rifle up and blasted a shot at the second enemy, but missed as the man dodged. A split-second later they were clashing hand-to-hand, Elaro wielding a short, straight, broad-bladed knife and the Sand King striking back with a wicked, long, curved dagger. The Egyptian-styled soldier drew first blood, the tip of his weapon nicking across Elaro's face. Then, as Arani looked on in surprise and wonder, Elaro executed a series of moves she had never seen before, culminating with a finishing blow that almost eviscerated the enemy.

Where did he learn that? she wondered. *Certainly not in my camp...*

Arani fired a shot past Elaro at a third enemy soldier who was approaching through the sand. The big man nodded at her and grinned, even as blood dripped down the side of his face.

Who is this man? Arani wondered, not for the first time since meeting him. *Why does he fascinate me so—and give me such pause for concern, too?*

At the same moment Elaro was battling the Sand King, Tamerlane turned to address Agrippa, but the big blond man wasn't there. Suddenly a whoosh of air, carrying with it the force of a small hurricane, nearly knocked him over. Looking up, he saw one of the hovertanks cruising by, its gun turret already swiveling around to face forward.

Agrippa stood atop its forward deck like some Viking prince at the bow of his ship. He called down to Tamerlane as he went by, "We are jamming all radio frequencies! If the Aether is still blocked—"

The rest of his words were drowned out by the roar of the tank' engines, but the general got the message. There was a chance this Sand Kings patrol had not been able to report their presence to their superiors. The element of surprise might still exist for Tamerlane and his expedition.

The Sand Kings formation, a moment earlier advancing confidently up the hill, now came apart at the seams as Agrippa's tank opened fire with its anti-personnel cannon, the smaller barrel situated to one side of the main gun. Rapid-fire, high-energy blasts cut the Sand Kings down where they stood. Those few who somehow managed to avoid the initial assault suddenly found themselves face to face with a huge, white-armored warrior bearing a heavy quad-rifle with one arm and wielding a short, broad-bladed gladius in the other hand. Agrippa roared and fired and swung his sword and the soldiers of Rameses, shocked to the core, fell before him like wheat before the scythe, most of them dying where they stood before they could even think to retreat.

Tamerlane couldn't let Agrippa have all the glory. He spotted two enemy soldiers running back down the hill, likely toward their hidden transport. If he was guessing correctly, they'd realized they had no Aether or radio comm connection and were hurrying back to the Heliopolis to report the armed intruders in person.

Can't allow that, Tamerlane thought.

Raising his arms, the General summoned up the fires of the Above that he now commanded and unleashed a stream of flame that arced overhead, curved down the hillside, and struck the two Sand Kings, surrounding and washing over them. Their uniforms combusted, as did their armaments a second later. Frantically the two men flung their superheated weapons away—the energy lances promptly exploded— and tore at their uniforms, rolling in the sand to put out the fires. By the time they managed to snuff out the flames, Arani's *Nizam* soldiers were upon them.

The fight was over scarcely seconds after it had begun.

"If that's the best the mighty Rameses can offer," Agrippa chuckled, "my estimation of our chances has increased."

"Let's not get carried away," Arani noted as her soldiers finished binding the arms of the two surviving Sand Kings. "That was just a patrol—not the palace guard."

"Very true, Colonel," Tamerlane said grimly. He motioned for the troops to gather around. "Nevertheless, I believe we stand a good chance if we strike hard and fast."

"When?" asked Elaro, blood still trickling from the wound across his forehead.

"There's no time like the present," Agrippa said with a grin.

"I wholeheartedly agree," Tamerlane said. "And I know what I can expect from each of you men and women." He turned to Delain where she stood silently off to the side, her black hood nearly obscuring her face. "Sister," he said, giving her a respectful nod, "what I don't fully know yet is what I can expect from *you*."

Delain raised an eyebrow. "The Grand Inquisitor has assured you that my loyalty—"

"No, no," Tamerlane interrupted, holding up a hand. "That's not precisely what I mean," he said. "I know we can count on you. What I don't know is what we can count on you to be able to *do*."

The black-clad woman gazed back at him, not understanding.

"For instance," the general went on, "I know you possess knowledge of all Imperial holdings. I assume that includes Rameses' Heliopolis complex."

Delain nodded once.

"Excellent." He paused. "I also assume you, like the Grand Inquisitor, gained some sort of extra-normal ability during our journey through the Above and the Below. But, in your case, I've never learned what that is." He smiled. "Now would be a good time to address that."

"Ah." The black-clad woman stared back at him for a long moment. Then she reached up and drew back her hood, exposing her delicate features, her red lips, and her long, black hair. She appeared to consider her response for a second. Then, "Your assumption is correct, General," she said. "In fact, I do believe I have been and can continue to be of great service to this mission. Because, as it turns out, my abilities tend toward obscuring from detection."

"Obscuring—?" Tamerlane absorbed this. He blinked. "You mean..." He paused, thought it through, and started over. "You mean you have the power to keep us hidden from—"

"Hidden from Rameses' scanners, sensors, and the like," she completed for him. "Yes. I have been doing so since we arrived. It seemed a wise course of action."

"*That's* why we haven't been crawling with Sand Kings from the moment we landed," Agrippa noted, his eyes widening as he gazed at Delain. "Well done, Sister."

"What about the attack we just faced, though?" Arani interjected. "Why were they able to spot us?"

"I assume they were simply a patrol that happened upon us," Delain replied. "I cannot make us completely invisible to soldiers who are standing only a short distance away and looking directly at us. But I can—"

The air around them became electric, a pressure wave expanding outward from a point nearby and nearly knocking everyone over. Sister Delain's statement would remain unfinished, for at that moment the fabric of reality split open and the swirling mouth of a dimensional portal opened a mere dozen meters from where most of them stood.

LEGION II: SONS OF TERRA

Weapons were raised, cover was taken. Such actions would not prove to be necessary. For only a lone figure—a woman clad in luminous white robes—stumbled out of the churning eye of the dimensional storm. She fell to all fours on the sand and the portal snapped closed behind her, disappearing as if it had never been there.

Tamerlane and Agrippa rushed forward and helped the woman back to her feet. Everyone stared at her, attempting to discern exactly who she was. Her hair was so light as to be almost white; her robes were diaphanous, floating about her in a seemingly weightless fashion. Her lips were pale, her skin porcelain. No one recognized her.

The woman looked around, her bright, sparkling eyes practically shimmering. They radiated an otherworldly energy, as if they were almost entities unto themselves. First they fell upon Tamerlane. "Yes," she whispered, "yes, I have found you. There is still hope."

The general had no idea what to make of this. "Who are you?" he asked, his voice as kind as he could make it, given the stressful circumstances. "Where did you come from?"

Her eyes continued to move across the others, those scattered survivors of the Lords of Fire, the Kings of Oblivion, and Tamerlane's secret *Nizam* Legion. "No sons of Mother Earth," she whispered. "I have come in time." She laughed a humorless laugh at that. *"In time!"*

"What are you talking about?" Tamerlane asked, attempting to hold his voice level and even.

"They will be upon you soon," she whispered, her eyes moving from Tamerlane to Arani and back. "But they are not the main threat." She laughed again. "Oh, far from it!"

"Speak sensibly, woman," boomed an increasingly impatient Agrippa.

The figure in white whirled and stared directly at the big blond general. She gasped. "You!" She stumbled back a step, nearly falling, and Tamerlane had to grasp her by the shoulders to catch her and help her stand. Then, straightening, pulling away, she moved a step closer to Agrippa, her eyes narrowing as she stared directly at him. "No—not yet. Not yet. But soon."

"What is this nonsense?" Agrippa demanded, scowling.

"Your destiny," she muttered. "So great. And so *dark*."

The big man was perplexed. He turned to the other general. "What is she talking about, Ezekial?"

His focus remaining on the woman, Tamerlane shook his head. "I don't know. But we don't have time for all this." He leaned in closer. "We're going to need you to be a little more plain-spoken," he said. "And we'll need that *now*."

"Yes, yes—of course," the woman in white replied. She paused, as if gathering her wits, and then gave Tamerlane her full attention as she spoke. "I have sought you out because only *you* can help me. We have an enormous task before us, but I believe I have arrived here in time that it can still be accomplished."

Tamerlane nodded slowly. "I...*see*." He stroked his chin, glancing back at Agrippa. The big man appeared extremely dubious. Then, "And what task would this be? Because, you see, we are already in the middle of a critical mission, and the longer we delay—"

"Your mission is important to you, yes," the woman said. "But, in the grand scheme of things, it is trivial. It pales in importance compared to what I have come to do. The danger you face is almost insignificant compared to what I must warn you of."

"Well," Tamerlane exclaimed. "You certainly paint a grim picture. What is this monumental danger we face?"

"I'll bet it involves the comets," Agrippa growled. "But we already know about them."

The woman laughed sharply. "The Phaedrons are terrible indeed," she said, "but they are merely a symptom of the larger problem."

The others all exchanged glances. *She knows about the Phaedrons*, they all seemed to be thinking at once. Her credibility increased ever so slightly with that.

"Then tell us," Tamerlane said. "Tell us what danger we face, that makes everything else seem so insignificant."

"I have come," the woman said, "to make one last-ditch effort, before it is too late. I have come to try to prevent the Shattering."

Tamerlane frowned. "The shattering?" he asked. "The shattering of *what*?"

"The shattering of the galaxy itself," the woman in white replied.

Karsis Station, located in high orbit above Chronos, was not the newest outpost in the Empire, nor was it updated with the most technological innovations as were some of the stations closer to the Inner Worlds. It couldn't boast the most powerful armaments or the most sophisticated tracking and detection systems. Truth be told, it even smelled pretty bad inside; it contained the musty air of a thousand inhabitants who had come and gone over the years, their various odors remaining behind, seemingly permeating the very walls and floors and ceilings of the crew space.

No, it wasn't the most glamorous or even pleasant posting for an officer of the III Legion. Nevertheless, Lt. Elizabeth McClure considered it home—it had been her home for some three months now, standard time, and would be for another twenty-one at minimum—and she had therefore resolved to embrace it and to try to think the best of it for as long as she was stuck inside it.

Little did she know how brief that time would turn out to be.

LEGION II: SONS OF TERRA

Out of all the glaring and visibly obvious deficiencies of the station, the one that would cost it and its crew the most was its outdated detection sensors. Had Karsis been outfitted with the latest units coming out of the fabrication stations over Tolkar, there might have been at least some sort of advance warning. Alas, no warning came, for those who needed to know, didn't know, and those who knew, didn't tell.

And so it was that the blood-red comets streaking in from outside the galactic plane dropped out of hyperspace and entered the Chronos system with hardly anyone noticing them at first. By the time they did, it was far too late.

As the comets closed in on Chronos they slowed, but not by very much at first. Three massive Imperial battlecruisers of the I Legion that rested at high anchorage were first to go, obliterated as the comets struck them like slugs fired from a sniper's rifle. The huge spaceships ruptured and spewed fire, atmosphere and crew into space as their hulls cracked and split, the several huge pieces that remained tumbling slowly away, either toward the planet's surface—there to do great harm as well—or off into the endless night.

Standing at an observation port to see these reported comets for herself, Lt. Elizabeth McClure gasped in shock and growing horror as the carnage played itself out before her. The three ships continued to erupt as their fuel and power cells combusted, one after the other, followed by their ammunition stores. The comets that had struck them continued on toward the planet, visibly slowing now, entering the atmosphere of Chronos with descent angles that looked more like spacecraft coming in for a landing than meteors crashing to the ground.

That in itself was a vital clue, and another that those who looked on missed entirely.

McClure stood there, rooted to the spot, and continued to watch as wave after wave of comets shot past, all on a direct course for the planet.

Within a short time, reports began to come in over Karsis Station's comm links that the comets were reaching the surface of Chronos, but many of them weren't behaving as ordinary astronomical bodies should behave when striking a planetary surface—that is to say, not all of them were obliterating themselves while blowing out vast craters and causing shockwaves that wiped out life and property for miles in every direction. Instead, the reports went, some were somehow drastically slowing as they fell, hitting the ground hard but not dangerously hard—and they were opening.

McClure turned up the volume and listened more carefully, but what she heard was not clear at all.

The reports grew garbled and uncertain then, filled with what sounded more like the hallucinations of the insane than actual, dependable, factual information. The people on the surface of Chronos—reports were coming in from both military and civilian observers—indicated waves of cold and ice radiating out from the landed comets, and strange creatures emerging. Without exception, the voices of the reporters became filled with horror, then transformed to babbling incoherence.

At that point, the reports all abruptly ended.

McClure recoiled and whirled about, suddenly afraid to look out the viewport of the station any longer. Explosions had been blossoming across the surface of the planet. Based on what she had heard, she felt more concern for the people in the areas not hit by the actual exploding comets. Whatever was coming out of the ones that landed sounded infinitely worse than mere instantaneous annihilation.

Lt. McClure resolved to go to the command deck of the station and ask the commander his opinion on all of this. She looked back out the viewport one last time, seeing the surface of Chronos mottled by impact craters and explosions, and then turned and ran for the lift.

LEGION II: SONS OF TERRA

She had made it halfway there when the comet smashed through Karsis Station and utterly obliterated it.

7

haos and death?" Governor Amon Rameses blurted, staggering back. "Are you *mad*?"

"Mad?" Goraddon gazed at him with amused disdain. He appeared to have grown far larger than his previous, human form; his presence virtually filled the vast throne room of the Heliopolis palace. "Mad?" he repeated. "I am not mad. I am a *god!*"

Rameses looked from the man in black to Zahir and back. "What—why—" he stammered. For his part, he seemed to have shrunk down to a shell of his former self. "Why my world?" he finally blurted, his voice small and pathetic. "Why me? Why *here*?"

"You possessed all the things I required," Goraddon replied. "A world. A legion of your own. And ambition— rebellious, burning ambition—that I could shape and mold as I desired." He smiled down at Rameses as an adult to a precocious child. "And so I nurtured you, just as I did the Emperor, to become my willing instrument in this universe." He reached out, his hand touching the governor's face, stroking it. "And you have served me well, Rameses." His expression hardened. "Until now."

Rameses blanched. He drew back, shaking his head, the honeyed words of the man in black crumbling within his mind as he reasserted his own will again. "No," he cried. "Stop it! Get out of my head!"

Zahir started toward the governor, his expression wrathful, but the man in black stopped him with a word. "No," he said. And as Zahir turned back to his master, surprise on his face, Goraddon motioned for him to move to one side. "No more violence here," the dark man said. "It is unnecessary. The Governor will come around. He will understand."

"Never!" Rameses cried. He ran to his Sand Kings guards where they stood in perfectly aligned ranks along one side of the throne room and shouted for them to go into action against the intruder and his lackey. Not a one of them moved a muscle.

"I'm afraid your soldiers are not so strong-willed as you are," Goraddon told him after the governor had run from one statue-like Sand King to the next, failing to persuade any of them to move—or even blink. "They all fully understand our cause, and are fully committed."

"They understand nothing! They are brainwashed," Rameses shouted. "You've taken control of their minds!"

Goraddon shrugged. "It amounts to the same thing," he said. He turned his attention momentarily to the ranks of soldiers, and in particular noted the six most elaborately-uniformed ceremonial guardsmen clad in gleaming gold accented with deep red and blue. "You six—stay," he ordered. "The rest of you—out of here. Await further orders. *Go!*"

"You cannot order my men around as if they—" Rameses' voice trailed off as the ranks of Sand Kings soldiers turned as one and marched out of the throne room, closing the huge double-doors behind them. The six ceremonial guardsmen remained standing, trancelike, at attention.

Rameses cursed. He cast his gaze about the chamber frantically, looking for anything that might help him. He saw the golden basin and thought of what he had endured while being wired into it these last few days. "I am a god, myself," he shouted. "Or very nearly so. Perhaps you didn't know—Zahir has been giving me treatments in order to—"

"You are an insect," Goraddon replied, seemingly amused by the entire performance. "Acting under my orders, Zahir has made you into a slightly more formidable insect, that you might wear the armor and bear the Sword as a soldier in our army, protecting the demon lord until he has fully formed and the princess has secured the throne."

"The armor!" Rameses blurted, ignoring the rest. He saw it then: the red cube, resting where he had set it earlier, atop a granite pedestal. He ran for it, snatched it up, held it out before him. No one made any move to stop him. Goraddon even smiled faintly.

Rameses closed his eyes and concentrated. The crimson light flared brightly. When it receded, he was again clad in the gleaming, not-quite-metal, seamless armor of the ancients. Artificial muscles bulging, he strode forward, confidence growing as he glared at Goraddon and Zahir.

"I want the two of you off my planet," he shouted, his face almost as red as the armor. "And I want you off it now!"

Goraddon's smile widened. "Excellent," he whispered. "At last you are ready to perform your remaining tasks for me— to fulfill your final destiny."

Rameses blinked at this. He scowled, starting to protest. He never got the chance.

Goraddon, his eyes burning with an eerie, internal fire, raised his left hand and snapped his fingers. Rameses, staring back into those eyes, stopped in his tracks. His arms slumped to his sides and his eyes glazed over.

Zahir glided forward and walked in a slow circle around Rameses, inspecting him carefully. "He is yours again, master," the vizier reported with a grin.

"Of course." The man in black moved closer to the governor. Clasping his hands behind his back, he leaned in. "Rameses—do you hear me?"

"I—yes," the governor replied, his expression impassive, his eyes unfocused.

Goraddon nodded. "Good. I have allowed you some small measure of free will beyond mindlessly obeying my orders." He tapped the side of the governor's skull. "There is still a tiny bit of Rameses inside there." He chuckled softly. "I don't dare trust you with much more than that. You have proven to be more difficult to control than I expected."

The man in the crimson armor continued to gaze straight ahead. His only response was a slight gurgling sound.

"Still," Goraddon said, turning away from him and toward Zahir, "that should be more than enough for what remains to be done." He stepped back, sweeping his eyes around the vast throne room, spotting the large screen off to one side that displayed the waves of starships in high orbit above the planet. "Listen to me carefully, Rameses, for my time here grows short. I have other duties to tend to before the game is complete." He snapped his fingers again.

Rameses coughed, blinked his eyes, and seemed almost to come back to himself again. He turned and saw the ships on the monitor.

"Your forces were never adequate to legitimately challenge both Tamerlane's and Agrippa's legions," the man in black explained. "You needed help, and I have given it to you." He continued to watch the fleets of ships flash past on the monitor. "Your Sand Kings were no match for two full legions plus Tamerlane's secret '*Nizam*' army," he said. "And so I took steps to see that at least one of those was utterly destroyed. To see that they were led directly into my trap."

"*Your*...trap?" Rameses continued to stare at the man, but his expression was slowly dissolving from robotic apathy to puzzlement.

"Yes, of course *my* trap," Goraddon barked. "I had Teluria lead them here, and I ordered your forces to set up the ambush that killed them." He smiled. "Meanwhile, I...*persuaded*...the crews of all the ships you see above Ahknaton now to come here—to serve in my cause. They have swarmed like flies about me for all the long journey here. They come from a hundred different worlds, but they all serve *me* now. Now—and for a little longer."

"Because the endgame is beginning, is it not, master?" asked Zahir, gleeful.

"Indeed," Goraddon stated. "With Tamerlane's secret legion wiped out and with these new ships here to assist Rameses, the two sides are in balance at last. The carnage, the destruction, will be utter and complete."

"What—" Rameses choked out. "What—of—"

Goraddon frowned and moved closer. "Yes?"

"What—of—Iapetus?"

Now the man in black laughed long and deeply. "Ah. The Sons of Terra." He shook his head in mock sadness. "I'm afraid the II Legion is pinned down on Holy Earth—" he pronounced those last two words with profound scorn and sarcasm—"and the other Inner Worlds by the threat of the comets—and our friends who ride inside. They have been quite effectively removed from the board, until such a time as other matters are settled and I am ready to turn my attention to them."

Rameses appeared to comprehend all of this. His eyes almost looked normal again, and his movements were growing less robotic.

"And now," Goraddon said, "I am needed elsewhere." He turned to Zahir. "Events are coming to a head. The pieces are being set up for the endgame. Victory is assured." He leered at Zahir and at Rameses, and his next words were spoken very, very softly. "The victory of chaos and death."

Zahir bowed deeply. Rameses coughed and blinked, as if fully waking up from a deep sleep.

"Wait, master," the vizier said suddenly. "What of—the *artifact*? Was it not your intention that our black king—" here he nodded toward Rameses— "should have it in his possession for the final confrontation?"

Goraddon looked back at the pale, slender man and laughed. "Oh, he will have it—fear not, my servant."

"But—?"

The man in black shook his head. "You must learn to have more faith, Zahir." He chuckled. "You will see. In short order, the great and mighty *Taiko* himself will hand the sword over to you—or, rather, to the dark king."

Wide-eyed, Zahir bowed again. "It will undoubtedly be as you say, master."

"Undoubtedly." Goraddon raised his left hand and, a short distance away across the throne room, the fountain erupting from the golden basin expanded into a coruscating, cascading sphere of shimmering light. Hovering at its center, vertically, a black circle formed; a null, blank, dead space that just as well could have been the doorway into Hell.

"You know what to do, Zahir," he said as he walked past the vizier and toward the swirling portal he had opened. "Do not fail me."

"You know that I will not, master."

Goraddon chuckled. "I know that if you do, you will suffer unending, unimaginable tortures."

Zahir blanched, his pale flesh growing even whiter. He bowed again, lower.

The man in black stepped through the dark circle and he, along with the circle itself, vanished. The fountain returned to its usual gentle tinkling.

Zahir turned to the governor. "So now you understand," he said—and it was not a question. "Now you see that each of us is but a pawn in our lord's great game. The game of chaos and galactic entropy!"

His muscles returning to his control now, Rameses coughed again and then looked away from the other man, staring instead down at the streaked marble floor. "I care nothing for your master's game, though I am now compelled to help see it through," he managed to croak through dry lips from a dryer throat. "But he has indeed left me some small measure of myself—my own free will— within this body. I will do as he commands, but I will also do as I desire." He looked up, his gaze settling on the monitor that displayed wave upon wave of starships circling Ahknaton. "If the end of everything has truly come— the end of my ambitions, of my world, and of the human race itself—I will gladly take my revenge upon Iapetus and Tamerlane and all the others along the way."

"The master will have no objections to that, Governor."

"Good." Rameses turned to look at the vizier then, his wild eyes burning, his features warped and distorted as he crowed, "I will see them all dead—all of them, you understand?" He scowled, turning to look at the demonic figure that was now descending slowly—oh so slowly— toward the unconscious body of the princess. He found that the sight no longer disturbed him in the least. "And afterward?" he asked. "I care not." He waved a dismissive, armored hand. "Let it all burn, Zahir. Let the galaxy burn around me!"

His right hand held up before him, the flames that crackled over his fingertips providing what little illumination his group possessed, Ezekial Tamerlane led the way along the narrow, winding, secret passage beneath the outer walls of the Heliopolis complex. Behind him came Sister Delain of the Holy Inquisition, her hands open and outstretched at her sides as she channeled her new powers to blanket the team from any electronic detection. Following Delain were Colonel Arani and Major Elaro, marching along in the midst of what remained of their troops; with Agrippa and his Bravo Squad gone, the number was now down to only three dozen.

"We're going to regret letting Agrippa and the Kings of Oblivion go," Arani was saying quietly to anyone who could hear and cared to listen.

"Going to?" Elaro whispered. "I already *do*."

"It's ridiculous," Arani went on. "How could they trust her? How could they let her take away the most powerful component of what we had left here—just before our assault?"

Elaro merely shook his head.

"I can hear you, Colonel," Tamerlane called softly back to her. "Just so you know. The acoustics are quite remarkable in here."

Arani reddened. "My apologies, sir," she whispered.

"Not necessary," Tamerlane replied. "I value your input, of course. But I know what I'm doing."

"Of course, sir."

As the team pressed on, following the hidden course Delain had suggested, Tamerlane felt a pang of nerves. *At least, I hope I know what I'm doing. Otherwise, this is all going to end rather badly, and for all of us...*

A short time earlier, Tamerlane, Agrippa, and the others had stood in a semicircle around the woman in white, struggling to understand who she was—and what she wanted with them.

"Perhaps if we started over," Tamerlane said. As the woman turned to face him—she still seemed somewhat distracted by and preoccupied with Agrippa—he asked, "What is your name?"

She seemed taken aback by the question, and appeared to have to consider it for a moment. At length she announced, "Aurore. My name is Aurore."

"You're sure?" Tamerlane asked. "Because you don't *seem* sure."

The woman smiled. Even in her disheveled state, she appeared radiant. "It has been a very long time since anyone has used it," she said. "I'd almost forgotten."

"Aurore?" Colonel Arani looked extremely dubious. "And you just happen to be named after one of the goddesses—"

"Named after?" The woman looked confused. "I assure you, I am the only one."

"You? *You* are Aurore?" Agrippa scoffed. "Aurore was one of the goddesses who were murdered. Everyone who keeps the old gods remembers this."

"No," the woman said, shaking her head. "No, I survived those terrible events."

"How?" the big man demanded, leaning in. "Seventy-five gods slain, and we are to believe you somehow survived?"

"Normally I wouldn't care what you believed," she snapped. "But—" She softened then, reining herself in. "—I need you to understand the truth."

"Speak the truth, then," Agrippa practically barked. "How could Aurore have survived?"

"What was my specialty? My Aspect?"

"Aurore's Aspect?" Agrippa stroked his chin, thinking. "Distraction, if I recall correctly. Disingenuousness. Deception."

"Yes. Precisely. And I deceived them all. I thought it was my only chance of surviving the slaughter." She met the big man's eyes, and her own sparkling, luminous ones seemed to see right through him. "I survived because I wasn't there," she blurted. "I didn't trust Baranak or Vorthan—those overgrown, arrogant children—before the murders, and I surely didn't trust Lucian after. So I went into seclusion—into my own private cosmos—before the murders began." She gave a slight shrug. "Later, after Lucian and Baranak did what they did, I simply remained in hiding, out of view of the others. Out of their perceptions. It still seemed safer. If three-quarters of us could be killed so quickly, so easily, why should I have thought it couldn't happen again? What if there had been more to the conspiracy even than was rooted out, so long ago? So I have kept out of sight."

"Hidden," Tamerlane said, "all this time."

The woman nodded. "Not finding me among the survivors, they must have assumed me dead." She spread her hands. "And so there I have dwelt, at peace for so very long, until I was visited by the ghost."

One of Tamerlane's eyebrows raised. "Ghost?" He glanced at Agrippa; the blond soldier's expression was one of extreme disbelief. "You were visited by a *ghost*, you say."

"That is one way of putting it, yes," the woman replied, "considering that the person it represented has been dead for thousands of years." She gave Tamerlane a hard look. "Do you know a better term?"

The general didn't reply.

"So you have come to us today," Agrippa rumbled, "at the behest of a ghost. And you are a goddess. And we are to believe you purely on faith."

"You saw how I arrived here!"

"You did not see how *we* arrived here," Agrippa laughed. "Are *we* gods, as well?"

The woman turned fully to face Agrippa, staring up into his glinting blue eyes. "Truly I say to you, destiny or no, I would strike you down for your impudence as soon as speak with you, mortal—but the need is too great."

"What ghost?" Tamerlane asked quickly, interposing himself between the two of them. "What ghost visited you?"

"The avatar of an old friend. Solonis the Seer."

"The god who could see the future," Arani interjected. "Supposedly."

"Yes indeed," the woman replied, offering Arani the hint of a smile. "And see the future he could—though imprecisely, and often outside of any reasonable context." She laughed once, humorlessly. "Seeing the future and understanding it are rarely the same things."

Tamerlane nodded. "And this ghost—the ghost of Solonis—asked you to come here? To find us?"

An increasingly agitated Agrippa leaned in. "Ezekial," he said, tersely, "I fear we are needlessly wasting our time.

Every second that passes means another opportunity for Rameses to discover our presence. Perhaps—"

Tamerlane raised a hand. "Just a moment longer, if you don't mind, Arnem." He ran his hand through his dark hair, thinking. "So," he prompted the woman who claimed to be Aurore. "You were saying: Solonis is a ghost—?"

"For all intents and purposes, yes," she said, seemingly forcing herself to be patient and explain things in detail. "He was killed during the times of trouble in the City, but much of his spirit never entirely occupied the present time. That was how he could see the future. The greater part of his life force actually existed at some point more distant in time and could occasionally communicate future events back to him. Though his body was slain, that future component of his personality remains—albeit now untethered from our present time." She smiled flatly. "On very rare occasions it has been able to reach back and make contact with *me*."

"Why you?"

She shrugged. "Perhaps I am the only one who can perceive him. Or perhaps I'm simply the only one who cares."

"So this future-god contacted you and told you something?" Agrippa asked impatiently, clearly anxious to get through the matter and move on.

"Yes. And he also told me where and when I would find you: here and now. And I need your help, for I cannot begin to do this alone. Goddess though I may be, I am not Baranak, nor even Lucian. I lack the wherewithal to effectively deal with a menace of even *mortal* parameters."

Tamerlane nodded. "Why us?"

"Solonis recommended you, and I assumed he had his reasons for doing so. Therefore I have watched you all for some time now. Your concern is for the welfare of the galaxy. You are trustworthy and wise." Her eyes flicked to

Agrippa and then away. "You are meant for great things. And tragic things."

"And what menace do we face," Tamerlane asked, "that is so great that it has demanded your attention, and ours?"

"She must be referring to the *things* in the comets," Agrippa said. "I have encountered them directly and they are...*disturbing*, to say the least."

"The Phaedrons?" She emitted a humorless laugh. "They are terrible enough, that is so. Would that they were the only threat this galaxy faced. But there is another, and much greater."

"A man," Tamerlane breathed, turning and staring away into the night sky. "A man all in black."

Agrippa looked at him, disturbed.

"I know nothing of that," the woman stated. "The menace I speak of is not of human origins."

"Then who—?"

"It is the Dyonari," she said.

Tamerlane almost laughed. "What?"

Agrippa did laugh. "The Dyonari are old enemies, it's true—but I have of late found them to be remarkably reasonable. Besides," he added, "they scarcely provide a threat of the sort you are—"

"They may *mean* well in this instance, yes," the woman said, her eyes meeting Agrippa's. "But what will that fact avail any of us when all of creation lies in shattered ruin?"

"What exactly are you talking about?" Tamerlane demanded, growing impatient and feeling a wave of sudden and inexplicable anxiety washing over him. "What are the Dyonari supposedly going to do?"

Aurore gazed impassively back at him. Slowly an expression of sadness crept over her features. "With every good intention and noble ambition," she said, her voice low but filled with power, "they are preparing the ultimate counterattack against the forces they perceive are poised to invade and conquer this galaxy. They are afraid. *Terribly* afraid. They believe that they—and *you*—cannot win in the long run. And they would see it all destroyed first."

"But," Tamerlane said, "they can't actually *do* that." He was suddenly unsure of himself. "Can they?"

"They *can*," Aurore said, "and they *will*. Soon. In the future-time of Solonis, they already have." She faced the assembled warriors and spoke in a voice that was audible to all. "That possible future *will* come true," she concluded. "The Dyonari will destroy *everything*. Unless *you* stop them."

"Him," Aurore said, pointing at the big armored man. "I want him. And his squad."

Tamerlane had taken a moment to think things through, even as Agrippa paced nervously, convinced they were allowing the enemy far too much time to locate them. Now the general in red whirled, startled, to see exactly where—or rather, *at whom*—the strange woman in white was gesturing. "Agrippa?" he blurted out, shocked.

"Me?" the blond general himself said, his tone conveying astonishment. "But—I don't even believe much of what you're saying! Surely someone else—"

"You," Aurore repeated. "You have a destiny, and I now believe part of it lies with me."

Agrippa had no idea what to say to that. He merely stared back at the woman in white, his eyes wide. A second later he looked to Tamerlane. "Ezekial," he said, "surely we have given this woman and her—shall we say, *imaginative* theories as much of our time as we can spare. Perhaps if we—"

"You can have Agrippa and his squad," Tamerlane interrupted, speaking to Aurore.

"*What?*" the big man exploded, aghast.

The woman smiled. "Thank you," she said. Then, "If?" she asked, knowing conditions were coming.

They were.

"If," Tamerlane said, "you can help us first."

As Agrippa continued to fume, Aurore gave a half nod. "I will consider it. What assistance do you require?"

Tamerlane moved in closer, his voice intense now. "Open a way for us directly into the palace, so that we don't have to fight our way in." He smiled, and now it was a cold, calculating smile. "You can open portals—we just saw it. Get us past the Sand Kings and right in on top of Rameses himself."

She pursed her pale lips, thinking. "If I do this, you will allow Agrippa to go with me?"

"I will. And his entire squad. I'll even throw in the tanks." His smile remained cold. "We won't be needing them indoors."

Agrippa had turned red, but he held his tongue.

"And, from what you've said," Tamerlane went on, "it certainly sounds like they will be assisting with a good cause." He barked a laugh. "What good is taking down the traitor Rameses when the whole galaxy will be blown up right afterward?"

Agrippa found his voice. "You believe this nonsense, Ezekial?" he asked, eyes wide. "You are going to order me and my Bravos to follow her off on some wild goose chase? You're going to assault the Sand Kings and the Heliopolis without our help?"

"If she can open a portal for us directly into the throne room itself," Tamerlane replied, "we won't necessarily *need* your firepower behind us."

Agrippa stewed at that but said nothing.

Tamerlane looked back at Aurore. "Well?"

The woman closed her eyes and stood motionless for several seconds. Her right hand came up, then her left, held just in front of her, the fingers reaching out, seeming to probe—at nothing but air. For several more seconds she did this. Then she opened her eyes and lowered her hands. "I cannot open a way directly into the palace," she told Tamerlane.

"There, you see?" Agrippa barked.

"But I can lead you as far as a large chamber," she went on. "Perhaps some sort of storage basement, underground, just outside the walls of the major complex."

"The Heliopolis," Delain said, closing her eyes and rapidly accessing her stored memories. "A city within a city. The palace lies within." She opened her eyes and looked at Tamerlane. "And I know of that basement. There is a hidden way from there, under the defenses. It is very old, but Stanishur has seen it, and thus I can see it."

"You mean—?" Tamerlane began to ask.

"I mean I can get us into the palace from there."

Tamerlane offered the female Inquisitor a tight smile. He did the same to an incredulous Agrippa. Then he turned to the woman in white. "We have a deal," he said.

emons?" Major Elaro asked, skeptical. "Here on Ahknaton?"

"That's what the lady said," Tamerlane replied. "She could sense them. Demons. Sorcery. Cosmic forces at work, right in the palace." Tamerlane shook his head. "We have to take it seriously. It's hard to imagine there are any threats more disturbing than those."

The three dozen soldiers had come to the end of the long, winding tunnel that had taken them under the walls and outer defenses of the Heliopolis on Ahknaton. Now they stood at the bottom of a stairway, carved from the very bedrock of the city, that reached up into darkness.

"How about the vast armies of aliens—and other human empires—fighting us on every frontier, sir?" Arani asked. "I for one find them plenty disturbing."

"Not to mention Rameses and the Sand Kings," Elaro said. "Let's not forget the current enemy—the one we're actually here to fight."

"The shocking thing is that all these enemies appeared at roughly the same time," Arani pointed out. "It almost makes you think they're connected somehow."

"I'm not certain they're not," Tamerlane muttered. Still generating their only light by summoning flames that flickered across his fingertips, he began to ascend the stairs.

Arani and Elaro exchanged glances at his remark; they'd heard it quite clearly. "Do you know something we don't, General?" Arani asked.

"No," he replied. "Just a feeling." But even as he said that, he frowned and asked himself if that was true. He kept almost remembering something... *someone*...

Onward and upward they climbed, the little procession of soldiers—some in red and gold, others in khaki—with their guns at the ready, and the Inquisitor in her robes of black, her power preventing them from being detected. The stairs were open on the right side and very quickly they all found themselves subconsciously hugging closer to the left-hand wall; in the darkness there was no way to be sure how far down the drop on the other side reached.

They moved mostly in silence, and the journey seemed to take forever. After an indeterminable time, they turned a gradual curve and a wall appeared on the right side, too. As much as the previous situation had been disconcerting with its blind drop-off, the new situation was increasingly claustrophobic, as the two walls gradually narrowed.

"It may have been a good thing Agrippa didn't come with us," Titus Elaro whispered to Arani. "I'm not sure his armor would've fit through here."

The Colonel couldn't argue. She squinted up and into the distance, beyond the shoulders of the troopers ahead of her, always keeping one eye on the flames generated by Tamerlane. The cold and the dark pressed in.

And then they came to a very abrupt halt.

Arani ran into the soldier in front of her, and Elaro bumped into her. It would've been comical if their lives hadn't all been on the line, here in the very heart of the enemy's stronghold.

Word came whispered down from one trooper to the next: they had reached a door. Tamerlane and the Inquisitor woman were examining it; obviously they wouldn't want to just fling it open with no way of knowing what they were walking out into.

Everyone waited, holding their breath. The seconds ticked by.

And then they were moving again, as silently as possible. As Arani reached the doorway, she saw the door itself swung out toward her, and she could tell that it was old; as ancient as anything she'd encountered in the old cathedral on *Ascanius*. It looked as if it hadn't been opened in a very long while. Obviously it was the final component, after the passage and the stairs, in a long-forgotten way that only the Grand Inquisitor still remembered. Arani found herself speculating on just how old Stanishur truly was.

Moving past the old door and through the low arched entryway it had guarded, she found herself and her troops standing at the rear of a long, narrow balcony that projected out over a large, well-lit open space. They had actually climbed up from the depths of the Heliopolis's basement levels and then beyond that, up inside the walls of the palace. And it had to be the palace; the main throne room, in fact. Nothing else looked like this. Down below, a handful of figures in gleaming gold with enameled red and blue accents stood at attention on a pale, veined marble floor.

"What—?" she started to ask, only to be motioned sharply to silence by Tamerlane. She saw then that two Sand Kings in the same ornamental dress uniforms as those below, with energy lances held at their sides, stood at attention on the edge of the balcony. Fortunately for the party, the two guards were facing away from them, toward the interior of the hall.

Sister Delain moved quickly and silently to the front of the group. She gestured with one hand and then nodded to

Tamerlane. "They have been silenced," she whispered, "nor can they now hear."

Tamerlane caught Titus Elaro's attention and motioned for him to follow. Together, the two men slipped up behind the suddenly isolated soldiers. The Sand Kings were just beginning to wonder what was happening—why they could no longer hear the sounds from below, nor even their own voices—when the two intruders brought them down with swift blows.

No sooner had they dragged the two unconscious guards away to bind them than Delain stepped into the spot they had previously occupied, near the balcony railing. She raised her hands high as she whispered words unintelligible to the others. *She's shielding us from view*, Arani understood. *Keeping the others below from detecting us in any way.*

Arani moved closer to Tamerlane, Elaro following behind her. "What's the plan, General?" she whispered.

Tamerlane said nothing. Instead he pointed down.

Arani followed his gesture. Now that they were out near the edge of the balcony, she could see nearly all of the vast open space below. In particular, she could now see a man in powerful-looking, dull-red armor standing near the throne. The armor was remarkable to look upon; it appeared to fit him like a glove, leaving only his face exposed. It appeared almost to be composed of some sort of liquid metal that had been poured over him, leaving no seams.

Then Arani recognized the face of the man in the armor. "Rameses!" she gasped.

Tamerlane didn't shush her this time. He only nodded. "Target acquired," he whispered back.

Arani stared down at him, also taking in the sight of the others around him: a pale, slender figure, shirtless, in Egyptian-style headdress; an officer in I Legion colors, lying motionless on his back on a strange platform; a young, blonde girl, also lying apparently comatose on a catafalque,

309

who had to be the missing princess; and a remarkably small number of Sand Kings in ceremonial armor and carrying ceremonial weapons. Arani studied the soldiers in particular and concluded that they might look like toy soldiers carrying toy weapons, but they were in actuality quite deadly.

Near all of them, a source of light radiated throughout the grand hall. Arani studied it momentarily. The brightness was coming from a golden bowl or basin resting on the marble floor. From it erupted a geyser not of water but of light and fire and pure, raw cosmic energy. Arani's mouth dropped slowly open without her realizing it. She wasn't sure what she was seeing, but something at a very basic level of her being sensed and appreciated that it was powerful beyond all reason.

"The Fountain," said Tamerlane, very quietly but with great conviction. "They've recreated the Fountain of the Golden City."

This didn't mean a lot to Arani. Vaguely she flashed back to some of the tedious lessons of her school days, when the Ecclesiarchy would send a priest to instruct the children on the basic tenets of the state religion. The Golden City was a sort of Heaven, she recalled, and the Fountain was an important feature of it. Beyond that, she couldn't remember very much. She hadn't paid a great deal of attention.

Looking still closer at the people milling about below, she detected one other figure—one she hadn't perceived at first. It was a man in red, she first thought. Then, to her horror, she saw that it wasn't a *man* at all. It was larger than any human, horns grew from its head, and its face was a fearsome scowl. She saw it and she knew: it was a *demon*.

It hovered over the princess. And it was descending towards her even as they looked on.

Realizing that fact, Arani gasped. At Tamerlane's puzzled glance she pointed with quick jabs toward the prone young woman and the creature. The general was clearly having a difficult time seeing it, or making out exactly what was happening. It was as if he had been somehow bewitched.

Arani hissed one word, sharply: "Possession."

And then the scales fell from Tamerlane's eyes. And he saw. And revulsion took him. He started to wretch. Before he could turn away, however, the room was flooded in a still brighter light. A swirling storm of fog and lightning erupted out of thin air, near the center of the chamber. A dark circle formed at its center. Human shapes could just be seen within the black. They were advancing.

"Looks like we aren't Rameses' only visitors," Arani noted in a low whisper.

As both the palace's official occupants and its hidden guests looked on, some two dozen armed soldiers rushed out into the throne room. They wore dark red uniforms with gold trim, and they carried blast pistols and energy rifles.

"It's my Legion," Tamerlane gasped, shocked. "The Lords of Fire! What are they—?"

From out of the portal, pushing his way past the I Legion troopers, came a somewhat shorter, stockier, and much older man also clad in the red and gold of the Lords of Fire. His hair was very short and gray and his expression was not one of the warrior entering combat but of the visitor confused by his surroundings.

"*Hideo?*" Tamerlane whispered, frowning. "Why would he come here himself? Has he lost his—"

Tamerlane's voice trailed off as he watched Nakamura raise the weapon he carried up high and out before him. It was a sword—a long, broad one—and it gleamed golden in the light of the fountain. Everyone there recognized it.

"He's brought the sword with him," Tamerlane exclaimed. "The Sword of Baranak!"

10

short while earlier:
"I fear I may have taken him too far, my lord,"
Teluria said.

Darkness and silence greeted her statement. She waited, there in her quarters aboard the I Legion flagship, *Ascanius*, the lights switched off and the door locked to any outside intrusion. Before her, mounted on the wall, hung a golden icon with the image of a man in contemporary clothing etched into it. She took a knee before it and gazed down at the floor, waiting, her words hanging in the air.

"My lord," she said again after an indeterminate time, "I find I cannot move the white king into position." She waited; still nothing. She dared to look up at the icon. It was cold and dark. "I believe he was weaker that we first thought," she continued. "He has deteriorated rapidly. He has grown entirely unresponsive."

She waited and waited but there was no answer forthcoming. She took this to mean one of two things: either her master was engaged elsewhere and too busy to commune with her right now, or else he was not interested in her problems and waited only for her to solve them herself. Either way, it amounted to the same thing: she was on her own.

Rising, she gave the icon one last look, her expression a combination of disappointment and annoyance. Then, drawing her crimson cloak tighter about her lithe form, she turned and strode toward the door. "Very well, my lord," she whispered very softly. "Your plans are jeopardized, here on the very cusp of victory. But if you cannot be bothered to—"

The room lit up, bright as noontime. Teluria spun around, staring up in awe at the icon. It was now glowing with an inner light that nearly overwhelmed her. The image of the man upon it seemed now to breathe, and to move.

"Teluria," came a deep, resonant voice from out of thin air. "You displease me."

Quickly she knelt and bowed her head. "My lord," she said. "I apologize."

"You cannot carry out your task?" the voice asked. "You have failed me?"

Teluria looked up defiantly, right into the eyes of the image on the icon. "I have done precisely as you instructed, lord," she said. "But we both misjudged the white king's resilience. He has lapsed nearly into catatonia now."

Silence for a long moment, as Teluria waited, anxious, fearing she had pushed things too far. A goddess herself, she knew full well her might paled before that of the one to whom she now spoke. Much as she might occasionally flirt with the idea of challenging his tyranny, she understood that she had joined her destiny with his, so many ages ago, and there was no going back now.

"And you would have me intervene?" the voice asked.

"I would have your plans come to fruition," she replied.

Another long pause, and then the light in the room grew even brighter. A swirl of dark clouds formed within the light, circling tightly around a central point. What looked like a tunnel appeared in the center of Teluria's quarters, and a figure emerged from it, walking out into the room.

Teluria bowed deeply. "My lord. Thank you for coming."

Not deigning to reply, the man in black walked past her. The door slid open as he approached. Teluria hurried to follow him out into the corridor.

Along the way, the crew members they passed didn't look at them or seem at all aware of their presence. No one so much as looked their way. Arriving at the entrance to the *Taiko*'s quarters, the man in black raised his left hand and the armed legionaries posted there instantly moved out of the way. The door hissed open.

The room was dark and stuffy. Only Nakamura was present, lying in seemingly deep sleep on a broad red sofa positioned against one wall. The man in black took one look at him and boomed, "Rise!"

Nakamura's eyes opened and he slowly sat up. He stared straight ahead, eyes glassy, not focusing on anything in particular. His breathing was shallow.

"Your time has come," the man told him. "You must rouse yourself. We have arrived at the endgame. Your final actions are required." He smiled. "And then you can rest. Rest for as long as you like." The smile widened. "Rest *forever*."

Nakamura nodded slowly and stood, at attention, still staring into the distance.

"The situation is critical," the man said, moving in close, his voice quieter now but just as intense, as if he were delivering important news to the *Taiko*. "The traitor Rameses acts without opposition. He has the little princess in his possession, and who can say what vile purposes he intends for her?"

At this, Nakamura's eyes focused a bit. "The princess?" His voice was weak and thin. "Rameses has her?"

"Indeed he does," the man in black said. "Furthermore, he has declared you deposed as *Taiko*. He has declared himself the new ruler of the Empire."

Now Nakamura seemed to wake, and his expression darkened. "How dare he? Traitor!"

"Yes."

"But—" The *Taiko* hesitated. "I have no armies left," he said. "They are all out on the frontiers, pinned down, fighting for the survival of the Empire itself. What can I do?"

"What can you do?" The man in black scoffed. "You are virtually a god yourself. You possess the Sword of Baranak! What can you *not* do?"

Nakamura's eyes lit up. "Yes! The sword!" He looked around. "Where is it?"

"It is on this ship," the man told him. "You made certain of that before you set out. Remember?"

Nakamura rubbed his face with his hands, still seeming to be waking up. "Yes, yes," he said. Then, "Guards," he called. "*Guards!*"

Teluria tensed at the *Taiko*'s shouts, but relaxed once the soldiers rushed in and Nakamura merely ordered them to retrieve the Sword of Baranak from its place of storage.

After it had arrived, accompanied by some two dozen heavily armed troops that the *Taiko* had summoned, the entire party filed into the strategium. There, the man in black gestured casually and another swirl of light and smoke filled the center of the big, open chamber. A dark, circular dimensional portal opened at its center.

Teluria motioned toward it. "That way lies Ahknaton," she said. "And Rameses."

"And retribution," Nakamura growled. Then he hesitated, looking down at the sword in his hands and then back at Teluria. Something clearly was bothering him. "The sword," he said, frowning. "If carry it through—will there be an explosion?"

"No," the woman in red told him. "Only a portal forced open by mortal machinery is vulnerable in such a way. When the *gods* open the way, there is no danger. Now go!"

Nakamura nodded. He raised the Sword of Baranak high, flames leaping up along his arm and along the blade as he did so. He faced the soldiers in their red and gold uniforms. "Men and women of the Lords of Fire," he called. "We go to capture—or *kill*—the traitor Rameses! *March!*"

Teluria watched them rush toward the portal. In only a few seconds, they had all passed through and were gone. As it started to close behind them, she turned to address her lord. "So much for the white king, eh, my lord?" But then she realized that the man in black was already gone. She frowned, but had to admit to herself that she was relieved he had simply departed without upbraiding her further.

The strategium was empty. She started toward the doorway to exit when a technician entered and approached her.

"Ecclesiarch," the man said, nodding respectfully.

"Yes?" she asked impatiently.

"You have a call."

Teluria raised an eyebrow. "A call?"

"Over the Aether. From the *Atlantia*, near Earth. Shall I put it through?"

Teluria blinked. "The *Atlantia*? The II Legion flagship? What—?" Absently she motioned for the tech to open the connection.

The strategium darkened and a larger-than-life face formed before her in midair, by way of the holographic projectors. Teluria regarded the man whose visage hovered over her. She felt her bile rising.

"Ecclesiarch," the rough-hewn man stated with no preliminary niceties, "your presence is requested aboard the *Atlantia*. Immediately."

She gazed back at the face. "General," she said. "We both know it will take some time for a shuttle to transport me all the way back to Earth. And that is even assuming I have the slightest intentions of jumping at your beck and call."

The big face distorted into a smug grin. "Let us not kid one another, Ecclesiarch. We both know you can come here virtually instantaneously. I require that you do so."

She reddened to nearly the shade of her cloak and hood. "You *require*? How *dare* you?" She exhaled slowly. "What in the name of the gods makes you think I would come running at your summons?"

"I note that you do not attempt to refute my larger point."

She stewed for a moment. "And you didn't answer my question," she said finally. "Why should I come to you?"

"Because you want to know what I could possibly be up to. Because you don't trust me at all—just as I don't trust you. But you're curious. So you'll come."

Teluria started to reply but before she could speak the image crackled with static, turned entirely to electronic snow, and vanished.

Her fists bunching up tightly, the woman in red exercised all of her restraint to keep herself from screaming her anger and annoyance. Instead, she relaxed her fingers and raised both hands, opening a portal before her.

"Oh, I'm coming to you, alright, Iapetus," she hissed.

She stalked through the portal and it snapped closed behind her. The strategium of the *Ascanius* was plunged into darkness. All that remained was the echo of her final words: "I'm coming— and you will sorely *regret* that fact, when I arrive."

11

What in the name of Those Who Remain does Nakamura think he's doing?"

The question, asked by a shocked Tamerlane as he looked down from the balcony at what was transpiring below, hung in the air unanswered for several seconds. Everyone could see exactly what was happening—but no one could explain it.

Seconds earlier, a dimensional portal had opened there in the center of the throne room. From it had emerged a battalion of I Legion soldiers, the *Taiko* Nakamura at their head, the ancient and powerful golden relic known as the Sword of Baranak held aloft and blazing in his hand.

As they entered the throne room, the few remaining Sand Kings elite guardsmen didn't attack but instead fell back, retreating into hidden spaces along the walls. Rameses and Zahir drew back with them, so that the invaders were the only ones left occupying the center space.

"Show yourself, Rameses!" called Nakamura. "Face me, coward!"

LEGION II: SONS OF TERRA

The I Legion troopers that had accompanied the *Taiko* looked around, moving in slow circles, their weapons up and at the ready, surprised by the utter lack of enemy resistance.

Tamerlane started to move, clearly intending to hurry to the *Taiko*'s side.

He never got the chance.

As the last of the ceremonial guards withdrew, leaving a throne room deathly still and quiet, a sudden flaring of light nearly blinded everyone who looked on. Standing behind the golden basin near the throne, the pale, slender man in the Egyptian headgear was executing a series of complex gestures. In response, from out of the basin erupted searing bolts of energy, like lightning moving horizontally through the air. The bolts forked across the chamber and cut savagely into the I Legion soldiers. Instinctively Nakamura brought the sword down, and indeed he managed to deflect the first couple of shots that had been directed his way. But then the third shot caught him in the leg and he cried out, dropping to the marble floor.

Tamerlane was up again at this, hurrying toward the balcony's edge, clearly intending to simply leap over and come to Nakamura's rescue. Titus Elaro leapt and tackled him before he could reach the ledge.

Rolling over onto his back, furious, Tamerlane glared up at the man. "What do you think you're doing? I have to help him!"

"It's too late for them," Elaro replied, his voice restrained and even. "You can see that. If you give yourself away, you'll give *all* of us away, and then it will have all been for nothing."

"But—we were going to attack them anyway," the general argued, his eyes frantic.

"We can't walk into that deathtrap," Elaro replied harshly. "We owe the *Taiko* a huge debt. He revealed exactly what would've happened to us if we'd launched a frontal assault on Rameses."

The general scowled and he looked to thinking of arguing—or wrestling the other man out of his way—but after a second or two of reflection, he calmed himself and nodded. "You're right. But we have to help him—rescue him—somehow..."

"Definitely," Elaro said. "But without getting ourselves killed in the process—right, General?"

Tamerlane didn't reply. He simply nodded once, reluctantly.

Elaro helped him back to his feet and the two men stared down in horror as the last of the I Legion soldiers was cut down by the murderous beams that struck from the golden basin. Some two dozen soldiers in red and gold lay still, scattered across the chamber like dried leaves. Tamerlane's hands were white where he gripped the rail of the balcony, and his teeth were bared. Beside them, Delain stood with her hands raised, chanting over and over a litany against detection.

Below them, Rameses in his crimson armor emerged from his hiding place and moved slowly and cautiously toward the prone *Taiko*. Opposite him, a tall, lithe form in Egyptian headgear glided out of the shadows. They began to speak quietly.

"What are they saying?" Tamerlane asked, his face flushed. "If only we could hear."

Delain glanced at him and offered him the tiniest hint of a smile. "Perhaps I can be of assistance with that, General," she said. And she rotated one hand slightly...

On the marble floor below, Nakamura lay unmoving, sprawled on his face. Some two dozen I Legion soldiers were scattered all around him, dead. The Sword of Baranak had fallen from his grip and now it rested on the marble floor a short distance away.

Zahir glided over and bent, picking it up. He held it for a moment, studying it.

"What do you have there, my vizier?" Rameses asked, moving forward in his seamless red armor. He took in the sight of the sword and he gasped. "Is—is that—?"

"The Sword of Baranak," Zahir informed him. "Nakamura brought it to us, just as the master told us he would. He brought it right to us!" The pale, thin man smiled broadly. "The final piece is on the chess board, as he foresaw. The endgame has begun." He strode several paces across the room and proffered the sword to the governor.

"To us? He has brought it to *me*," the armored man snapped. He reached out and seized the sword, wresting it away from the vizier. "It represents his final capitulation. The old Empire is dead. Nakamura has brought the symbol of power to the one who is his superior—to the one who replaces him as supreme force in the galaxy! *To me!*" He held the golden blade aloft. "Witness now the birth of a living god!"

His sneering unnoticed by the other, Zahir bowed low. "Rameses—the living god," he proclaimed. "Let it be written; let it be done." He turned and gazed at the princess where she lay on her palanquin; moving ever so slowly, so carefully, the ethereal demonform had descended more than halfway into her body. The girl's eyes were open and her mouth locked in a soundless scream. "For a short while yet, at least," he murmured softly, almost inaudibly. "Then comes the ascension of the Empress, the reign of the demon lord—and all the galaxy at the feet of great Goraddon."

Watching from the balcony above, Tamerlane cursed violently. Delain had magnified the thin man's words so that all of the team could hear him, and now they truly understood what they were up against.

"Madmen," Tamerlane growled. "Cultists! Demon worshippers!"

"I believe they are more even than that," the Inquisitor woman whispered to the general.

"What do you mean?"

"I detect vast power swirling about and within the vizier," she said. Her arms still aloft as she projected a shielding effect, she nodded with her head. "This one called Zahir—I believe there is more to him than we have seen thus far." She hesitated. "The same is true of Teluria, the Ecclesiarch. I was not certain at first; she is very skilled at hiding certain telltale signs. But now—"

"They're gods," Tamerlane stated flatly. "I know it."

Standing beside them, Titus Elaro and Arani exchanged startled glances.

"Gods?" Arani said.

Elaro blinked. "You mean—you're saying they're two of Those Who Remain?"

"Exactly," Tamerlane responded. He turned and faced them. "We've always heard stories that some of them had survived all the way into the present day, and dwelt in our dimension, rather than in the Above or some other private cosmos. I believe that's what these two are."

"There is another," Delain said. She had spoken before she could stop herself to think it through; had she reflected for a moment, she realized with a start, she wouldn't have allowed herself to say it. *Why is that?* she wondered. *Some built-in reflex that would've caused me to not speak the thought aloud? Yes—almost as if I'd been put under a...* spell...

Tamerlane started at her last words. Eyebrows knitting, he turned and stared at her, his eyes meeting hers and seeming to bore in. "Another," he said. "No. No. No other. N—" He choked, coughing violently for several seconds. "Yes. Yes!"

Straightening, he looked from the extremely puzzled Arani and Elaro to Delain. "Why couldn't I say it? Or *think* it?"

"Because he didn't *want* us to," the Inquisitor replied. "Because he wouldn't *let* us."

It all came back to Tamerlane then, with enough force to nearly knock him over. "The man in black!" he gasped. "He was there—he was *always* there! Why did I always forget him?" He shook his head. "Because he wanted me to," he said before Delain could. "At the cathedral, speaking to the Emperor. In Nakamura's quarters. Everywhere. A man in black."

"Goraddon," Delain said. "Goraddon, the god of persuasion."

Tamerlane brought his fist down hard onto the railing. "All along. It was him, all along. Pushing Rameses—using him as a pawn."

"As a dark king," Delain whispered. "And Nakamura the king of light—lying face-down on the floor now." She closed her eyes. "He's already won."

"Not by a long shot," Tamerlane snapped. "This is no chess game. There are more than two sides in the fight. And Rameses and his manipulator have yet to hear from *me*."

"To battle this foe, General," Delain said, "you will need more than just we few here. Even an entire legion would not be enough—"

"It would be a good start," Tamerlane replied, his mouth twisted in anger.

"There are no more legions to be had," Arani pointed out.

"There's one," Tamerlane stated. "And it's time they got in the game."

The others all exchanged glances.

"You mean—?" Arani said.

"I mean it's time to give Iapetus a call," the general said. "It's time the Sons of Terra were heard from in all of this."

"He won't listen," Elaro said quietly.

"Oh, he'll listen—and he'll come," Tamerlane replied, eyes burning. "Even if I have to go and drag him and his entire legion here by myself."

BOOK EIGHT
WHO WATCHES?

1

The darkened strategium of the *Atlantia* lit up again as it had some time earlier, bathed in the sickly yellow light of eldritch fire and the smell of smoke and metal. As the light faded, a human form shrouded in dark red became apparent to anyone who was looking on.

As it happened, only one person was there waiting. As the red-clad figure stepped out of the open tear in space and time, the other waited patiently, eyes downcast.

The light faded away to nothing, the wound in reality closing. The figure in red stood there, alone, hooded and robed.

"Lady Teluria," Colonel Piryu said, drawing near and bowing low. "My lord Iapetus thanks you for coming on such short notice."

Teluria gazed at Piryu, her mouth twisted in a pout. "What is the meaning of this?" she demanded, looking around the empty, dark chamber. "I do not appreciate being perfunctorily summoned—by anyone!" She frowned. "Where is Iapetus? He has much to answer for."

"The General is otherwise engaged at the moment, Lady," Piryu said, still half-bowed and looking not at her but at the metal plating of the floor. "He sends his assurances that he will attend you very shortly."

"Unacceptable!" Teluria all but shouted. "How dare he demand I appear here, on his flagship, and then ask me to wait upon his pleasure?" She stalked across the broad room regally, chin jutting out. "He must be taught some manners!"

Piryu bowed low again. "As you say, Lady. In the meantime, I have been directed to take you to the lounge, where you will enjoy—"

"There is nothing about this that I *enjoy*, lackey!" Teluria glared at the colonel for a long moment, then turned away. She stood there for several seconds. "I cannot quite believe that Iapetus would impose upon me in such a blatant manner. Apparently I have woefully misjudged him."

"That may be," said Piryu quietly.

Teluria's gaze snapped back around, locking onto the colonel with a burning intensity. "What?"

"If you would follow me, ma'am," Piryu stated formally, gesturing toward the door, "I will be honored to lead you to the lounge."

Very slowly and very reluctantly, Teluria allowed the colonel to lead her out of the strategium and a short distance down one corridor to the luxuriously appointed suite that had been prepared for her. As she glided along, the woman in red continued to mutter curses and imprecations against Iapetus and his entire Legion.

Perhaps half an hour passed before Teluria would have no more of it. Scarcely containing her fury, the imperious woman sat up from where she had been languorously lounging on a well-cushioned chaise and rose to her feet. She wore only a skintight, blood-red leotard woven of some unrecognizable material. Reaching over, she snatched up her robe from the chair on which it had been draped and refastened it about her neck. Then she moved to the door and waited for it to open.

It did not move.

"Have the idiots locked me in?" she wondered aloud. "They wouldn't dare," she answered herself. Raising a hand, she gestured toward the door. This time it slid silently open.

Just outside stood Piryu. Seeing her, the colonel bowed low. "My Lady," she said, her voice now carrying a hint of nervousness, "can I be of assistance?"

"Yes," she said, walking past her. "You can direct me to Iapetus and otherwise stay out of my way."

"I—err—yes, of course," she replied. Quickly she accessed the Aether. In doing so, she lost a couple of steps behind Teluria as the woman stalked away, and she hurried to catch up. "The general can see you now," she reported. "He awaits your pleasure in the strategium."

"Oh, does he, then?" She scoffed. "I'm afraid he will find little pleasure with me." Leaving the hood down, her sour expression plain to anyone who dared look at her, she followed the officer back along the corridor to the strategium.

She entered the darkened room again, this time not via a trans-dimensional portal but by way of the sliding doors. Teluria followed her in and stood next to her, waiting.

A short distance away, seated on a plain metal chair that had been brought in, was General Ioan Iapetus. He sat unmoving, his dark eyes piercing through the dimness and unflinchingly meeting hers.

"What is the meaning of this, Iapetus?" the robed woman demanded. "Have you become so deluded that you think you can simply summon me to your presence whenever you see fit?"

The general said nothing in reply. He simply gazed back at her, watching. The golden eye emblem on his black uniform gleamed in the semi-darkness.

Teluria took a step toward him, anger spilling out now. "Will you speak, then? Will you answer for yourself?" Then she saw that he had two objects resting on his lap. One object was a small box, about the size of a packet of the cigarettes he usually carried.

The other was a gun.

This gave her pause. She halted, frowning, one eyebrow lifting curiously.

The doors slid closed behind her, and she realized that Piryu had exited. Only the two of them remained in the vast, empty room.

"You seek to threaten, to intimidate me—*me!*—with a pitiful blast pistol, General?" she asked—but her voice now betrayed her uncertainty. She knew all too well how wily, how unpredictable, and how dangerous this man could be. She told herself to tread carefully, at least until she fully understood what sort of game he was playing.

She waited, and their eyes remained locked, like some vicious predator with its prey. The question of which of them was now the predator and which was the prey remained hanging in the air between them, unspoken and unanswered.

"You will perform a service for me," Iapetus stated quietly, breaking the silence at last.

"Oh, will I?" Teluria responded.

"Yes."

She chuckled once, but there was no real force behind it now. "And if not? What follows?"

Iapetus's expression remained flat, his composure utterly calm. He reached up, into a pocket on the breast of his uniform, just above and to the left of the golden eye emblem. He drew out a small, shining gemstone, dark red in color. He held it up for her to see, then lifted the strange pistol from his lap with his other hand and fitted the stone into a recessed cavity in it. Having done so, he held the gun so that it was not *exactly* pointed in her direction.

"If not," he said, "I will shoot you with this."

She blinked, puzzled, and stared at the gun. And then she realized what it was.

Gasping, Teluria stumbled back a step, two steps. Her expression dissolved instantly into one of fear and panic.

"*Wha*—where did you *get* that?" she demanded, though her tone no longer carried any sort of commanding force. "*How* did you get that?"

"You know of it," Iapetus said. "Good. That will save me the need for any sort of demonstration. Because, to be honest with you, I wasn't certain how I could stage an effective demonstration without killing you in the process."

She glared at him.

Now Iapetus smiled. His smile, however, was cold, reptilian, and not something designed to bring any degree of relief. "I have been dispatching expeditions to locate one of these for many years now. Having become general of the entire II Legion, I found my resources vastly increased." He gave a slight shrug. "The story goes that Lucian commissioned many of them to be made. I suspected a few of them remained behind after the Revolt in Heaven. It was only a matter of time until one turned up."

Teluria wasted no time. She raised one hand and uttered mystical incantations in a long-forgotten tongue; incantations that would open a trans-dimensional portal for her.

Nothing happened.

Now she raised both hands, gesturing more broadly, her voice louder as she chanted.

"You do realize I can shoot you down right now, as you do that, right?" the general asked, looking suddenly bored.

"What has happened?" the woman demanded. Her eyes were wide now, wild, frantic. She tried a third time to open a portal, that she might escape this mad mortal. Again, there was no effect whatsoever.

"What has happened is that I fully understand what you are," Iapetus said. He held up the other object that had rested on his lap: the small, black box with flashing red and green lights along its sides. "In addition to the gun," he told her, "I also possess this."

She finally ceased her efforts and looked at the little box. Her eyes held the specter of defeat in them. She didn't ask.

He told her anyway. "This scrambles your ability to open portals," he said. "There is no escape—until you have performed the job I have set for you."

"Impossible!" she cried. "No mortal device can restrain the powers of a god!"

"And yet," Iapetus said, shrugging again, "here you remain."

Teluria glared at him. "May the demons of the abyss drag you screaming into the depths of the Below," she muttered, her teeth bared.

"Perhaps that will happen," Iapetus replied. "But I doubt it. And not while there is still work to be done." He smiled again. "There needs to be a clear understanding between us. You will do as I say. You will perform a small service for me. And then you are free to go." He paused. "Provided you go back to your own realm and leave this dimension forever." He held up the pistol again. "Otherwise, understand that I have no qualms whatsoever about shooting a goddess point-blank, drawing out her soul, and imprisoning it forever in that little red crystal."

Huddling back from him, she now resembled nothing so much as a snake driven into a corner and raring to strike at the first opportunity—but afraid to try.

"You should have been one of us," she growled at him then. "You have the traits. You would've fit right in."

"I have no interest in the gods or in godhood," Iapetus replied, standing. "I simply wish to protect the precious and sacred Earth. And to do that, I will require your help."

Teluria stood there, facing him, for a long several seconds. She breathed in and out, her eyes burning like hot coals. At last she nodded once. "One favor. Granted by your Ecclesiarch." She stuck out her lower lip. "Call it a reward for your loyal service to the Empire."

"Please," he scoffed. "I know you care no more for this Empire than I do." The pistol remained held easily in his left hand. "I have been nothing but honest with you; please afford me the same courtesy."

"Fine," she spat. "What would you have me do?"

He smiled, and this time the smile actually seemed warm. Warm for him, at any rate.

"I would have you open a way for me and for my legion," he said.

"Oh? To where?"

Now he laughed. "Why, to the one place you seem hell-bent that I shouldn't go."

After Teluria had grudgingly allowed herself to be escorted back to the quarters prepared for her, Iapetus strode in the other direction, toward the bridge. Colonel Piryu hurried along at his side. As they neared the entrance to the command level, the junior officer couldn't help but observe, "That went well, General."

Iapetus nodded. "Still, it was a narrow-run thing. If she had decided to test my jamming device only a couple of minutes earlier, she might have exposed everything."

Piryu looked puzzled. "Exposed? How is that? If you don't mind my asking, sir?"

Iapetus laughed. "She was quite right that blocking her power with any sort of man-made device is virtually impossible."

"What? But then—how were you able to—?"

Iapetus held up the little black box with the red and green lights. "Simple," he said, dropping it to the floor and crushing it with his boot. "I tricked her. It was fake."

"Fake?" Staring aghast down at the broken pieces of plastic on the floor, Piryu shook her head. "But she wasn't able to open a portal!"

Iapetus laughed harder. The doors to the command level opened before them and they walked out onto the bridge. On the main viewscreen directly ahead, the tan semicircle of a planet loomed large and near. The general pointed to it. "There's your answer, Colonel."

The other officer stared at the mottled surface, studying its pattern. "That—that's Candis, isn't it?" she asked.

"Indeed it is," Iapetus replied. "And we just dropped hyper and pulled into orbit a few moments ago. Just seconds before Teluria entered the strategium, in fact."

Piryu considered this. Slowly a smile spread across her face. "Candis," she repeated. "The safeworld. The one place in the Empire where no dimensional portal can be opened, by god or man. The place where the walls of spacetime are too thick."

"Correct on all counts," the general agreed. He nodded greeting to the ship's captain and sat down in an auxiliary seat situated off to one side.

Piryu shook her head in wonder. "Well played, General," she said. "Very well played. Still..."

"Yes?"

Piryu met his eyes and then looked away, nervous. "I suppose we'd better hope she doesn't figure it all out."

Z

I f you're so sure they can't detect us," Tamerlane whispered, "why are we sneaking around like this? And whispering?"

Inquisitor Delain sighed to herself. The two of them lurked in the shadows behind a massive stone column that towered up into the heights of the domed throne room. Just ahead of them lay the golden basin that still bubbled and spewed cosmic energies some fifteen meters into the air. Beyond that, the bodies of the Princess Marens and Colonel Belisarius lay unmoving, the hideous, ghostlike shape of the demonform slowly descending and merging ever so slowly into the body of the young woman. Only a fraction of the demon remained visible now; the process would not take much longer. The six ceremonial guardsmen had reemerged but the bulk of the Sand Kings forces were still absent.

Delain had her right hand outstretched in front of her. "Because," she answered, "while I am capable of obscuring us from the view of mortal man, I have no idea if the same can be said of a god. If the vizier there is truly one of Those Who Remain, the possibility exists that he could detect us at any time."

Tamerlane nodded, agitated. He was staring straight at the princess and the demon, and his face was contorted with anger. "How dare they do this?" he muttered to himself. "It's *inhuman.*"

"Zahir is *not* a human," Delain pointed out. "And, based on his words, Rameses must now believe the same can be said of himself."

"We'll see about that," the general snapped.

"We must hurry," Delain said. "I'm sorry it took so long to get us down from the balcony." There had been a large group of Sand Kings standing at attention directly in front of the doorway that led from the balcony's stairway down into the throne room. Delain had insisted she could find another way, but it had taken a seeming eternity of repeated backtracking—and then another forever when they had run into yet another patrol and had had to take cover and wait. Tamerlane had felt he could have taken down either group—particularly with Delain's able assistance—but he wasn't ready to reveal his or the rest of his team's presence just yet.

"Colonel Arani and the others on the balcony are well-concealed from casual view," Delain said, "but without my powers to blanket them entirely, they could be discovered at any moment."

Tamerlane nodded again. "So—let me make sure I understand. All we need to do is get to this bowl thing, and you can use the power from it to sort of boost the signal so that I can contact Iapetus via the Aether?"

"Essentially, yes," Delain agreed. "I anticipate that it will be more difficult given the interference clogging the Aether. But I will do my best."

"I know you will." Tamerlane gave her a wink. "Alright. Let's do it."

Right hand held out before her, the Inquisitor led the way, keeping the two of them as invisible as she could. So far, no one was looking their way, which certainly helped.

They crouched down behind the golden basin and Delain offered the general her left hand. He gave her a look but shrugged and took it in his right. Then, closing her eyes, she touched the basin with her own right hand.

"Open the Aether link in your mind," the woman told him quietly.

Tamerlane braced himself for the onslaught of painful static he'd experienced earlier. He closed his eyes and concentrated.

There was no pain. The interference was gone. The Aether opened itself to him without protest. Then Delain began to draw cosmic energy from the fountain, allowing it to flow into Tamerlane. In reaction, the general gasped. The resonance, the depth of his senses increased a hundredfold—a thousandfold. He found he could reach with his mind through the infinitely branching pipeline that was the Aether net, to find—to touch—almost anyone who was connected to it.

"Is it working?" Delain asked.

"*Nnnggh,*" Tamerlane responded, unable to form words in the physical world as his mind expanded throughout the AetherSphere. All the recent talk of godhood had meant little to him, but suddenly he felt he understood, ever so slightly, what that might be like. His mortal frame still sat hunched down, hidden behind the golden cauldron, but his consciousness traveled throughout the cosmos in the blink of an eye. To inhabit all of even one narrow sliver of the Above—to have one's consciousness filling the entire network, all at once—was to become in some ways a living god.

"General," came the voice of Delain as if from far away. "General!"

He felt something then—felt something with his nearly-forgotten physical body. He blinked his eyes open and saw her, hunched over, leaning towards him. She was kicking him in the shins.

"General!" she hissed again. "You have to control it—don't let it carry you away. If you go too far down that path, you might not come back."

Tamerlane's eyes focused on her. He understood—understood all too well, now. Steeling himself, he closed his eyes again. This time, though, he did it with purpose, with focus. This time, as the Aether enveloped him, he knew exactly what he was doing, where he was going, for whom he was searching.

Iapetus. Iapetus!

Where are you, O commander of the Sons of Terra? Where are—

There.

The link opened and the mental "voice" of Ioan Iapetus echoed in Tamerlane's head. *"Who is this? What is happening?"*

"General," Tamerlane said, his voice a carefully-contained thunderbolt striking across the cosmos. "I need you. You and your legion. Now."

To his credit, Iapetus seemed to grasp what was happening—and to whom he was speaking—remarkably quickly.

"So. Tamerlane. Again you request my assistance."

"This is no *request*, General. You will bring your legion here, now, if you wish to see the Empire—and the galaxy itself—survive."

Iapetus did not reply for a moment. Then, *"What is this grave danger you need my help in confronting?"* He laughed. *"Have Rameses and his Sand Kings proven too much for your own soldiers to handle?"*

"It's not just Rameses. It's the people—if *people* they truly are—that he serves."

"And who would that *be?"*

"The gods," Tamerlane said. "Three of them, we believe." He paused. "They have the princess. She's in the process now of being possessed by a demon lord."

"By a what*?"* Iapetus's voice betrayed his skepticism.

"There is no more time," Tamerlane barked across the link. "If you don't want to see the galaxy laid waste, with a creature of the Below reigning over the ruins, you must act. And you must act *now!*"

Iapetus laughed again.

"Why do you laugh?" Tamerlane demanded. "Do you discount the degree of danger we face?"

"Oh no, not at all," Iapetus replied. *"I believe you. It's just that your timing could not have been more fortuitous."*

"Why is that?" Tamerlane asked, barely holding his anger at the man in check.

"Because I will be there in mere moments," he replied.

"You—*what?*" Tamerlane couldn't quite believe what he was hearing. "You're already on the way?"

"You are in the throne room now—is that correct?"

"Yes, but—"

"Rumor has it Rameses possesses a weapon of awesome might within the throne room," Iapetus went on, ignoring Tamerlane's objections. *"If it can be disabled, the force I have here with me should be sufficient."*

"The force you have with you?" Tamerlane was taken aback. "We may require the better part of your entire legion."

"I doubt that." He continued on before Tamerlane could object. *"Can you disable the weapon in the next few moments?"*

"I think so. Yes."

"Good. Do it."

The link was severed on the far end. Tamerlane opened his eyes.

"Success?" Delain asked.

"It...*sounded* like it," Tamerlane said, "but then again, it was Iapetus, so—" Tamerlane started to say more, but a cry from the gangly vizier, Zahir, caught his attention.

"The demon lord will soon arise! The process is nearly complete!"

At Zahir's shout, Rameses turned from where he had been standing over the body of Nakamura. He had been gazing down at the broken *Taiko*, mixed feelings nearly overwhelming what little remained of his own personality—the parts Goraddon hadn't violently and permanently suppressed. Part of him was thrilled to see the presumptive, arrogant Nakamura brought low—and even more thrilled at the possibilities for himself that now lay open. But another part of him, buried deep inside, was extremely disappointed. "I—I didn't get to *do* anything," he whined softly, so that no one else could hear. "I only got to stand there, in hiding, and—"

"Lord Rameses," Zahir called, his kohl-rimmed eyes meeting the governor's, seeming to appraise him carefully. "Did you hear? The process is nearly finished."

"What's that?" Rameses asked, blinking as he roused himself from his musings.

"It is almost irreversible now. Come and see," Zahir said, beckoning with skeletal fingers.

The crimson armor moving smoothly, as though it were but a suit of silken clothing, Rameses crossed the short distance between them and stared at the body of the little princess on her palanquin. The demonform was no longer visible above her, save as a vivid, glowing red halo about her. Somewhere inside Rameses a voice screamed objections, but that part of him was locked away forever. Instead he merely nodded. "Very good," he said. "What next?"

Zahir had turned and was stepping over the bodies of the Lords of Fire soldiers that lay dead on the cold marble floor. "First we must have the Sand Kings remove this... *debris*," he clucked, kicking at one of the bodies disdainfully. He turned. "And then—"

Nakamura was sitting halfway up. His eyes burned with hatred.

Zahir gasped and stumbled back, tripping over a body, going down in a heap. His Egyptian headdress toppled off and skittered across the floor.

"Monster!" Nakamura shouted. "Loathsome creature!" He brought his hands up, directing both of them at Zahir. "How dare you harm the princess?"

Zahir scrambled to get back—to get away. He was entirely too slow.

Flames lashed out from Nakamura's hands; cosmic flames that were not of our realm but of the Above. The fires set into Zahir with all the fury of their master who had conjured them.

Erupting like an oil-soaked torch, Zahir screamed.

Still ensorcelled, the guardsmen only stared straight ahead, lacking any coherent commands from Zahir.

All eyes moved to the blazing man as he staggered back, shrieking, his features obscured by flames. All eyes, that is, except for one pair.

Rameses was staring directly at the Sword of Baranak where it lay on the marble floor. He moved toward it, reaching out.

Tamerlane saw what was happening—it was all only a short distance away from him—but he couldn't quite believe it.

"He's alive," he said to Delain, voice strained with emotion. "He's *still alive!*"

Delain knew what the general was going to do but, before she could attempt anything to stop him, he raised up from cover, taking one step in Nakamura's direction, clearly intending to come to his assistance. "*Taiko!*" he called. "Are you—?"

Rameses, encased in the cosmic crimson armor, came forward and into view. He held something in his right hand, raised high. Something gleaming and golden. Too late, Tamerlane realized it was the Sword of Baranak. He raised a hand to unleash his own cosmic flame.

The sword came around, not slowed in the least by its passage through Nakamura's neck. The head separated from the body and dropped to the marble floor, followed a second later by the body itself. Both parts burst into flame.

Tamerlane screamed.

From her post on the balcony of the throne room, Colonel Niobe Arani saw it all unfold with mounting horror.

General Tamerlane and the Inquisition woman, Delain, were crouched behind the golden basin, busy in their attempt to contact General Iapetus. The pale, lanky vizier, meanwhile, was standing over the little princess, supervising—and reveling in—the near-completion of the process that would bind a demonform to her forever. Then, unexpectedly, Nakamura the *Taiko* had risen up, his wounds apparently not fatal, and had unleashed a blast of fire at the vizier. The vile man had stumbled back, falling over the bodies of former soldiers of I Legion, his every visible surface area bursting into flame. He'd shrieked, and he'd burned.

And then the most horrifying development of all: Governor Rameses, encased in the strange, red armor and wielding the Sword of Baranak that Nakamura himself had brought with him to Ahknaton, had swung the cosmic blade and decapitated the *Taiko*. The man's head and his body had each burst into an uncontrollable blaze. Within seconds, only ashes remained.

In reaction, General Tamerlane had stood and screamed in horror. Arani couldn't blame him. If someone who had meant as much to her as she knew Nakamura meant to Tamerlane had just been killed—and killed in *that* manner, and right in front of her—she, too, likely would have thrown caution to the wind. Unfortunately, doing so revealed his presence to the bad guys—and it would surely make them look for others.

In short, Arani understood in an instant that the jig was up. Coming to terms with that fact and all of its ramifications very quickly, she took Titus Elaro's rifle from him before he could object. She hefted it, sighted down it, and fired.

Rameses was just advancing on Tamerlane, the sword held high and ready to strike again, when Arani's shot caught him in the lower ribcage on the left side. It didn't penetrate the crimson armor at all, but the force of the blast spun him around and sent him backwards a step.

Tamerlane stood now like some vengeful god, his hands blazing with cosmic fire. Still standing on the other side of the golden bowl, he directed his arms in the direction of Rameses and let loose a column of flames that crossed the short distance between them in less than the blink of an eye. The fires washed quickly over him.

"That is the best you can do, Tamerlane?" Rameses barked. The flames were settling down and it appeared now that the armor was entirely undamaged.

The last of the flames vanished and Rameses stalked forward again. As he moved, however, he cast a quick glance toward Zahir, intending to ask the vizier how he was; to ask him if Nakamura's attack had caused him any harm. What he saw took him aback and stopped him in his tracks.

Zahir lay on the floor, his body a burned, molten mess. There was no way the poor wretch could have lived long in that state. As Rameses looked on, however, the vizier-god's eyes turned upward and stared directly at him; it was enough to give anyone who saw it nightmares for years to come. And then the blackened body rose from the marble floor, the mouth opening and closing, no intelligible sounds emerging but only an animal-like hiss.

Rameses gawked. He dithered, his eyes moving back and forth from the shambling wreck of Zahir to the infuriated Tamerlane.

Then, as Arani prepared to take another shot before leading the troops down into the throne room in one last act of defiance, several things happened at once:

The air a short distance away swirled about, slowly forming a vertical circle of clouds and light.

Rameses, not seeing this, focused his attention on Tamerlane and started forward again, the sword up and ready to strike.

And Tamerlane, his rage overtaking him yet still somehow allowing him enough sanity to remember the other job that needed doing, grasped the lip of the golden basin with both hands. Acting purely on instinct and anger, but with all the strength he possessed, he lifted the edge of the cauldron and tipped it over in the direction of Rameses and Zahir.

A wave of sloshing, foaming, raw cosmic energy poured out. The leading edge struck Rameses and bore him back and away. Then it washed over the zombie-like form of Zahir, and the already-ragged figure screamed in agony. As the energies engulfed him, his flesh bubbled and boiled away. A second later, the wave had passed, leaving behind only his bones, which began to crumble to dust. Within seconds only a charred spot remained where once the vizier had stood.

Rameses, regaining his footing and protected from the onslaught by the cosmic armor, gaped at the rapidly diminishing remains of Zahir—a god he had believed could never die. "The fountain," he murmured, realizing the truth. "The energies. They were not tuned. In their raw state, they can destroy even a god." He looked down at himself. "Only the armor saved me," he exclaimed, patting himself all over as if to be sure all his parts were still there. "Only the armor…"

Tamerlane ignored all of this. His fury was undiminished. He started toward Rameses, even as Arani and Elaro and the rest of the company rushed down from the balcony to help.

Rameses stood in his gleaming crimson armor, the mighty Sword of Baranak clutched in his hand. He regarded Tamerlane and laughed heartily. "You—you *attack* me, General?" he asked, incredulous. "I wear the armor of the gods. I wield the mightiest weapon in the galaxy. I am a living god! And you—*you*—are *unarmed*." He laughed again. "Why in the name of Those Who Remain should I fear you?"

"Because I can make you *burn*," Tamerlane barked. He gestured with his right hand and flames leapt up across Rameses' back and the side of his head.

The governor of Ahknaton scoffed, ignoring the fire, entirely untroubled by it. "Your meager powers do not concern me, Ezekial," he said. "Start all the fires you like. Inside this armor, I cannot be harmed!" He plodded forward, raising the sword high. "But I can certainly harm *you*!"

Colonel Arani and her team rushed down the stairs and onto the floor of the throne room. They had expected to encounter resistance from the Sand Kings, but only a scant half-dozen of Rameses' soldiers occupied the vast chamber—and those stood still as statues, staring off into space.

Arani and Elaro gawked at the heavily armed and armored ceremonial guardsmen for a moment, uncertain of what to make of them. Then, concluding that, for whatever reason, they did not represent a threat—at least for the moment—they dashed past them towards Tamerlane.

The general saw them coming out of the corner of his eye, even as he kept the other glued on the advancing Rameses. He waved them away. "The princess," he shouted to them. "See to her. See if it's not too late!"

Arani hesitated, then complied. She ran to where the young girl lay on the platform, her entire body surrounded by a bright red glow. "I don't know," she called, almost frantic as she beheld the horror that was occurring before her. "I have no way of knowing." She turned to Titus Elaro, who stood behind her, looking on with an expression of disgust. "What can we do?"

Sister Delain appeared between them suddenly, as if she'd been conjured like some ghost or spirit of the netherworld. She raised one hand, palm facing outward in the direction of the little girl. "It is as I feared," she murmured, her voice barely audible. "This process—it is alien to me." She looked up at Arani, despair evident on her face. "It may well be irreversible now."

"Try *something*," Elaro almost shouted.

Arani put a hand on his arm to calm him, then said to Delain, "Do what you can. We may not have much time before Rameses' army rushes in here."

Frowning but nodding, Delain moved closer to the glowing girl and bent over her, hands moving in gestures both subtle and complex.

Meanwhile the other soldiers that had come down with Arani from the balcony moved quickly up behind Tamerlane, seeking to help him against the armored enemy. Again Tamerlane motioned them back, even as he slowly gave ground himself.

"You retreat," Rameses laughed.

"I stall for time," Tamerlane replied.

"Time?" Rameses regarded him with an expression that portrayed mostly scorn and contempt, but revealed a slight degree of curiosity. "Time for what?"

"For them," Tamerlane said. He nodded toward the spot in midair nearby that was currently in the process of rending itself open.

Rameses, sensing a trick, hesitated for only a second. Then he turned his head quickly and looked. He gasped.

Lightning was flaring out of a hole ripped in the fabric of spacetime. A dimensional rift had been torn open in the midst of his throne room, and to Rameses' shock and horror, a veritable army was rushing through. Men and women alike, their faces bore grim determination if not outright fanaticism. Their black uniforms shone in the light of the chamber's artificial illumination and open flames, and the golden eye insignia on each of their chests was unmistakable.

It was the II Legion—the Sons of Terra. And at their head, the infamous commander himself, General Ioan "The Unyielding" Iapetus, led the way. Beside him walked the Ecclesiarch, Teluria, in her red robes and hood, very obviously unhappy to be there. Iapetus held a pistol in his right hand, aimed casually in her general direction.

Rameses gawked at the intruders, and he stopped his advance. The sword drooped slightly in his hand as he fully appreciated exactly who had invaded his inner sanctum. "You—!" he managed at last. Anger and resentment almost overtook him. "*You!*"

"Us," Iapetus said. Then, more formally, "We are the Sons of Terra," he intoned. "And in the name of sacred Mother Earth, Governor Amon Rameses, we are here to accept your surrender." He smiled his cruel smile. "And if, as I hope, you choose *not* to surrender, we are here to render you very, *very* dead."

3

Chaos reigned in the throne room.

Only seconds after the Sons of Terra appeared, pouring in through the portal, the six elite guardsmen of Rameses awoke. Seeing the intruders, the six let loose with their power rifles and energy lances. The blasts cut into the leading edge of the Sons' line.

The Sons scarcely seemed to notice. Their numbers were too great, their focus too intense. They closed up their ranks and opened fire.

The exceptional nature of the elite guardsmen's armor protected them for somewhat longer than an average trooper's suit would've, allowing a mere six to hold out for over a minute rather than only seconds. Soon enough, however, the unyielding barrage of firepower from the Sons' guns began to have an impact. First one and then another of the guardsmen went down before the onslaught, gold and enamel armor shredded by particle beams, slugs and energy bolts.

Rameses, reeling from this unexpected intrusion into his throne room, his palace, and his world, retreated in confusion. Tamerlane was almost entirely forgotten to him now. His focus instead was on Iapetus—hated, despised Iapetus, with his arrogance and his condescension and his cursed legion. A legion that now seemed to be transporting its entirety right here onto Ahknaton.

"I still have the sword," he reminded himself as he backed away. "And this armor. And—" He turned and looked about. "—my own legion," he finished, frowning, looking around as if realizing for the first time that no other troops were present in the chamber. "What?" he asked no one. "Where—where are the—?"

And then he remembered. Remembered the man in black sending them away, closing the door behind them. Leaving him here with only six guardsmen to protect him.

"Guards!" he cried, running for the entrance. "Come to me! You are needed!" He reached the doors and fought the locks, attempting to force them open. Something had been done to them; something had fused them solid.

The man in black, he realized. *He did this.*

A part of him—buried deep, deep down inside—wanted to scream in defiance. But he couldn't. He simply could not. He was incapable of fully formulating coherent thoughts one way or the other about the man in bl—about—about that man who—about—

Shaking his head as if lost in a fog, Rameses shouted wordless anger and raised the Sword of Baranak. He swung it around and down against the doors. Lightning flared and sparks flew, but Goraddon's seals held.

"Sand Kings!" the mad governor shouted. "I need you!" He swung the sword again, and the sound of its impact resounded like a thunderbolt within the confines of the throne room.

"General," Arani called a few moments earlier. "We need you!"

Next to her, Delain ceased her efforts and leaned heavily against a column, almost fainting from exhaustion. The body of the princess lay unmoving and unchanged on the flat platform, a red glow still surrounding it.

Tamerlane had thought to pursue Rameses, but with the chamber rapidly filling with II Legion troops and with Arani calling him, he decided to let Iapetus have first crack at finishing off the governor. He hurried over to where the colonel and her little entourage were gathered around the platform.

"I cannot do it," Delain managed to get out as she gasped for breath. Her black hood was pulled completely back and sweat ran down her pale, smooth face.

"Then what—" Tamerlane began.

"She has an idea," Arani said, interrupting her commanding officer. "Sir."

Tamerlane looked from the colonel to the Inquisitor. "Well?" he asked, impatient.

"The demonform has not yet fully manifested into our plane of reality," Delain said. "I can open a way into its dimension, but I am unable to harm it—or affect it at all, really—once I do so."

Tamerlane took this in and nodded. "Alright. And?"

Arani looked at him. "You're the answer."

"Me?"

"Your fire."

Tamerlane took this in, blinking. He thought he understood, more or less. "Very well," he said. "What do I do?"

Delain quickly explained. Then, even as energy blasts and tracers sliced their way back and forth across the huge chamber, the three of them got to work.

"Wait, wait," Delain whispered, leaning close over the body of the princess. "Be ready..."

Tamerlane gritted his teeth. The thought of a demon lord mere inches away from Delain made his skin crawl. And—

if they were successful in this impromptu exorcism, would the creature erupt right out of the little girl's body, doing the gods knew what harm as it did so, and would it immediately attack those nearest to it, namely Arani, Elaro, Delain, and him?

Tamerlane inhaled deeply and tried to put such thoughts out of his head. This little girl was the only living heir to the throne, as far as he or anyone knew. With Nakamura very obviously dead, there was no one else left to pull the disintegrating Empire back together. No wonder Rameses wanted her under his control! She had to be saved—freed— no matter the cost to him or anyone else. "I'm ready," he breathed. "Just tell me when."

As Arani and Elaro stood guard over them both, Delain shook her head, continuing to chant as she moved her fingers in complex gestures above the little girl's comatose body. "Wait," she hissed, between incantations. "Wait—"

The plan as the Inquisitor lady had explained it was simple enough—yet insanely dangerous. Delain would open a small dimensional portal through the girl and directly into the underverse from whence the demon lord had been summoned, and where most of its metaphysical body likely still resided. Tamerlane's job was to unleash a blast of his cosmic fire through the girl and into the portal, with the goal of driving the rest of the demon out of the princess and back down the hole into its own realm. Theoretically the fire would travel within and along the pathway of the portal and would not touch or harm the girl's physical body. Also theoretically, the demon would be trapped in its own dimension once again, as it had been before the late Emperor and his party had brought it and its brethren back. That was entirely too much "theoretically" for Tamerlane, but what else could he do? It was all well outside of his base of expertise. And in truth there were only a couple of variables: Would Tamerlane's flames be enough to dislodge the monster, or would it all be for naught? And, of course, would the fire truly pass harmlessly through the little girl and not harm her—or would Tamerlane himself be the one who actually killed her?

None of them had any way of knowing, and no time to experiment. So they did the only thing they could: They tried it anyway.

The Inquisitor ceased her incantations and curled her fingers into a tight fist. She gritted her teeth and grunted. At that moment, a swirl of light formed directly above the little girl's chest.

"Now!" shouted Delain.

Carefully containing and regulating it—and grateful that he'd spent so much time in recent weeks refining those abilities—Tamerlane poured a column of flame down the narrow tunnel of light, and directly into the little body that lay before him.

The princess opened her eyes and screamed.

Unnerved, Tamerlane gasped and stepped back, the fire instantly cut off. Delain stopped her gestures and opened her hands, palms outward, toward the girl. She was breathing heavily.

Princess Marens cried out once again, then collapsed limply onto the palanquin.

"Did it work?" Tamerlane demanded, moving instantly to the girl's side. He took her hand, feeling for her pulse. "Was that enough? When she screamed, I—"

"I—I do not know," Delain gasped, sweat now pouring from her brow.

"How will we know? *When* will we know?" Arani demanded.

The Inquisitor recovered enough to give the colonel a sharp look. Under normal circumstances, no one would ever dream of speaking that way to an official of the Holy Inquisition. The present circumstances being the farthest thing from normal, however, Delain appeared to take the questioning in stride. "I'm sorry," she managed to say, her voice ragged, "I simply don't know. All we can do is wait and see."

"That's not good enough!" Arani almost shouted. "This little girl—"

Tamerlane leaned in between them. "Colonel Arani. I appreciate your concern for the Princess. But I believe your energy and passion could be put to better use." He nodded toward the horde of black-clad Sons of Terra still swarming into the throne room, their guns blasting away at the remaining two guardsmen, who had taken cover behind marble columns. "Unless you believe General Iapetus will be easy to manage once this is all over."

Arani looked at him. She blinked. "I understand, General. My apologies." She turned to Delain. "To you as well, Inquisitor. I shouldn't have—"

Delain raised a hand and shook her head. "It's alright, Colonel. I fully appreciate your concern." Then she looked back at the girl. She frowned. "The red glow is gone."

"That's good—right?" Tamerlane asked, looking from Delain to Arani and back.

"I suppose so, but—"

Delain was interrupted by Titus Elaro, who leaned in front of Tamerlane, his blast pistol unholstered and in hand. "General," he said urgently, "the Sand Kings. They're in."

Tamerlane looked up. He absorbed the tactical situation instantly.

As the last of the elite guardsmen held the Sons of Terra assault force off, Rameses had finally managed to unseal the massive double doors at the end of the throne room. The twin portals burst open and an army of Egyptian-styled soldiers rushed in, past the exhausted Rameses. Still clad in his crimson armor, he stood off to the side, the sword resting tip-down on the floor as he leaned upon it like a walking stick.

"Kill them!" he shouted, pointing at the II Legion troops in their black and gold. "Kill the intruders!"

The two armies sized one another up in less than a second, Sand Kings on one side and Sons of Terra on the other, and then the guns of both sides opened fire. The throne room became a killing zone. The Battle for Ahknaton was truly engaged.

4

As the Sand Kings in their red and blue enameled body armor charged into the throne room, General Iapetus and his unwilling companion moved quickly aside, seeking cover. The need to lead from the front was now over, and the priority became simply to survive the conflict. Victory would be nice, too, but survival above all else.

"You will suffer for this," Teluria growled at him. Her dark red robes were pulled tightly against herself and her hood nearly obscured her face as well as the rest of her head. "No one treats me this way."

"Obviously *someone* does, since I'm doing it presently," Iapetus replied as he pulled her behind a column. The god-slayer pistol rested loosely but comfortably in his hand, and it wasn't exactly aimed at Teluria—but it wasn't exactly aimed anywhere else, either. "Just be patient and we will be finished here shortly."

"What if you don't win?" the woman hissed vindictively. "What if Rameses beats your army?"

Iapetus snorted. "I seriously doubt that outcome is a likely possibility." He offered her a half-shrug. "But, should it somehow occur, I will need you to open a way out of here for us, and in record time." He smiled. "That's the main reason I've had to impose upon you to stay close to me a little longer."

She glared at him but said nothing. Just beyond them, the firefight only amped up higher, bright and deadly red and yellow and green streaks of coherent light and whizzing projectiles crisscrossing the open interior of the chamber.

Seeing nothing more to be done for the princess, Tamerlane and Delain had moved out into the midst of the battle and were contributing what they could to aid the cause of the Sons of Terra. It felt extremely odd to Tamerlane to actually help the soldiers in black; in recent days he'd nearly come to think of them as yet another enemy. But that was ridiculous, of course. They were one of the three major army groups of the Empire, and he told himself he could not allow his personal dislike for the abrasive Iapetus to cloud his attitude toward II Legion. He wasn't entirely sure how convincing he was, though.

So Tamerlane hurled fireballs at the Sand Kings and Delain confounded them with illusions and distortions, causing them to shoot at their own men or run into walls. It didn't amount to a lot in the grand scheme of things, but it made them both feel as though they were genuinely contributing to the effort against Rameses—that he was being beaten at last.

Tamerlane, nonetheless, couldn't shake an odd feeling that somehow he was causing himself more trouble in the long run. But all he could do was to dismiss the feeling as paranoia and redouble his efforts. So he fired blast after searing blast of cosmic flame into the ranks of the Sand Kings, melting their armor and weapons and driving them back.

LEGION II: SONS OF TERRA

For another fifteen minutes at least, the battle raged unabated, though it felt to the participants like hours. In such a confined space—even one as large as the massive throne room of the Heliopolis—the two armies were pressed together tightly and the fight grew brutal almost immediately, with hand-to-hand combat replacing stand-off-and-shoot fighting more and more often as the minutes passed by. Rifles were slung onto backs as the two legions' almost-frictionless *gladii* came out of their sheaths—short stabbing swords that could penetrate even the finest plate armor.

Movement was limited, and attempts were made to break open the congested little battlefield; a half-dozen Sand Kings with flight packs lofted into the air and attempted to fly over the Sons, likely in an effort to get behind them and squeeze the invaders between two lines. It never came close to succeeding. The Sons had brought a few extremely heavy-duty, tripod-mounted energy cannons with them, and they swiveled them upwards, blasting the fliers, causing still-smoking pieces to rain down on the marble tiles. Seeing this, the Sand Kings didn't attempt any more aerial attacks.

Black, acrid smoke filled the broad chamber. Tamerlane and Delain were both coughing nearly every breath, as were many of the soldiers who hadn't brought breathing equipment. Fires had erupted in spots behind the Sand Kings front line where Tamerlane had directed the brunt of his flaming assault. The dead and wounded lay everywhere, in some cases layered over the casualties of Nakamura's first attack. There wasn't as much blood; the weapons being employed mostly tended to self-cauterize the flesh as they did their damage. Nevertheless, the marble tiles were growing slick and spots of clean, open floor were becoming scarce.

The portal Teluria had opened to bring the II Legion to Ahknaton was closed now; what the Sons had with them in terms of troop strength was what they had. The numbers had appeared to be more than enough at first, but with casualties mounting so quickly, one had to start to wonder: Who will run out of troops first, Rameses or Iapetus?

In the event, it was the Sand Kings who at last gave way.

The battle had been an epic one, with heroic and cowardly deeds in equal measure on both sides.

Ultimately, though, the Sand Kings faltered, their morale never the equal of the fanatical Sons. Sensing victory at last at hand, Iapetus issued new orders over the now-clear Aether link and the black-uniformed horde responded, redoubling their efforts in key spots.

One thing about their approach was very clear to Tamerlane from the start, and only became magnified as the battle raged on: the Sons had no intentions of taking any prisoners. They lashed out with a fanatical fervor Tamerlane had rarely seen from trained Imperial forces. They were utterly brutal. Any of the Ahknaton soldiers who attempted to surrender were simply shot.

They're operating according to a different set of rules from my Lords of Fire or Agrippa's Kings of Oblivion, he understood fully then. A cold dread moved up from his stomach and began to grip his heart. *What have I gotten myself—and the Empire—into, bringing this crowd into things?* he wondered. *Can they be managed—controlled—at all, once it's all over?*

It was a fair question—as Tamerlane would discover soon enough.

Tamerlane stood looking down at the princess. Behind and around him, a few shots still rang out here and there, but for the most part the Battle of Ahknaton was over. The Sand Kings had been routed, their best forces defeated— *slain*, Tamerlane corrected himself—and the entire

LEGION II: SONS OF TERRA

Heliopolis secured by II Legion troops. Scattered units still operated outside the city, but they could be mopped up at any time, later on. Tamerlane sincerely hoped that meant "persuading them to surrender and change sides," rather than "kill them," because, in addition to simply not wanting to have to kill anyone else, manpower was becoming increasingly scarce. They needed every soldier they could get.

Of Rameses there was no sign. He had disappeared during the melee. Elite Sons of Terra units were searching the palace for him now. Iapetus, meanwhile, was nowhere to be seen, either. The good part of all that was the number of Sons troopers in the throne room was down to a bare minimum, as well.

Tamerlane gestured toward the little girl and looked to Inquisitor Delain. "What's her status?" he asked. "Do you know yet if she—?"

Delain shook her head. "The telltale signs are gone, and she appears to be resting normally—pure sleep, not an induced coma—but I have no way of truly knowing, and I still fear—"

"Right." Tamerlane didn't want to hear the rest. He spared a glance at the body of Belisarius lying on the other palanquin. The man still appeared as stiff as a statue; he might as well be dead. He had no idea what that might mean.

The general ran a hand through his graying hair and turned to where Colonel Arani and Titus Elaro stood, their guns slung over their shoulders and their faces dirty with soot and blood from the battle. He started to ask them about the status of the *Nizam* forces when a veritable battalion of II Legion soldiers in black and gold marched up, boots crashing on the marble floor. At their head was not General Iapetus but Colonel Barbarossa—a sight that warmed Tamerlane's heart. Though it had only been days, it felt like weeks or months since he had dispatched Barbarossa back to the man's own legion to keep an eye on Iapetus—to "watch the watchman." This, he felt, was a Son of Terra that he could do business with.

Thus he was somewhat nonplussed when Barbarossa motioned and the Sons behind him all drew their weapons, leveling them at Tamerlane and his little group.

"What is the meaning of this, Colonel?" the general demanded.

"Orders, sir," Barbarossa replied with a slight shrug. "The Princess is to come with us, back to the *Atlantia*."

Tamerlane gaped. "*What?*"

Several Sons started forward toward the nearer palanquin. Tamerlane stepped in front of them, hands raised. "Hold on. I've given no orders that II Legion is to take custody of—"

"The orders came from General Iapetus himself, sir," Barbarossa said casually.

Tamerlane frowned. "Iapetus has no authority to issue an order such as that," he barked. "*I* am the ranking officer here."

Barbarossa offered the general a half-smile. "I'm afraid you may find some things have...*changed*, sir," he said coldly.

Tamerlane reddened. "You have no love for Iapetus. You've said so. You were helping me—serving the Empire, not that egotistical—"

The general's angry objection ended in mid-sentence as Barbarossa merely laughed. "So you were to believe." He chuckled. "Iapetus feels strongly that any foe—real or potential—should think he knows more than he actually does about our legion's doings. Should have a, shall we say, false sense of security. Thus he arranged for double-agents in all the most critical locations across the Empire." His smile widened now. "That would, of course, include me." He looked directly at Titus Elaro. "Among others."

Tamerlane and Arani blanched. They turned, staring at Elaro. The Major appeared extremely uncomfortable; he was sweating and his skin was red.

"Major Elaro," Barbarossa ordered, "secure the princess and let us depart."

"You were a mole?" Arani gasped, astonished. "You're part of the *Sons*?" To her credit, given what had happened between them, she didn't react violently or emotionally. She stepped away from Elaro but closer to the princess, her rifle unslung and at the ready. "You're not taking the girl," she said, glaring at him.

Elaro looked from Arani to Barbarossa and back. He appeared uncertain.

"It's not too late for either of you," Tamerlane asserted, moving forward. In reaction, the Sons brandished their weapons in his direction; he ignored them. "Iapetus is committing high treason by doing this. You don't have to go down with him."

"Treason?" Barbarossa scoffed. "Against whom?" He motioned toward the piles of bodies around the throne; one of them had been Nakamura's. "The so-called *Taiko* is dead." He nodded toward the princess. "This little girl is the only legitimate authority remaining in the Empire. Whoever controls her is, by definition, legitimate—and whoever opposes them is, by definition, an insurgent. A rebel." He looked from Tamerlane's face to Arani's to Delain's and back. "So, if I were you, I would be very careful about just whom I accused of committing treason, General."

Tamerlane bunched his fists together but didn't move—yet.

"Now," Barbarossa continued. "Major Elaro—if you would?"

Elaro looked down at the little girl, then up at Arani. He breathed deeply, then shook his head. "I'm sorry, Colonel," he said, "but I can't do that."

Barbarossa frowned. This was the first thing to go against Iapetus's carefully laid plans, and it took the colonel by surprise. "What did you say, Major?"

"I can't help you abduct the princess. It's wrong. General Tamerlane is right."

Barbarossa shook his head sadly. Then he motioned. In response, a half-dozen Sons of Terra rushed forward. One clubbed Elaro in the head with the butt of his rifle in a quick and savage move. The others grabbed the girl quickly but securely and lifted her up, even as Elaro collapsed to the floor, bleeding.

Colonel Arani cursed loudly and raised her weapon to fire at the Sons, but another of their legion moved up behind her silently and knocked her down in the same fashion as Elaro. The two lay side by side on the cold floor, eyes closed.

Tamerlane was utterly furious. He got up in Barbarossa's face, his finger jabbing the man in his chest. "You're going to be court-martialed," he said. "You and your general."

"It will be the other way around, I'm afraid," Barbarossa replied, still smiling.

Tamerlane watched as the soldiers carried the little girl away. "How do you know she's not still possessed? You may be taking a demon lord with you, back to Earth."

Barbarossa shrugged. "We will deal with that eventuality if and when it presents itself."

"You fool," Tamerlane breathed. "You have no idea what—"

"IAPETUS!"

The cry came from across the chamber—from a lone figure in red who was emerging from a heretofore hidden room behind the throne.

"TAMERLANE!"

Everyone looked up. Tamerlane saw the man standing there and he only shook his head. "Of course," he said. "Of course he would reappear now. The *idiot*."

Rameses strode out into the chamber, crimson energy crackling over the surface of his cosmic armor, the golden Sword of Baranak swinging in his hand.

LEGION II: SONS OF TERRA

"Zahir thought I did not know of his secret reserves of cosmic power hidden away in there," he muttered, his words barely audible. "But I have tapped into them—the Power fills me, overflows from me—and now I will have my vengeance!" He stalked toward Tamerlane, the sword coming up as he moved. "Where is that *dog*, that *barbarian*, Iapetus? I would have a reckoning with him, as well!"

Tamerlane shook his head. "I don't know."

Rameses scowled. "You first, then," he growled. He rushed forward, sword held high.

The Sons of Terra that had backed up Barbarossa moved in front of him and opened fire, almost point blank. The blasts all struck Rameses but deflected harmlessly off the armor.

Rameses roared in anger and whirled. He focused his attention on the soldiers in black and gold that had attacked him. When he moved, it was almost faster than the eye could see, the armor boosting his muscles and reflexes. The gleaming sword lashed out, slicing effortlessly through the ranks of black-clad soldiers. In mere seconds, they were all dead.

Barbarossa himself stumbled backward, trying to get away.

Tamerlane moved between them.

"If your issues are with me, Rameses," the general said, "then let us settle them together, you and I."

Rameses roared wordlessly and swung the sword. Tamerlane barely dodged. He raised his right hand and unleashed a blinding blast of flame directly into the governor's face. Rameses choked and stumbled back, but the armor somehow protected him even where it didn't appear to; perhaps, Tamerlane thought, it *did* cover his face, too, but was simply not visible there.

As the others hurried to move back out of the way, Tamerlane and Rameses circled one another, looking for an opening. Rameses struck again, the Sword of Baranak singing as it sliced through the air, barely missing the general's chest. Tamerlane followed with a column of fire he directed at the floor beneath the governor's feet, half-melting the marble and sending the armored man down onto his hands and knees. The sword remained clutched in his grasp.

Rameses jabbed with the blade as he fought his way back to his feet. He started to attack again, and Tamerlane prepared another counter-attack.

And that was when the demon lord erupted from Belisarius's body in a shower of blood and flame.

5

oth Tamerlane and Rameses whirled at the horrendous, inhuman, unearthly sound of a lord of the Below fully manifesting itself into our universe and tearing itself free of the ruined body of Colonel Belisarius.

It expanded rapidly in heft as well as in height, until within only a matter of seconds it towered over them, some four or five meters tall at least. Naked, its skin was the dark red of drying blood. Horns protruded from its forehead, and fangs from its mouth. Its eyes burned like fire, and when it roared, the sound was enough to crack the foundations of the palace itself.

"It must have retreated back into Belisarius," Tamerlane guessed, though no one else could hear. "That means the princess is safe, at least." He allowed himself some small measure of relief at that thought. Only a second's worth, though—the situation had just gone from very, very bad to infinitely worse. "Surrounded by every conceivable enemy, all at once," he added. "I suppose we can have one final reckoning, then." He found the thought oddly comforting. He was *tired*, he realized. So *very* tired. He felt as if he'd been carrying the entire Empire on his shoulders for months; come to think of it, in some ways, he *had* been. If he was about to go down—and, frankly, he couldn't imagine any other outcome of all this—at least it would be *over*. And, if nothing else, at least the little princess wasn't going to transform into the hideous creature that confronted him now. That much was a victory.

The hideous creature. Yes. That thought brought him back to the present with a start. The demon lord was here, now. It strode forward on reverse-bending legs, roaring its fury.

"We need to work together," Tamerlane called to the armored man across from him. "It's the only way anyone here survives."

Rameses looked as if he were about to reply in the affirmative. Then, with a blink and a sudden shake of his head, his expression hardened. "What care I for this thing?" he shouted back at the general. "Let it wreak its havoc. I seek only revenge!"

The mad governor rushed forward, ducking a taloned hand that swept out from the demon, and lunged at Tamerlane. The general dodged to one side and rolled. He raised a hand and blasted Rameses back with an erupting column of fire.

The two men got to their feet almost instantly, just ahead of the demon's next attack. Again Tamerlane was forced to defend himself from both threats; the demon lord, meanwhile, seemed to sense that Rameses wasn't seeking to harm it, and it turned all of its attention to Tamerlane.

"Listen to me," Tamerlane cried over the bellowing roars of the demon. "You can't simply let this creature—this *abomination*—win! It will conquer your entire world!" He moved again to dodge razor-sharp claws and conjured a wall of fire between him and the creature. "You must have *some* remaining bit of compassion or concern for this planet and its people!"

Rameses frowned at that. His expression began to change to one of increasing confusion. He looked back at the demon lord and halted, no longer attacking Tamerlane. "What—what is *happening*?" he muttered. "Why—?"

The red monstrosity, perhaps sensing that something about Rameses was changing—that he was questioning the layers of mind control that had been laid down within him by Goraddon—appeared to conclude he had become a threat once more. The demon brought its long arm back and swept it around, striking Rameses hard and sending him hurtling across the floor and into one of the columns with a resounding crash. The seemingly indestructible armor he wore protected his body from most of the potential physical harm, but he was shaken severely. By the time he had regained his senses and raised up onto his haunches, his mind had cleared at last.

"*This* is what they desired to see ruling here, on *my* world?" he exclaimed, horrified, as he stared up at the towering creature. "And they somehow convinced me I should go along with it—?"

"It was Goraddon," Tamerlane said. "We saw him. We heard him. He's been controlling you—influencing you. He wanted you to help him implant this thing within the body of the princess. That was his goal all along."

"Goraddon?" Rameses reacted to this news as if he'd had no idea whatsoever. Then his mouth opened and closed and twisted into a horrified expression. He gasped. "Yes! Goraddon! It's true—it's all *true!*"

The demon clearly understood what was happening. A beast it was, but it was cunning, possessed of a keen if crude intelligence already, only moments after its "birth" into our universe. It bellowed again, louder, and rushed at both of them.

Fortunately, at that moment, the remaining Sons of Terra troops in the room appeared to have concluded that the hideous abomination that had erupted out of Belisarius was perhaps a more immediate enemy than Tamerlane or Rameses. They opened fire at it, their blast pistols and quad-rifles slashing and searing into its mottled flesh.

The monster turned slowly away from the retreating duo it had been fighting and sized up the dozen or so black-clad II Legion soldiers who were firing at it. A second passed; two. A long, forked tongue emerged from its mouth and licked upward, touching a spot where a particularly powerful blast had struck the side of its face. Then it moved, and it moved like lightning. Before the Sons could fall back or find any sort of cover, it was in their midst, raking its talons here and there, its tail lashing like a heavy bullwhip, its fangs clamping down on whatever it could get between them.

In a flash, half the Sons of Terra who had opened fire were dead, their smartcloth uniforms torn open, their weapons as mangled as their bodies.

Tamerlane rushed around to where the creature was facing. He shouted and hurled a steady rain of fireballs at the thing's face. Rameses watched him, hesitated for a moment, and then raced up behind the creature. He swung the Sword of Baranak—that legendary weapon of the gods—in a broad arc that took the blade directly into the demon's back.

The inconceivably sharp edge bit in, carrying with it the cosmic force of the Above. The demon lord screamed, and the sound was enough to shatter windows and send grown men to their knees, clutching their ears and clinging frantically to their sanity.

Like a manic lumberjack assaulting a stubborn redwood, Rameses pulled back and swung again.

Inquisitor Delain watched what was happening across the chamber in mounting horror and fascination. The general and the governor were somehow holding their own. She thought to go and help them, but then she looked down at the unconscious bodies of Colonel Arani and Major Elaro. They were entirely too exposed to danger, simply lying there in the floor of the throne room. Grasping first Arani and then Elaro by the ankles and gritting her teeth each time, she dragged first one and then the other out of harm's way, into a recessed alcove nearby. There she leaned back against the stone wall, closed her eyes, and breathed heavily, recovering.

When she opened her eyes she saw that Arani had awoken and was looking up at her, obviously puzzled.

"What's going on?" the colonel asked, slowly pulling herself to her feet and reaching up to rub at the knot on her head. "Did somebody—?"

"They knocked you out," Delain told her. "Him, too."

Arani gazed down at the still-unconscious Titus Elaro and pursed her lips. She stared at him for several seconds. It wasn't clear whether she intended to help him or shoot him—and whether she meant to wake him up before doing either of those things.

At that moment, Elaro solved at least part of the problem by waking up on his own. His eyes fluttered open and he groaned.

Arani kicked at him, and not delicately. "Get up," she barked.

Frowning, still partly confused but starting to comprehend the situation, Elaro did as he was told. He stood there, rubbing at the large bump on his head just as Arani had done, and waited. "Well?" he asked finally. "Where do we stand now? Am I your prisoner—or still your teammate?" He chewed his lip. "Or are you just going to execute me?"

Arani hesitated for another moment, as if weighing those options. Delain looked on, a bemused half-smile creeping across her pale features. At last, Arani shrugged. "The situation is critical," she told him. "We good guys need all the help we can get—even from the likes of you."

"Hey—I'm a good guy," Elaro protested.

"You're a Son of Terra," Arani snapped. "And a fraud. And a liar. That automatically rules you out of the good guy camp, as far as I'm concerned."

Elaro looked to be about to say something, but then he reconsidered and kept quiet, simply following the two women back out of their hiding spot and into the thick of things.

They did so not a moment too soon; the demon had drawn back from Rameses' assault with the sword, which had slowed considerably. It had circled around, and now had both of its antagonists cornered.

And before Arani and her two associates could move another step, things got infinitely worse: the air crackled and split, a dimensional vortex swirled into existence, the temperature in the throne room dropped several degrees, and Goraddon—the man in black; the god of persuasion— stepped out of it and into the room. He surveyed what was happening before him and realized he had arrived only seconds too late. He opened his mouth and screamed.

Tamerlane had moments earlier been driving the demon lord back with a relentless, sustained onslaught of fire blasts, even as Rameses had kept the creature from pressing its attack by fending it off with the Sword of Baranak. That being said, both men were obviously wearing down. Rameses, despite the boost in strength and stamina provided to him by the energies with which he had been infused and by the crimson cosmic armor he wore, was tiring. Tamerlane's flames were running low; he'd never come close to using his power so often as this, nor in such a short time, nor with such intensity. Already he felt his body weakening, as though he'd been wandering for days through a barren desert with no food or water, slowly burning up all of his reserves of strength.

Clearly the demon perceived these things. It hadn't tired at all, and its only injuries appeared to have come when Rameses managed to strike it a pair of times with the sword. Flames still gutted out of the slashes he'd left in the creature's back and side. Now the monster rushed forward, talons outstretched, intent on ending the battle quickly and decisively.

Tamerlane felt the wall behind him—he was quite literally up against it— and he knew the decisive moment had arrived. There was no more retreating; the final confrontation would happen in the next few seconds. He had to give his all, regardless of consequences, and hope for the best. Raising both hands, he aimed them into the gaping maw of the demon as its hideous head descended toward him, fangs dripping.

The fire blast rushed out, flowing mainly into the creature's mouth and down its throat, and in reaction the monster recoiled, parts of its head burning now with the cosmic flames of the Above.

Rameses seized the moment. He advanced, slashing and stabbing with the Sword of Baranak. His first strike was a swing that opened a gash across the creature's chest that spat fire and smoke instead of blood. The second strike was a lunge that ran the demon through, from one side to the other.

The demon lord howled bloody murder. It swung its scaly arm and swatted the armored governor away, just as he drew the blade out. Rameses tumbled over the mounds of dead bodies that lay in a heap near the base of a column, the Sword of Baranak sliding to a stop next to him.

Tamerlane sprang forward, acting on instinct. He shoved his right fist into the burning hole that gaped open in the demon lord's chest.

Across the chamber, the newly arrived Goraddon saw what was happening—what was about to happen—and screamed in outrage.

"For Nakamura," Tamerlane breathed. Then he let loose every bit of flame he had left within him.

The demon jerked away, suddenly afraid, but it was far too late. The holy fire of the Above filled it, expanded, bloated the massive creature beyond recognition—and consumed it. The demon wailed one last time and then exploded, spraying untold gallons of burning blood and ichor across the throne room.

When the carnage ended, the demon lord was gone. All that remained were small, burning puddles across the marble floor.

Goraddon saw it all happen, was powerless to prevent it, and screamed in wordless rage again.

Tamerlane had slumped forward, onto his knees, breathing hard. He felt as if the flame power had been drained from him forever, though he had no idea if that was truly so. He raised up and saw the man in black glaring at him with unbridled fury. He wanted to do something—*anything*—to express his anger, his hatred, his contempt for the evil god. Unfortunately, he couldn't move a muscle. He was utterly exhausted.

Rameses, however, was not. The governor of Ahknaton climbed back to his feet and ran forward, his eyes locked on Goraddon, the Sword of Baranak held high. He swung it.

The blow didn't come close. Goraddon struck him down with a single, casual, almost dismissive gesture of his left hand. Rameses crashed to the floor to Goraddon's right; the sword skidded across the marble to his left. The armored governor lay stunned, his head spinning.

Standing over the Sword of Baranak, Goraddon looked down at it.

"No!" cried Rameses. "No—that's *mine!* It belongs to *me* now!"

The man in black simply laughed. "Pathetic human. Even if it did belong to you—*you* belong to *me!*" Goraddon said this, and returned his gaze to the sword, yet still he did not pick it up. Instead, as he seemed to become aware for the first time that he and Rameses and Tamerlane were not alone in the room, he raised one hand high and snapped his fingers. Ice instantly formed on the floor and the walls as his overwhelming psychic power reached out and robbed everyone there of the ability to move.

Locked down, still as statues, the others in the chamber looked on, witnessing what they could perceive of the events playing out. It wasn't easy; to even turn one's eyes toward Goraddon was to find one's vision blurred and fuzzy.

"You have failed me, Rameses," Goraddon was saying. "You have failed me utterly and completely. Not only did you fail to live up to your portion of the plan, you actually helped destroy the last of the demon lords available to me here in this misbegotten universe." He snorted a cynical laugh. "You scarcely could have done more if you'd possessed all your senses and had been intentionally trying to thwart me."

Rameses gurgled an attempted response.

"Oh, by all means—share with me your brilliant riposte." He nodded towards the governor, freeing his body.

Rameses found that he could move again. He raised himself to his feet slowly, eyeing the man—the god—as he did. Then, roaring with rage, he rushed him.

Goraddon snapped his fingers.

The crimson armor instantly abandoned Rameses, peeling away from his body. It reformed itself in midair into a crimson cube, and the cube flew across the short distance to land in Goraddon's open, outstretched hand.

"No," Rameses murmured, stumbling to a halt midway. "No—not the *armor*, too..."

"Oh yes," the man in black laughed.

"*Yyyyoooouu*—" came a drawn-out sound from the left. Someone was attempting to speak, despite the psychic lockdown Goraddon had imposed on the entire chamber.

Intrigued by the willpower being displayed even by the utterance of such a simple sound, the man in black turned.

Tamerlane was attempting to rise. He was up on one knee now, his face contorted with the effort, as though he had to fight ten gravities or more to stand.

"Ah," Goraddon intoned. "General Tamerlane. Of course. Most impressive."

Tamerlane glared back at him, still attempting to speak, still mostly failing.

Goraddon shook his head and raised one hand. "No, no— don't strain yourself overmuch, General. You have more than made your point. Your actions have spoken quite loudly and clearly to me. And, truly, I should've known," he added enigmatically. "I should've anticipated. You are resilient. Stubborn. Very like your illustrious ancestor." He nodded once. "This round goes to you," he said, his voice casual but tinged with a growing anger and menace. "Twice now you have proven to be a more formidable opponent than I expected. Rest assured—I will not make that mistake a third time."

Tamerlane's body was practically frozen in place, but his mind whirled as he considered exactly what the man in black could've been possibly talking about. *Illustrious ancestor?* He couldn't guess.

Goraddon strolled a few leisurely steps forward and looked down again at the golden Sword of Baranak where it lay on the floor. He frowned deeply this time, then gave a sort of shrug and turned back toward the swirling dimensional gateway through which he'd entered. Just before he stepped through, he glanced back at Rameses. "Oh," he said, matter-of-factly. "I also reclaim the tiny bit of the Power you were granted by Zahir. You were never anything approaching a god, Rameses, but now you are entirely mortal again."

"*No!*" the governor shrieked. He fell to his knees, pitched forward, and screamed as waves of light radiated out of his body momentarily. "No—*please!*"

The man in black stepped through the portal and it closed behind him, as if neither he nor it had ever been there.

Rameses lay face-down on the marble tiles, sobbing. "I—I was a *god*," he gasped. "I was a god..."

Tamerlane could move again. He stood, his muscles aching from the strain he'd put on them, fighting the psychic lockdown, and looked from the spot where Goraddon had vanished to the broken form of Rameses. Then he saw the sword still lying where it had fallen. No one else had noticed it. He hurried toward it.

He didn't reach it in time.

Another figure appeared, moving out of the shadows and into the light like a specter. A pale hand reached down and grasped the hilt of the sword, lifting it and holding it casually to one side.

"I believe it's time this thing was stored away," stated General Ioan Iapetus with a chuckle as he studied the gleaming weapon. "It's done more than its share of damage today." He looked from Tamerlane to Rameses and back. "Now it's *my* turn."

Regent?" Tamerlane exploded. "*You?*" Anger seemed to pour from him as he glared back at General Iapetus. "Have you lost your mind?"

The two rival generals stood facing one another in the now mostly empty throne room of the Heliopolis palace. Behind Iapetus stood red-robed Teluria and Colonel Barbarossa, as well as some two dozen elite soldiers of the II Legion, their black and gold uniforms immaculate despite the very rough fighting that had raged across much of the planet as the last of the Sand Kings had been, in Iapetus's words, "pacified or converted."

Behind Tamerlane stood only the two women, Colonel Arani and Inquisitor Delain, with Major Titus Elaro off to one side, remaining near Arani but utterly ignored by her. Of the surviving members of the team Tamerlane had led into the palace—I Legion troops and *Nizam* soldiers—there was no sign. The general fervently hoped they had been merely taken into temporary custody while he and Iapetus worked out their differences, and nothing worse—though he would scarcely put anything past the Sons of Terra commander at this point.

"Lost my mind?" Iapetus repeated Tamerlane's words, regarding him sidelong, appearing to give the question serious consideration. His hands were clasped behind his back and he bowed his rough countenance, staring down at the floor. Then he raised his head, met Tamerlane's eyes, and, "No," he said. "No, I believe I am perhaps the only sane person left among the leadership of this Empire. Certainly the only competent one."

Tamerlane bristled at this. "Your arrogance is breathtaking," he growled.

"Watch your mouth," Colonel Barbarossa snapped, but his commander raised a hand, settling him down.

"Arrogance?" Iapetus snorted. "Scarcely. I merely deal in facts." He smiled again. "And the facts are these: I have the Sword of Baranak. I have Princess Marens. I have Ahknaton." He leaned his head back as though attempting to peer upwards through the domed ceiling of the great hall. "My legion's fleet has arrived in orbit above us, and the shuttles are bringing reinforcements and heavy equipment down even as we speak." He looked back at Tamerlane. "I have Holy Earth, and the Inner Worlds—all in the custody of my legion, all safe. It makes perfect sense that I should assume the position of regent until the young lady comes of age." He smiled his cruel smile. "You, on the other hand, my dear Ezekial—along with the late Nakamura, of course—have lost most of the Outer Worlds to invaders, and virtually everything you have attempted has failed—or has actually made matters worse."

"The Empire wouldn't be in this state if you had agreed to help out from the beginning," Tamerlane almost shouted.

Iapetus shrugged at this. "Perhaps. I doubt that's true, though. Had I come rushing to aid—had I dispatched whole companies of my legion to assist you in your lost causes on the frontiers—it's quite likely Earth would be in enemy hands now, and all of the Empire lost."

"That's garbage," Tamerlane shot back—though, deep inside, a small part of him wondered if there was some grain of truth to it. Had Iapetus been right all along? Right to hold back his legion until the situation became most critical—

No, Tamerlane told himself. *He didn't hold his forces back until they were most needed. He held them back until the situation could most benefit* him—*until the rewards for him and his legion grew large enough that he could walk in and take them; take the entire Empire, plucking it like an overripe fruit.*

How did I let things come to this? Tamerlane wondered. *How did I let everyone down, and lose everything that mattered?* Frowning, he bowed his head, feeling utterly beaten for the first time in his life. Beaten, and alone.

But he wasn't alone, as his companions reminded him then.

"You can't get away with this," Inquisitor Delain interjected, her expression as animated and dark as Tamerlane had ever seen it. "The Grand Inquisitor stood up to Barmakid and stopped him, and he will stop you, too." She glared defiantly at Iapetus. "How effectively do you truly believe you can govern this falling Empire with the Inquisition—and likely the Ecclesiarchy, too—set against you?"

"The Ecclesiarchy is firmly behind me," Iapetus replied with a smirk. He turned and looked to the red-robed woman behind him. "Isn't that so, Teluria."

"You're supporting him in this?" Tamerlane asked her, almost incredulous. "I thought you had more sense than that."

The woman met Tamerlane's eyes briefly and looked away. She appeared remarkably uncomfortable and unhappy. She looked back at him again, then at Iapetus— and particularly at Iapetus's waist, his belt. A holster hung there—one that Tamerlane didn't recognize as part of the general's usual outfit. He didn't at first recognize the pistol that rested within it, either. But then something in his memory clicked, and he began to understand.

"As for Stanishur," Iapetus continued, shrugging, "Well—he's had a lengthy tenure as Grand Inquisitor. Perhaps it's time he had a vacation. A long vacation, far from Earth. Or perhaps simply a retirement."

Delain cursed.

"Your job," Iapetus went on, moving next to the woman in black, "is to tell him that. Make it clear to him. I know that you are close to him. Make him understand. I would like him on my side, but I will not hesitate to replace him."

The Inquisitor glared at him but said nothing.

"You're retreating, aren't you?" Colonel Arani said then, scorn dripping from her words. "You're pulling back. Everywhere." She looked from Iapetus to Tamerlane. "It's the end of the Empire, general," she said. "He's going to retrench across the Inner Worlds, and to hell with the rest!" She gave Iapetus a sour, disapproving look. "It's so stupid—so blind, so short-sighted."

"She's right," Tamerlane said coldly. "You're making a terrible mistake, Iapetus. One that will bring you and your legion down. The gods forbid it also brings down the entire Empire."

"Your mistakes have already brought the Empire to this state," Iapetus snapped, growing visibly perturbed for the first time. "But," he said, raising one hand, "this is all pointless. Decisions have been made. Processes are already underway. I merely wished to inform you of them, out of respect for your years of service." He smiled again—enough to chill the blood—and added, "Those years are now *over*, of course." He motioned and four Sons moved forward, guns at the ready. "Take this little group into custody," he ordered. "They are all under arrest."

"What?" Tamerlane started forward, but two Sons bracketed him roughly, holding him by the arms.

"That one, too," Iapetus added, nodding toward Titus Elaro. "His loyalties have become divided, I believe. I cannot trust him any longer."

Soldiers in black surrounded the two women and the double-agent major.

"What of the governor, sir?" Barbarossa asked, pointing toward the doubled-over form of Rameses where he sat on the floor nearby, abandoned and ignored. "Should I arrest him, too?"

Iapetus regarded the broken Rameses, lips pursed in thought. "No," he said at length, striding across the tiles to stand over the wreck of a man. "No, I think his usefulness is done now." He drew a blast pistol and fired a single shot into Rameses' head. The governor slumped to the cold marble tiles, dead.

Tamerlane and the others jumped, startled and shocked. The Sons of Terra didn't react at all; for them, it was as if this was standard procedure.

"Hmm," Iapetus said, looking down at the body. "It appears he wasn't a god after all."

Tamerlane cursed. "He deserved better than that," he barked.

"*Better*?" Iapetus laughed. "You've been out to get him for months. Isn't this what you wanted all along?"

"It wasn't entirely his fault," Tamerlane replied, still angry. "There are other forces at work here. The gods—"

Iapetus regarded Tamerlane with a smile. "Even the gods do not want to mess with me now." He glanced back at Teluria. "Isn't that right, Ecclesiarch?"

The woman in red said nothing, but her complexion darkened to almost match her robes.

Iapetus seemed to have said all he intended to say to his prisoners. He turned to consult with Barbarossa. Meanwhile Tamerlane struggled angrily against the hold of the two Sons. He nearly slipped as he did so; the marble floor had become suddenly slippery. He ignored it at first, what with everything going on, but then frowned. Had he stepped in a puddle of blood left over from the earlier battle? Looking down, he saw it wasn't blood... but *ice*.

Ice. Again, and more of it. And with Goraddon long gone.

"Iapetus," he murmured, looking to the rugged general in black. Then louder, "Iapetus! I believe we have a serious problem developing." He motioned toward the spreading patches. "Ice. Don't you see it?"

The air had grown noticeably colder in the throne room. Delain had perceived it quickly; her brow furrowed, she raised a hand in an attempt to sense what was happening, only to have one of the Sons slap it down. She glared at the man in scarcely contained rage.

Iapetus and Barbarossa had been joined by a third soldier, who was whispering something frantically to them. The last part of it he said loud enough for all to hear: "Thank the gods the fleet is here."

Iapetus was scowling, seemingly uncertain of what to do. He realized then what Tamerlane had said to him a second earlier. He turned back to the other general, now obviously disconcerted. "What was that?" he asked. "What did you say?"

"Ice," Tamerlane repeated, nodding toward the sheets of it forming on the columns and across the floor. His breath was a cloud of white now. "You *know* what that means."

"It's a by-product of the manifestation of psychic energy," Barbarossa offered.

Iapetus whirled on the man. "I'm well aware of that, Colonel. Thank you."

Stung, Barbarossa bowed and backed away a step.

Another Son approached Iapetus and spoke the word Tamerlane had expected. "Comets," he announced loudly and clearly. "Comets are incoming. Hundreds of them."

"Comets?" Iapetus repeated this, nervousness manifest in his voice. "Here?"

"Goraddon's parting gift," Tamerlane breathed. "He wasn't done with us after all."

The first impact, some distance away, shook the foundations of the palace. The next two were closer.

The throne room was plunged into chaos. Ice covered every surface and the Sons of Terra were having trouble moving about as the general ordered them to form up and join their compatriots at one of the landing areas outside the Heliopolis.

They never got the chance.

A comet, its velocity greatly reduced by the astounding telepathic power of its inhabitants, crashed down just beyond the Heliopolis, and in reaction the wall on that side of the palace buckled and collapsed, chunks of stone and glass and metal raining down. The chamber was now open to the early-morning air of Ahknaton—to that, and to an eerie, crimson light that flickered over the landscape.

Tamerlane gazed into that light and was horrified by what he saw: dark shapes, specter-like, with gleaming silver faces in the shapes of alien skulls. It was as Agrippa had described. It was the Phaedrons. They had come to Ahknaton.

Iapetus recognized them as well. He whirled about and barked orders at Barbarossa and the other Sons officers nearby. "Get the men back onto the shuttles. Load everything and get it all back up to the *Atlantia* and the other ships as quickly as possible."

"Everything?" Barbarossa asked, frustrated. "Everybody?"

Iapetus remembered then that Barbarossa had never personally encountered the Phaedrons, so he couldn't truly understand. He was therefore extra-patient with his assistant. "Everything and everybody, yes," he answered.

"Are we simply to abandon Ahknaton, then?"

"To hell with Ahknaton," Iapetus growled. "This is not a fight I'm the least bit interested in having. Certainly not out here in the outer periphery. If these things want this lump of sand so badly, they can have it." He raised his voice and addressed all the Sons of Terra still present in the throne room. "Back to Earth! Get out there and get the transports loaded." He glanced over at Barbarossa, realizing the men wouldn't move as quickly as they needed to, unless he took a hand himself and pressed the need for haste. "The Colonel and I will help," he added.

"What of the prisoners, sir?" asked the ranking officer among the group holding Tamerlane and the others.

"Bring them along. When all is ready—when I am satisfied—and the main bulk of our forces has lifted off for the fleet, the good Ecclesiarch here will open a direct passage for us back home." He flashed Teluria a quick and tight smile and then he and Barbarossa hurried from the throne room, leaving only a handful of his soldiers behind.

"Alright, then," the ranking Son barked. "This way, all of you."

They started forward, along the same path Iapetus had taken out of the chamber, but then more chunks of masonry tumbled down, the sound like gunfire as the big pieces impacted the marble tiles. Between that and the horrific sounds coming from outside, the guards grew somewhat distracted and lost their focus, ignoring their prisoners for a precious few moments.

That was all the opening those captives needed. Tamerlane struck with what little of his flame power he had recuperated, while Delain warped their vision, causing them to lose track of their charges. Arani and Elaro seized weapons from the startled soldiers and fired. Within only a few seconds, no one was left standing there except the former prisoners—and Teluria.

"We need to move," Arani said, sizing up the tactical situation. "What can we do?"

"Teluria is getting us out of here," Tamerlane told the others, only then turning to face the woman in red.

"And why am I doing that?" she asked archly.

He laughed without humor. "Because the Phaedrons are coming—and I think even *you* fear dealing with them if you don't have to. And because you despise Iapetus as much as we do. And because you don't like being a prisoner."

She took this in but her expression still appeared skeptical.

"And," Tamerlane concluded, "because I will never point a *gun*—a gun that actually could *hurt* you—at your head and order you to do my bidding."

"You saw it?" she whispered, eyes widening. "You *know*?"

Tamerlane nodded. "I saw what Iapetus had in his holster, and I know the story. The gun that can kill a god."

The ice was everywhere now. Cold winds blew in from outside. Teluria shivered, but it had nothing to do with those physical things.

"What's it going to be?" Tamerlane asked, reaching out his open right hand toward her.

The red lights were all-pervasive. An eerie, howling sound echoed across the sands of the desert. The horrific Phaedrons were descending upon the Heliopolis and would be there at any second.

Teluria considered all of this, and considered Tamerlane's words. Then she shrugged, and even offered him and his companions a minuscule smile. Raising one hand, she began to conjure a dimensional portal; swirling smoke and lights appeared in midair just beyond them. With her other hand, she clasped Tamerlane's.

"Where would you like to go?" she asked.

EPILOGUE:

In a darkened room in a darkened corner of an otherwise dazzlingly-lit celestial city, an ornately-designed and crafted chess board sat on a small granite table. The pieces were of ivory and obsidian, the board itself a slab of veined marble. The game in play upon it looked to be near its finish; many pieces on both sides had been removed from the board and set aside, killed, while those that remained were in place for a swift endgame that clearly favored the black side.

A hand reached down and caressed the black queen for a moment. It did so gently, almost tenderly. Then it grasped the edge of the board and in one smooth motion lifted it up and dashed it against the wall of the room.

As the dust and debris and shattered pieces settled to the floor, a man clad all in black turned on his heel and strode from the room. The door clanged shut behind him.

The spiral of lightning, fire and smoke dissolved around them and left them standing on solid ground again. The ground, however, was the only thing solid within view.

General Agrippa touched the visor of his helmet and it slid soundlessly up and out of the way. His breath immediately became visible as a white cloud in the cold.

385

Cold. He tensed, suspecting what that could mean. He reached for his quad-rifle.

"No, no," Aurore said, motioning with her right hand for him to relax. "It's not psychic energy making it cold here. It's simply *cold.*" She placed the hand on his arm and leaned on him for a moment, as if the exertions of getting them all this far had drained her of her energy.

The other eleven members of Agrippa's Bravo Squad moved up around the two of them and waited, most with their visors still down, tiny lights blinking along the sides of their helmets and air circulation systems hissing softly. They looked about them in wonder; it appeared as if they stood within a tunnel of fluffy white clouds that led off in either direction into infinity. The effect was extremely disconcerting.

"Where are we now?" the general asked, his eyes moving from the swirling mists that surrounded them to the face of the woman in white. Big and muscular and clad in the Deising-Arry Mark 5 combat plate, he towered over her frail-looking form. "How much longer until we reach our destination?"

"We are very close now," she replied, seeming to recover a bit. She gazed in one direction down the tunnel of clouds and then the other. "I think."

"You *think*?" Agrippa frowned at this. "You've led us across half the multiverse to get this far," he rumbled. "Don't lose the way now."

"No, no," she reassured him, offering a wan smile. "The Dyonari are nearby. I can sense them. They naturally channel a tiny bit of the Power at all times. As you can imagine, they make quite a vivid impression in the fabric of spacetime."

Agrippa couldn't imagine any such thing, and didn't want to try. Instead he offered, "Perhaps you could use a break? We could stand guard here while you recover more fully, and—"

"I am perfectly fine," Aurore snapped back, almost sharply. Then she softened. "Your consideration for my health is appreciated, General," she said, patting him on the heavily-armored forearm, "but I am a goddess of the Golden Realm. I require no rest, no sleep. Merely unobstructed access to the Power of the Fountain."

Agrippa nodded uncertainly at this. "And—um—how can we make that happen?"

"It happens constantly," Aurore said, smiling at him maternally as though he were a small child being instructed on the most basic facts of life. "The Power radiates out from the Fountain in the City, high in the Above. It reaches everywhere in the multiverse, always. It—" She faltered again, this time actually grasping his arm and hanging on it for a moment.

Startled, Agrippa brought his other arm around and caught her, keeping her from falling.

"Aurore?" he said, growing more concerned. "My lady, are you—"

Her eyes were closed. They fluttered open once and she murmured something unintelligible before they closed again. Her skin had already been pale but now it was growing almost translucent.

Agrippa easily lifted her up in both of his powerful arms, cradling her like an infant. He looked up at the others; their faceplates were all up and they were staring back, eyes wide.

One last time her eyes opened and she strained her head upward. Agrippa leaned his own down to hear her. She whispered something. He hesitated, then nodded.

Light flooded out from her. He almost dropped her in surprise, so blinding was it, and so unexpected.

And then her body came apart, literally shattering in an instant into thousands of tiny shards of what looked like glass. The shards cascaded down, sparkling as they fell. The troops instinctively all moved back a step, startled. A second later, the shards were gone. Agrippa's arms were empty. Nothing remained of the woman in white at all.

"What—what *happened*?" the nearest of the soldiers—Torgon—asked his general. "Where did she *go*?"

Agrippa shook his head, only now relaxing his arms back down to his sides.

"She'd better come back, and soon," Harker said, gesturing with one arm at the fog and clouds that surrounded them, constituting the entirety of their world now. "I'd prefer not to have to settle down and live out my days here." He spat to one side. "Wherever *here* is."

"I don't know that she *is* coming back," Agrippa growled. "Something has gone wrong. *Very* wrong."

The others all nervously looked at one another, increasingly discomfited by the surroundings and the situation.

"What did she say, there at the end?" asked Obomanu hopefully, a second later. "Was it anything helpful? What did she whisper?"

"She said pick a direction and go," Agrippa replied, his forehead creased with worry. "She said finish the mission. Save the galaxy." He looked at the others, thrust out his jaw firmly, and began to exude a bit of his usual confidence and bravado. "And that is precisely what we will do, Bravo Squad."

Agrippa gazed first one way and then the other along the tunnel of smoke and fog. Then, as if detecting some telltale clue that provided the correct answer, he nodded once to his right and set out in that direction at a brisk and steady pace.

The others spared only a moment to glance at one another in uncertainty. Then they all quickly followed along behind their commander, weapons at the ready.

The Kings of Oblivion disappeared into the fog.